VOICES
IN THE
DARK

Andrew Coburn

VOICES IN THE DARK

A DUTTON BOOK

DUTTON

Published by the Penguin Group
Penguin Books USA Inc., 375 Hudson Street, New York, New York 10014, U.S.A.
Penguin Books Ltd, 27 Wrights Lane, London W8 5TZ, England
Penguin Books Australia Ltd, Ringwood, Victoria, Australia
Penguin Books Canada Ltd, 10 Alcorn Avenue, Toronto, Ontario, Canada M4V 3B2
Penguin Books (N.Z.) Ltd, 182–190 Wairau Road, Auckland 10, New Zealand

Penguin Books Ltd, Registered Offices:
Harmondsworth, Middlesex, England

First published by Dutton, an imprint of Dutton Signet,
a division of Penguin Books USA Inc.
Distributed in Canada by McClelland & Stewart Inc.

First Printing, February, 1994
1 3 5 7 9 10 8 6 4 2

Library of Congress Cataloging-in-Publication Data
Coburn, Andrew.
Voices in the dark / Andrew Coburn.
p.   cm.
ISBN 0-525-93644-0
1. Police—Massachusetts—Fiction.   I. Title.
PS3553.O23V65   1994
813'.54—dc20   93-27924
                                    CIP

Printed in the United States of America
Set in Janson and Kabel

Designed by Steven N. Stathakis

For Bernadine, without whom nothing would be possible; our daughters Cathleen, Krista, Lisa, and Heather; my sister, Julie; and my toughest critic, Nikki Smith.

VOICES
IN THE
DARK

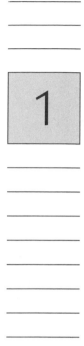

ON THE LAST DAY OF HIS LIFE HE READ A WARNING IN HIS horoscope and cast the newspaper aside when a woman asked if she might share the bench. Sitting close, her shirt open to a dash of white, she doubled a leg beneath her and said, "Let me guess, you're fourteen." He was sixteen, he told her, which was the exact truth, though he was slight for his age and wore braces on his teeth. It was his birthday, which he didn't tell her. She said, "I was never sixteen."

His involuntary smile revealed the braces. "You must've been, once."

"No, I skipped it."

They were in the Public Garden, where daffodils flung out bells and tulips were cups awaiting offerings. Beyond, in the direction of the lagoon where swan boats carried children and tourists, brilliant forsythia clashed with red rhododendron. The Boston sky was veined marble.

"My name's Mary. What's yours?"

He would have guessed something less ordinary, Naomi or

Daphne. Her auburn hair flowed from each side of the center part, and her left cheek bore a small blemish, like postage, as if she had come a way. Her face, expressive, was a puzzle beyond figuring. His was delicate, marked by pallor, and harbored an air of privacy. His name he meant to keep to himself, but it came out anyway. "Glen."

"Fits you," she said.

He hoped not. It was too light a syllable, too quick a sound, which seemed to dismiss him as soon as he said it. He would have preferred Anthony, which had strength and was the name of someone from school.

The woman, her tone winsome, said, "I love Saturdays, don't you?"

Not particularly, and he let the click of a heel claim his attention. An extremely attractive black woman with dangling chains of hair strutted by on legs as splendid as those of his stepmother, whom he thought the most beautiful creature in the world. Then came a rush of guilt, for his loyalty lay with his mother, with whom he lived.

The woman touched his arm. "Are you all right?"

His heart was racing, his breathing was dense. More than a year ago, a Saturday, the doctor had given him the odds and the minister had laid his future in the hands of God, which made him feel like a tossed coin that would eventually land heads or tails. Heads was hope, tails a tunnel at the end of which, some people claimed, was a blast of light. He didn't believe it. "I'm fine," he said.

"Are you sure?"

What had struck was already passing, leaving him with no epiphanies, only vague understandings he didn't bother to sort out. Instead he watched a trim man with gray locks and dimples feed bread to pigeons. The man didn't scatter torn pieces but sailed out whole slices onto the grass, which raised a clamor and provoked battles.

The woman said, "Would you rather be alone?"

Though his horoscope hung heavy, warning of a false friend, he said, "No, ma'am."

"Call me Mary."

Looking her full in the face, he likened the flaw on her cheek to the bruise on a windfall apple: Eve tempting a callow Adam. She looked thirty-five, but he was no judge. She could have been much older or much younger. With a frown he read his watch. "I'm waiting for my father."

A shape advanced, but was not familiar. It passed, followed by sauntering youths with legs muscled into jeans, baseball caps worn askew. Pigeons racketed around the man who had finished feeding them, some pied, some shedding fluff, a few nursing hurts. Several, beating their wings, seemed set to fly up at the man. Bigger birds might have done it.

Mary's whisper heated his ear. "He's not coming."

"What?"

"I would bet on it."

Her smile, a challenge, went unanswered, for he presumed that all contests were fixed, all events predetermined. Adults kept score. She pulled her leg from under her and softened her smile.

"People tend to disappoint us. Isn't that the first thing you learned when you were little?"

The question was meaningless, for he had doctored most memories and lately had learned to walk a wire from one mood to another. A drop of rain spotted his shirt, though the sun continued to shine. A sudden breeze raised a disturbance in the woman's hair.

"We mustn't let it bother us," she said. "Worst thing is to dwell on it."

Dwelling on nothing, he drew in sights and sounds existing only for that moment. Sparrows sprayed from a Norway maple and took flight. Children near the weathered statue of a warrior raced and rolled on grass, arms and legs flying out as if detached.

"The trick is to relax, accept what comes along. Can you do that, Glen?"

He held out a hand to feel for more rain, but his palm stayed dry. The breeze vanished, the world went on. From other benches old men, craning their necks, sunned themselves like turtles on logs.

"You're an only child, aren't you?"

Everything she said was a sort of surprise that gave him a turn, as if they had met in another life, planet Pluto, winds whistling around them. "How did you know?"

"Something in your eyes."

He was interested. He wanted to know more about himself, particularly on this special day, with candles yet to be lit. "What else do you know about me?"

"You'd smile more if it weren't for those braces."

"They don't bother me," he lied and concentrated on people parading by, the intensity of this man, the lack of it in that one. Here was a woman with effortless steps, another with labored ones, the sun scalloping her. Suddenly he was tired. An eye twitched as he flung his watch a final look.

"I told you," she said.

She was on her feet, as if a little clock had chimed. Her shirt, plum with white buttons, traced her breathing. In her face was a kind of caring, aloof but vivid, alive but contained, leaving him without thoughts, only sensations.

"Your age, every problem is magnified."

He knew that, he didn't need to be told. He had graduated the past week from Phillips Andover, the youngest in his class, fitting into no social cluster, possessing only his own thoughts, with the sin of Onan to put him to sleep at night.

"You mustn't fear anything."

"I don't," he boasted, but the truth was that he suffered nightsweats, had demons in his dreams, and didn't feel wholly human in the morning. But the feeling always passed.

"And you won't. Promise."

He didn't want her to leave. Sunstruck, her face was a palimpsest of feelings, with no way for him to read through the rough to the original. Her blemish acquired the textured translucency of a watermark. "I won't," he promised, his tone rash, as if he had bitten into the apple with no thought of the worm.

"I won't forget you," she said.

Each moment expecting her to look back, he watched her stride toward Beacon Street. A few minutes later he rose reluctantly and strode in the opposite direction, past dogtooth violets and coral bells, to Boylston, where cars bumper to bumper honked and fumed. At a crosswalk girls with riots of glazed hair and candy faces colored the air, their torsos in the squeeze of tank tops and bicycle pants. He picked out the prettiest and stashed the image for another time.

In the gray air of the subway station, he sidestepped a derelict who smelled like old fish and bumped through a turnstile. On the platform, people compacted around him. A train flowered with graffiti reverberated by on the opposite tracks, the cars like massive coffins destined for slots in hell. On one side of him was an Hispanic youth with the consumed look of a user and on the other an elderly woman preoccupied with her pocketbook. From behind a man's voice, private in his ear, startled him. Twisting, he glimpsed gray locks and a dimpled smile aimed at no one.

The crowd shuffled and, at the rumble of an approaching train, pressed forward, forcing him to the verge of the platform, the view of the rails naked. The Hispanic youth gave off a cloying scent of cologne. The woman clutching her pocketbook exuded lilac.

"Better worlds are coming," the dimpled man whispered in his ear.

The beam of the train, an unearthly eye, appeared abruptly, and in the prick of the moment Glen's mind filled with childhood drawings his mother had preserved for him on a wall, like cave art. The colors were brilliant, primary, waxing in his mind with the roar of the train.

"Now," the man said in his ear.

A half hour away in the bedroom town of Bensington, Police Chief James Morgan was crossing the village green while watching robins worm the ground. With his loose, easy stride, he was a limber figure in an old sports jacket and narrow chinos. His step slowed when he glimpsed a woman near a billowing red maple, and his spirit quickened when she lashed her thighs over a boy's bicycle, bent forward, and pedaled toward him. But then she glided past him without a word, only a slender smile one might have given a stranger. Picking up speed, she vanished behind explosions of forsythia and moments later reappeared on the street.

From a bench, he craned his neck and watched her sail by the white facade of the town hall, by the Blue Bonnet Restaurant with its window boxes of geraniums, by the war memorial near the ivy-matted library, by the pink brick of the post office. Then he lost sight of her behind a curving bank of parked cars beyond the Congregational church.

Waiting for her to reappear on the far side of the green, he stretched a leg and viewed with mixed feelings the backdrop of chic little shops that had sprung up in the long stretch between Pearl's Pharmacy and Tuck's General Store. Brand-new, Minerva's Tea Room announced itself in tasteful gold leaf lettering. Relatively new, Prescott's Pantry sold gourmet food and catered private parties, and Elaine's dolled up children in designer clothes. The Gift Shoppe featured crystal and Wedgwood in its window.

Burger King had sought entry near the green but was relegated to the outskirts of town, near wetland that now harbored a fleet of Japanese cars.

From his vantage point Chief Morgan watched comings and goings of Saturday shoppers at Tuck's. From the street came the toot of an old station wagon's horn. A familiar hand waved from the open window, and Morgan waved back. He knew nearly everyone in town, certainly all the natives and not a few of the wealthy newcomers who occupied the Heights, a prestigious area once unmolested woodland and now groomed with extended lawns, ornamental ponds, and geometric gardens surrounding grand houses. As a boy, pretending to be a pioneer blazing a trail, he had wandered those woods.

He pulled his leg in when he heard the crunch of grass. Surprising him, the woman on the bicycle had breezed up from behind and was now wheeling in front of him. Abruptly she braked and stood straddling the crossbar. She was tall, husky, and athletic. Morgan could almost see the gallop in her legs, the spring in her toes. She was from the Heights.

"Are we speaking?"

"It'd be foolish if we didn't," he said, his head full of her. A widower, he enjoyed women, and with them he had a livelier voice, a warmer smile, special eyes. Each new woman in his life was a tonic.

"I didn't mean to stand you up," she said. She had thick blond hair bundled back, a striking and aggressive face, and an orotund voice thrilling to men and intriguing to other women. Before marrying and moving to Bensington three years ago, she had been a television reporter in Boston. "I'm sorry," she added.

"It's okay," he said, though it was not. Yesterday he had waited two hours for her in the lounge at Rembrandt's, a restaurant in neighboring Andover. It would have been their first date. "Did you get cold feet?"

"Something like that."

"You could've called."

"Yes."

"But you didn't."

"It wasn't convenient. Harley was in and out." Harley was her husband. The marriage, which was not working, was her first, her husband's second. She shifted her weight over the bar of the bicycle and said, "Did you wait long?"

"No," he said and wondered what it would be like to be greedily in love again, to wear his whole heart on his sleeve. She had turned thirty, which he knew from a check of the voting list, and he was well into his forties, but with no gray in his hair, he was proud of that. And proud too that he still had his looks, though his nose played slightly too large a part in his face.

"But you're angry."

"Maybe it's all just as well," he said without meaning a word of it. His truths he told with a smile, his lies with solemnity. "Still friends, aren't we?"

"I hope so, James."

"And no reason we can't bump into each other at the library."

The library was where they had got to know each other, where she read out-of-town newspapers and borrowed biographies. Fitting herself back onto the bicycle seat, one foot on the ground and the other poised on a pedal, she said, "No reason whatsoever."

He did not want her to leave, not so quickly. The anticipation of loss was with him always, the chill rooted in childhood when his father was killed in the war and reinforced tenfold when early in his marriage his wife was killed on a winding road. "I suppose you have to go somewhere," he said.

"A party," she replied. "The Gunners."

"Paul and Beverly."

"You know them?"

He knew what they looked like, he knew they were rich as God, and he knew they had had a loss of their own, two, maybe three years ago. "Not really," he said, watching a monarch wobble in an errant breeze, its flight redirected. "I don't suppose you'll be at the library on Monday."

"Let's not plan anything, James. That way neither of us will be disappointed."

Too much truthfulness in her face. He would have gratefully accepted a lie, the sort he told, which gave hope and fleeting comfort. He watched her pedal away, her torso flung forward, her bottom arched over the tiny seat, and her legs shedding light. Then he was on his feet.

"Kate," he called. But she did not hear him.

Mary Williams lived one flight up in a brownstone on Beacon, near Charles, near the Public Garden, a mere walk from the Ritz, where her grandmother used to take her to breakfast and taught her to eat her egg from a porcelain cup, the continental way; where her grandmother had read the *Times*, which had no comics she could borrow, though waiters had occasionally amused her and dowagers had made much of her. On days such as this, it did not seem that long ago.

Light streaked through the tall front windows and struck ceramic vases and crystalware, picking out the prettiest. The apartment was spacious, airy, with many rooms, the furniture her grandmother's. The paintings on the walls of the wide passageway were her own creations, the ones she felt she could show: a meadow imbued with the calm of a Corot, a maiden with a Modigliani neck, a street scene reminiscent of Hopper, nothing that would upset her friend Dudley.

In the kitchen she made herbal tea in a pot smothered with delicately etched forget-me-nots, the tints not as striking as when her grandmother was alive. As she poured the tea into a chipped china cup, she pondered the dynamics that would impel one woman to throw the cup out and another to keep it. It was, she felt, as worthy of study as anything else.

Carrying cup and saucer with her, she passed through the dining room, where a bowl of potpourri emitted a strong fragrance, and into her reading room, where walls of books threw out titles in a learned way. The rolltop desk had been her great-grandfather's and still sheltered some of his papers. She paused only to trail a hand over the humps of an open Oxford dictionary, as if her fingers absorbed words.

She glanced into her studio, where like bad children, canvases were stacked with their faces to the wall. Her mother had called it her therapy room. In the works was a sketch of a nude male, the model an ex-soldier with a shaved head and a quilt of belly muscles.

Her bedroom faced her friend's. She went into hers. The bed was an old-fashioned four-poster of dark oak and fretwork, beneath which, for effect, was a chamber pot. On the night table were pencil stubs, a wind-up clock, and a candle rising from a tarnished wreath of gilt. Small ornately framed photographs of family members lined a mantelpiece, her father and her grandmother in the forefront. Sitting on the window seat with a partial view of the street, she sipped her tea and waited.

The grandest house on the Heights belonged to the Gunners. Built on the converging lines of an English manor and a Dutch colonial, it was approachable through a stone gateway. The driveway was an avenue of tapered arborvitae, which concealed video scanners. The cocktail party was at five, and on the hour automobiles of note began arriving. In a foyer of rosy marble the Gunners greeted guests, who gradually would include nearly everyone from the Heights and many from Andover.

Beverly Gunner's hair was a golden shell perfectly in place, Paul Gunner's collar bit into his big neck. He shook the hands of the men and planted kisses on the cheeks of the women. His heavy face was wadded with an importance he deserved. A graduate of MIT, he had worked for a software company only long enough to form his own, which he sold seven years later in a deal spectacular enough to put his picture in *Forbes* and *Fortune*. Later he made killings in commercial real estate and got out before the market collapsed, for he heeded the signs the greedy ignored, among them Myles Yarbrough, whose hand he was now pumping with a superior grip. Phoebe Yarbrough, a willowy elegance in waist-cinching silk, he slobbered with a kiss.

"You're lovely," he said. Pleasure enlarged his face and further fattened his whole look.

Beverly Gunner greeted people warmly but tentatively, her manner shy and uncertain. A gift from her husband manacled her wrist and embarrassed her when it drew the attention of Regina Smith, who was shrewd enough to guess that she would have chosen a small packet of understanding over a diamond bracelet.

"It's stunning," said Regina, whose steel smile was a sullen force. Her own jewelry was minimal, exquisitely noticeable by degrees. Her dress left her shoulders bare. Paul Gunner, who had once likened her to a frozen delicacy, suddenly corralled her, but with a subtle shift she avoided the full weight of his kiss.

By six, the foyer clock striking the hour, the party was in full swing. Guests numbering nearly a hundred thronged the long dining room, where high windows stood deep in the walls. Breezes delivered fragrances from the garden, and trimly uniformed Hispanic women served hors d'oeuvres and wine. Stronger drinks were available at the bar in the billiard room, where a crowd surrounded Crack Alexander, the former ball player who stood five inches over six feet and had gained thirty pounds since retiring. Gripping an imaginary bat, an elbow cocked behind him, the big fellow demonstrated the legendary stance that had earned him super salaries with the Boston Red Sox.

His wife, Sissy, stood by herself in a short flare of chiffon, her lurid legs fleshy above the knees, her mouth stiffened into a smile to last the evening. She knew she was an afterthought, an insignificant addition to the gathering. Put a drink in her hand and forget her. Only a pretty Hispanic woman with a tray of delicacies took pity on her, pausing frequently to feed her. Then a small semibald man came up to her on springy feet.

"Excuse me," he said and reintroduced himself. She had met him before, briefly, another party. He was a mathematics teacher at Phillips Academy, brainy and bespectacled, though in no way intimidating. Inside his neat little beard his grin looked like a woman's. "What's it like, Mrs. Alexander, being married to a famous athlete?"

An anchovy glued to something hot went down hard. Ginger ale, which she drank fast, pricked her nose. Behind her someone was telling a joke, and she flinched as if each burst of laughter were at her expense.

"I suppose you've been asked that a thousand times."

Her face, round and wholesome, seemed to contract. "Please," she said, "could you get me another ginger ale?"

Kate Bodine, her blond hair negligently bundled back, arrived late, shot smiles at those she knew, and was surprised to glimpse her husband. He was deep in conversation with Paul Gunner, their posture stiff. Harley lacked an eye for art and an ear for music, but he had a sure head for business, and he was Gunner's lawyer.

They broke away, and she, lifting her wineglass high and dodging elbows, went to him.

"I didn't think you'd make it," she said.

"I came here directly." He was tailored tight in a sober suit uncompromisingly correct. Inside he was diffuse, never one thing she could put her finger on but always a series of hedges, a reservoir of suspicions.

"How did it go?" she asked.

"I got tied up. I didn't see him."

"He must be very disappointed."

"I'll make it up to him."

"I don't see how, Harley."

"Don't make me feel more guilty than I do," he said in a tone to remind her the boy was his son, not hers. His gaze roved; his dark, supple face changed expressions. "I'm going to the bar, do you mind?"

"Do as you like, Harley."

Myles Yarbrough, his nerves shot, his stomach deranged from money losses, sneaked away early. Free of his jittery eye, Phoebe Yarbrough mingled with the weightless gait of a dancer. Voices rose rich and bubbly, eroding an inhibition or two, and she recklessly started a conversation with Ira Smith, his face owlish behind horn-rims, his voice warm.

"I saw Myles leave," he said.

Her eyes absorbed him. Here was a man she could love, perhaps deeply, perhaps forever, but she knew he would not have it. Nor would Regina allow it. They were, if appearances counted, a happy couple. She said, "He has a lot on his mind."

"Is there anything I can do?"

Like her husband, Ira Smith was a Boston lawyer but without the greed that might have propelled him into precarious situations. He headed the firm his grandfather had founded, his life laid out for him the day he was born. "Myles is a big boy," she said. "Big boys take care of themselves, or at least they should."

"Everybody can use help now and then."

"I'll buy that." Her smile brought out bones while a melancholy twinge made her wonder what he would think if he knew that in her youth she had conducted business out of a Manhattan apartment. Her clients were corporate executives who booked her in advance, flowers arriving before they did. "But I'm not sure Myles would. His pride would get in the way." "I can understand that."

His horn-rims reminded her of a client who at Christmas time had given her a glossy catalog of jewelry, no prices listed, and told her to choose something. The order form was in back, coded, so that his company would get the bill.

"In tough economic times, Phoebe, you learn to live smaller."

"As long as others don't notice," she said and privately brushed his hand, which had the whiteness and dry hairs of a scholar or a minister. Her fingers latched on to three of his.

He pleated his brow and spoke softly. "This isn't wise."

"It's not even possible," she agreed.

Lighter on her feet after a second drink, Kate Bodine glided into the company of two bankers from Andover, subtly balanced her attention, and charmed them both.

Near a marble mantel graced with silver candlesticks, she joined a clutch of aging men and full-bodied matrons. A white-haired man in a cashmere jacket stared at her without restraint, and she edged away to sample a serving dish of choice little meats. Dick English, under an abundance of silver-streaked hair, gave her an extravagant smile, stepped in, and whispered, "When?"

"Get off it," she said and moved away.

Someone stepped on her toe. New arrivals shifted patterns and rearranged scenes, and she sought her husband through a whirligig of heads and faces. Young Turks—go-getters in managerial positions at Raytheon, Gillette, and the like—surrounded him, held him in an eddy of talk.

Angling out of the drawing room, Kate sought a bathroom and found it occupied. Another was close by, but she went off track looking for it, the heels of her pumps tapping the oak floor of a passageway that abruptly deposited her into a room of period pieces. A large gilt-framed mirror displayed the tarnish of authenticity, chairs looked appropriately fragile, and Germanic

faces from another time peered out of photographs. A solitary
figure stood near a baroque lamp. Beverly Gunner was smoking
a cigarette.

"Don't tell. Paul doesn't like it." Under the golden shell of
hair a smile worked loose. "Is everything all right? Is there
enough food?"

"Everything's fine," Kate said quickly.

"Paul wants it to be perfect."

"It always is."

"He'll find something." The cigarette held high, the smoke
escaped like a ghost going out on its own. "He's too smart for
me, Kate. He's too smart for all of us."

"No man is that smart."

The cigarette was snubbed out. "He'll smell the smoke, he
always does. Is my face all right, Kate?"

The skin around the eyes was worn, exhaustion written into
it. The thin lips looked as if they had been stamped hard with
permanent red ink. Kate said, "You look lovely."

"Then we must get back. Let me go first."

Kate found a bathroom off the kitchen and used it. The
seat was cold. A wall mirror faced in on her, and with a bit of
a start she discovered what she looked like sitting on a john. In
the lighting, the ivory curve of her hip was bone. The roll was
down to its cylinder, and she ripped away the last tissue, more
token than whole. At the sink the water ran cold, then too hot.
She took out a tube and hurriedly made a mouth as if a camera
awaited her.

Returning to the party, she did a double take. Chief Morgan
was standing at the edge of the crowd. Despite a wineglass in
his hand, he looked very much an interloper with his searching
air and the queerness in his expression. A bit of tattered lining
hung loose from his sports jacket. She went to him with a challenging smile.

"You a guest or a crasher?"

He drained the wineglass and gave it to her. "I have to talk
to your husband," he said, the words full of weight.

"James, what is it?"

He gazed beyond her. "He's here, isn't he?"

"Maybe the billiard room, I'm not sure. James, tell me what it's about."

"I think it should come from him." He edged past her. "Don't worry, I'll track him down," he said, and for a wild second she imagined him scampering on all fours with his nose to the floor.

She tried to follow him, but others got in the way. Regina Smith touched her arm and said, "We must see more of you and Harley." She nodded and weaved, heads bobbing around her.

She still had the chief's empty glass and placed it on a table. Strong fingers gripped her arm. "Kate, I'm sorry," Paul Gunner said. The words and the tone frightened her, and she pulled away, bumping shoulders with someone. Then she saw the stricken air of her husband.

"Harley," she said, bearing down.

Chief Morgan edged back into the double doorway of the billiard room, where he became a shadow. Her husband stood in bright light, his arms slack, as if the movement had gone out of them for good.

"My son is dead," he said.

2

IT WAS THE HEART OF SUMMER, THE DOG STAR ADDING ITS HOT breath to the sun's. On Beacon Street, traffic was packed into a heated whole. From a tall window in the cool of her studio, Mary Williams gazed down at it with a sadness that had to do with other things. When she turned to the man behind her, the endless brow of his shaved head shined in her face. With a smile, he stripped down to his Jockey shorts and tensed his stomach into curling muscles, which he displayed challengingly.

"You can't hurt me here. I see the punch coming, I can take it every time."

"Why would I want to punch you?" she said.

"You'd be surprised those who'd like to."

She watched him flex his arms, the muscles ropes, not a bit of him wasted. His presence was pronounced and emphatic, which made him seem taller than he was. His nude head was the bone handle of his body. The only evidence that he was approaching sixty was the netted skin around his deep-set eyes, like the wingscape of butterflies.

"Where's the fag?" he said, and she stiffened.

"Don't call him that. I'd find it offensive even if it were so."

"Did he leave you?"

"He's away for a while. He'll be back."

"A guy like that, you don't know what he'll do."

"You don't know anything about him," she shot back.

"I got eyes, that's enough."

Bending, he unzipped a rugged gripsack and pulled out a set of camouflage clothes, which was what she wanted to capture him in. His name was Eaton, but he called himself Soldier. Nearly twenty years out of the army, he still imitated the life.

"I shouldn't need more than an hour," she said and watched him reclothe himself into a warrior and blouse his pants with stretched condoms square-knotted at the ends.

"I got the cap," he said. "Do you want me to put it on?"

"No need," she said, her gaze fixed on him. His ears lay flat as if in babyhood and beyond they had been taped. A violet hue burned through his suntanned scalp. His temple pulsed.

"Where do you want me?"

She stationed him in the strong light from the windows, where he stood in a way that looked hostile, not exactly what she wanted. "Relax. Act as though you were waiting in a line."

"I was doing that, I wouldn't relax. I'd want to get to the front."

"Okay. Be that way."

She perched herself on a high chair, with a sketch pad in her lap and a collection of charcoal pencils in the pocket of the paint-smeared shirt she wore over shorts. Her feet were bare, the toes curled over a rung. Quickly, the edge of her hand scuffing the rough paper, she began sketching him but without verve or confidence, without the fire with which she could pretend she was Goya etching madness, Munch darkening a scream. She tore the sheet from the pad, tossed it aside, and started afresh.

He winked at her. "I like it better when you do me in the raw."

With quick strokes she strove to capture from his stance

someone lonely, displaced, and rootless, but produced only caricature. Her nerves were out of order.

"You got nice toes," he said, "but you ought to paint the
nails. Give 'em character."

Her pencil concentrated on his face, weathered and shatter-
proof, and on his deep-set eyes, which could go conveniently
vacant, immunizing him from criticism and insult. Every line in
his brow seemed to have a purpose that defied translation. She
was better doing women. Women she understood.

He said, "I know somebody could give you a nice pedicure."

"I don't want a pedicure, Soldier. I just want to get this
right."

"You'll never get me right. I'm nobody you ever knew."

"You're commoner than you think," she declared, shutting
the sketch pad and slipping off the chair. "But you're right, it's
not working. Maybe the next time."

"Tell me the problem," he said, "maybe I can solve it."

She pattered to a table, where she opened a leather bag and
extracted bills from a wallet, half the usual amount, which she
offered up. "Will this do?"

"Yeah, I'll accept it." He deposited the money into a deep
pocket. "I know the problem," he said. "Your friend's not here,
right?"

She took herself to a window and gazed at the traffic, which
the city endlessly sucked in and dribbled out. Sometimes her
head hurt thinking about it. Pedestrians herded themselves along
a crosswalk, their steps quick and their eyes wary, for the change
of lights did not guarantee safety. Without turning, she said,
"Your girlfriend, Soldier, I'd like to meet her."

"You would, huh? Why?"

"I'd like to do her."

"It's not her thing." He came up behind her and caressed
her back with the heel of his hand. "You're sad, aren't you? How
long has he been gone?"

"Two weeks," she said.

His breath closed in on her. "You got different bedrooms. How come?"

"That's none of your business, Soldier."

"Don't get mad, I'm just asking. When will he be back?"

"I don't know," she said, unable to muffle the worry in her voice or cloak the tension in her shoulders. He rubbed her back in a circular motion. Leaning over, he brandished his unwanted face.

"You know what I like best about you?" His lips went to it. "This little mark on your cheek."

She stepped away, nerve-worn, uncertain, vulnerable, all of which heightened her sense of the absurd. His splotchwork of clothes presented farce rather than force. His arms hung long. He was not tall, only middling.

"You want me to go, just say so."

Her mind veered from one thing to another as she flung a final look out the window. "There's no rush," she said.

Holly Pride at the library may have been the first to take note of the fellow, his appearance scruffy then but not yet derelict. When he breezed through the twin doors, she knew he was no townie and surely no resident of the Heights, but where others might have seen merely untidiness and eccentricity, she went beyond the stubble and rumpled clothes and surmised refinement and poetry, a story within a story.

"May I help you?" she asked when he approached the desk, bringing with him a bath of air, hot and humid. She was ready to rummage shelves for him, but all he wanted was a street map of the town, which she provided with a timidity that arose at vital times, a curse to her, a bit of amusement to him. Seated at a secluded table, he pored over the map and later scanned the town's ill-written weekly, *The Crier*.

Only she seemed struck by him. Fred Fossey, the part-time veterans affairs officer, was deep into a war book and never looked up. Other patrons ignored the stranger, but occasionally, with bent brows, Fossey glanced at them.

He stayed an hour and in leaving thanked her with the sort of smile into which she could have read anything. Shifting to a window, she watched him ambulate the green, pausing to admire the rockery of flowers lovingly maintained by the Bensington Garden Club. She was sure he would return the next day or soon after, but he didn't.

He did, however, reveal himself in the leafy little neighborhoods beyond the green. Mildred Crandall, the town clerk's wife, answered a knock at the back door and laid eyes on him when his appearance had deteriorated to whisker and grime. He astounded her because she had not seen tramps in Bensington since Depression days, when her mother had hurried them away with table scraps. She sent him walking with a powdered doughnut cocooned in plastic wrap.

May Hutchins let him sit a spell in her gazebo, where she served him a bowl of high-fiber cereal weighted with strawberries and drenched in low-fat milk. He wore a signet ring she hoped was not stolen. The best time of day, he told her, is when the dew is still on the grass. "Yes," she said, "I'm an early riser too." A robin's egg, he went on, is more precious than a pearl. She shied away from the unpleasant odor that flew up at her but relished his words.

Dorothea Farnham, whose husband was a selectman, would have no truck with beggars and threatened him with a bone knitting needle when he failed to move fast enough from the back step. Then she cursed him roundly, which was a mistake. A while later, stepping out the front door, she saw something on the porch that heated her face. It approximated shit and, on closer inspection, was exactly that.

Sergeant Avery responded to her incensed call and cruised the neighborhood in one of the town's two marked police cars. The sergeant came up dry, but early that evening, five miles away, a man fitting the description was seen bathing his feet in Paget's Pond, which was conservation property, no swimming allowed.

At the selectmen's meeting, second Monday of the month, Orville Farnham told the board that a person of disreputable ilk, no apparent abode or income, in other words a bum, was infecting the town. A motion was made, seconded, and Farnham brought his gavel down on a unanimous vote for the police chief to handle the matter forthwith. Chief Morgan, not present, got the message in the morning.

In his investigation, which carried through the week, the chief learned that the fellow had been here, there, and everywhere, including the Heights, where he had been seen plucking flowers. Everett Drinkwater, the funeral director, glimpsed him reading stones in the cemetery, and birders with binoculars spotted him in purple loosestrife behind Wenson's Ice Cream Stand on Fieldstone Road. Tish Hopkins, an elderly widow with a farm farther up Fieldstone, found him sleeping with her hens, rousted him with a pitchfork, and offered him a meal for an hour's work, which he declined. She fed him anyway.

Toward the end of the week the man was sighted several times on rural roads near the West Newbury line, which gave the chief a fair idea where he was taking shelter. "I'd better come with you," said Sergeant Avery, who was off the clock. It was late afternoon, the heat high, with two fans whirring in the station. The chief said, "He's not that big a deal."

The chief's old car, unmarked except for the faded town seal on each side, ran rough. He rode it around the green, turned right onto Pleasant Street, and drove with the sun in his eyes until he reached County Road, a long and lonely stretch through pinewood, with only occasional frame houses to break the view. The sky was irreproachably blue.

A mile from the West Newbury line he slowed at the sight of a weathered post that had once supported a mailbox and angled onto a dirt road that crept into the woods and came abruptly to a clearing. A battered pickup smeared with pine needles squatted on four flat tires. Nearby, the rusted handlebars of a bicycle protruded from weeds like the horns of a slain buck. To the left was a shack of a house with a ruined front step and torn window screens. The persons who had lived in it, Dogpatch types, a father and son, were dead, and another son, who lived in Florida, had forsaken it. The chief slipped out of the car.

Robins sang, jays made noises. Wild raspberry canes, thick with thorns, sprang at him. He ambled toward the house, his eyes on the windows. The door hung loose. Avoiding the rain-rotted step, he edged directly into a kitchen inundated with the hot and gamey smell of animals. Skunks had long had their way with the rubbish, and raccoons with half-human hands had ransacked the cupboards. Beneath the stained sink was the murk of a rat hole. The chief stood still, breathing soundlessly, aware that someone was in the shadows of the next room. He squared himself.

"Come out of there," he said forcefully. "I'm a policeman."

He waited, listening to the mad scampering of squirrels on the roof, at least two, maybe three. A dense spiderweb near the ceiling flaunted the remains of moths. From the other room came a silence not of emptiness but of indifference.

"Come out or I'll shoot."

A voice sounded. "You don't have a gun."

"I'll get one."

"What kind?"

"Never mind what kind!"

A floorboard creaked, and a man emerged, his hair matted and his whiskers like needles. The chief drew back from the reek of him, humid like fruit past its time, the juices fermenting.

"Who the hell are you?"

The man was smiling. "Your prisoner."

Regina Smith spent the afternoon playing golf at the Bensington Country Club with Phoebe Yarbrough, Anne Lapierre, and Beverly Gunner, but she did not leave with them. She went into the clubhouse to make a phone call, glimpsed Harley Bodine sitting alone, and, with a surge of compassion, joined him at his table. She had not seen him since his son's funeral.

"It's not something you can get over," he said. He was drinking a martini. A smiling waitress brought her white wine. They were the sole patrons.

"In time you will," she said. "Not entirely, but enough to go on."

He looked unconvinced, wary, and she, uncharacteristically, reached out to touch his forearm. Actually she had never liked him, too ambiguous, too furtive, but now she was dealing with someone who had lost a child, which changed the rules. He was costumed for golf, but she knew he had not been on the green.

"Where's Kate?" she asked.

He shrugged, ill at ease with her presence. He did not look at her directly. A certain hauteur on her part had always kept him at a distance, but now, for the moment, she wished to draw him closer.

"How's she taking it, Harley?"

"He wasn't her son."

"But she loved him, I'm sure."

A seal broke, and his face altered. "Things haven't been good between us, you probably know that."

She had suspected it. Kate Bodine was too vital, too spontaneous for him, perhaps even too young, more in attitudes than in years. "I had no idea," she said.

He brought out a cigarette, which surprised her. She had not known it to be one of his vices. "Do you mind?"

Actually she did. She detested the smoke and the smell. "No, go ahead."

He lit up and said, "I think she's seeing someone."

She was somewhat taken aback because people, particularly men, did not confide in her about such matters. Her aloofness, along with her impeccable looks, tended to have a belittling effect on the cares and concerns of others. She tilted the wineglass and sipped.

"I won't tell you who," he said. "It's too ironic."

She wanted to know, though she despised details, for there was decorum to maintain, dignity to uphold. She reasoned that it must be someone unlikely, and for a stunning instant she wondered about her own husband, though that was absurd.

Bodine flicked an ash. "I think I know where they meet." His fingers fretted a napkin. "I could be wrong. It may be nothing, but I can't count on it. Right now I can't count on anything."

He was, poor man, being hit with too much too fast, and she gazed at his lowered head with interest. His brownish hair had a chalk part. His ears were prominent. Something about the shape of the whole head suggested the asceticism and celibacy of a monk from another century.

"I'm not up to another loss," he said.

He needed propping up, as Ira occasionally did, as all men do, though loath to admit it. The wine was not to her liking, and she stopped sipping it. "Everybody's life," she said, "has cracks. The strong fill them, the weak fall through."

"Now you sound like Gunner."

"Heaven forbid."

His face loosening, he met her stare. "What I told you about Kate, I wouldn't want that to get around."

"I don't reveal confidences," she said, her tone chastising him. The smoke bothered her, and she was glad he was finally stubbing out the cigarette, a nasty thing. She and Ira had never had the habit, unlike her first husband.

"When Glen was killed, it was as if someone had raised a hammer over my head," Bodine said suddenly, his face opening. "And I feel it's still there, ready to come down."

"The loss of someone we love can do bad things to us," she said with a clear memory of the boy's mother, pretty but worn, done in by the tragedy. She had met the first Mrs. Bodine just that once, at the wake, a funeral home in Brookline. Bodine had stood beside her as if still married to her while Kate had tried to make herself inconspicuous, no easy task for someone of telegenic bearing.

"I was supposed to see him and didn't. It was his birthday. That's a guilt I'll take to the grave," he said, and she imagined he would, no way to mitigate the regret, no way to bring back the day. "I'll never know if he stumbled or was pushed. I don't want to believe he jumped."

"Jumped?" That surprised her. The boy had been a classmate of her stepson's at Phillips, top of his class, his heart set on Harvard, the medical school. "I don't think he would have done that, Harley."

"So much was going against him," he replied distractedly. "I thought he was in remission."

"He was coming out of it." He sighed. "His mother says he wouldn't have taken his life, but I can't be sure."

Regina stayed silent, for he seemed to have fallen into a tolerable mood of impassivity he did not want broken. She let her gaze wander over vacant tables. The waitress, who wore her hair high, a take-off of tarnished gold, was joking quietly with the bartender.

"Good of you to listen to me," Bodine said abruptly, breaking his own spell. "I usually keep things to myself."

With concern, as if somehow she were now responsible for him, she watched him finish off his martini. "You're not going to have another, are you?"

"I know when to quit," he said, and she more or less believed him. Anxiety leaped into his eyes when she glanced at her watch.

"I really must," she said and rose with a graceful swing and the certainty that even in sporty clothes she carried an imperious and peremptory air, as if others came alive only when she arrived and faded once she left.

"I wish you wouldn't."

She peered down at him. "What is it, Harley?"

"I don't want to be alone. I don't quite know what to do with myself." Tension worked its way across his face, like a wire. "Am I asking too much?"

"Probably."

"There's no logic to depression. It can eat anything."

"Only if you let it." The dark of her eyes and the sullen force of her smile challenged him. The waitress was heading toward them. "Check, please," she said, and the waitress turned back. "When's the last time you've been to Burger King, Harley?"

"I never have."

"Then it'll be a first for each of us," she said.

Chief Morgan, who did not want the man beside him, stuck him in the back, tilted the rearview to keep an eye on him, and with all the windows open ran the car out onto County Road. The sunlight of early evening tore through the pines. Needles blazed. Docile enough, the man said, "You arresting me?"

"That's what I'm doing," the chief said. "You smell."

"You arresting me for that?"

"The charge is vagrancy."

"I have money." The fellow pulled out a crumpled bill from a pocket in his pants. It looked like a ten, but it might have been a one.

"There's another charge," the chief said, his eyes sweeping from the mirror to the road. "Defecating on private property. A resident's porch."

"I deny it. Categorically. Do you have a witness?"

The chief pressed on the gas. A few minutes later he rounded the green, cruised past the library and the Blue Bonnet restaurant, and made his way into the lot behind the town hall. He parked in a reserved space a few feet from the police sign that sprang over a side door of the building. Looking into the mirror, he said, "Get out."

The man said, "Shouldn't I be manacled?"

"If you run, I'll shoot you."

"I haven't seen the gun yet."

The chief took him into the cramped quarters of the station but did not get far. Meg O'Brien, the civilian dispatcher who worked long hours, some unpaid, and exerted authority beyond her duties, leapt up from her desk. Her pony teeth erupted from a narrow face. "You can't bring him in here!"

"I have to put him somewhere, Meg."

"Then clean him up first, for God's sake. He reeks."

The man smiled through his whiskers. "I've already been told that."

Swiping at her hair, the color gone from it, she stepped from the desk. "What's his name?"

"He says it's Dudley. Nothing more. Just Dudley."

"Does he have a wallet?"

"No wallet. Meg, let me handle this."

"If you keep him here, you'll have to feed him."

"I know that."

"I'm hungry," Dudley said.

"Clean him up first, Jim. Please!"

The chief took him out, walked him through the lot, guided him through a gap in the back hedge, and marched him across a narrow street to the fire barn. Chub Tuttle, a volunteer, and Zach Unger, a permanent, looked up from their card game and gawked at Dudley. The chief said, "I wonder if you boys could give me a hand."

The two glanced at each other. Chub, whose regular work was roofing and carpentry, had a plump face boiled by the sun. Zach's was grained like walnut. Zach scratched his head.

"Don't let me put you out," the chief said.

Chub took off his shoes and put on black rubber boots, in which his feet slopped. Zach unwound the garden hose used to wash down the pumper, which usually got a wash whether it needed it or not. Dudley said, "I'm not going to do this."

"You don't have a choice," the chief replied, and presently a filthy jacket with crested buttons and split seams fell to the concrete floor. The chief kicked at it, read the label, and muttered, "Brooks Brothers, for Christ's sake." The shirt came off like skin and then, reluctantly, everything else. The socks were stiff at the toes and heels.

"I don't much care for this," Dudley protested. "I was molested once at a boys' camp."

"No one's going to bother you," the chief assured him and flipped him a bar of Ivory Chub had provided. Zach activated the nozzle of the hose. When the water hit him, he shrieked, for it was cold. Then he began to like it. "Use the soap," the chief commanded. "Scrub it on!"

The water ran rich. Chub, swashing through it, said, "Ain't much of a man, is he?"

"Hell, he's got more than you," Zach said, increasing the spray.

"How do you know what I got?"

"Your wife told me."

"You shut your mouth!"

Crouching, the chief picked through the discarded clothes at arm's length. Nothing in the pockets except the bill Dudley had brandished, a one, not a ten. The shoes, which were English leather, were ruined.

"He's pissing!" Chub shouted.

"Everybody pisses taking a shower," Zach said.

Straightening, the chief waited awhile and then said, "That's enough. Get him a towel." He looked behind him. "He'll need something to wear. Anything hanging around?"

Twenty minutes later, hollow jaws stark from a shave with a disposable razor, Dudley was making himself at home in a flannel shirt too big for him and jeans broken at the knees. His belongings, including his shoes, had been shoveled into a barrel. Zach had hosed away the dirty water into a drain, and Chub, flopping in his boots, was swabbing the remains.

"I owe you fellas," the chief said.

He took his charge out of the firehouse. The air was humid, the heat of the day still plugged into it, though the sun was setting fast. Dudley, barefoot, walked gingerly. "Where's my dollar?" he asked, and the chief, shortening his stride, gave it to him.

"That won't get you far, will it?"

Cutting through the hedge, Dudley stumbled, recovered, and smiled as if immune to injury. Padding through the lot, his eye out for pebbles, he rolled his sleeves to the elbows and gave a hitch to his pants. When they entered the station, Meg O'Brien looked up and said, "Is that the same creature?"

"I'm not decent," Dudley declared. "I'm not wearing underwear."

"You're not wearing shoes either," she said, pushing her chair back. She had long feet and, in the bottom drawer of her desk, a pair of old sneakers she sometimes wore for comfort. She hauled them out. "They might fit him." Her gaze remained critical. "He could use a haircut."

"I think I've done enough," the chief said.

"You lock him up, you'd better consider something. He might hang himself."

"You wouldn't do that, would you, Dudley?"

Dudley was crouched. He had put on the sneakers, a fair enough fit, and was tying the laces. "I might," he said. "I might do anything."

"Look at that," Meg said. "He's got dimples when he smiles."

"If he answers a few questions, I might go easy on him," the chief said. "If he gives me facts instead of fairy tales, I might even let him go."

Meg said, "That would save us all a lot of trouble."

"I want to eat first," Dudley said, rising.

"You want too much," the chief said and took him by the arm, not to the cell, where cleaning supplies were stored, but into his office, where he activated a ceiling fan. Then he seated Dudley on a hard chair and himself behind his desk, atop which papers were fluttering. He anchored them with a coffee mug and a pencil holder. "All right, what brought you to Bensington?"

"Breezes," said Dudley.

"Give me a straight answer."

Dudley pressed his lips in rigid concentration, then said, "I must've been on a toot."

"Where'd you get those clothes you had on?"

"Stole them off a line."

"That's a criminal offense. Another charge against you. That ring you're wearing, did you steal that too?"

"Better throw the book at me," Dudley said with a smile that brought back the dimples. "When do I eat?"

The chief dropped back in his chair, an old leather-cushioned rotary that grated on its wheels. "Dudley your first name or your last?"

"I don't know. It's the only one I remember."

"You're a strange fellow, Dud."

"Yes, I've always known that."

"Where do you live?"

"The woods, the roadside, chicken coops."

The chief lifted his face to catch the cool from the fan. "What do you do in the winter?"

"I freeze."

"And what do you do when you're not freezing?"

Dudley smiled. "I kill kids."

"I hear we got a prisoner," Floyd Wetherfield said eagerly when the chief stepped out of his office without entirely closing the door behind him. Floyd, who had good looks but bad posture, as if someone long ago had bent his back against his will, was the youngest member of the Bensington Police Department, less than a year on the job, the evening shift. He wore his uniform with prideful aggression, the cap squared, the revolver hitched high. "Can I have a look at him?" he said and, slipping by the chief, peered through the space at the office door. "He's not cuffed."

"He's not going anywhere."

"You gonna lock him up?"

"Soon as you clean out the cell."

"You mean you're holding him?" Meg O'Brien said with surprise.

"In a manner of speaking," the chief said with an odd expression on his face. He glanced at Floyd. "When you finish with the cell, get him something to eat from the Blue Bonnet."

Floyd looked at his watch. "It's closed by now."

The chief looked at him. "Somebody will still be there. Rap on the window. Get our fella what he wants."

"What's he want?"

"Cookies and milk," the chief said.

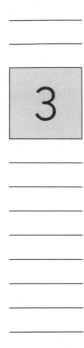

3

THE MORNING BROKE BRIGHT OVER BENSINGTON, MORE HEAT
and high humidity predicted. May Hutchins, who had slept
badly, turned with a groan and flumped a pink arm across the
bed when her husband rose. For a half hour, off and on, she
dozed in and out of quick little dreams, one bearing no involve-
ment with another, though all were vaguely unpleasant. She was
running a bath when her husband drove off in his work van, and
she was sipping her first cup of coffee, her hair in curlers, when
he returned unexpectedly—back from the Blue Bonnet, where
he breakfasted most mornings with the early regulars, a bunch
of townies gabbing across a communal table, Fred Fossey probably among them.

"Guess what?" he said. "They caught the tramp you told
me about. The chief locked him up."

What tramp? Her mind was still fuzzy. Then she remembered. "The chief arrested him?"

"He's just holding him."

"What's the difference?" she snapped and chided herself

for being short, but she couldn't help it. It was her age, her time of life, her uneasiness with it. She swallowed coffee. "What's the chief doing—making a federal case out of it? Hasn't he got anything better to do?"

"The tramp could be dangerous, May. You must've heard about that business with Dorothea Farnham. He did a mess on her porch."

No, she hadn't heard, and she laughed. "Poetic justice. Dorothea thinks her own is odor-free."

"That's not nice, May. She was your good friend in high school."

"That was then." Then was thirty-six years ago, too upsetting to think about, which was the reason she despised birthdays. Each was a thief. "Roland, stop doing that!" He had a habit of clicking his teeth. Thank God she still had her own. "Did you make a special trip back just to tell me about the tramp?"

"I thought you'd like to know."

"It could've waited," she said, a raw nerve loose in her voice. She liked the house to herself.

Roland peered at his watch. "I guess I got time," he said and poured a cup of coffee. He joined her at the table, which forced her to draw her feet in.

"What did you have for breakfast?"

"Scrambled eggs," he said, "fresh from Tish Hopkins's farm."

All that cholesterol—but she couldn't tell him anything. He ate what he wanted. "Who was there?"

"You know, the regulars. Malcolm Crandall, Eugene Avery, and the rest of 'em."

"Fred Fossey?"

"No, come to think of it. He hasn't been showing up lately."

"Why not?"

"Don't know."

"Maybe he gets more gossip at home than an ear can take."

He slurped his coffee. "I thought you liked the Fosseys."

"Fred's all right, but Ethel's a big mouth."

"You shouldn't talk that way."

"I'll talk the way I want."

She didn't mean to be short with him, but what did he know of the great gusts of sadness that swept through her at odd hours, of the dreads that snatched at her heart? At twenty, she had been rightly proud of secretarial skills acquired from McIntosh Business School in Lawrence. The school, like her skills, no longer existed. At twenty, her life had seemed so large. Now it wavered small.

She watched him finish off his coffee sooner than he had intended and carry the empty mug to the sink to rinse it out. His chubby arms worked like flippers out of a gray short-sleeve shirt that matched his trousers. He was a master electrician with his own business, a good provider throughout the marriage, a fine father, all of which must've mattered once, but now the children had families of their own. She wondered what she was still doing with him.

"I'm not sure what time I'll be home," he said, flipping through a pocket notebook, his work schedule.

"Can't you give me an idea?"

"Seven, I guess." He kissed her cheek, which she barely felt, for she had trouble staying in the present. The past was more attractive. "Anything the matter, May?"

"Nothing's the matter. What would be?"

So little of a person can be shared with another, that was the problem, the whole ball of wax. In the beginning you have your mama and in the end only yourself. She quivered with impatience, her lips apart. She was anxious for him to leave.

"Well, I'm off."

About time, she thought with a sigh. He gave her a tentative smile out of his full rosy face and turned away, poking in his pockets for his keys until he remembered they were in the van. At that moment something tore at her. Perhaps it was the slump of his shoulders or the mere confusion of her own emotions.

"Roland!"

He wheeled around almost in terror. She came out of her chair and, curlers dangling, gave him a hard kiss on the mouth, which knocked him off balance. His eyes went one way and then another.

"What was that for?"

"Nothing," she said.

Chief Morgan strode through the growing heat of the morning past the library and the post office and all the way to the Congregational church, which overlooked the far curve of the green, its hickory spire a whiff of whitewash against the Bensington sky. Morgan stepped onto the wide walkway, his gait turning loose and casual, a shade irreverent. Churches did not make him think of God. Apple blossoms did.

He moved from the walkway to a pebbly path alongside the church that took him beyond to the minister's quaint little cottage anchored in a surround of shrubs. The sun pounded the latticed windows, in which a few quarrels were broken. Affixed to the front door was a miniature cabinet sheltering paper and pencil for volunteers to leave messages when neither the minister nor his wife was home.

Morgan went not to the door but around the side to the garden, where the Reverend Austin Stottle was watering flowers with the hose held high, the spray playful. Without looking at the chief, he said, "When you splash water in the sun, you see nothing but jewels."

"It looks like fun," Morgan said.

"Would you like to try it?"

"Another time."

A black spider, lush with fur, scampered about in the home it had made for itself in the dusty miller. Red roses wallowed in their shrill beauty. Reverend Stottle killed the spray, tossed aside the hose, and assumed the stiffness of a prayer book. "I hear you have a prisoner. A lost soul, I gather."

"He could well be that," Morgan said. "An interesting fellow."

"Most people are, Chief. Some are very interesting."

"This one's wearing a class ring from Harvard. He could've stolen it, but I tend to think otherwise."

"As you grow older, the more astonishing life becomes," Reverend Stottle said with a smile. His hair was wispy, his narrow chin dented.

"This fellow might not be all there."

"Some say that about you, Chief, and I suspect many say it about me."

"I was going to let him go, but he said something that blew my mind. He claims he kills children."

"Good gracious, does he?"

"I doubt it," Morgan said. "I think he's putting me on. He likes attention."

"We all crave that. Some of my parishioners brood all week if they don't catch my eye during the Sunday sermon. I shouldn't say this, but Ethel Fossey is one."

"I don't know his whole name," Morgan went on patiently. "He won't give it to me."

"Stubborn chap, is he?"

"Sergeant Avery has fingerprinted him, and a friend of mine with the state police is sending the prints to the FBI. That will tell me if he's on record. I've a hunch he isn't."

"Is there anything I can do?"

"I thought you might talk to him, draw him out, give me more to go on."

Reverend Stottle drew himself tall with purpose, a mission to perform. "I'll do it right now, if you'd like."

"That would be great." Then Morgan lowered his voice. "Everything I've told you is confidential."

"Of course."

They began walking away in unison, Reverend Stottle's stride the more determined one, his shoes crunching pebbles when they reached the path. Then he stopped abruptly and looked back at the house.

"I'd better tell Sarah first."

In the luxury of her large bathroom, where fancy soaps exuded fragrances, Regina Smith brushed her black hair and did her nails. Rising from the dressing table, she moistened a monogrammed facecloth and patted her brow. Her face gripped a beauty that her thirty-eight years had only slightly loosened. Elegance escaped her by a few tantalizing flaws, one of which was a barely perceptible cast in one eye.

Dressed simply in a summer thing, she stepped to the window and gazed down at the pool, where her daughter and her stepson were lounging on rubber rafts. Each was in a minimal bathing suit, which upset her. Patricia, a tender outburst at fifteen, was her prize, the only value that had come out of her first marriage. Anthony, Ira's only child, was sixteen. His good looks provoked her, angered her. Anxiety whitened her face as she sought in theirs hints of intimacy, which was her worst fear. Boys wanted only the one thing.

Neither should have been here for the summer. Patricia, through her school in Connecticut, had arranged to stay with a French family outside Paris, but with no knack for a foreign language she had grown homesick and returned after a single week. Anthony had been enrolled in an Outward Bound program in Maine, which he detested. When he came home for the Bodine boy's funeral, he decided not to go back, much to her chagrin.

Her gaze focused on him. His mother had died several years ago, which meant that she had had to assume a responsibility. His room was at an opposite end of the house from Patricia's, she had seen to that, but she had to be on constant guard. How often had she reprimanded Patricia for coming to the breakfast table in only a long T-shirt? How many times, especially in the past weeks, had she sorted through Patricia's intimate laundry for telltale evidence? She had even pawed through his.

He was out of the pool. Patricia was joining him. Regina moved back slightly in order not to be seen, but their attention was with themselves. They were talking, laughing, but she did not like the way they stood poised, as if their bodies were scenting each other. She was on the verge of shouting, but good sense prevailed. Order and control guided her life. With invincible calm she turned away.

Downstairs in the breakfast nook she dipped a spoon into

a melon half and chided herself for letting pressures build, but she did not want anyone putting hands on her baby. Even with Ira, she always alerted herself for nuances in his behavior with Patricia. One could not be too careful. For all his maturity, dignity, and reserve, Ira could be contrary, like a boy in new shoes splashing through puddles.

Finishing the melon, she munched on an unbuttered scone. She took care of herself, ate the proper foods, worked out twice a week at the health spa at the country club, though some of the women got on her nerves, especially the ball player's wife, who was silly and shy, definitely out of place. And Kate Bodine was not entirely to her liking: too much of a presence, too much of the working girl still in her. Even Phoebe Yarbrough seemed lacking at times, as if something there didn't quite mesh.

Pushing aside the remains of the scone, she sipped from a cup of decaf. She was well aware that aloofness was her natural air. As a child she had chosen her friends carefully and had had few—sometimes none. In adolescence she had let her guard down with boys unworthy of her. The choice of her first husband had been reckless, a mistake rectified with Ira.

He always left a morning paper for her, usually the *Globe*, occasionally the *Times*, never the *Journal*. Today it was the *Times*. She attempted the crossword puzzle, but it was difficult, unlike the easy ones at the beginning of the week, which she often completed without a pause. Her pencil moved slowly. Twice she erased. The ring of the telephone shattered her concentration.

The voice on the other end was Harley Bodine's. "I don't mean to be a pain in the neck," he said.

She filled a plunge of white squares with the missing word in a Shakespearean line but was annoyed that she couldn't remember the play from which it came. "What is it, Harley?"

"Please," he said, "can we talk?"

After introducing them, Chief Morgan left them together in the little cell. Dudley, whose clear eyes showed the benefit of a good night's sleep, was sitting on the edge of the cot and flexing his

toes inside Meg O'Brien's sneakers. Reverend Stottle held a fat
orange. "This is for you," he said, bestowing it. "A gift from
my wife."

"I don't believe I know the woman," Dudley said, "but
thank her for me." When he began peeling the orange, it
squirted its juices. "Would you like half?"

"It's all for you," the reverend said, making himself at home
on a gray metal chair. He had imagined the lockup would be an
ominous dungeon furnished only with a wooden stool and an
unemptied chamber pot. The cot looked quite comfortable, actually, with a pillow provided for the prisoner's head. A fan with
rubber blades stirred the air, and magazines had accumulated on
a wall shelf. The old *Newsweek*s, he guessed, were the chief's and
the *Playboy*s, he figured, belonged to Sergeant Avery or Officer
Wetherfield. He said, "How are they treating you?"

"I could use a TV."

"They probably won't keep you here long."

"They don't intend to let me go," Dudley said with no
apparent alarm.

The reverend wished he had not been introduced but had
sneaked up on the man all at once. A person caught unawares
can never be sure what lies on his face. It could be a vital clue
to what lurks in the soul. "Otherwise, are you comfortable?"

"They could've dressed me better," Dudley said, crossing
his legs. The sneakers gave him feminine feet.

"Where do you go to the bathroom, I'm just curious."

"They let me use theirs." He was eating the orange with
gusto, both halves, the peels deposited beside him.

"I understand you don't remember your full name."

"Dudley's more than enough."

"A Harvard man, I hear."

"It may have been Dartmouth."

The reverend took into account that mental illness could
give a person false selves. Indeed, it could provide access to a
whole wardrobe of personalities. He himself had once donned
the robes of Jesus, not a comfortable fit and definitely not a

pleasant time for his wife, upon whom he had forced the role of Mary Magdalene.

"Or Yale," Dudley said. "It's uncertainty that keeps me young."

"How old are you?"

"I've touched fifty."

"I've scraped it," Reverend Stottle admitted. He was closer to sixty and subject to moments when everything saddened him: the look on a weary woman's face, the slant of shadows across the green, the aimless trot of a dog without a collar. With sympathy he said, "It mustn't be pleasant being locked up."

"But I'm not," Dudley said cheerfully.

The reverend looked around. "This is a cell. There are bars on the door."

"It's never locked. It only looks it."

"Then you could walk out anytime you pleased."

"The chief has said as much, though he hinted I wouldn't get far."

Reverend Stottle came up a bit in the metal chair and solemnized his voice. "You said a strange thing to him."

"For his ear only."

"It was rather bizarre, you must admit."

"He shouldn't take seriously everything I say."

The reverend winked conspiratorially. "Does that mean you tell whoppers?"

Dudley smiled mysteriously and wiped his fingers, the scent of the orange embedded in his nails. The reverend gazed at him full in the face with all the shrewdness he could muster. In a way it was a pretty face more suited for a young man.

"Can we be friends?"

"I believe we already are," Dudley said.

"Can you tell me anything about yourself? Perhaps where you come from?"

"That's not clear."

"Perhaps Dudley isn't your real name at all."

"I'm sure it is."

The reverend felt vaguely that he was not in charge. Either God was not guiding him, or an invisible hand was working against him. "I'm not disturbing you, am I?"

"I enjoy the conversation," Dudley said.

"But something's not working here, Dudley. Perhaps you don't trust me."

"Trust must be earned."

"I agree, absolutely." Patience and a greater degree of wile, the reverend realized with some misgiving, would be necessary. "Is there anything you want?"

Something seemed to surge inside Dudley's head. His face gained force. "I could use something for irregularity."

Reverend Stottle brightened, for here he had answers. When he was a child, his mother had always fed him things she said were good for his bowels. Fresh fruit, she claimed, made you happy on the toilet. "The orange should help," he said. "Tomorrow I'll bring an apple."

"Promise?"

"I do." He rose from the chair, his posture relaxed and meditative. A wondrous feeling of usefulness pervaded him. "Would you like to pray?"

"Next time," Dudley said, "when you bring the apple."

He stepped to the cell door. When he rattled it, it flew open. The chief was waiting for him with folded arms near Meg O'Brien's desk. Meg ripped a tissue from a floral box and blew her nose. "I'm afraid we have a lost soul in there," he said, his eyes on both.

The chief said, "Thanks for trying."

"It's my job," the reverend said, with a suspicion that the chief had been listening in. "I promised him I'd be back."

"That's good," the chief said, and Meg O'Brien looked the other way.

After the reverend left, the chief loosened his arms and scratched the back of his head with his middle finger. Meg rose and stood taut in a dress that hung crooked. "I'm not going to say anything," she said, but then she made a disapproving *tsit-tsit* with her tongue and teeth.

"All right, Meg. Say it."

"I just don't know what that was supposed to accomplish —bringing in a fool to talk to a loony bird."

"It was worth a try."

She looked at him gravely. "No, it wasn't."

In the hot Boston sunlight, Mary Williams and Soldier passed doorsteps with decorative iron rails. Someone had chalked a swastika in a handicap parking space. Soldier, whose politics were repugnant to her, smiled. They had left Beacon and were walking past Commonwealth Avenue toward Newbury. She had on a net jersey, a thin swishing skirt, and sandals. Soldier, wearing a tank top and khaki shorts, paraded an overcharge of muscles in his arms and legs. His tennis shoes lacked laces.

"Feeling better?" he asked.

"Yes," she said, turning her face from the traffic. She had woken with a headache, which aspirin had only half killed. On Newbury Street traffic was heavier. Vibrations engulfed her.

"You sure?"

"Yes, I'm sure," she said.

They took refuge under the canopy of a crowded sidewalk café and threaded their way to an unoccupied table, lucky to find one. Soldier ordered sweet rolls and grapefruit juice; Mary asked for coffee only. He said, "If you're feeling better, then what's the matter?"

She watched a bearded man rattle a newspaper, a young couple touch hands. The man was reading the theater section, the couple each other. Everything seemed right with the world, but inside her were anxiety, division. When her coffee came, she said, "He's never been away this long before."

Lowering his shaved head, Soldier tore into a roll. "You got me, what more do you want?"

She heard a deep voice and imagined Heathcliff, but it was only a waiter, not theirs, repeating an order. "That nurse of yours . . ."

Soldier laughed. "We have an open relationship."

"I see. She doesn't mind."

"Wouldn't matter if she did."

She watched the young couple kiss, their movements a slow melody from another time. "And where do I rate with the nurse?"

"Higher." He downed the grapefruit juice as if it were whiskey. "You got a beauty mark."

"It's unlovely," she said.

"You're wrong, but if you don't like it, have it removed."

"Why should I? It's me."

He was grinning, showing sturdy white teeth. "You've got another asset. Your grandmother's bed."

"Don't get used to it," she said and hurled her gaze toward the sidewalk. Faces swarmed, traffic rushed. "When he comes back, you're gone."

He laughed, and she strained to stay on top of her emotions while envying his arrogance and independence. He had no apparent worries, no baggage. He didn't work. He lived on an army pension and off women, currently the nurse. "Who knows," he said, "you might want me to stick around."

It was that cocksure immediacy that she tried to trap in sketches of him, with only varying success. His life was all in the present tense, no past. Sometimes he alluded to his military service, but he seldom talked about it. Once he mentioned a sister but gave her no face.

"You support him, don't you?" he said, gathering crumbs and eating them. "I know you do."

"It's none of your business."

"What is he to you? I still don't get the relationship."

"It's not for you to understand or even think about," she said, sweeping her hair back. The couple had quit kissing and were leaving. The woman had a rich, confident laugh, as if life could never be cruel to her. The young man's face was alight. She was saddened to see them leave.

Soldier said, "What if he doesn't come back?"

"Then I shall die."

He snorted. "I know bullshit when I hear it, and that's bullshit."

"Then you shouldn't ask questions that require lies."

"How long have you known him?"

"Always," she said, which was not true, but was true enough. She swallowed coffee, wishing it were her own herbal tea.

Soldier said, "The guy's got a secret life."

"We all do."

"But maybe he's crazy."

"Maybe."

"Maybe you both are."

"That would follow." She put her coffee cup down. The bearded man, with the air of a connoisseur, was staring at them over his newspaper; then he withdrew his eyes as if he had seen enough.

"You finished?" Soldier said and snapped his fingers at a waiter, not theirs, and asked for a check. When it came, Mary paid with a bill fresh from an automatic teller machine, the newness sticking to her fingers. Soldier reached the sidewalk before she did.

"You go on," she said. "I'm going the other way."

He contrived a smile. "What do you mean? Where are you going?"

"I'm going to look for him."

"You're right," he said. "You're crazy."

They met at Paget's Pond, five miles from the green. Kate Bodine drove up in a Mazda, the seat pushed back for leg room, and was out of it when Chief Morgan pulled up with a small smile of gratitude, for it was she who had phoned. Stepping out, he said, "Crazy summer. One whole dog day."

"No season is perfect, James. Always too much of one thing, not enough of another."

They moved away from their automobiles, skirted a weathered picnic bench and a No Swimming sign, and followed a path toward the pond. Birds gave voices to the pines. Canada geese were distant buglers. When they reached the water, she yanked her hands from her pockets.

"I don't know why I'm here."

"Give yourself time, it'll come to you." He was enchanted as ever by her eyes, the blue from a crayon stub. The sun spangled her hair. "I've looked for you at the library."

"I haven't been there."

"Holly Pride mentioned you have an overdue book."

"Who in hell is Holly Pride?"

"The librarian."

"My God, were we that obvious?"

"Only to Holly, I'm sure. She's a romantic."

Kate looked away. Morgan did too. The surface of the pond, toward the distant middle, was restless, swirling in places, as if from a dynamo of hidden fish. From the opposite shore came faint traces of voices, which startled her.

"Girl Scouts," Morgan explained. "The camp's in the woods. Were you a Scout, Kate?"

"A Bluebird. I flew up and never landed."

He stared at her with much wishful thinking and too much purpose. In his head was the ring of a hammer, which another time might have driven her back a step. Now she was distracted. "Kate, what's the matter?"

"I don't know."

He embraced her for the first time ever. He kissed her chastely on the cheek but held her too tightly, despite a resolve to make no uninvited moves.

"I'm all right, James. Let me go."

Walking side by side, they stepped over bumps of earth, mosses, stunted weeds. Pungencies from the pond filled the air. A blueberry bush yielded a bird, and a chipmunk, visible one instant, vanished the next.

"It's Harley," she said suddenly. "Something isn't right with him."

"I would think so. He's lost a son."

"It's that and something more. He's turned secretive and suspicious. When I come into a room, he jumps. His eyes try to cut holes in me, like he wants to hone in on exactly what I'm thinking."

"Maybe he knows about us."

"What's there to know? We haven't done anything."

"Only we know that."

She shook her head. "If it was that simple I could deal with it, even dismiss it, but it's deeper. I've become his enemy, and I don't know why."

"Could you be imagining it?"

"No."

High in the pines came a creak and then a loud crack, eerie because they expected to hear a crash but none came, which raised in Morgan a memory of his wife and their shepherd, wintertime, the pond frozen. Belly rumblings from faults in the ice had unnerved the dog, and the dog fled. He said, "Are you afraid of him?"

"Only because I don't know him, not the way a wife should. Too much is missing in the marriage—a child, for one thing. He led me to believe he wanted one, but he doesn't."

"Do you love him?"

"Bells don't ring, if that's what you mean."

"If you're unhappy, leave him."

"It's not that easy," she said, without explaining. Her smile was ironic. "I should be talking about this to another woman. Instead I choose you."

"A police chief has many functions."

"Let's get out of here," she said when voices from across the pond grew louder, some distinct. She had the lead as they made their way back along the path. Over her shoulder she said, "It's my problem, James. I don't mean to make it yours."

He felt too old for her, but he wanted her anyway. He wanted to be drawn into the whirl and heat of a romantic act of madness with a woman he could love. A mosquito whined in his face, and he repulsed it. He wanted too damn much.

The police radio was crackling in his car. He ignored it. She leaned against the fender and folded her arms. "You listen to a woman, James. Few men do. When we first met, something about you struck me as authentic and honest. I still feel that way. Why are you blushing?"

"There's deceit in all of us."

"But less in you, I think. I sense strength."

He took the compliment for what it was worth. Endurance, a kind of strength, was among his qualities, and women were his safety ropes. He did not mention that on evenings when he was alone, depression was a punctual visitor, arriving uninvited, staying as long as it liked, and leaving unnoticed, its absence only gradually sensed.

He smiled to hide his thoughts, and she reached out and touched his arm. "You have a nice smile, James, the kind that can glue a woman to you."

"The women don't seem to stay."

"You deserve better."

"I take what's given."

She leaned toward him. Her kiss was light, but it was on the lips and lingered. Then she climbed into the Mazda, shut the door, and gazed out. "I tell you my problems, James, you never mention yours. Maybe you don't have any."

"I've got a fellow locked up I don't know what to do with. His crime is telling scary stories."

"If I were still working in TV, I'd interview him, though no guarantee it would run. James, thank you."

She twisted the ignition key. The motor murmured power, and Morgan's ear, usually deaf to such matters, detected a degree of anxiety in the hum, something to be checked. He stepped back as she pulled onto the road, and then he watched the car climb a hill. The hill was fairly steep, a blind rise, and in the instant he envisioned disaster at the top. A sudden crash. A burst. Another woman taken from him.

The Mazda simply and soundlessly vanished over the hump.

In one of her nicer summer dresses, her lips painted, May Hutchins entered the police station and gave Sergeant Avery her friendliest smile, though she didn't think much of him, especially as a police officer. He was too dumpy for the uniform. His pants, too small or something, rode up on him, and his shirt was half untucked. She glanced at Meg O'Brien's unoccupied desk and at the chief's vacant office. "Where is everybody, Eugene?"

Sergeant Avery slammed shut the drawer of a file cabinet in which he'd been pawing for something he'd squirreled away and now couldn't find. He swigged root beer from a can and said, "The chief I don't know where he is, and Meg's gone home to do something with her cats."

"How many has she got?"

"Three last I knew, one died."

"Hope she didn't go into mourning. 'Course, she doesn't show her feelings like the rest of us. What are you staring at, Eugene?"

"You look different. Your hair, right? A different color, sort of orangy brown."

"You don't like it?"

"I didn't say that." He took another swig and then tattooed the soda can with his thumbnail. "What are you doing here, May? Something I can do for you?"

"I hear you got a prisoner. I want to see if he's the poor bugger came begging at my door."

"He leave you a present too?" Sergeant Avery asked with a smirk, and May arched her back.

"Just because Dorothea Farnham makes an accusation doesn't mean it's true. He came to my house, he was a perfect gentleman. Christian charity is what he got from me. You going to let me see him, or don't you have the authority?"

Sergeant Avery hesitated, then shrugged. "Sure, I got the authority. You want to see him, what do I care?"

She followed him through a doorway and down a short passage, a broom closet on one side and a lavatory on the other. At the end was the lockup. Peering through bars, she saw the prisoner napping comfortably on an army cot, a pillow under his head, a small table fan providing a breeze. "He looks different, but that's him," she whispered. "Sleeping like a baby."

"That's what he does best."

"Does he have a name?"

"Dudley."

"It suits him," she said, tilting her head for a better look. "I let him eat a bowl of cereal in my gazebo. He had perfect manners and a wonderful way of speaking. He said the best time of day is when the dew's still on the grass."

"All I know," Sergeant Avery said, still clutching the soda can, "is he's locked up for uncouth behavior. That's how the chief put it."

"Chief should talk. His is X-rated if half what I hear is true." She shifted her gaze to magazines on a shelf and found herself scowling. "Some of that reading material doesn't look proper."

"Must be Floyd's."

"I've a mind to tell his mother."

The prisoner was awake. A single blue eye stared at her from the comfort of the pillow. Over her shoulder, a blast in her ear, Sergeant Avery belled, "How's your stomach, Dudley? Any better?" In a lower voice the sergeant confided, "He's constipated. Poetic justice, the chief says."

Dudley sat up with a start, as if coming out of a dark place, and pulled at his ill-fitting shirt, which may have been disarranged in a dream. May watched him swipe the forelock from his face, which for a full moment suggested an old clock without the will to tick. Smiling through the bars, she said, "Do you remember me?"

A strange expression diminished his features, as if he were debating his own existence. Then he brightened. "Did you bring me anything?"

"Sorry," she said, wishing she had. His eyes were coins spending themselves on her. "Are you in much discomfort?" she asked with real concern.

"I want one of those," he said, pointing at Sergeant Avery's root beer.

"Go get him one, Eugene."

"Hell, no," Sergeant Avery said, "they're Meg's. One I'm drinking I gotta pay for."

"For God's sake, I'll spring for it."

He shuffled off with a grumble, and she peered through the bars. What was she doing here? What did she want? As we grow older, she asked herself, do we all drift into some kind of nonsense? Dudley was looking at her curiously, his signet ring catching her attention, and once more she wondered whether he had stolen it.

"Are you a good person?" he asked.

She was as good as the next but nobody special. In church she sang without a voice and at home played the piano without talent. She had never learned to knit, which prevented her from emulating Dorothea Farnham, who brought her needles to town meeting and gave the impression that her life was devoted to doing two things at once.

"Are you a happy parent?" Dudley asked.

What a queer question! "My children are grown," she said. "I don't see much of them." She did not mention that her son, only twenty-six, was beginning to bald, which made her feel ancient, and that her daughter, living in California, had made a mess of two marriages.

"Not everyone," Dudley said easily, "should have children. Chronos devoured his. Agamemnon sacrificed his to make war. This isn't anything I'm making up. It's mythological fact."

The names sailed over her head, but his smile warmed her, as if he understood everything and judged not. Sergeant Avery returned and thrust upon her an unopened can of root beer, cold to the touch. She poked it through the bars. "For you, Dudley."

"Something for you to remember," Sergeant Avery warned, working wisdom into his round face. "No good deed goes unpunished. That's what the chief says."

May said, "Screw the chief."

In facing chairs in her sitting room, Regina Smith listened to Harley Bodine talk in low and measured tones. He was in his dark lawyer's suit, his back stiff, his legs crossed. His movements were formal. "Kate and I don't fuck enough," he said. "That's one of the problems."

The crudity did not disturb her, merely surprised her, though the look she returned was impersonal, almost as if he were a tradesman. "Whose fault is that?" she asked.

"I don't think it matters."

"That sounds too casual."

"It's not something I can talk about with her."

"There's the real problem."

His face, monotonous in its grimness, looked used up. "We've never been truly open with each other. My fault, no doubt."

She could readily believe that, for people invariably summed him up as a tightass. Phoebe Yarbrough had speculated that his butt was a hairline fracture.

"I'm not easy to get along with," he added.

She could well imagine him as one person at the office, another in the privacy of his home, and a third here. His work world, like her husband's, was high up in one of those verticals of concrete and glass, in a suite of dark mahogany, stainless steel, rich carpeting, and abstract art. She had heard that he could wither an underling with a look.

"I don't know how to get close," he said. "The sexual act is only an illusion of closeness. No one can truly get into another person. We die strangers, one to the other." He flicked an ash into the dish she had provided. "Thanks for letting me smoke."

She had served iced tea. His was gone. "Would you like another?"

He shook his head. "Does Ira know I've been taking up your time?"

"I've mentioned it."

"Good, I wouldn't want him to think . . ."

They sat through a few moments of dead silence, which was broken by approaching voices. He stubbed out his cigarette, and Regina, relieved that her daughter was wearing something over the bikini, said, "You remember Patricia?"

Rising, Bodine had obvious trouble reconciling the memory of a child of ten or twelve with an adolescent of burgeoning maturity. The girl was lovely, lovely, like her mother. Same glossy black hair, same dark and indifferent eyes lacking only the mysterious cast in one. He lightly shook her hand. "You've grown."

"That's what they tell me," she said.

"And of course you know Ira's son," Regina broke in. "Anthony. Though he prefers Tony."

The boy, wearing a T-shirt and swim trunks, had the torso of a greyhound. Bodine shook his hand with vigor and feeling and said, "You knew Glen, didn't you, Tony?"

"Yes, sir. He was in some of my classes."

"All you boys who came to the funeral, I appreciate it. You were one of those he looked up to."

"Oh, I don't know about that, sir." The boy looked embarrassed. "More like the other way around. His grades were far above mine."

"All the same, I know he admired you."

Patricia leaned over her mother, said something, and left. Tony stayed because Bodine's eyes held him. Each stood tall, and the air in the room seemed to tighten around them. Regina sat motionless in her chair. Bodine said, "I'm going to ask you something I shouldn't, Tony, but maybe you can appreciate my state of mind. Do you think Glen took his own life?"

"No, sir. I don't think he'd have done that."

Bodine went silent, as if something infernal were picking at him. Regina spoke. "Why do you say that, Anthony?"

"It's what I feel."

Bodine spoke. "That's all?"

"I know he was sick and all, sir, but he never made much of it. Just the opposite. He said he was going to become a doctor."

"I know," said Bodine. "He had his heart set on Harvard Medical School."

The boy slung back his hair, which he wore long. His handsome face was a slant of light. "Wasn't it an accident, sir?"

"That's my problem, Tony. You see, I don't know what it was."

The boy left. A travesty of a smile seemed to detach itself

from Bodine's face as he busied himself with private thoughts. Regina noticed that his eyes were red-rimmed. "I should be going," he said but stood rooted. "I should be working things out on my own."

"Shouldn't you be doing that with Kate? Give her a chance, Harley."

"No," he said. "I can't trust her anymore."

Regina now had other things to do and rose from her chair. With a gentle but firm grip on his elbow, she took him from the room and guided him over an expanse of gleaming hardwood and then of dense carpeting. He moved with a heavy gait and some reluctance. At the front door he turned to her.

"I told you Kate's been seeing someone. He's not one of us. He's a townie."

"Then it can't be serious," she said, wondering who in the world among the locals would interest Kate, from whom she had expected better taste.

Bodine said, "Do you remember the man who came to the Gunners' party to tell me Glen was dead?"

"You're joking. Not the—"

"Yes," he said. "The police chief."

Racked with a fear that Dudley was lying somewhere dead, Mary Williams roamed the Public Garden in the hope of glimpsing him alive and well. She approached a man sleeping on the grass and then veered away. The heave of the sun hurt her eyes, and she almost stumbled into a great bed of marigolds that her fancy took for heaps of gold coin unloaded from a pirate's ship. Blazing begonias her mind made into the hemorrhage of battle. On the walkway a vagrant held out a raddled hand, but she was too distraught to grease it. When two children ran in front of her, she nearly tripped over them. She had to get out of there. Too much pressed upon.

On Arlington Street she remembered that Dudley sometimes spent hours in train stations and airline terminals, a pretender among travelers. On Boylston Street she hailed a taxi that had jousted too long in Boston traffic. Its front was jagged, its windshield cracked, and its trunk sprung. It looked savage. She climbed in anyway.

The taxi crept through Chinatown, where hot street air wafted in on her and Asian faces paid her passing attention. Chatter from the sidewalk reached in like a hand and took hold of her. Plaster-doll children with rolling eyes raced across the narrow street, but the driver was careful. Several minutes later, angling out of traffic, he pulled up at South Station. She spoke to him in an appealing voice through the opening in the clear panel that separated them. He was a middle-aged black man with warm brown eyes, who did not mind waiting.

"As long as you can pay the fare, ma'am."

Inside the great stone station her footsteps echoed over old marble. Nerve-worn, uncertain, she avoided undesirables loitering near the entrance to the public toilets and scanned the concourse. Men on benches goggled at her. Walking fast, she surveyed concession stands and gave a fleeting glance into a pizzeria. Two elderly women quailed at the raucous sounds of youths near the gateway to Track 4. That was when she fled.

"Logan Airport," she said, settling herself back into the taxi. Then she changed her mind and gave another destination, much closer. The driver looked at her.

"That's where you want to go?"

"Yes, I do," she said.

He eased into traffic, fell behind the reek of a slow-moving bus, and, much to her relief, escaped it with a quick turn at the first intersection. Without comment, he drove to the city morgue, the facade gray and granite. Twisting his neck, he said, "This is it. This what you want?"

"Yes," she said. "I'm looking for somebody."

His expression was sympathetic. "Somebody you hope isn't there?"

"Yes," she said, climbing out.

Inside the building, instinct showed her the way. Sculpted sphinxes flanked a stairwell, which she descended into a chill that made her think of polar snow. A passageway delivered her into an office where the furniture seemed to have been frozen into rigidity, like pieces in a museum. A man with a quiet, relaxed face and hair shaded zinc and nickel stood ready to help, though appointments were customary, some authorization mandatory.

"Do you have any unidentified . . ." Her voice failed, then half returned. "I have a friend who . . ."

"Are you up to it?" he asked, and she nodded. He took her into a long, lurid room of white tile and naked plumbing, where the taint of mold laced a greater chill. Her gaze swept banks of compartment doors, one of which was open, a vacant body tray visible. "Male or female?" the man asked.

She shivered as she spoke. "Male."

"White, black, or yellow?"

"White," she said. "Very white."

"Then you don't need to look," he said.

When she stepped out of the building, the heat came at her like a blast. The city sun drenched her. The driver turned to look at her as she pushed herself into the back of the taxi. She did not close the door right and slammed it the second time. "He's alive," she said.

"He's alive in there?"

"He's alive somewhere," she said. Instead of relief, she felt strain, which told on her. Her color was high, her hands trembled. "One more stop," she said and told him where.

He drove her without enthusiasm into South Boston, past fireplugs around which youths tended to gather, past a window display of dinette furniture, then through a preponderance of four-decker houses, where whoops of children could be heard from the alleys. When a man on a corner made a hawking-to-spit sound, she swiftly turned her head.

"My friend," she said, "he lived here for a while when he was a boy." She didn't know exactly where. It might have been this tenement house or that one, for they lacked definition, as if anything could be going on inside, or nothing. Pointing, she said, "It could've been there."

The driver kept his eyes straight ahead and drove all the way to the ocean edge, Day Boulevard, L Street Beach. He

parked near the beach, swimming temporarily prohibited because of a high coliform count. Nobody was in the water, but
people were on the sand, many women and children, a few
young men, and scattered elderly persons. The driver kept the
motor running and turned in his seat. His face was toil-worn,
the skin burlap. "I think you'd better pay me now," he said.

"I won't run away. Come with me if you like."

"This is not my neighborhood."

"Then I won't be long," she promised.

She removed her sandals on the sidewalk and plowed into
the heated sand, a yellow grit that stung her feet. The sky over
the ocean gave her bigger feelings of things, along with a sense
of the brink, the stepping off to anywhere. Her steps were
scissor-like, her trespass onto the beach duly noted. The faces
were Irish and struck a note. Where had she seen them before?
Then she realized she had seen them everywhere.

A man with a face blown big with good cheer gave her the
once-over. His tight trunks had a boastful pouch, as if holding
all his belongings. Beachwear gave the women shapes that were
overly honest. One stood explosive in pink, and another lay
gummed in stretch nylon that look irremovable. Wandering
among them, she felt like Cinderella, the feeling reinforced by
the blemish on her cheek, soot from a chimney.

At the ocean's edge, where a passing gull screeched like a
wronged woman, she let all the pain from Dudley's absence
come to bear, which hours earlier might have driven her to her
knees. Dangling her sandals from one hand, she stepped back
when spume from a broken wave touched her toes. Turning, she
came face to face with squalling children whose mothers
screamed at them not to go into the water. One child did.

She would have retrieved the girl herself, but a mother
reared up from a towel and charged forth, straps flying, breasts
bolting a useless harness. The flesh was milk brought to a boil.
The child, yanked by the arm as if it had no socket, stumbled
on the wet sand. Punishment was swift, the second slap reverberating louder than the first. Each left a rose on the skin.

Trying to remain frigid and detached, she could watch no

more and scurried away with the memory of another child nearly the twin of that one, the same flaxen hair and frail face and maybe even the same ruffled bathing suit. A child preserved in her sketch pad, eyes wondrously big, marvelously expressive. Midway up the beach her legs lost speed, and she paused to slip her sandals back on.

As she climbed into the taxi she noted a canteen truck across the street. Her driver, finishing a Fudgicle, tossed the stick out his window. "I took a chance," he said.

"I don't know your name. What is it?"

"It's a simple name, the kind you forget. John."

"Mine's Mary."

"Yes," he said, peering at her in the rearview. "You look like a nice old-fashioned girl. Where to now, ma'am?"

"Take me home, John. Beacon Street."

Traffic was rough, at times impossible, but no annoyance to her. Her eyes were closed. When the taxi finally pulled up at her brownstone, she rendered the fare with grace, the tip with generosity. She took two steps on the sidewalk and swerved back.

"Do you have a family, John?"

He leaned across the seat. "Children and grandchildren, ma'am. My wife works in an office building on State Street. She's a cleaning lady, night work. Those buildings never sleep."

"I'm a painter, John. An artist." She hesitated. "I think you'd make a fine model."

"I probably would, but I don't need to go looking for trouble, do I?"

"I'd be willing to—"

"Thank you all the same, ma'am, but this isn't my neighborhood either."

Soldier was waiting for her at the top of the stoop. He stood at parade rest, with the sun shooting rays at him. He said, "What the hell was that all about?"

She smiled wanly. "Dudley's alive."

Malcolm Crandall, who functioned as both town clerk and tax collector, left the town hall by the front door and went around the side to the police station. Meg O'Brien was on the phone and paid him no attention, which irked him, especially since the call sounded personal. He placed a buttock on the corner of her desk to force her to look at him. They did not particularly like each other. When she got off the phone, she said, "What's your problem, Malcolm?"

"It's my plumbing," Crandall said in an ugly voice. "I can't remember the last time I had a happy piss."

"Spare the details. What do you want?"

He shrugged. He was heavy-set, gruff, ill-tempered, and usually in a pucker. Nipples showed through his drip-dry shirt. When he was much younger, military age, a sucker punch had disfigured his nose. With a disparaging glance at the chief's vacant office, he said, "I see he isn't in. Must be banging somebody. Anybody we know?"

A movement in Meg's pony face perceptibly quickened. Her loyalty was ironbound. "Why don't you ask him yourself, if you've got the guts?"

"That guy you locked up, is he arrested or just living off the town?"

"What's it to you?"

"I pay taxes as well as collect 'em. Let me take a look at him. Might be somebody I know."

He didn't wait for permission, for the phone was ringing and she was reaching for it. Nor did he need to be told the way. He tramped the passageway to the end and peered through the bars, pleased with nothing he saw and outraged over what the prisoner was reading. His voice was controlled.

"They give you everything, huh? Even dirty magazines."

Startled, Dudley quickly smiled. "I don't have a TV."

Crandall felt a throb. The little prick wanted hotel amenities.

Dudley said, "I like to watch the soaps."

A fag to boot, a stinking flower, enough to make Crandall

want to retch. "How about a boy? Would you like a little boy in there with you?"

"No, thank you," Dudley said equably, sitting on the cot with his back to the wall. "But I see where you're coming from."

"You got no idea. Weren't bars between us, I'd smear the floor with you, wipe you up with a rag."

"I've been beaten up before. People like you."

"If it was people like me, you wouldn't be walkin'."

That said, Crandall passed a hand over his flat hair and would have stomped off if the creep had not mocked him with another smile. Abruptly he gripped the bars, and the door jumped open. When he stepped into the cell, the moment was electric, power he hadn't felt in years.

"Smile again," he snarled. "Let's see those dimples."

Dudley sheltered his head in his arms and raised his knees protectively, displaying the ability to accept immediately what was irrevocable. The blows never came, for a voice barked at Crandall. It was Meg's, which would not have stopped him, but another voice did. It was Chief Morgan's.

"You've got no business here, Malcolm."

The chief's presence pulled Crandall from a state half reverie and half rage. Calming the motion in his face, he aimed a finger at Dudley, whose head was still buried. "Another time," he said.

From his office Chief Morgan said, "We've got to get a lock for that door."

"I've been telling you that for years," Meg O'Brien replied from her desk. An hour later she was still at the desk because Bertha Skagg, her relief, had called in sick. With a glance at the wall clock, she shouted, "Somebody's got to get him something to eat."

Morgan, who had been on the phone, came out of his office. "Nothing on the prints," he said. "Our friend's still a zero."

"So what are you going to do?"

"Get rid of him. In the morning I'll drive him to Andover and dump him off at a bus stop with a couple of bucks."

"That sounds humane. In the meantime, you'd better feed him."

The chief left the station and crossed the green. From the church came the peal of an organ; then great chords were struck. Reverend Stottle's wife was practicing. Either that, or a tuner was busy. Morgan entered Tuck's General Store and went to the deli counter, where he was waited on by George Tuck, the only one of three brothers to stutter. George said rapidly, without a hitch, "I hear you've got a pervert locked up."

"Not for long," Morgan said. "I'm going to free him tomorrow and run him for selectman."

"That'll l-l-liven things up."

"What's on sale, George?"

"Ch-ch-ch-ch—"

"Yes, I'll have it."

Morgan returned to the station with a container of fried chicken legs and wings. The station was unattended. Meg was in the lavatory. Walking to the cell, he heard two voices. Entering the cell, he saw only Dudley.

"What are you doing?"

"Talking to myself," Dudley said.

"When you do that, you become two persons. Which one is you?"

He smiled. "I'm the one without the answers."

Morgan gave him the container and watched him lift the lid. Steam rushed up, the aroma filled the cell, and Dudley's smile widened. "I can use my fingers, can't I?" Morgan provided a napkin. "Hot!" Dudley said, gingerly handling a wing.

"I've a question," Morgan said. "Are you an alcoholic?"

"I'm a bit of everything," Dudley said, his teeth tearing flesh from a flimsy network of bone, which for some reason provoked an unease in Morgan. "It's good!" Dudley pronounced.

"I thought you'd like it."

"A picnic, almost."

"I'm letting you go tomorrow," Morgan said, and the look he received was angular.

"You don't have to."

"I'll add a couple of dollars to the one in your pocket and send you on your way, out of town."

"Maybe."

"Maybe? What do you mean, maybe?"

"You might change your mind."

"I don't do that easily."

Dudley licked his fingers. "I might change it for you."

4

SWEEPING ASIDE A SINGLE COVER, BEVERLY GUNNER ROSE WITH no awareness of dreams, a blessing. Too often baby demons invaded her sleep, pink-fleshed creatures born wrong and gathered for revenge, her daughter among them. Fay, who had entered the world defective, left it eight years later in a splash no one heard. Motors were revving, they said. Attention was elsewhere. No longer could she look at a body of water without imagining her child's soul in it. And only surreptitiously could she open the album preserving Fay's short history, for her husband did not like to see her poring over it. Nor did their two sons, the spit and image of him.

Stepping onto a lambskin rug, she stared at the wall picture she had not put there and had never dared take down. It was a color photograph framed in silver, bride and groom blown big. The bride was full-figured and dewy, encapsuled in a time when she had trusted the sentiments of popular songs and took faith from happy endings in movies. The groom, gripping her, was a tawny bear.

She looked at her watch. Gunner was still asleep but would soon need waking. They had separate bedrooms, hers the larger one, not because she had preferred it but because he had wanted one less elaborate, more masculine, more in tune with a self-image that exalted his bloodline, Prussian on his father's side and Hessian on his mother's. Her blood, Dutch and Danish, had been acceptable.

She stepped into her bathroom, which adjoined his, though the door was locked on his side. His privacy was sacrosanct, his foibles supreme. Like the rest of the house, a manor befitting him, her bathroom was his design, which the builder and sub-contractor had executed to the letter, overwhelming necessities with luxuries, a sauna she could have done without, a whirlpool she never used, a bidet the gilt likes of which embarrassed her. His bathroom was spartan, with a shower stall that barely contained his big breathing.

Bathed and dressed, she did her hair, a puff of gold, over which she sprayed a shell. Moments later, she left her bedroom and quietly entered his. The only extravagance was a water bed. "Paul," she said, and he came out of the covers like a whale surfacing to spout. The bigness of his belly sheltered his sex. His feet hitting the hardwood floor were fat thuds.

"Boys up?"

"No."

"Let 'em sleep."

His bullying voice she had long grown used to. His eyes were mere dents in his face. When he moved the flesh swam. It floated and drifted. It followed currents and tides and rode waves, everything a-quiver except his buttocks, which were concrete. From his bathroom, he told her what he wanted for breakfast, though it never varied.

Breakfast was on a low balcony, near which a trellis bled roses and honeysuckle drew hummingbirds. She buttered his toast, poured his juice, and served him jumbo eggs scrambled into a fluff. She would eat later when her stomach settled. Coffee suited her for now.

"God damn it," he said, looking beyond the honeysuckle.

A grubbing skunk had left divots on the billiard-cloth lawn. "Make sure they see that," he said, and she nodded, for it was her job to pass on instructions to the men who came weekly to tend the grounds, though he frequently interfered, as if she were sure to leave something out.

He scooped egg and crunched toast. He was a fast eater, with a need for his napkin, which he kept poised in one hand. She stared at his lowered head, at the thinning spot in his fair hair, and dearly missed the years his software company had consumed his life, his absences long, his presence a surprise and not always unpleasant. Now that he was home most of the time, she was attendant on wishes often no more than whims.

"Bodine will be dropping by later," he said, which both surprised and pleased her. "I'll see him in my study."

She was surprised because late yesterday he and Harley Bodine had talked for hours, much longer than usual, and she was pleased because she would have time for herself, no interruptions. Then she remembered that the boys would be up, each with his own demands.

He wiped his chin. "Did you hear me?"

"Yes."

"Then why are you so quiet? What the hell's the matter now?"

"Nothing," she said but knew what he was accusing her of. Perhaps it was always there in her eyes, ingrained in her face, the intractable grief she was no longer allowed to express. Whenever she tried, he raised a hand to ward off the words. If she persisted, he turned his back on her. In her heart she knew he had never forgiven her for having had an impaired child.

He finished eating, quaffed what remained of his juice, and was ready for coffee. She poured. Glancing at his watch, he said, "Maybe you'd better wake 'em."

The boys were his defense, the proof of his pudding. Their IQ's nearly rivaled his while hers was average. Fay's had been pitiful.

"So what are you waiting for?" he said.

Their bedrooms were in the west wing, a hike to get there,

a dreaded chore to wake them. As babies they had been piglets and as burgeoning children whiners and tyrants. Now, as adolescents, eighteen months separating them in age, they were more so. She rapped on the door of her younger son and opened it without looking in, for it was always suspect what either might be up to. "Time to get up," she said and briskly stepped away. When she repeated the performance with her elder son, he challenged her.

"Who says?"

"Your father."

God forgive her, but she would have sacrificed the two of them for the return of her daughter.

An hour later, she ushered Harley Bodine into the foyer and tried to convey in her manner the sympathy she felt due him, for undoubtedly his loss was no less than hers. It struck her as strange that he carried no briefcase from which to pluck facts and figures for Gunner's consumption, though neither, she recalled, had had one yesterday.

"This way," she said.

Halfway to Gunner's study, he touched her arm. "Beverly."

"Yes, Harley?"

He had stopped; his posture was wooden. "I know now what you've gone through."

"Yes, I'm sure you do." Out of habit she viewed him with reserve, though one could not distrust everybody. "Harley, do you have a cigarette?"

He glanced toward the study. "Yes," he said and sneaked her one.

It was their first shared secret.

Sergeant Avery brought Dudley his breakfast from the Blue Bonnet: coffee with extra packets of sugar and two bran muffins with extra pats of butter. Pulling up a small table close to his cot, Dudley said, "This may be my last meal here, Eugene."

"I thought I told you to call me Sergeant."

"I feel we're friends now," Dudley said, buttering a muffin

with a plastic knife that had come wrapped in a napkin. "I don't mind sharing one."

"They're both yours, you can thank Meg O'Brien. Her treat, not mine." Sergeant Avery left the cell but soon returned with underwear and socks. The undershirt was V-neck, the shorts boxer, and the socks argyle. "Compliments of the chief."

Careful of crumbs, Dudley wiped his mouth and fingers and inspected the goods. "They're not new."

"Just make sure you wear 'em. Chief doesn't want you leaving here indecent."

Twenty minutes later, Meg O'Brien, who occasionally cut the chief's hair, seated Dudley in the metal chair, draped a towel over his shoulders, and began snipping with thin scissors. "It's like I'm going to be executed," he said in a cheerful air of martyrdom. "I think I'd like bangs."

"Be happy with what you get," she said and gave his head the same attention she'd have given the chief's. When she finished, she handed him a mirror.

"It's lovely," he said, lying only a little. His eyes filled.

"What's the matter? It's not that bad, is it?"

"I miss my mother."

"Yes, Dudley, I miss mine too."

His final visitor was Reverend Stottle, who came bearing another orange and a medicinal vial the reverend claimed was a sure-fire physic guaranteed by Mrs. Stottle. Obligingly Dudley took some on a plastic spoon, made a face, and said, "I'll be leaving soon."

"Do you have anything to confide?"

"No," Dudley said, peeling the orange. He gave the reverend half. "But I have a question. Should we, any of us, be afraid of death?"

"No, indeed. I believe at a preordained time the soul flees the body like a tainted breeze, and death purifies it for the light beyond."

"Cleans us all up."

"There you have it. God looks after his own."

"And our souls are immortal."

"That's what they tell me."

Approaching footsteps sounded in the passage. Dudley sat quite still on the cot, eyes flickering, as if looking at himself in some inner mirror. "They're coming for me," he said.

May Hutchins and Fred Fossey arrived minutes apart at the library and sat at the same table but not directly across from each other, a ruse that didn't fool Holly Pride standing on heels higher than usual behind the checkout desk.

May opened a copy of *Mirabella* and flipped a page. Fossey, who had scarcely spoken since sitting down, leafed deeper into *Newsweek*.

"What's the matter, Fred? You got a hair across your ass?"

He looked up slowly, his face rumpled. The left lapel of his ill-fitting sports jacket bore a flag pin and a VFW button, backups to his title of veterans affairs officer. "It wasn't right what you did," he said in a low rasp.

May almost laughed. "What did I do?"

"Bad enough you fed that freak in your gazebo, you had to go visit him in jail."

"You mean Dudley?"

He skewered her with a look. "How would I know his name? What I'm saying is you should've shown more sense."

"He's one of God's creatures."

"He's a pervert."

"You're not my husband, Fred." She turned a glossy page and skimmed an advertisement promising feminine comfort from an intimate product with the scent of flowers. Nearly inaudibly, she added, "You're not even my lover."

He tucked in his chin, burying the loose knot of his tie.

Closing her magazine, she said, "I'm leaving."

"Please, don't." His head jerked. "I didn't mean anything."

"Roland doesn't talk to me that way. What gave you the right?"

"May, I'm sorry." He hesitated. "You know how I feel about you."

"You look ridiculous. You're red."

"Can't help it."

Staring at him critically, she could not determine which was the plus half in the vague disparity between the two sides of his face. Though the shine had worn away, he still had a full head of hair. That was a plus. And, unlike Roland, he did not carry in his pocket a little coin purse, the kind you pinch open.

"Say something, May. You know I put you on a pedestal."

"I don't belong there," she said with perverse satisfaction. At age ten, she had shown an older boy her bum for a quarter, and for another quarter had let him run a finger along the crack. Good God, she had been only a child, but what could she have been thinking of! A whore at ten, if only that one time.

"Guess what," Fossey said sheepishly. "This is our first fight."

"Yes," she said, unready to forgive him. She scraped her chair back and returned *Mirabella* to the rack. Passing the desk, she nodded to Holly while gazing pointedly at the peaks in the younger woman's blouse. Outside, Ben Foxx was staring up at the war memorial, though he knew all the names by heart and all the families. He turned with a smile as she approached.

"Good thing I don't run a gossip column," he said.

"Go to hell, Ben."

His face fell. "I was only joking, May."

She strode onto the sidewalk. She passed the Blue Bonnet and approached the town hall, indecision slowing her stride only for a moment. She went around to the side and entered the police station.

Sergeant Avery looked up in surprise. Meg O'Brien was on the phone and gave her only a glance. She swept past them both.

"Where are you going?" Sergeant Avery called out.

"To see that poor man."

"He's not there. Chief let him go."

She stopped in her tracks. "Good," she said. "You could tell just looking at him he was no criminal, just a lost soul. Where is he now?"

"Chief's running him out of town."

May shivered in protest. It was as if Dudley had come to her out of the air, a bird from a tree, to sing in her ear, a serenade of sadness and loss, a hymn to her—and now they were driving him away.

Meg O'Brien put the phone down and went to her, slinging an arm around her. "What's the matter, May? Why are you crying?"

"You've been smoking," Gunner said as he showed his lawyer into his study and shut the door. "I can smell it on you."

Harley Bodine made no defense. The movements in his face were uneasy, wary, as if only black threads held his mind together. Weariness clung to him.

"And you're wearing the same suit you had on yesterday. That's not like you." Paul Gunner stood near a round table occupied by two sets of toy soldiers, the plastic figures from Gunner's childhood and the lead from his father's. They faced each other on a field of green felt, the plastic pitted against the lead, the battle stillborn. "Which war do you think was more barbaric, Bodine? The Kaiser's or Hitler's?"

"I'm not interested in military history."

"Nor I. I'm pleased only by the toys." Gunner billowed toward a club chair and overfed it with his bulk. "What's your blood, Bodine? Who are your people?"

He remembered a grandfather who had worn work shirts buttoned at the neck and had spent days on an assembly line and evenings in a union hall. The strongest memory of his father was that he had smoked Raleigh cigarettes, saved the redeemable coupon slivered inside the cellophane of each pack, and promised him a bicycle as soon as enough coupons were amassed. The bicycle, he remembered, was the toy he never got.

"Don't you know?" Gunner asked. "Or do you choose not to?"

"They're not me." He spoke with his body thrown forward, waiting for permission to sit, which finally came with a nod.

"Nothing was handed to you, right? You rose on your own. Brains got the scholarships and put you through Harvard."

"I also waited on tables."

"I wondered whether you'd tell me that." Gunner saturated him with a look. "Uptight about it, aren't you?"

"Not at all."

"My great-grandfather earned his living killing cattle with a sledgehammer. People said with that swing of his he was to slaughtering what Babe Ruth was to baseball. Do you believe that, Bodine?"

"I have no reason to doubt it."

"My father had his brawn and got his brains from the other side of the family. I always thought he was durable as iron, but a heart nobody knew was bad took him. He had all the right genes, but you never know, do you?"

Bodine had come to talk, but instead he listened, his face now adhering to a fake composure emptied of meaning. He felt that recent events had been taken from a dream and made real. Without thinking, he said, "Don't you ever get depressed, Paul?"

"I'm too smart for that, and you should be too busy. You're spending too much time out of Boston. Get back to your office. Operating at high pressure, isn't that your strength?"

It had been, but now he saw it as horrendous tedium for which he no longer had the will. "I've had bad dreams."

"Time shuts up everything," Gunner said with impatience.

"I thought I could handle it."

"You telling me you can't?" The voice had a crust. "What *are* you telling me?"

He was telling too much, but Gunner was the only one in whom he could confide, though he expected no sympathy, none whatsoever. He watched Gunner's hand chop the air.

"You make a decision, you live by it. You're not sleeping well, take a pill. That doesn't work, take the whole bottle. Then you have no worries."

"I'd never do that," he said and felt the cramp worsen, like punishment.

"Then take some advice. Don't complain—who cares?"

He managed a smile. "My mother used to say that. She was

an amateur singer. The songs she sang the most were from musicals."

"I don't want to hear about your mother," Gunner said and heaved himself to his feet. For moments his breath came out poorly. "Now get out of here, I've got things to do."

Bodine gripped the armrests with an effort that produced nothing. "I can't get up."

"Then sit there till you can," Gunner said and left the study.

"I don't like none of it," Soldier said, holding the large sketch pad at arm's length. "And I'm big, but not that big."

In her latest likeness of him, Mary Williams had over-endowed him, and she had garbled his muscles, cluttering them into miscalculations of the body. Besides that, she had narrowed his shaved head, scratched menace into his eyes, and thrust savagery into his posture.

"It's not me," he said angrily, as if she had turned him into pornography.

"Yes, it is, but something's missing." She took the pad from his hands and set it aside. "That's why I should meet your friend. I need to see what kind of woman would live with you."

"She doesn't know me any better than you do."

"Maybe nobody knows you, Soldier. Would that please you?"

"I know myself. That's good enough." He rubbed a bare shoulder, near the strap of his tank top. Just under his chin the skin was the color of common clay, and the rest was red. A sweat band broke the endless sheen of his forehead. "I ask nothing of anybody. That's been a rule."

"Thank God for rules," she said and watched him paw idly through canvases stacked with their faces to the wall. "I'd rather you not do that."

Before she could stop him, he lifted a canvas from the stack, extended it, and sought perspective by poising it this way and that. "What the hell is this? I don't get it."

It was an abstract convulsion of acrylic colors, mostly red flaring into shocking pinks, garish yellows, and burning blues. Mary had the dismal feeling that something bad was going to happen, but nothing did. Her voice was sharp. "Don't look at a painting, Soldier. Look into it!"

Squinting, he pulled a face. "I still don't get it."

"I painted water as if it were gasoline, and in my mind I put a match to it and let the brush do the rest."

"Looks like the brush didn't do what you wanted." He spotted letters scratched into the rough wood of the frame. "Says, 'Swimmer.' I don't see any."

"There isn't one, Soldier. Only a face, but you need eyes to see it."

"Whose face? Yours?"

"Doesn't matter if you can't see it." Much rumbled in her head, but she didn't let it bother her.

He slid the canvas back into its place and began poking about, disturbing things, prying. His sneakers slithered over a length of tarpaulin to a cluttered table, where he picked up an art magazine and riffled for nudes. Then he turned his attention to a folio of travel photography, some of it exotic. "You been to these places?"

She had never been out of the continental United States; had never been on the ocean, fear of the depths; had never been on a flight, fear of the universe. "My grandmother, not I."

A watercolor she had done years ago kept her grandmother alive for her, but it was not for his eyes. It showed her grandmother struggling with a corset, a woman warrior donning pink armor, with thighs pocked, starred, and chewed from the rigors of battle.

"I've been all over the world," Soldier said. "Eighteen when I joined the army, thirty-year man when I got out. Little I haven't seen."

"Don't touch that," she said, for he was opening an old sketch pad, the pages brittle and the edges tattered. She moved swiftly over the tarpaulin but not in time to stop him, and she knew immediately the sketch that engaged him, a painful one of herself at sixteen, the only personal evidence that she had ever been that age. He stared harder.

"Is this you?"

"No."

"There's a mark on the cheek, like yours."

"Then maybe it is." She slid the pad from his grasp and closed the cover, but he was already snatching up another, not as old but not new. She grabbed it from him and flipped it open. "What do you think of this?"

He tilted his head. "It's a kid. So what?"

Pastels gave the little Gunner girl a shell pink complexion, quince yellow hair, and Wedgwood eyes, along with a gossamer air, as if the drawing had been done in a false light. The girl could have almost passed as a childhood doll long preserved in tissue and now making a tentative gift of herself. "You don't know, do you, Soldier?"

Her voice had deepened, and he gave her a curious look. "It's not you, I know that."

Her smile was uncanny. "I've shared a secret with you," she said, "and you don't even know it."

Kate Bodine spent the afternoon on the telephone, calls to Boston, each of the television stations, letting people know she wanted to get back in the business, though no one offered hope. Times were tough. Station managers were laying off, not hiring, which of course she had known. Her old boss, a fatherly sort, said, "Otherwise, how are things, Kate?"

She was seated at a little desk in a bow window. Without warning, tears sprang into her eyes, but she kept them out of her voice. "The mere fact I'm alive always excites me."

"That sounds like you. How's married life?"

"Fine, Charlie. Sunshine and roses." She spoke too flippantly, and he was quiet for a few seconds. She ran a finger along the crust of a notepad where pages had been ripped away.

"I'm sorry, Kate. If things change here, you know I'll keep you in mind."

"But no promises."

"You know what promises mean in this business."

"Then you're sweet not to make any."

Consulting a directory, she jotted down the numbers of Boston's two dailies. She spoke to Driscoll at the *Globe*, afterward to a lesser personage at the *Herald*. Neither, though graciously polite, could offer anything. Each asked about her marriage, and the lies she told tightened the mask on her face.

Later she carried a glass of chablis outside and sat in a canvas chair under a dogwood. The day was still hot. The sun bled. Roses, fed all the right ingredients, luxuriated on a vine. Brick paving girded a riot of flaming hybrid lilies she had planted in the spring. Gardening had produced the only fruit of her marriage.

She had finished her chablis and may have dozed off, for when she raised her eyes she saw her husband. His jacket was off, his tie loosened, and his lips pinched around a cigarette. His footsteps marked the grass. Moving without vitality, he dropped himself into a chair away from hers. She had no idea how long he had been home.

"You surprised me," she said.

He shrugged. The heat dimmed his eyes, and she was unsure whether he was looking at her or only seeming to.

"That cigarette, Harley, it's not you."

"I am what I am," he said almost inaudibly. "Nothing more, nothing less."

She tried to recall what she had seen in him, other than that he had been a departure from others in her life, men in love with themselves, a sportscaster for one, a weekend anchor for another. "Help me, Harley. Tell me what's wrong."

"If something's wrong, you tell me." His tone was distancing, as if she were a stranger.

"Do you want to talk about Glen?"

"Why should I want to talk about him? He's dead."

"I know that, Harley. I know that as well as you."

He leaned an arm over the side of his chair and snuffed out

his cigarette. He was constrained, silent; then his face went crooked. "Are you seeing anybody?"

The question, which should not have surprised her, took her aback. "If you're asking whether I'm having an affair, the answer's no."

"If you're not having one, why are you seeing the police chief?"

She could not stop herself from coloring, for the blood came too fast. She did not want to lie, but neither did she want to reveal anything that was only half true. "I'm not *seeing* him. He's someone I met at the library, and we chat now and then. That's as far as it goes."

"What's he been asking?"

"I don't know what you mean."

"What do you tell him about me?"

Much more than he would have liked, but she had never mentioned his meanness with money, the way he shortchanged waiters and waitresses, cheated the paperboy, evaded payments to merchants and repairmen, as if everyone were trying to put something over on him. Nor had she mentioned his restlessness in the night, which had driven her into a bedroom of her own.

"Well?"

"What is there to tell?" she said.

"When's the last time you saw him?"

Her thoughts eddied, and her mind shouted at him to shut up, for she did not want to answer any more questions. "I don't remember."

"It couldn't have been long ago."

"Maybe it wasn't."

"Maybe you don't want to talk about it."

She remembered thinking that marriage was the only ir-revocable step she had taken in her life, a one-way adventure into a new world, the possibilities boundless. She forced herself to speak. "I'm looking for a job."

Without comment he looked away. Flying insects, silver-bodied in the sun's brilliance, swarmed over emerging mums, and bees were at the roses. The humid air was rhythmic with the activity. She lifted herself up.

"I'm going in."

He rose too and approached her. He looked at her with tired eyes and spoke too close to her face. His breath had turned. "How would you like a child?"

"I wouldn't," she said.

Windows were open, and the heat of the day, laced with pollen, lay dense in her bedroom. Emerging from the chaos of a sneeze, she plucked a Kleenex from the night table and blew hard. Wiping her nose, she said, "Put on the air conditioner."

"No," he said. "Then we can't hear anything."

They were sitting cross-legged and barefoot on her bed, library books between them. She reached behind her head and fantailed her heavy black hair. Her shirt was open, the cups of her inadequate bra overfilled. "I was going to knock on their door last night," she said, "but they were getting it off."

"Why shouldn't they? They're married."

"I know, but doesn't it make you feel kind of itchy? My mom. Your dad."

"You're too much, Hannaford." In private he called her by her surname because it isolated their differences. What he liked best about her was the high promise she carried of her mother's likeness.

"I wish we had a joint," she said.

"Your mother would smell it in a minute."

"Forget her. You worry too much."

His own mother had died when he was nine. When he was eight, he had seen her in her bath and had waited for God to strike him dead. He had glimpsed the tense line of a breast and had anticipated a thunderbolt.

"What time is she coming home?" he asked.

"How do I know?"

"Where'd she say she was going?"

There was a laugh. "Are you afraid of her, Tony?"

"Don't be silly," he said.

"Do you have a thing for her?"

"Cool it, Hannaford."

He asserted himself by leaning over the books, breathing her air, expanding his chest. She lifted his T-shirt and counted ribs, then pinked his stomach with a sharp finger. He squeezed her feet. Her painted toes glittered like candy. She kicked free, her legs leaping from a denim skirt.

"What do you think of my new panties?"

"Jesus, Hannaford!"

She wasn't wearing any. Her private hair was a narrow wedge pointed down at a bare cleft, the price paid to accommodate the brevity of swimwear, the currency hot wax. Her brown eyes gained luster as she snapped forward to sweep the books off the bed. "Do you want me to do you?"

He was nervous, apprehensive, his ears wide open for threatening sounds. "Not now. It's too hot."

"Then do me," she said, dropping back.

It was as if she were offering him a cup from which to staunch a thirst. Jaws thrust forward, he felt the growing weight of his head on the back of his neck, with an opposing force coming from the sudden clamp of her hand. He exulted in the thrilling odor of her but twice thought he heard a car and another time footsteps behind him. Still, he brought her off, or perhaps she brought herself off. He was never sure.

"I'd better get out of here," he said with a fast look at his watch. He leapt away, struggled with his sneakers, then the laces, and grabbed books that were his. She smiled languidly from the bed and scratched an ankle with the toe of the other foot, as if he were no longer essential to a mood or relevant to her life.

"You did your duty," she said in a teasing tone.

He slipped out of the room, leaving the door ajar. Carpeting in the wide corridor, which soaked up his footsteps, also muted the *plocks* of Regina Smith's high heels. His breath caught when he saw her round the top of the staircase. Approaching him, she cast fiercely maternal eyes toward her daughter's room.

"What were you doing in there?"

A book slipped from his grasp. His T-shirt was sweat-soaked. "Talking."

Her face contorted. "It better not be what I think," she said and swept past him.

Chief Morgan crunched the key into the ignition lock and told Dudley, who was sitting beside him, to buckle up. Dudley did so with a vacancy in his smile, as though a major portion of him were on automatic. For no obvious reason, Morgan took the long way around the green, past the post office, the church. As they neared Tuck's General Store, Dudley pointed. "Fellow in there stutters."

"You know a lot about us," Morgan replied. "I wish we knew something about you."

"Are you really letting me go?"

"That's the idea."

There were better routes to Andover, but Morgan meandered onto Summer Street, where dense hedges separated small properties and trellises supported overloads of roses. House fronts, set close to the sidewalk, shone with respectability.

"Some people I haven't said good-bye to, like those fellows at the fire station."

"Chub and Zach. I'll do it for you."

Morgan made an elbow turn onto Spring Street, where the gory remains of a woodlot animal lay on the road. He drove around it, almost onto the walkway to an old Victorian with gingerbread trim.

"Woman in there was nice to me, gave me a powdered doughnut."

"I'm glad you didn't mention that to her husband. He's the town clerk, the fella who wanted to take you apart."

Spring Street took them to Ruskin Road, which eventually led them into the Heights, where a yellow trash truck was grinding up the litter of affluence. Grand houses on rolling grounds, some with stone beasts lounging at the gateways, celebrated their worth with balconies and cupolas, arches and columns. An estate of manorial pretensions loomed on a rise.

"People named Gunner live there," Morgan said with a gesture. "He's a genius, they say. Three years ago their little girl drowned in the Charles River, Cambridge side."

"Then that's where her spirit is."

"She's buried here, Bensington."

"It could be in both places."

A little later Morgan gestured again, with a slower hand. "The man here lost his son not long ago. The boy, only sixteen, was killed by a subway train in Boston. You must've seen it in the papers."

"I never read those kind of stories."

"His name was Bodine. That name mean anything to you?"

"No," Dudley said with a shrug, "but it has a good ring. Could be a character from a historical romance, the sort my mother read. And Gunner. That could be from a World War I poem."

Several minutes later they crossed the line into Andover, bigger than Bensington in scope and population, with numerous enclaves of affluence. The roads were wider, the traffic swifter, especially on South Main, where overblown development occupied the memory of an apple orchard. Phillips Academy lay ahead, its bell tower a beacon. When they drove by the campus, Dudley looked left and right, for it sprawled on each side of the divided street.

"I went there," he said.

"You went here?"

He paused. "It may have been Exeter."

Downtown, Morgan parked across the street from the bus stop and glanced at his watch. "We've got a few minutes," he said and settled back. A knot of young businessmen with a harmony of short haircuts and broad smiles were gabbing near Andover Bank. Outside Brigham's an elderly couple shared an ice cream cone, one lick for her, two for the old gent. Morgan said, "Do you still have your dollar?"

"You said you'd give me more."

"When you get on the bus."

A young mother, high-hipped, all legs, scooped up her child

in crossing the street and set him down near the bus stop, where the sun netted her and diminished him. A racial mix of summer students from the academy sauntered by.

"The bus will take you to Boston," Morgan said. "Will you be all right there?"

"That's too much to think about." Dudley creaked his neck for a wider look at the elderly couple. "I wouldn't mind an ice cream."

"There's no time." Bothered by the heat, Morgan heaved a sigh. "I don't know who you are, Dudley, but you worry me. I wish you didn't."

"I'm a puzzle, I don't deny it."

"I can make things add up, but I have to force the figures. You see, I just don't know. That stuff about killing kids, it's easy to talk cold-bloodedly in the abstract."

Dudley conveyed a look that could have been this or that, Morgan had no way of telling, no skills, he felt in dealing with him. The businessmen were dispersing, one into the bank, the others elsewhere, the sun beating on them.

"Ease my mind, Dudley. Tell me you wouldn't hurt a flea."

"You're the policeman."

"But I don't solve crimes. What I do is my best, which most of the time is enough."

"You look tired," Dudley said with an undercurrent of fellow feeling.

"I am." Which was the whole truth. The last couple of nights he had slept poorly, allowing old sadnesses to come to bear, some in dreams. And Dudley, whom he had first viewed as a challenge, was now a burden.

"It was his birthday," Dudley said quietly.

"Excuse me?"

"And he wore braces on his teeth."

"Who did?"

"The boy killed in the subway."

The mammoth approach of the bus was sudden and tumultuous. In the clamor brakes hissed and wheezed, and the back of the bus steamed. Faces peered through the square windows, some featureless because of the glare of the glass. Morgan waited for something inside him to take command.

No one got off the bus. The woman, lifting her child, got on with money ready for a ticket. With a fixed gaze Morgan watched the transaction, which seemed to take an ungodly long time. Then the bus snorted into readiness as the driver waited for the woman to find seats. Morgan stirred uneasily, as if scuffling with a decision too big for him. The bus rumbled away with a reek in its wake.

"Do you still want an ice cream?" Morgan asked.

5

MARY WILLIAMS WOKE WITH A START AND COULDN'T TELL whether it was the verge of day or the pull of night. Soldier was beside her, which startled her, and she shook him awake. "You weren't supposed to stay," she said angrily, watching him rub his eyes. He left the bed with a spring and pattered into her bathroom on the balls of his feet. A few minutes later, after letting in the full morning light, she joined him in the shower. "This is my home, not yours," she said as he worked the soap over her back. "I set the rules, not you."

"I hear you."

He dried himself quickly in a small towel and her vigorously in a huge one that was rough on her skin, evoking memories of her grandmother, who had tossed her about in the same sort of towel. Her grandmother's presence lingered in closets, in the sunshine that poured through the big windows, in the phantom creaks of floorboards.

She stepped on a scale, dampening it. "I've gained two pounds."

"It doesn't show."

She stepped off. "You have no rights here except those I give you." Then she began to cry.

Soldier lifted his sinewy arms. "It's him you're mad at, not me," he said and gathered her in.

"Sometimes I'm scared, so scared," she said.

"You got me," Soldier said.

Left alone for a while, lips critically pursed, she got hold of herself and gazed in the mirror with only mild degrees of discontent and melancholy. Her hair, blown dry, was brushed. Her shirt dress was pima cotton, with faint blue stripes on white. Stepping out of the bedroom and glancing into the facing one, Dudley's room, she nearly slipped back into a mood.

Soldier awaited her at the breakfast table. Coffee was ready, juice poured, toast kept warm under a plastic dome. Sensitive to his stare, she said, "Something the matter? My dress maybe?"

"You're beautiful," he said.

Sitting down, she scowled as he poured coffee from a Silax. "I prefer tea," she said.

"I forgot."

She accepted the coffee and drank the juice. With deliberation she spread jam on oatmeal toast. "You're spending too much time here. What's that friend of yours, the nurse, going to say?"

"I might as well tell you," Soldier said offhandedly. "She kicked me out. Nothing to do with you, Mary. She's a screwed-up lady."

"We're all screwed up, every one of us. It's the way we come out of the womb. Then it's the way we're handled and touched. It all makes a difference."

"Nothing wrong with me," Soldier said.

Later, with a wave of resentment, she watched him clear the table, rinse off plates, bunch up cutlery, open the dishwasher. Those were Dudley's chores, the kitchen more his than hers. Without a word she slipped away.

In Dudley's room, the bed primly made, closets closed, drapes partly drawn, she dredged up the memory of a dream in which she had teetered on the edge of a roof, ready to take a plunge, but someone unseen had held her back, hands unfelt had kept her in place. A few days later, in the Public Garden, she had met Dudley.

Soldier called to her. "Where are you?"

In the Public Garden, hours had wandered off without their knowing it. She saw in Dudley a depth others didn't, and he glimpsed the ghost of the lonely little girl serving pink cupcakes and glazed cookies to her dolls and playing favorite to none, unlike her mother, who favored her older sisters. Dear Dudley, he saw everything. When she suffered cramps, some of her pain appeared on his face.

Soldier embraced her from behind. "So here you are."

Dudley was not all there, her mother had said, but neither was she. At Radcliffe teachers had thought her strange, and classmates had called her "Mental Mary." She finished Radcliffe but quit art classes at the museum after the instructor said that her paintings lacked audacity, that the colors lay too comfortably on the canvas, that her nudes lacked the inner roar of life. Little did he know that she was holding back, bottling energies he could not possibly understand. Only Dudley would.

"I won't be in your way," Soldier said in her ear. "He comes back, I'll leave. Simple as that."

"Nothing is ever as simple as that," she said. With Dudley her thoughts could anchor in the pleasant, in the ripples of a dreamy smile.

"My duffel bag's packed. All I got to do is go get it."

Dudley was precious wine, Soldier a bargain bottle of scotch she wished she had never opened. Her father had drunk only the finest, while her mother had satisfied herself with brandy and Dubonnet. Tea had been her grandmother's beverage, and a little wine on bad days.

"Do you want to be alone here?" Soldier said. "You can tell me if you do, but I won't believe it."

Her head swayed. "You know how to play your cards."

He left a little later, a snap to his step, and she made her way to her studio and, in the full force of the morning light, perched herself at a drawing board. From memory she tried to sketch the boy, Glen Bodine, and for inspiration sank into memories of her own young years spent dressing dolls, memorizing popular songs, racing through homework, and, after her father's death, reading legends on gravestones. She worked a solid hour with the failed efforts accumulating on the floor. Too much escaped her: the set of the boy's eyes, the unwillingness of his smile, the thoughts in his head.

She tried to sketch her father, as she remembered him in the closet, but gave up after a single effort. She had better luck with a female face. Quick strokes of the charcoal brought it to life. Smudges deepened the eyes, and keen points awakened them. She would have finished it had footsteps not startled her.

Soldier was back. Everything he owned was crammed into the duffel bag propped on his shoulder. "What room?" he asked.

"Not his," she said in the instant.

"I didn't think so." Despite the weight of the bag, he moved closer with a nimble step and peered at the nearly completed drawing. "Anybody I know?"

"Only I know her."

"She looks mean."

The drawing was ripped from the pad and crumpled. "She's my mother."

Outside Brody's Hardware Store, which was not open yet, Orville Farnham said, "What are you doing with the fella messed on my porch, Chief? First I hear you let him go, then I hear you didn't. What's going on, people want to know."

"Few things I have to find out about him," Chief Morgan said. "I want to make sure he's not a threat to society."

"We got to know what he's charged with."

"I haven't decided yet."

"Jesus, Chief!" Farnham's face, never at rest, leapt up, with contours shifting. "To hold him, you have to charge him, then he's got to be arraigned. I don't need to be a lawyer to know that."

"The cell's not locked, he's free to walk," Morgan said.

"I'm just giving him a place to stay for a while, call it a kindly act."

Farnham was nonplussed. "What if he walks?"

"Then I'll really arrest him."

"I don't believe this," Farnham said, his face mobile. As a selectman, he had an oath to oblige and standards to uphold. The public good was in his trust, the chief accountable to him. "Look here," he said, mustering authority.

The hardware store was opening for business. Old man Brody smiled at them both and proclaimed that the day would be another hot one. Morgan strode toward him, and Farnham called out, "I don't like the way you're handling this."

"I don't know another way," Morgan said over his shoulder.

Some minutes later, he left the store and crossed the green with a weighted paper bag. The sun beat through the ribs of a cloud, the rays warming his back all the way to the station. Inside, with a quick glance at Sergeant Avery, he said, "Get the Polaroid."

Sergeant Avery scurried. "Whose picture?"

"His."

Dudley sat on the edge of his cot with a tray in his lap, one of the Boston papers beside him, compliments of Meg O'Brien, who had brought him breakfast. He was eating Wheaties, doused with coffee cream, from the box, an individual serving. He had wanted a bowl, and Meg might have scrounged one up had he put up a fuss. "Did I miss a beat somewhere?" she asked. "I thought we were rid of him."

"I decided against it," Morgan said, tired of the question.

Sergeant Avery took several pictures of Dudley, who, wiping his mouth, smiling, was a willing subject. He had on a different shirt, a blue button-down oxford, one of Morgan's which gave him a gentle look and almost a boyish cast. A necktie might have made him a scholar.

"That's enough, Eugene," Morgan said and ushered him and Meg from the cell. Morgan also stepped out and secured the cell door with a chain and lock from Brody's, which Dudley viewed with a mix of amusement and alarm.

"How will I go to the bathroom?"

"You holler, we'll hear," Morgan said. Two small keys went with the lock. He pocketed one and gave Meg the other. He had scarcely looked at Dudley but now looked at him fully. "I'm not locking you in, I'm locking others out."

"All I have to do is holler?"

"That's what I said."

Dudley crimped his brow, years returning to his face. "You mad at me?"

Morgan was already turning away. "I'll let you know."

In his office, he rang up the Boston Police Department, District A, and after a number of delays reached the detective who had investigated Glen Bodine's death. "Chief who?" the detective said. He sounded busy, harried, put upon, his attention split several ways. Morgan spoke rapidly and sensed disdain when he asked about the possibility of homicide. "We got no evidence of that," the detective snapped.

"Could you check something for me in the medical examiner's report?" Morgan asked.

"I don't have it handy."

"Could you tell me if the victim wore braces on his teeth?"

"Beats the shit out of me."

"I've somebody here," Morgan pressed on, "who might know something. Problem is, he won't give me his real name. Can I send you his picture, see if it means anything to you?"

"You do that," the detective said and was gone.

Morgan stared momentarily into space and then, slowly, tapped out a local number he kept in his head but had never called before. Elbows on his desk, he listened to the rings; the back of his neck went prickly when Kate Bodine answered. Recognizing his voice, she was not pleased. "What is it, James?"

"There's something I need to know about your stepson. Maybe you can tell me."

"Why do you need to know anything? What's this about, James?"

"Just something I have to clear up. Did he wear braces on his teeth?"

"What?"

"Please, Kate. Just tell me if he wore them."

"How did you know?"

Hanover House, situated off a bucolic byway in a secluded part of Andover, was a private care facility, exclusive, almost secretive, quietly appreciated for its elegant comfort. The venerable stone building, generations ago the mansion of a textile tycoon, stood on grounds etherealized by the haze of willows and the listing presence of birches. Ground pink flanked the walkway, and brass studded the impressive front doors. Paul Gunner, his visits infrequent, was unexpected.

The reception hall contained fine period furniture, though Gunner was unsure of the period. The curvature and fancy footwork of the tapestry chairs impressed him, and the appearance of the administrator, Mrs. Nichols, a tall figure in dark colors, unsettled him. Hanover House was the only place in the world where he felt at a disadvantage.

"How is she, Mrs. Nichols?"

"Doing fine, Mr. Gunner."

He let out his breath. "No problems, then?"

"There are always problems," Mrs. Nichols said with a faintly superior smile. She was of uncertain age, wore round eyeglasses, and vaguely reminded him of Phoebe Yarbrough, perhaps because of her height, which exceeded his.

"Do I dare ask?" he said and waited. Her scent was heavy, rich, musky. He wondered what ingredient of an animal, what furtive juice, had gone into it.

"She claims aliens took her on a spaceship and had their way with her."

"I see."

"She says she was sodomized."

He was embarrassed. "What can I say?"

Mrs. Nichols was realistic but not unsympathetic. "Not much, I'm afraid."

Eschewing the birdcage elevator, he progressed slowly up the grand stairway. At the top, replenishing his breath, he paused to look at a painting of nymphs bathing in a brook and, as always, admired the melodious play of light on skin. Then he moved on with a plodding step. Most of the doors were closed or ajar, but his mother's was wide open. Her weak eyes grappled with the sight of him.

"Yes, it's you," she said. "Don't just stand there."

The lofty room reflected Mrs. Gunner's tastes. The drapes were too heavy a maroon, and the furniture, massive and dark, seemed more suitable for a club where old men might mumble outrageous things to one another. A mirrored door led to a private bathroom, but Mrs. Gunner had insisted on a chrome potty chair near the bed.

"I'll come back," he said.

"No," she said, and he fidgeted, an inappropriate presence while she peed. "Fat like your father, same flubby lips," she said. "You'll die like him, too much blubber around the heart."

He remembered the problems with the casket, the way his father had seemed to swell out of it.

"There," Mrs. Gunner said and, rising, made herself right. Her white hair, worn wild, had yellowed, prompting her to believe she was blond again. Her eyes, small and private, yet rife with inner light, were free of most worldly cares and free certainly of anxiety over death. Indeed, she awaited death with untoward glee, as if it were tantamount to a holiday. "Did Nichols tell you? I was buggered."

"Are you all right now?"

"I hurt in the asshole, otherwise I'm okay."

They moved to club chairs not unlike the ones in his study, but at the last moment she chose a plum armchair to sit in. He sank into leather. "My father," he said, "was a genius."

"He was a bully. I don't want to talk about him."

Gunner let his gaze wander. A heavy overstuffed sofa drank up much space. Unread books lined a shelf. With a furtive glance at his watch, he told himself he would stay ten minutes more, no longer.

"How's Fay?" Mrs. Gunner asked.

"She's dead, you know that."

"That little girl was the only good thing in your marriage."

He looked at his watch, which had grudgingly donated less than a minute. "She was defective, Mama."

"You're not?"

Through the years, since his father's death, his mother's tendency to wound had sharpened into a precision instrument. At the funeral he had suffered intense grief, she none at all. "Beverly sends her love," he said suddenly. When he got no response, he added, "My wife."

"I know very well who Beverly is. She's me when I didn't know better."

He was relieved when a knock came on the open door and a woman wearing linen of bone white entered the room. The voice was stark. "Am I intruding?"

"If you were, I wouldn't let you," Mrs. Gunner said. "You remember Isabel, don't you, Paul?"

"Of course he remembers me. *He's* not the one who forgets things." Isabel, who resided in the next room, spoke from a rigidity of too many face-lifts. Her skin looked as if it had been sized with glue and fitted to each bone. Her eye holes were punctures free of whites, her nose a blade. Her whole face seemed fictive inside a clarity it did not deserve. She and his mother were deadly friends. "How are you, dear Hilda?"

"You know what I've been through!" Mrs. Gunner said.

Isabel smiled at Gunner with red lips that looked ignitable. The points of her fingers were crimson. "Did she tell you she was violated?"

"He knows," Mrs. Gunner said with a testy look.

"Your mother, poor dear, wants her adventures to be operatic, but they're vaudeville." Isabel dropped herself into the club chair facing his and crossed her legs, which were still intact and shapely. She clutched a packet of long cigarettes, a slim lighter wedged in the cellophane wrap. "Do you mind if I smoke?"

"I prefer you don't," Gunner said sternly.

"It's my room, you smoke all you want," his mother said in the instant, her chin held high with an authority never exerted in her marriage. Isabel lit up, and he drew in his chins with a shiver of disgust. His mother's eyes flared. "You going to die on the spot? Look at him, Isabel. I had him too late in life. I never should've had him at all."

He read his watch, his mother's voice drilling a hole in his head.

"Your last-born, Isabel, how old were you?"

"I don't think it matters, dear."

"Of course it matters. Look what you're saddled with. The devil put a mark on her face."

Isabel Williams blew smoke. "Let's leave my Mary out of it."

Gunner felt himself gagging on the smoke. His rise from the chair took stupendous effort, which stained his cheeks. Both women were gazing at him with what could only be taken as mockery. "Is there anything you need?" he asked.

"Don't talk nonsense. Everything I need is here, I have only to snap my fingers. Here we're queens, aren't we, Isabel?"

"We're fucking beauties," Isabel said.

When he leaned forward to kiss his mother, her head butted up and struck him. "No, you don't!" she said.

His exit was ten minutes on the dot. Reaching the stairway, he ignored the nymphs and gripped the banister, which almost slid away from him. His descent was cautious. At the bottom, Mrs. Nichols's eyeglasses refracted light.

"What's the matter, Mr. Gunner? You don't look well."

He said, "When is she going to die?"

"That's rather up to her," Mrs. Nichols said.

Chief Morgan drove to Boston, to State Street, a funnel made miniscule by towering office buildings in which, he suspected, the world was governed. He pulled into a lot, where the attendant, whipping cars around like toys, paused to take his money. Minutes later, escaping the heat of the street, he passed through glass doors that had opened for him, padded over marble in his soft loafers, and at a bank of elevators stood among men in traditional custom suits of varying sobriety. No one glanced at him. It was as if he were not there.

He rode the elevator to a lofty height and stepped out into a reception area, where glass reflected him kindly but obscurely. A woman with stiff features but a pleasing voice took his name, spoke into a telephone, and then, looking up, said, "Yes, he'll see you." Another woman, her hair drawn in a chignon, showed him the way.

Harley Bodine's office was elegantly spare and chaste, with a single piece of artwork on the wall and a great window that seemed level with the sky. Morgan almost expected to meet the eye of God. He was not asked to sit. Bodine came forward in the splendid fit of a suit that matched those of the men at the elevators. "My wife mentioned a picture," he said in a brisk voice, and Morgan passed it over. Bodine stared at it intently. "This person knows something about my son's death?"

"It's possible."

Bodine gave the picture a last look and returned it. "I've never seen him before. Who is he?"

"He calls himself Dudley, that's all I know. I picked him up for vagrancy."

"How stable is he?"

"Not very, but he knew your son wore braces. The picture the papers ran didn't show that."

"What else about my son?"

"That's all he would say."

Bodine's eyes were thrusts of ice returning nothing, and his tone of voice possessed the same cold quality. "What do you think he's holding back?"

"At this point I don't know."

"You're quite right about the newspapers, Chief, but you've forgotten television. My son had little to smile about, but occasionally he did. The picture used on Channel Seven, eleven o'clock news, clearly showed the braces. How seriously do you take this man?"

Morgan faltered, wondering whether he was scraping air, questioning his own competence.

"Is he playing you for a fool?"

"That's crossed my mind."

"Have you told me everything?"

"Yes," Morgan lied. "I may have overreacted."

"Are you playing *me* for a fool?"

The air had altered between them. Morgan's smile was incongruous, accidental, transitory. "I don't know what you mean."

"Why have you involved yourself? What's your interest?"

"It's my job."

"How far does your job go?" Bodine's white teeth glared between thin lips, and in the instant he no longer seemed of sound mind. "I'll make it plain. Are you screwing my wife?"

Guilt strained Morgan's face, for the answer was *Many times in fantasy.* "No, sir," he said, feeling absurd.

"I don't believe you."

"There's something I haven't told you," Morgan said. "The man claims he kills children."

Dudley's state of mind was not good. His hands shook. His breakfast, eaten too fast, threatened to come up. Lying on the cot, the pillow doubled under his head, he scarcely responded when the woman with pony teeth asked whether he wanted an aspirin. Her face was fussed up for him. "Is it your bowels?" she asked solicitously, and he said, "No, I've had my poops." She lingered outside the cell, eyeing him with concern. "Is there anything I can do?" she asked, and he told her not to worry, it comes and goes.

"What does?"

"Me," he said.

The fan kept him cool. Closing his eyes, he slipped into an air pocket of a past kept alive by a false sun, a protected place where long-ago voices rang, clocks ticked without moving their hands, and he was his mother's pet and his father's pride. He was curls, ruffles, and short pants and kept his bottle until he was four and his teddy much longer. His mother used spit to clean the corners of his mouth. His father fixed his wee-wee when the skin stuck. The town was Exeter, the world at war. His father said he was going to kill Hitler, but Hitler killed him.

He opened his eyes when the sergeant they called Eugene brought him lunch, a chef's salad he nibbled at before pushing it aside and returning his head to the pillow. He was eight when he and his mother moved from Exeter to Boston, the part called Dorchester, where families lived on top of one another in four-deckers, which he had never seen before. Nor had he seen before so many women wearing kerchiefs and dungarees and holding babies. Overheard women's matters filled his ears: the whispers about cramps, the revelations of pregnancies, the asides about birth. "You're the spit and image of your father," his mother told him, but it was her spit on his face.

He was thrust into a strange public school, a brick building with no grass around it, no drawings taped to the classroom walls. He developed a crush on the girl seated beside him and exposed himself to gain her attention. The girl immediately told the teacher, an aggressive slip of a woman who summoned him to the front and announced to the class: "Dudley has something to show us."

His eyes fluttered open at a sound outside the cell. "You're back," a woman said through the bars. She was the one who had visited him once before, with hair that looked as if it had just come out of curlers. It still looked that way. The padlock and chain disturbed her. "If they're not treating you right, let me know," she said, and he nodded, his heart beating hard, people caring for him. She was on her way to the library and offered to bring back books. "What's your preference?" she asked, and he named a children's book, which surprised her. "Really?"

"I don't know your name," he said.

"May," she said.

"May," he repeated. "It's almost Mary but not quite."

His classmates had been bullies, and Sweeney with a big moon face was the worst. In daily acts of terror, Sweeney bent his arm back, jabbed his privates, extorted his milk money, stomped his lunch box, and defaced his books. Cruelest of all, Sweeney stole his cat. In the backyard he saw the calico hanging from a crude gallows that brought a scream to his lips and his mother to the window. His mother did her best, but the only comfort came from his teddy bear, which he hid under his jacket when she took him to the child psychologist, who gave him crayons and paper and told him to draw. Afterward, an ear to the door, he heard that the boiling purple sun he had drawn was rage and betrayal felt from his father's death. The puny stick figure snared in tendrils was his own insufficient self with no-where to grow.

A sound stirred him, and through his eyelashes he discerned the gaunt figure of the reverend, who was offering him some-thing through the bars. His stomach was better, his hands steady, and he pulled himself up. The peach was a hybrid, no fuzz, and he polished it with his palms. "How much of me is real?" he asked. "Can you guess?"

"It would be a wild one," Reverend Stottle replied. "We are, all of us, stardust."

He nibbled. "Why are you staring?"

"I'm trying to understand you."

"Why?"

"It's my business."

"I wasn't born, Reverend. I was a trick out of a magician's hat, a card drawn from my father's sleeve."

"Are you lonesome?"

"Not very."

The reverend said, "How are you, May? Is that for him?"

He finished the peach and deposited the stone in his breast pocket. Wiping his hands on his jeans, he accepted the book and carried it to the cot, his touch respectful as he flipped pages. The print was large, and the illustrations of Jerry Muskrat and Jumper the Hare were in color. He pressed the open book to his face and breathed deeply, inhaling his childhood. He had no fear of Sweeney, whose name was etched on a tombstone. The dead sink into the depths or float off into the universe—either way they're gone for good.

May Hutchins said, "When you finish it, I'll bring you another."

"This will do," he said.

Looking in on her daughter, Regina Smith presented an intense face at odds with itself, arguments going on behind the dark eyes, nothing resolved, as the keen cut of the mouth vividly showed. Patricia was painting her nails, the fingers done, a few toes to go. Stepping over the threshold, Regina said, "Time we talked, young lady."

"Please, Mom, not again. We went through it yesterday." Patricia spoke over a raised knee, her lashes lowered, her concentration on her foot. "Nothing happened."

"I don't believe you."

"You're entitled to your opinion. God knows, you have enough of them." She had on a camisole top and string bikini briefs. Her beauty was undeniable.

"What you're wearing's hardly decent," Regina said with a sense of frustration while breathing in too much scent. You could cut it with a knife. "I don't want you walking around the house that way."

"I don't see what you're so upset about. Tony's my brother."

"Your *step*brother. That's a world of difference, as you know very well."

"You're making too much of it." Bending her head, her raven hair cascading, she blew on her toes and then rose with a suppleness seen only in the young. "And you always have."

Regina watched her angle to the dresser with a movement of her buttocks no man would ever ignore, her body a bright thing framed in sunlight from the window. This was her only child, her only recompense from a marriage in which she had been deceived from the start. She said, "I won't tolerate him in your room."

"Okay, I hear you." Patricia squirmed into designer jeans, a yank needed to force them over the flare of her hips. The cutting teeth of the zipper nearly nipped bare skin. "You ought to ease up, Mom. Trust me, for God's sake."

She left her daughter's bedroom and traveled the distance to her stepson's room, where she stepped into the screech of a rock singer, savage to her ear, an affront to her sensibilities.

Anthony killed the stereo in the instant, which did not appease her. A rumpled sheet trailed off the bed, and soiled socks and a stained jockstrap lay on the floor, another affront. She could see into his bathroom. The toilet seat had been left up, and a towel festooned the tank. She regarded him silently, with the frozen lips of a statue. "Sorry," he said and began to pick up.

"Look at me," she said, and he unfolded from a crouch, his height exceeding hers, his uncut hair hanging in his face. "No more lies, Anthony. They taint your tongue, make your breath bad."

He wore a loose shirt over ballooning slacks that tapered to his slim naked feet. With both hands he palmed his hair back. "I don't know what you mean."

"The truth about yesterday."

"I swear, we were just talking."

She had practice looking a liar in the eye. Her first husband had been one. "This is not something I want to discuss with your father," she said. "Don't force me to."

"We didn't do anything."

"If I learn otherwise," she said, "you're gone."

Mary Williams read some Flaubert to Soldier and then a meaningful scene out of D. H. Lawrence. "I don't need to be put in the mood," he said. "I'm already there."

An undertow of melancholy threatened to carry her away, but a sense of absurdity, perhaps her own, held her steady. Putting the book down, she asked, "Whom would you want, Madame Bovary or Lady Chatterley?"

"Both, same time," he said with a growing hoarseness. "Three-way snarl."

"That's greedy."

"It's interesting."

He spoke from a chair, she from the bed, the bottom sheet bared. Between them, a shaft of sunlight swirled with motes of dust like a universe in miniature, all the principles intact. She raised an arm as if to feel on her hand the breath of God guiding the debris. Soldier took it as a gesture to him and uncurled from the chair, aroused before he touched her, ready before she was willing or able. Her arms were rigid, her torso the white of a lunar moth.

Her mind slipped to other things, to strip poker at summer camp, where other girls had conspired to get her naked first, her shyness part of the allure, her humiliation measured into the fun. An older girl snared the moment with a camera, the picture later bandied about, last seen among the kitchen workers.

Soldier said, "You're not with it."

"I will be," she promised, remembering icy jewelry worn by her mother, lush welcomings from her grandmother, and wistful farewells from her father, who had kept a noose in a closet for when he would find the nerve, though her mother had assured her he never would. She was fifteen when he hanged himself and sixteen when she suffered a breakdown, from which she emerged like an actress seeking a role.

Soldier was on his knees and leaning forward from the hips. "What's the matter?"

"I fear loss," she said evenly. "Loss is emptiness."

"What kind of talk is that?"

Under the careful probing of his eyes, she lay like someone slain until he lifted her legs and drove them back to the exclamation mark of parted cleft and anal bud. "What are you doing?"

"I'm interested," he said.

Then he was on her, kissing her with an open mouth, which she endured with the knowledge that he was not integral to her life but merely a collage on the surface of it. Her thoughts were clear, bright, loud inside her skull. Soldier was chosen but unwanted. Without someone, anyone, she was a stranger to herself.

When she felt him dissolve inside her, she waited for him to hop away like a soldier on the run. Instead, overstaying his welcome, he shrank out of her and then propped himself up to look into her face. His eyes were bloodshot, with the same thready redness clinging to the stone of a peach.

"You didn't come," he said.

———

Chief Morgan keyed open the padlock, loosened the chain, and opened the cell door. Dudley was napping again. Morgan gently shook him awake and said, "Someone to see you."

His color was pale, disinfectant, with sleep marks withering a cheek. "Has my time come? That's not an undertaker, is it?" Then his eyes went small in a yawn big enough to threaten his jaw. "I wish he wouldn't."

Smoke twirled from a cigarette.

"I had asthma as a child."

Harley Bodine, spooled silent and tight in pinstripes, viewed him with ferreting eyes, as if reading the fine print of a contract.

"My mother almost lost me." The cot creaked. Sitting up, Dudley scratched an underarm and smiled at Morgan. "I was dreaming. Little animals were everywhere, and I knew their names."

"What's mine?" Bodine said and received a look empty of substance. "He's not connecting."

Morgan stepped in. "Answer the question, Dudley."

The cot creaked again. "I know it's not Sweeney."

Bodine's gaze went to a book that lay open on its pages. "Is that what he reads?"

"This is Mr. Bodine, Dudley. It was his boy who was killed by a subway train. Did you know him?"

"His name was Glen," Bodine said in a voice that sounded ripped from a bone, menace in his unblinking eyes, and for a bare second something in Dudley's face altered, as though heat and cold had collided. Dudley was slow to gather words.

"It doesn't ring a bell."

"But you knew he wore braces," Bodine said with dry intensity.

Moments of confusion passed, and Dudley's voice came out small, with a spin. "Was it in the paper?"

"You tell me."

Morgan's attention wavered from one to the other, from Bodine's chalk part and silky tie to Dudley's restless forelock.

Dudley was concentrating on his thumb, and Morgan hoped he wouldn't suck it. He did.

Bodine's shoe scraped, as if a nerve had leaped. "I've had enough."

Morgan, disappointed, held the door as Bodine stepped from the cell. The chain was left to dangle, the padlock to fend for itself. Meg O'Brien looked up when Morgan passed by her desk without a word, Bodine in the lead. Outside, in the gloom of the heat, they stared at each other as if for an instant their feelings matched.

"I don't need this, Morgan. I'm trying to put what happened to my son behind me."

"I think he fakes some of that foolishness."

"He could've fooled me. Not you, though, huh?"

Morgan, compelled to defend himself, said, "Two children with Bensington connections have died in apparent accidents. Your son and, three years ago, the eight-year-old daughter of Paul and Beverly Gunner. Both deaths took place outside of Bensington. Boston and Cambridge."

"What am I supposed to make of that?"

"I'm a policeman. I have to consider outside possibilities."

"If they're reasonable, yes. That man in there isn't."

Morgan walked him to his car. The car was elegantly free of exterior accessories. He remembered when every automobile had been an overenthusiasm of ornament and chrome, the tires big and fat, the horses under the hood chomping at the bit.

Bodine opened the driver's door and slipped into quiet luxury. The window lowered itself as if from a verbal command. "My wife and I plan to have a child. Has she told you?"

"No reason she should have."

"My mistake. I thought it might interest you."

Morgan watched the automobile glide around the sweep of the lot and vanish through the gateless opening in the shrubs. "It's nothing to me," he said to himself, and the words had weight but not reality.

———

It was cocktail time when Harley Bodine entered the busy lounge at the country club. Carrying a wineglass and a smoldering cigarette, Bodine mingled easily, with a renewed sense of himself, for he'd been challenged and tested and was stronger for it. He felt experienced, felt about him almost an aura of immortality. Here and there he returned smiles. Phoebe Yarbrough was a Calder mobile in a sequin dress. Illusions shaved and contoured her; her height diminished her husband's. "Where's Kate?" she asked.

"Working on something," he said. "She fancies she's a writer."

Myles Yarbrough wore an aspect of worry and unease and offered a handshake. The small diffident knot of his tie squeezed up a cleft of skin when he spoke. He was hard to hear, for his sentence frayed at the end.

Phoebe said clearly, "I didn't know you smoked."

"Does it bother you?" Bodine asked, unaccustomed to the bold way she looked into his eyes.

"May I?" She took a drag from it, and her face flared out of a pageboy, hollowed dramatically under high cheekbones, and seemed in a pending state of foreclosure. She was not beautiful, he decided, merely vaguely bizarre.

He moved on, abandoning his cigarette in the nearest ashtray, and spotted the Gunners near the buffet table. Paul Gunner was eating bleeding meat off a skewer, his stance preemptive, unopposed, supreme.

Seconds later Gunner plodded toward the men's, and Bodine followed.

The mirrors were ice, the floor a checkerboard of black and white. He and Gunner spaced themselves a urinal apart, and Gunner pissed without looking, without touching, shivers running through his shoulders. Bodine stood straight, like a priest being watched.

"I have something to tell you."

"Not now," Gunner grunted.

"It's about my son."

"This isn't the time."

"It's also about your daughter."

Gunner shook himself dry by jiggling his stomach. "I don't discuss family in a shithouse. Call me later."

They moved in unison to the mirrors, Bodine to rinse his hands, Gunner to pull a hair from his nose. The nostrils were strawberry, as if he'd had a bleed. Bodine subjected his hands to the fierce breath of a blower as Gunner heaved away.

"My private line."

Bodine nodded.

Peering through the bars, Chief Morgan watched Dudley consume an apple. Dudley ate it to the core, to the pips, which he spat into his hand and deposited neatly in a saucer. Then he looked up and said, "I could use a clock."

"I'd like a million dollars."

"I'd like a cuckoo clock."

"You're cuckoo enough," Morgan said, opening the cell door, both ends of the chain banging against the bars. "How about a stroll outdoors?"

"Yes," Dudley said, popping up from the cot. "I could use the exercise."

Moonlight drifting through clouds was a kind of spiderweb holding the night together. In front of the town hall the emerald eyes of a raccoon glared, then vanished. Morgan crossed the street with a hard step. Dudley's seemed weightless, and when they entered the green he moved as if some half-heard music were drawing him along, giving his step a slow lilt, his breathing a mild beat. He touched Morgan's arm.

"I won't run."

"If you do, I won't chase you," Morgan said wearily, stiff in the joints. The night delivered its own sounds, its liquid tastes, its touches of the unknown. Shrubs charred by shadows stood jagged. "It would settle a lot if I knew who you were."

As they moved deeper onto the green, Morgan's gait became more like Dudley's, almost somnambulistic. The darkness had various shades and shapes, the deepest dark lurking in the trees. Dudley said, "Are you angry?"

"I think you like making a fool of me."

"Yes, you are angry."

"I think you rehearse your lines."

Dudley gazed up at drifting clouds, all resembling slow barges bereft of goods. "We'll never see eye to eye, Chief. That's because you only have two."

Morgan spoke softly. "Would you agree to a polygraph?"

"A lie detector? I wouldn't want to be strapped in."

"It isn't like that."

"I wouldn't want anyone getting into my mind."

Morgan felt a greater stiffness in his legs. The texture of the air had altered, and a breeze strolled toward him. Suddenly he stopped in his tracks and looked around, for Dudley was no longer with him. "What are you doing?"

His hand was out. "I felt a drop."

Morgan was glad of the distance between them. It seemed to lessen a tension, and he spoke in his coolest voice. "In this town we like our eccentrics harmless, not homicidal."

"I go where there's a need."

"What does that mean?"

"I'm a professional," Dudley said, only a part of his face visible. "A hitman."

"You don't look like Mafia to me."

"I only do children. Reasonable rates."

Morgan felt a greater weariness than before. Who is this man, he asked himself, and why am I listening to him? "I see. Contract stuff."

"Yes. I'm quite good."

"How do you get business? You can't advertise."

Dudley smiled through the dark, teeth and dimples showing. "Word of mouth."

At eleven-thirty Harley Bodine left his wife's bed, partially clothed himself, and paused to listen to the rain. A wind chafed the trees. From the bed, her face tattered in shadows, Kate said, "Close the door when you leave."

He descended the stairway deliberately in minimal light,

entered semidarkness through a double doorway, and, picking up a cordless phone, went to an open window. He wanted fresh air on his skin and in his lungs. He rang Gunner's number, and promptly Gunner's voice was in his ear.

"What's the problem?"

"That friend of yours is in town. The police chief has him in a cell."

"I should have warned you. He tends to be unpredictable afterward."

"The chief took me to see him. The silly son of a bitch looked me right in the eye."

"And?"

"Nothing," Bodine said. "It was like we were feeding each other lines. It was a stage play. What's with him?"

"He likes to hold a razor against his throat," Gunner said.

"I felt it was against mine."

"No danger of that."

Bodine found a cigarette and lit it. "How can you be sure?"

"The man's certifiable, and so's the woman. That's always been the kicker. I thought you understood."

Exhaling smoke, Bodine enjoyed the twirling sensation in his stomach, that of a man operating beyond the ordinary pitch of life. He said, "The chief mentioned your daughter."

"But our friend didn't."

"No."

"It's late," Gunner said. "Go to bed. Enjoy your lovely wife."

"I already have," said Bodine.

6

MRS. NICHOLS LOOKED IN ON HER. THE ROUND EYEGLASSES and dark colors stood static in the doorway, like sculpture, but the scent of musk marched in. "How are we this morning?"

Sitting up in bed, Mrs. Gunner scratched a whiskery underarm. A cockled leg eased out of the cover. "I'm an old lady, so you figure it out."

"Did we have a good night?"

"I wasn't ravished."

"Wonderful," Mrs. Nichols said. "Are we joining the others for breakfast?"

"I'll eat here."

Maria, new at Hanover House, came in later to make the bed, pick up soiled clothes, run a bath, and empty the pot. Then she helped Mrs. Gunner into the tub, toys floating on the water, metal bars within range for Mrs. Gunner to hoist or lower herself. Within reach was a button to press in the event she was alone and in distress. When she slipped deep into the water, a rubber duck floated up and nudged her chin.

"I suppose you think I'm cracked."

"I think it's grand," the young woman said.

Mrs. Gunner let herself sink into her shapeless past, so many years running together. Here she was a girl, there she wasn't. Here was her husband, who didn't want conversation, only the physical, and there he was in another light, the complete edition of the child they had produced.

A luxuriant towel awaited her; then a rubdown to smarten her flesh, against which she held a grudge. It had submitted too wantonly to age and mocked her cruelly in the mirror. An outsize dress obviated a bra. Moccasins accommodated her bare feet. Maria came forth with a comb, but she warded it off.

"I want my breakfast."

Gustav had been her husband's name, his brutality always casual, spontaneous, part of a moment that passed. Later her bruises surprised him, angered him a little, as if she were throwing them up in his face. But he forgave. She did not.

Much that had been forgotten came back.

Maria returned with breakfast on a gilt tray, which she placed on a café table near the window where the sun angled in with the grace of a tiger extending a paw. Seconds later Isabel Williams entered with a steaming mug of coffee and a fresh-lit cigarette and, snatching up an ashtray available for her, joined Mrs. Gunner at the table. Her voice was sere. "You could've done your hair, Hilda."

"Who's to see?" Mrs. Gunner tapped the shell of a soft-boiled egg. "I don't smell, that's what counts with old people."

Isabel sipped coffee, the red of her mouth splotching the edge of the mug. Thicknesses of mascara gave her eyes the look of bullet holes in a pâpier-maché face. Her nose expelled smoke. "Did you sleep through the rain?"

"Never heard it."

"The thunder was like racehorses charging 'round the bend."

"Didn't hear that either." Mrs. Gunner fired a look at Maria, who was dusting crystal figurines and examining photographs in stand-up frames. "Don't break anything."

Maria lifted a picture framed in silver. "Big boys."

"Swines," Mrs. Gunner replied, shocking the young woman. "Ill-mannered and repulsive."

"Her grandsons," Isabel said evenly.

"No better than their father," Mrs. Gunner stated, egg yolk on a corner of her mouth. Her eyes narrowed from an image of her final month of pregnancy, when her belly had been a globe of the world. A phantom cramp made the recollection hurtful. "I'm a great expense to him now. I'm glad."

Maria said stoutly, "In my family we revere children."

"You're in America now," Mrs. Gunner said, picking up toast that had been buttered for her.

Isabel dashed her cigarette. "Are you Hispanic, dear?" she asked, and the young woman nodded. The ashtray was porcelain. The ashes were fastidiously deposited in a single corner, the lipstick-soaked butt put to rest nearby, as if Isabel were the cleanest of cats. "You sound quite intelligent. Where's your accent?"

"I was born here."

"But you're still a spic," Mrs. Gunner said, "same as I'm a kraut. Mrs. Williams here is Mayflower, a bit too la-di-da for my liking."

Maria, boy-figured, picked up another picture, this one in a small, insignificant frame. "Such a pretty girl," she said. "Is this your granddaughter?"

"The child is dead," Isabel interjected. "Mrs. Gunner sometimes forgets."

"I know she's dead!" The voice was harsh, blistery. "They put her under three years ago." The voice dropped. "But she's alive in my heart. Put the picture back."

The young woman returned the picture to its place and continued dusting. Crunching toast, Mrs. Gunner gazed in a wounded way out the window. The grounds were greener from the rain, the flowerbeds overfull. A crow gracefully beat the air. Isabel said, "You have egg on you," and wiped it off with spit.

"He never shed a tear," Mrs. Gunner said. "He wanted her dead."

"Let's not get on that subject."

"Can't help it. She was my sweetie." Mrs. Gunner's face heated up as memories ramified feelings, and feelings tangled her mood. Her breath came out hot. "I don't blame the mother, just him."

"Not in front of a stranger, Hilda dear."

"He'll go to hell, the little girl's in heaven," Mrs. Gunner said.

Maria, stepping back from her dusting, started to speak, but Isabel, with a gesture, went momentarily cross-eyed to indicate that Mrs. Gunner wasn't all there.

"He'll burn," Mrs. Gunner said with satisfaction, and Isabel lit another cigarette, the flame leaping high from the disposable lighter.

"Won't we all, dear."

Chief Morgan left his car near the chapel and, seeking the administration building, approached a gaggle of summer students. A girl whose face black eye pencil gave arguable drama pointed the way. The Phillips campus was a hamlet of venerable brick and well-behaved greenery sweetened by wafting fragrances of phlox. The grandeur of the bigger buildings, fronted by stately columns, evoked memorials. Morgan felt like an obtruding presence and a loud voice inside the echoing personnel office, where a man of measured formality studied the Polaroid of Dudley and said, "Sorry, no one we know. Should we be worried?"

In the alumni office a rose-haired woman obliged him with old yearbooks, in which he tried to match a young face with Dudley's dimpled one. Resemblances popped up, but none panned out. "It was a shot in the dark," he confessed to the woman. He asked to be put in touch with someone who had known the Bodine boy. The name she gave him was Pitkin.

Aerobic shoes gave balding and bespectacled Ted Pitkin a bouncy step as he and Morgan walked over campus grass golden green in the sun, every blade in place. Trees stood brassy. "I recognized you right away," Pitkin said. Roomy short sleeves diminished his arms. His mouth was liver inside a wiry beard of

dubious color. "I was at the Gunners' the evening you brought
the bad news. Glen Bodine was a brilliant student, one of my
best."

"Tell me about him," Morgan said, shortening his stride.

"Polite, sensitive, shy . . . and brave. Yes, very brave."

"Was he depressed?"

Pitkin shrugged small shoulders. "If so, it was his secret.
Are you asking if I think it was suicide?"

"Yes."

"People with treacherous illnesses are inscrutable. They live
within themselves. I have a theory, Chief. I believe people carrying such burdens are prone to macabre accidents, violent
deaths. Life sneaks up on them with an air of combat."

"But the boy was brave, you said. He would have fought."

"Bravery is usually foolhardy. Cowardice is calculated. It's
what keeps most of us alive."

They paused in the shade of a rhododendron grown to magnificent proportions. Morgan lifted his face, his skin absorbing
the breath of dark green foliage. The sky was aggressively blue.
"Tell me about his father," he said.

"I scarcely know him."

"But you know the Gunners."

"I tutor the two boys, advanced mathematics. Mr. Gunner
wants them to be a credit to him. He looks upon them as his
little thoroughbreds, though of course they're not so little.
Rather gross, I'm afraid."

"The family lost a daughter."

"The boys never mention her, nor does Mr. Gunner. Mrs.
Gunner did once, but she was talking more to herself than to
me. Are these questions leading to something, Chief? Has something new come up?"

"I'm just gathering opinions."

"Why?"

"It seems to be my job," Morgan said, and they moved on,
but not far. A beech tree offered more shade. A shed condom
of shocking pink lay near the trunk like a wad of bubble gum.

Ignoring it, Morgan produced the Polaroid. "This face mean anything to you?"

Rising on his toes, Pitkin looked at it one way and then another. His mouth blossomed in his beard. "Is there a connection? Who is he?"

"Maybe make-believe."

Pitkin seemed to enjoy a puzzle. "Fictional?"

"Funny pages," Morgan said. Vague noises ripened into voices. Students were passing, boys and girls in lollipop colors. Morgan returned the picture to his breast pocket. "He could be nothing more than a coincidence."

"In your work," Pitkin said, straining to help, "I'd assume all coincidences are suspect till proven otherwise."

Morgan stepped into sunlight, tossed a last look at the students, and said, "That's my theory."

When Beverly Gunner crept into her husband's bedroom to wake him, the immense stillness of his body frightened her. At first she thought he was dead—and, God have mercy, she hoped with all her heart it was so. Then the mass of a belly, visible through his open pajama top, rumbled. Profoundly disappointed, she backed out of the room and soundlessly shut the door.

Still in her robe, she carried coffee outdoors and sat in a canvas chair wet from the night's rain. A lemon veil of sunlight gave the flower bed the aura of a fairy tale. She tried not to think, tried not to see or to hear, but near the honeysuckle a fanciful figure hopscotched on the grass. Her daughter as image and metaphor. Song and dance. A smile christened the little face, a scab emblazoned each knee. She tried to hold the vision, but her hand shook. Coffee slurped.

"I'm here, darling."

Birds spurted from a fruit tree and dissolved in the air, as if sunlight, not feathers and wings, had whisked them off. From the house came sounds of her sons, which activated a nerve in her face. She finished her coffee, rose from the chair, and tightened her robe, her bottom soaked from the chair.

They awaited her at the breakfast table, much ill humor in their identical full faces. What in Christ had she done now? The elder, Gustav, named after his grandfather, was scornfully good at staring her down. When he grinned, his eyes closed. The younger, Herman, was best at pouting. Both looked as if they were still in the suckling stage; both were subject to tantrums, often in competition. The elder said, "Your hair's all scraggly."

One of them had spilled sugar, which she found unnerving to walk on. "I haven't done it yet," she said, glugging milk into a bowl, cracking eggs into a mix.

"She looks like Nana," the younger said.

"Something's jumping in her face," Gustav observed.

She was nobody on her own, simply a mechanical part of a family composition.

Gustav glimpsed the back of her robe. "Did you piss yourself, Mama?"

Herman the younger broke up. "She needs Nana's potty."

Their births had been easy. Fay's had been the difficult one, the doctor joking to the nurse as he forced the delivery, then cursing himself, panic stitched into his brow. Her baby, her child, always she had dressed her in happy clothes.

She placed a platter of pancakes between her sons, with the unavoidable thought that she was slopping hogs.

When she returned to the outdoors, weariness embraced her and set her down hard in the canvas chair. The honeysuckle yielded shivers of light but no images, no phantoms. Her coffee, a fresh cup, was steady in her hand. Her husband barked from an upper window. Why hadn't she woken him? He wanted his breakfast, his newspapers. She raised her eyes and saw a quarter of his face, more than enough.

"Did you hear me?"

In a voice nearly as loud as his, she said, "Ants look out for their dead, Paul? Why can't we?"

"What?"

"Why can't we talk about her, Paul? Why can't I ever mention her name?"

"Shut up," he said. "You want the boys to hear?"

The man holds the greedy seed, the woman the selective egg. He blamed her, not the doctor, not the nurse, for Fay. "She's alive, Paul. I see her every day."

He closed the window, shut her out of his hearing.

She screamed.

Chief Morgan drove into Boston, made his way through the noontime snarl of Kenmore Square, and crossed into Brookline. The street he had trouble finding was off Commonwealth Avenue, directions provided by the first Mrs. Bodine, whom he had phoned from the academy. She lived in a complex of brick called Dexter Park, fronted by pruned trees and ivy ground cover. An electric buzzer let him into the foyer, and a security guard indicated the way to the stairs, which he conquered two at a time to the second floor. Midway down the long corridor a door opened, a woman waited.

"Morgan?" Her voice lacked tone. Her narrow hand came out. "Do you have identification?"

Satisfied, she let him in and led him to a chair near a trumpet vase of lilies. He sank into the cushion. She stayed standing, her face pinched tight under an upsweep of hazy hair. She was short, petite, with the overbright eyes of an insomniac and the diaphragm of a wasp.

"I don't understand," she said. "It happened in Boston. Why should you be interested?"

"The police here got in touch with me about your son. I broke the news to your former husband."

She was poised quite still with her legs together, as if her body were a single muscle, its only function to hold up her head and hair. "Glen was an expense, that's how Harley viewed him."

After a moment's hesitation, Morgan said, "Are you satisfied with the police account of your son's death?"

"My only child has been taken from me, that's all I'm sure of." Her eyes refocused and dwelled on him in a way they hadn't before. "You don't look like a policeman."

"I did when I was young," he said. When he was young he had worn a uniform and a revolver on his hip. The holster, brand-new, shined like a shoe. When he was young his wife had been alive and the world had been wider.

"Did you know my son?"

"No," he said but wished he had. Perhaps now he would be drawing conclusions instead of dealing with suppositions.

"Not an hour goes by I don't think of him. Sometimes he fills the hour and then the next one. Do you have children, Morgan? No? Then you stay a child yourself." She moved to a captain's chair, though he knew she wouldn't sit in it. Her hand, dry and colorless, gripped the top of it. "What is there about you I don't trust? Are you holding something back?"

He rose stiffly and showed her the Polaroid, but she needed glasses to see it. They were behind her on a table. When she fitted them on, they consumed her face. Slowly she shook her head.

"I don't know him. Should I?"

"He may have seen exactly what happened in the subway station."

Her glasses slipped to the tip of her nose, and she removed them. The fullness of her grief was in her eyes. "Do I really want to know? Will it bring Glen back?"

"I'm sorry I had to bother you," he said.

She reached out, and her faint touch on his arm had the same weight and ungiving warmth as winter sunlight. "Stay for a sandwich," she said. "I need the company."

In the kitchen he trod over octagonal tiles that seemed to spring up at him. They drove him to a table, where he drew a chair and sat with an elbow near a veneer basket of fruit that had passed its time. The wall clock could not be counted on. It varied radically with his watch, which he knew to be true.

"Glen liked corned beef," she said and unwrapped some. The bread was rye. Her back was to him, and he stared at her shapely head and undersize shoulders.

"May I ask you something brutal?"

"It won't matter. I've already been brutalized."

"In his heart of hearts, do you think . . ."

She uncapped a squat jar of mustard. "Go on, Morgan. I'm listening."

"Do you think your ex-husband might have wished the boy dead?"

She concocted two sandwiches he knew neither she nor he would eat, and then she added a slice of pickle to each plate. Turning, she said, "Why did you ask that?"

"It was unworthy," he said.

"No," she said. "No, it wasn't." She placed the sandwiches on the table and stayed on her feet. "Harley and I divorced six years ago, and he has seethed over every nickel he's had to lay out for Glen. He's never been normal about money, but it got worse when Glen was diagnosed with leukemia. The insurance coverage is limited."

"Still and all, his own son."

"After the divorce he ceased to have a son. He identified Glen with me, and me he hated. Claimed I was sucking him dry."

His voice level, Morgan said, "Do you think he could have been involved in some way with Glen's death?"

Her face tightened in the instant, as if a key had been turned. "If you know something, tell me."

"I don't. I have only suspicions."

Her fist, gripping the back of a chair for support, looked like the skull of a small animal. "You have suspicions, Morgan. I have nightmares."

Alone in the big house, Regina Smith entered her daughter's disheveled bedroom, read cryptic entries in Patricia's diary, surmised meanings, and shuddered. Her anger was deep, bitter, and specific.

Her stepson's bedroom had been picked up, the bed made, things in proper places. In Anthony's clothes closet her slim hand dug deep into pockets. In his bathroom she touched soap that had dissolved into a tattered lump and from a hamper dragged up sweat socks that would never come clean and briefs that had the pungent smell of an orange peel. In her mind she imagined his tongue eaten up by lies he had told.

A mirror loomed, and in a refracting moment she saw herself at Patricia's age, full of upheaval and change, of fleeting moods complex and expressive, with lapses into the vulgar. The first boy in her life had been less a lover than a mechanic checking her oil. The second had grinned the whole time from his good fortune.

She clumped downstairs with memories that could still make her cringe and stepped to a window, where she swept a dead hornet from the sill and stared out at the faultless morning, the sky unwaveringly blue, which gave the grounds a surer green. An automobile of note rounded the drive.

Harley Bodine climbed out with an air of recklessness and, approaching the house, glimpsed her in the window. A cigarette was snared between his teeth. He chucked it. "I don't mean to bother you," he said.

She spoke through the screen. "But here you are."

"May I come in?"

"I'll come out," she said. They followed a footpath of crushed white rock, strayed from it, and took sanctuary near an oak cursed with gypsy moth blight. Flecks in his otherwise somber necktie caught the light. His close-shaved chin, she noticed for the first time, had the hint of a cleft. "The police chief is making moves against me," he said with a cocky smile that surprised her. Much about him was beginning to surprise her.

"What moves?"

"He's keeping my son's death alive."

"How?"

"He has his ways," he said mysteriously, and she wondered whether he was growing paranoid. His voice ran on a single note, and he seemed to gaze at her in a code he expected her to break. "Morgan's playing policeman. Kate's the prize."

"Is he harassing you?"

"He thinks he is, but he's out of his league." The jolting cry of a jay startled her but not him. He crept closer. "Kate and I are fucking again."

"Congratulations," she said in a temperate voice. His eyes slid over her without restraint, an affront to the dignity of any decent woman. "You could get arrested for that," she said.

His hand reached out vaguely. She wasn't sure what he hoped to touch. His breath was in evidence, neither good nor bad, mostly cigarettes. "I wish Kate were you."

She brushed his hand away. "But she's not."

Beverly Gunner felt she had to talk to someone and, though not on intimate terms with any woman in the Heights, chose Phoebe Yarbrough. Phoebe lived in a contemporary that had long walls of glass and sheets of skylights to exorcise darkness. "Light is life," Myles Yarbrough said. She had not expected Myles to be there. Myles, according to her husband, was a loser. His eyes were jittery, his voice thin. Taking her by the elbow, he piloted her over hardwood floors free of carpets and then told her to continue on herself, straight out to the pool. "That's where the fun is."

She did as she was told, the heels of her beige pumps clicking over the hardwood. When she swished open a slider, she heard a spate of voices, which almost made her turn and run, but heads were already pivoting from a semicircle of colorful poolside chairs.

"Bev! How nice!"

Phoebe instantly erected an extra chair, practically sat her in the sunken seat, and served her a brimming glass cup of punch laced with rum. Crossing her legs, she felt painfully overdressed, though only Anne Lapierre, proudly displaying the scar tissue of an old Caesarian, was in a swimsuit. Sissy Alexander, the ball player's wife, was in something that resembled a sunsuit, and Kate Bodine and Germaine English wore loose shirts over shorts. Phoebe's slender neck, careening out of a tank top, was nearly long enough to make her head independent of her body.

Phoebe said, "Kick your shoes off, Bev."

She would have done so if her pumps had not been so tightly clamped to her swollen feet. The chlorine odor of the pool was strong, and the bright water looked as if blueing had been added. She heard Anne Lapierre say, "I had walls to scale, but Armand didn't want me to. He was afraid men would look up my dress."

"So what?" said Phoebe. "As long as you had something on underneath."

"I often didn't," Anne Lapierre said wickedly, her red frizzed hair a small fire.

The first swallow of punch loosened a knot. They, Beverly suspected, were on their second or third cups. Germaine English's shirt was tailored, Kate Bodine's was not. She admired their strong youthful figures, no sallow skin in their cleavages, no penciling on their smooth legs.

"We all had our dreams," said Germaine English. "Mine was to get on a horse bareback and ride naked. In the moonlight, of course."

"Your hair flowing," offered Kate Bodine.

"Yes, it was long then."

Anne Lapierre said, "My first lover was a graduate student. What I remember most about him is that he said dry witty things none of us had answers for. The real problem was that he painted me as pure, which meant I had no place to go but down."

Relishing their droll smiles, Beverly wanted to speak but feared some absurdity would leap out. She was out of their beat, but she was not stupid. She read poetry. Wordsworth pleased her, Eugene Field's "Little Boy Blue" brought tears to her eyes, and James Russell's rhetorical and immortal question about the month of June raised her to a higher plane.

"My first romance didn't last the winter," Germaine English said. "I couldn't tolerate sleeping with a man who closed the windows tight. I like air. I like pulling the covers over me for warmth, not kicking them off for breath."

She admired Germaine English, whose charm emanated from her soulful eyes and slow smile, and she enjoyed looking at Anne Lapierre's clean little ears and saucy large mouth. Phoebe had beautiful fingernails. Glancing at her own, she resolved to treat them better.

"Did I tell you about my second lover?" Anne Lapierre asked. "He always went at it at top speed, like we were on a railway track with a train coming."

"He must've been married," Phoebe said.

"No, I was. Not to Armand, to my first husband."

Beverly's glass was empty. She had blotted up even the dregs, which doubtless accounted for the feeling that was washing through her. It lifted her in a phantom way and left her suspended, though the weight of her pumps was a drag. Phoebe's ankles were long and shapely, splendidly tapered, and her own, she began to suspect, had never been as trim as she had thought. Afloat, she felt bulky and clumsy. Surprising herself, she said, "I don't like my arms."

No one heard her.

"Eight inches, I swear, and this big around," Anne Lapierre said, curving a childlike hand.

Kate Bodine stirred. "That doesn't sound pleasant."

"Often it wasn't."

Listening, Beverly uttered a laugh that came out unattractive and wished she could take it back. Uncrossing her legs, she then swept them aside to let Phoebe pass. "Why didn't you say something?" Phoebe said to her, returning to fill her glass. Phoebe's long, flawless face with its raised cheekbones seemed borrowed from a magazine.

Sissy Alexander, sitting as if shackled, round knees nailed together, shyly allowed that her husband, the ball player, had been her first man. "He was my childhood sweetheart. We've been through good times and bad, all the highs and the lows." The voice was wholesome, like bread baked at home. "Now I know the marriage will last forever."

Wonderful words. Paul was Beverly's first man, her only man, and their sons parodies of him. Lifting an arm, sloshing punch, she could feel her dress sticking. Phoebe stared hard at her, and the blue-green of Phoebe's eyes became fixed in her mind, perhaps forever. In a loud voice, rocking in the chair, she said, "I hate my husband!"

———

"So there you are," said Mary Williams in a hearty voice as she entered the common room at Hanover House. A couple of elderly women whose heads were too weighty for their frail shoulders smiled from chintz chairs. Each had nothing to lace thoughts together but relished the passing attention she gave them. A man sitting with a cane between his knees grabbed a look at her. She kissed her mother's tightened cheek, the skin stretched from twig to twig, and glimpsed the thin telltale scar racing from ear to jaw like the red margin on a sheet of notepaper.

"I didn't think you were coming," Mrs. Williams said, thrusting aside the *Wall Street Journal,* which she had read religiously for as long as Mary could remember.

"I told you I was."

"You're not reliable."

She let that pass, from long habit. "You look marvelous, Mother."

"I keep up. One has to."

In younger years her mother could stand still, not move a muscle, and pull people to her. The poet Robert Lowell had aggravated a dicky heart by falling in love with her, and the president of the First National Bank of Boston had been a personal adviser, but all the men in her life had had a temporary look, including her own husband, Mary's beloved father. Mary could forgive her for many things but not that.

"How's your friend?" she asked.

"I have all my marbles, Hilda doesn't. She was raving about her husband, so they had to hit her with a hypo." Seated upright, Mrs. Williams adjusted the hem of her dress, which was fashionably short. Her knees were shiny. "And how is *your* friend?" she asked. "Still living off you?"

Her mother despised Dudley, had detested him on sight and called him a pearl. *You know what a pearl is, don't you, Mary? It's a sick thing in an oyster.*

"Can't we keep this friendly, Mother?"

"I don't trust you, dear. You were your daddy's girl, not

mine." Mrs. Williams's face, distorted by the travesty of a smile, looked fired upon, the marksman drilling black holes on each side of her thin nose.

Sounds in the room collected, the ticking of an antique clock, the gurgling of an aquarium of tropical fish. Whispers came from the chintz chairs. The man lashed out with his cane, as if to score the air, and then, the strength leaving his arm, he dropped it. He stared at Mary as if he wanted to reveal himself, to divulge his preoccupations, to lay out the thoughts that came to him in the night. "He married into the Rockefellers," Mrs. Williams confided. "He used to command boardrooms, now he has to have his face wiped after he eats."

Mary pictured his lost world of dark business suits with faint stripes, of corporate carpeting muffling the hardest footfalls, of sleek-limbed women bending over Canon copiers, of disembodied voices speaking to him in elegant English from Brussels and Berlin.

"He's Exeter and Yale," Mrs. Williams said. "He's Skull and Bones."

His hair reduced to a trace of cigar smoke, his uncertain legs elementary, he struggled to his feet, fumbled open his pants, and projected himself. Unabashed, the two women in the chintz chairs smiled at each other.

"He thinks we don't know he's had an implant," Mrs. Williams said coolly. Then in a louder voice: "That's wonderful, Mr. Skully. But we've seen enough."

"I think I'd better go," Mary said.

Mrs. Williams rose with ceremony, smoothed her dress— she always wore linen in the summer—and touched her hair. Leaving the common room, mother and daughter progressed through the oak-paneled passage, encountered the scent of musk, and ran into Mrs. Nichols, who appeared so abruptly she might have stepped out of the woodwork.

"Mr. Skully was exhibiting again," Mrs. Williams said.

Mrs. Nichols frowned. "I'll restrict him."

"No need, my dear. We're all quite used to him."

Mary blurted out, "How is Mrs. Gunner?"

"Quite well," Mrs. Nichols said. "She's having a little nap."

Seated on the cot's edge, Dudley tore a sneaker off, then the other. When he stripped away Chief Morgan's old argyles, his feet looked like fish plundered from the cleanest waters, though an odor arose. His shirt was open to an anemic chest, which he scratched. "I feel dirty," he said.

"Perhaps you are," Morgan said.

"I need a shower. A real one. Not with a hose."

Morgan stood over him with a notepad and pencil. "Everything you've told me, I want you to put it in writing."

He looked up with a smile. "I can't, Chief. It was all in confidence. Between you and me. Our secret."

"That's not the way it works," Morgan said harshly, his tolerance exhausted, his irritation building. "The free ride is over."

From Dudley came silence; between them lay an emptiness. Morgan stepped back and viewed him from an oblique angle, a different perspective that yielded nothing except a glint of irony, like light that shoots off ice.

"My problem, Dudley, is I'm beginning to believe you."

"Yes, I thought you might." He seemed pleased, in a modest way triumphant. "I didn't need to push the boy. He was open to suggestion."

"That's hard to accept."

"You weren't there." Dudley's smile gave a lift to his words. "He went on his own."

Morgan stood fixed. "How about the little girl?"

"That was slightly different, but just as easy."

"Any others?"

"One, but that was long ago."

"People hired you?"

"That's confidential."

"Too late for that." Morgan tossed the pad and pencil on the cot. "I want it all written out, your hand. You don't have a choice." Morgan strode to the cell door, yanked it open, and stepped outside. "I'll be back in an hour. If it's not all down on paper, I'm turning you over to the state police."

"That doesn't frighten me."

Morgan spoke through the bars. "They won't treat you the way I have."

Dudley's smile, a gash, began to heal when he picked up the pad. "I've never used weapons. I wouldn't know how."

"I believe you," Morgan said.

Ira Smith came home early, his face in its usual pleasant mold despite problems. A senior partner in his law firm's Washington office had committed improprieties with several trust accounts, and he needed to fly down there, to do what he could. In the bedroom he slipped an extra suit into a garment bag. "This might take a couple of days," he said calmly.

Regina Smith placed a hand on the back of his shaved neck. Dear Ira. He was a paragon of reasonableness, no wild cards in his deck, no jokers. In a shuffle he always came out the same. "Must you leave now? Wouldn't tomorrow do?"

"I'm afraid not." He closed a small suitcase bearing necessities and moved to a dresser to use a pair of hairbrushes on his head. "A limo will be here in an hour."

"Then we have time for a sherry."

Downstairs, in a room recently redone at great expense, they took chairs near casement windows set in lustrous walls. The afternoon light streaked to crystalware that fired back hard little rays. Brass objects became gold. Regina took a sip of sherry and sat back.

"What do you hope to accomplish down there?"

"Damage control. That's the Washington buzzword." He adjusted his horn-rims and gazed beyond her. "Anthony and Patricia, they're not around?"

"They're at one of the beaches, Rye, I believe. That's a matter we must settle when you come back." She did not need to explain. She had voiced her concerns several times. Changing the subject, she said, "Harley Bodine seems to be coming out of it."

"It's been good of you to look after him."

"I haven't exactly done that, and I wouldn't want him becoming dependent on me."

"Is that a possibility?"

"I may have to wean him," she said lightly. She felt free to tell Ira nearly anything. She trusted him. He was void of jealousy, incapable of malice, and slow to judge, in comfortable ways a perfect husband who would always be there for her. His first wife had raced through one red light too many and had died of head trauma.

Their sherries drunk, she heard him say, "I never wanted to open a Washington office."

"Why did you?"

"I didn't listen to myself."

She waited with him outside, his garment bag draped over his suitcase. In a maverick breeze silver birches sprinkled the air with little leaves. Some of the lilies were molting, which brought to her a momentary sadness. As a child she had wanted it always to be summer—blue skies and meadow flowers. As an adolescent she had occasionally let silly stuff consume her. She had wanted to die on a dance floor, in someone's arms.

Ira said, "I'll call you."

"Yes, please do."

Through the shrubbery flanking the long drive came flashes of creamy white and the intermittent glare of a windshield. Ira retrieved his garment bag. A robin offered up a song as the endless automobile, floating on scented air, curved toward them. Ira reached for his suitcase.

"Nothing more ugly than a stretch limo," she said. "Detroit with a hard-on."

He looked at her with surprise. "I've never heard you talk like that before."

"Sometimes I do."

Beverly Gunner pulled a small color photo from her bag and held it up for the ball player's wife to see. "This was my daughter," she said, and Sissy Alexander, childless, viewed it with shy politeness. Then she swiftly returned the picture to her bag. No one could know the depth of her grief, the loneliness of her situation. Phoebe Yarbrough looked at her with extreme kindness.

"You mustn't brood, Bev."

Sitting hot and immobile, her punch glass empty, Anne Lapierre said, "Why aren't we in the pool?"

Germaine English and Kate Bodine rose in unison, followed by Phoebe and then Sissy Alexander, all with bathing suits under their clothes. Kate Bodine came out of her shirt and shorts in splendidly large proportions and shook her blond hair free. Her suit was the sort Olympic swimmers wear, and Germaine English's was the white of lingerie worn under wedding dresses. Sissy Alexander was a butterball in ruffled yellow. Phoebe stripped down to an off-white bikini, the top and bottom no more than breaths in winter air.

Phoebe said, "Come on, Bev."

"I can't." Everyone was on her feet except she. "I don't have a bathing suit."

"Go in your underwear."

Anne Lapierre, tugging at the sturdy bra of her suit, said from the diving board, "Go naked."

"I'm not beautiful," she said, her feet glued into her pumps.

"No woman is *not* beautiful," said Phoebe.

Her body was vernacular, Phoebe's was the King's English. And the dancer's harmony of flesh and bone. "I'm afraid of water."

"Then get it over with," said Anne Lapierre.

The pool's surface looked like colored glass too precious to break. Anne Lapierre shattered it with an awkward dive. Kate Bodine's was more coordinated. Sissy Alexander squeezed her nose and jumped in, making the biggest splash. Germaine English tested the water with her foot and slid in. Phoebe held back.

"You don't have to, Bev. It's up to you."

She heaved herself from the chair, her dress sticking to her bottom, her pumps pinching her toes, which made her unsteady.

She could enter the shallow end of the pool, wade up to her waist, and ease her bladder. But no, it would show. And she'd suffer the shame of a pup caught piddling on the carpet.

"Maybe you shouldn't," Phoebe said. "Are you tipsy?"

At the deep end of the pool, removing nothing, not even her watch, she felt the skin tighten across her face to the point she feared something would pop. Her inner ear picked up the rhythm of her husband's soundless anger, and her mental eye witnessed a hitherto unimaginable degree of hate. The isthmus of sex was their only meaningful connection, but his lovemaking was primitive. She loathed the doggy position.

Someone from the pool yelled to Phoebe. "Watch her!"

Phoebe grasped her arm. "Come back, Bev."

Tearing free and tumbling forward, she committed the first rash act of her life and made the biggest splash.

Chief Morgan lunched late at the Blue Bonnet and returned to the station with a sense of mission, immediately aborted when he encountered the faces of Meg O'Brien and Sergeant Avery. "Don't tell me," he said in a low voice and proceeded down the corridor to the cell. The door hung open, the chain dangling from the bars. He went to the cot and snatched up the pad of paper. Drawn with care was the cartoon face of a boy, which easily could have been a girl.

Sergeant Avery and Meg O'Brien had come up behind him. Meg said, "I was on the phone, James. My back was turned."

"It was my fault," Sergeant Avery confessed. "I let him out to go to the toilet, and then I had to use it. I was in there for a while."

"He had one of those *Penthouse*s with him," Meg said. "*Didn't* you, Eugene?"

"You mean you didn't lock him up?" Morgan said and sailed the pad of paper back onto the cot. "No one's to know. We have to find him."

Meg said, "Do we really want him back, James?"

"Yes, Meg, we really do."

———

Climbing into the rear of the taxi, Mary Williams woke the waiting driver, who pulled himself erect behind the wheel and turned the ignition. The motor stuttered, then found a voice. "Not to worry, ma'am."

"I'm not, John. I feel perfectly safe." On the way to Interstate 93, she studied the solid back of his neck, the heavy curves of his ears, and the rough graying head of hair. "When are you going to let me sketch you?" she asked. "It really would be worth your while."

Their eyes met in the rearview. "I'm not for sale, ma'am."

"Then do it for free."

"I was going to do it at all, it'd be for the money."

On the interstate, she felt the shock of passing cars. John drove with both hands on the wheel, his eyes straight ahead. She said, "May I ask you something?"

"I'm used to questions."

"Is it difficult being black?"

"Being blind would be worse."

"I've read everything by James Baldwin."

"I've never heard of him, ma'am."

"He found peace in Paris, but he came home to die. That's what Dudley will do."

"That the fella you told me about?"

"My soul mate, John."

"Did he go to Paris too?"

"He's nowhere."

John screwed his head around to look at her. "Everybody's somewhere."

"No," she said. "In madness, you're neither here nor there."

7

DARKNESS FELL FAST, WRAPPING TREES, ROLLING AWAY FLOWER beds, and stashing lawn chairs. Phoebe Yarbrough, casting a long shadow by the lit pool, collected empty punch glasses and placed them on a tray, along with crumpled napkins. Myles Yarbrough, financial worries tangling his mind, sat in the chair Beverly Gunner had occupied. "The most that can happen," he said, "is we lose the house."

The pool reflected her image and elongated her legs, which quivered in a breeze. On her face was a rigid smile, as if someone were taking her picture.

"I'm not saying it'll happen," he went on abruptly. "I'm just laying out the worst scenario."

He spoke always in a breath of certainty, even when delivering bullshit. That they would lose the house was a given, for she had seen the ultimatum from the bank. "There are condos in Andover that are quite nice, Myles. I've already made arrangements to look at one."

"Yes, just in case." He spoke too fast, the words beaten

together. Then his eyes sought reassurance, like those of a show dog that had failed to perform. He had come from money but not as much as she had thought. "Not sorry you married me, are you?" he said through the pretense of a laugh.

"It's a question I could ask you," she said in a tone meant to calm him. He had been a client, one of those who had sent her flowers before arriving, fellows who ran operations, took chances, walked tightropes, in her business the guys with the big balls. Now all those clients, except Myles, were a compound image in her mind. Had she not married him, he would be lumped in the glue of the others. "For better or worse, Myles, weren't those the words?"

"I'll bounce back, you'll see." He was a lawyer who directed his energies toward loopholes, went into deals with a vision of endless returns, and cooked the books of paper companies he had helped form. "You believe me, don't you?"

She neither believed him nor loved him but had affection for him and was loyal. Picking up the tray of clinking glasses, she saw the moon emerge through the dark of distant trees. Rising, he followed her into the house, where he trod softly on a floor meant for sound.

"You ought to call Gunner," he said, his voice as low as he could make it.

"She doesn't want me to."

"You don't have a choice." Seams showed in his face, hope in his eyes. "And while you're talking to him, you might mention—"

"No, Myles."

"You didn't let me finish."

"I'm going to look in on her," she said.

Beverly Gunner lay on a bed in a guest room, her head on two stacked pillows, her ruined shell of hair radiating its spill. Myles's robe consumed her. "I feel like such a fool," she said in the feeble light of a bed lamp. "And I've wrecked my watch. Paul paid a fortune for it two birthdays ago."

"Maybe it can be repaired."

"He buys me everything. Should I be grateful?"

Phoebe seated herself on the bed's edge. Shadows in the room hung still. Beverly Gunner's face was high red, as if dramatic necessity had brought them together.

"He never fights me with words, only cold silences. That's why he always wins. Where's my bag, Phoebe?"

Phoebe gave it to her and watched her bring forth the color snapshot she'd seen before. This time she got a better look at it. The eyes of the child were shallow yet inexplicable, the smile madcap yet tender. The face bespoke Beverly's, except for the chin, which lacked precision. "She was beautiful, Bev."

"He said my best thoughts were for her, not for the boys. He claimed she wasn't worth it." The picture went quickly and safely back to the bag. "She was an embarrassment to him."

"Shouldn't you phone him, tell him you're here?"

"I don't know. What time is it?"

Phoebe told her and received a puzzled look, as if the hour belonged to another day, the day to another year. Myles could be heard in another room.

"I live an interior life, Phoebe. Paul's not a part of it."

"Would you mind if I call him?"

"It's not clear what I want, but you do what you wish."

Phoebe used the phone in her own bedroom. Myles approached her from the side and stood much too close until she edged him back with an effortless movement. "At least tell him I'm the one pulled her out," he whispered.

"She did what?" Paul Gunner's voice rose to preemptive volume, slicing Phoebe's explanation short, demeaning his wife's worth. Phoebe suspected he never used his entire brain when listening to women. He said that the foolishness at the pool was beyond him. How could anyone have been so clumsy? "All I know," he said, "is the boys and I had to eat at Burger King."

"Paul."

"What?"

"She's staying here the night." She spoke quickly so that he'd get it, and then she waited because nothing was coming from him except the sound of his labored breathing. She pictured his eyes shuttered, his pink lips pursed. Suddenly he responded.

"Somebody better come over here and explain."

The line went dead, and, still holding the receiver, wondering how she had gotten into this, she looked at Myles, who had heard everything. Myles said, "You go."

Sergeant Avery, told to be discreet, searched for Dudley behind the stores on the far side of the green. Hank Brody, who owned the hardware store, poked his head out the back door and asked whether he was scavenging. The droll and stylish white-haired woman at Roberta's Ladies Shoppe asked whether he'd like to step in and try on an ensemble. She thought he might look chic in a short-sleeve patterned jacket with black shorts, which she had been saving for a customer from the Heights.

Officer Floyd Wetherfield reconnoitered book aisles at the library, pausing to examine an art folio someone had left on a reading table. He slapped the cover shut when the librarian, Holly Pride, came upon him and asked whether she could help him.

Later he parked his cruiser near Pearl's Pharmacy, slouched behind the wheel, and kept his eye on the green until the approach of darkness when Fred Fossey, commander of the local Legion post, stood in respectful attention among Boy Scouts for the lowering of the flag. A bugle sounded. The flag cascaded down the pole like paint.

Chief Morgan drove to Pearson Grammar School, behind which men, young and not so young, were acting out fantasies in a slow-pitch game of softball, each assuming the mannerisms of Crack Alexander in his prime. Another time Morgan might have joined them.

On Summer Street he slowed at Dorothea Farnham's house, viewed the porch Dudley had desecrated, and spotted Dorothea chinning with a neighbor over a dividing hedge recently barbered. At the end of the street, vaulted by maples, he made a U-turn and found his pulse beating abnormally from an

anxiety he hoped was unwarranted. On his shoulders was a burden he felt he had put there himself.

It was dark when he finally quit looking and returned to
the station. The nighttime dispatcher, Bertha Skagg, a large
woman whose floral dress shouted attention to her unfortunate
size and shape, was ensconced behind Meg O'Brien's daytime
desk with her usual air of being put upon or of being left out
of things, grievances that had put a permanent twist to her
mouth.

She said, "You let the tramp go?"

Fiddling with papers on Sergeant Avery's desk, he sort of
said yes.

"Good, it was creepy having him here," she said. "Eugene
called in. He said to tell you, 'No luck,' whatever that means. I
guess you know, 'cause I don't."

"How about Floyd?"

"Floyd doesn't tell me anything. You got a call from a Mrs.
Bodine. The number's on your desk."

He entered his office, shut the door behind him, and looked
at the number. Brookline. The first Mrs. Bodine. She answered
immediately, and when he identified himself she said, "What
kind of man are you?"

The agonized voice was raw enough to freeze his ear and
arrest his other senses. He ripped a page from his calendar block,
on which he seldom wrote anything, a dental appointment perhaps, a reminder to pick up dry cleaning.

"You had no right," she said. "It was cruel what you did."

What had he done other than his job, or what seemed his
job? One did not do what was necessarily right but what seemed
poignant. A rule, he supposed, every policeman followed.

"Why didn't you tell me you're having an affair with Harley's wife? Is that supposed to be your secret?" Her voice was a
needle with no thread, simply an instrument of puncture, nothing worth stitching. "You tried to use me, Chief."

It seemed pointless to defend himself. Expostulation seldom, if ever, worked. Besides, she was no longer on the line.

A while later, with a rumbling effort, her heaviness a burden on her legs, Bertha Skagg heaved herself up, poked open his door, and looked in. "I thought you were sleeping," she said. "Don't you have a home?"

This was more of one, his choice since his wife's death. At times he could not remember his wife's face, as if time had burned the memory to ash. Other times it was more vivid than when she had been alive. "Where do we go from here, Bertha? Where do we go when it's all over?"

"You asking me?"

"It's a reasonable question."

"I have no lofty thoughts," she said, resuming a frown. "My mind is like my legs. It can't climb stairs."

He looked at her in a warmer light, remembering when she had lost her cat and for a solid year sought its return through a boxed ad in *The Crier*. Offered a reward. Signed herself *Heartbroken*. Meg O'Brien offered one of hers, but it wasn't the same. He said, "Close the door after you."

He picked up the phone and called the second Mrs. Bodine. He heard someone lift the receiver and immediately replace it. He repunched the number, and his eyes fainted shut when she answered.

"This is James."

"Yes, I know your voice."

"Anything the matter?"

"I was undecided," she said vaguely.

"Can we talk?"

"All night if you wish."

An hour back from the beach, a plate of cold chicken and tomato wedges consumed, Anthony Smith was flopped in one of his bedroom chairs and reading Chaucer when Patricia, her unscraped face moistened with a lotion, stepped in uninvited. "Prithee, get the fuck out of here," he said.

"Don't talk to me that way, you prick." Her cheeks glistened, her nose was a dab of light, her eyes flashed. "My chemistry teacher would murder for what you get."

"Your chemistry teacher, huh? Man or woman?"

"A man, you asshole." She plunked herself into the other chair, her legs thrown out, and stared at him with undeflectable eyes. "What are you reading that shit for? It's archaic."

"It's on my list."

"Anais Nin's on mine. What do you think of that?"

"Never heard of her."

"Figures. Do you love me, Tony?"

He flipped a page. "Why do you want to mess it up?"

"Because five years from now you'll wish you'd said yes."

He lifted his eyes, but with his grip firmly on Chaucer. "You know I do," he said, the wallop of truth in his face.

"Then say it."

"No."

"What are you so afraid of? My mother?" Her eyes were trained on him, her smile tense, disruptive, truant. "You're scared to death of her, aren't you?"

"With reason," he said.

"This way," Paul Gunner said, and with the pressure of a thumb on her arm he guided Phoebe Yarbrough deeper into the house, past a mirror that gave a good report. She was wearing black jeans; her legs were ink strokes. Her heels sank in the carpeting; a club chair reared up and possessed her, and in that instant she wished she hadn't come. He gazed down at her from his bulk, and she guessed that he didn't want to talk about his wife. "Let her stay the night if that's what she wants," he said. "Maybe she's going through the change. What do I know?"

"It may have been the punch I served," Phoebe suggested.

"Let's talk about Myles," he said, stepping back, sinking into a chair the twin of hers, which he overfilled. "How's he doing?"

"Since you ask, not well." Her back was straight, her legs crossed. "But I'm sure you already know that."

"I could help him, I suppose. Low-interest loan to tide him over. After all, what are neighbors for?"

"Nice of you to offer," she said, "but Myles can stand on his own two feet."

His eyes narrowed to nothing, but his mouth was swollen big in a smile, as if his teeth were sunk into the rubber guard of a boxer. "You really think so?"

Stretching her long neck, she glanced about the room, densely masculine with its dark wood, extra-plush drapes, heavy furniture, and brass lamps that produced more shadow than light, all of which made her suspect a trap, one with steel jaws if she was reading him right.

"Tell me about yourself," he said. "What did you do in New York? Career woman, weren't you?"

She had been through this before with him, but in a crowd, safety in faces, always others to interrupt. "I did publicity."

"Ah, yes, you did mention that once. What company?"

"I was free-lance."

"When I owned my company, I was in New York a lot. Stayed at the Pierre. It suited me." There was no movement in his face, but his smile was effusive. "Myles says your father was in government. Treasury."

Her father had stood in a New Jersey turnpike booth and handled money all day, hands beaten and bruised from it. "Low-level," she said.

"Is he still alive?"

He had had high blood pressure and had been lax about his medication. The day he died his face looked like a flash burn. "No," she said, aware how drastically the dead fade with the years and distance themselves to a degree she wouldn't have thought possible. But then in a random dream or the triggering of a memory they return larger than life, more vital than ever.

"My father," Gunner said, "was a genius."

"So I've heard."

"And so am I."

"I've heard that too." She disliked Gunner's lips. Fatty morsels. That he was brilliant had impressed her but not intimidated her. She sensed something was coming and waited.

"You don't remember me, do you?"

What was he saying? Did she want to hear? Her own silence pressed upon her, along with a boding of danger.

"I had a beard then, and I wasn't as heavy." Each shift in his smile was a tactical maneuver. "Funny, I never forgot you."

With nothing to say, she sat like a cup of tea gone cold, his lip print on the rim. She remembered some clients as series of eager thrusts alternating with pauses recommended by their doctors, some as vulgar voices lining the shell of her ear, others as eyes going awry, no longer true mates, lust putting them at odds. She remembered no faces.

"You were the only woman I know could undress with an air of decorum."

His voice was intrusive, a key digging in, twisting loose secrets, though she felt nothing other than lightheadedness, somewhat like a forger relieved at being unmasked.

"I remember," he said, "we smoked marijuana of a particularly heady variety."

She had done that a few times with men she guessed would be a chore. Or when she felt she might be pitched into a situation she couldn't handle. Cannabis could calm.

"I reckon you married Myles for respectability. Too bad you picked a loser."

Respectability had been a major factor, but so had the tender way he had handled her breasts, treating her as a woman first, the other second. Unlocking her thighs, gripping the arms of the chair, she rose. Clumsily, Gunner rose too.

"I'm not the type to spread tales."

"What do you want, Paul?"

"For myself, nothing. But it's time my oldest boy learned what it's all about. He's got a birthday coming up. I can't think of a nicer present, can you?"

She saw in his face the fat that runs through steak and the gristle that can't be chewed but must be discreetly spat into a napkin or casually placed on the side of the plate. Her composure was amazing.

"It'll be worth your while," he said. "And I can call it secretarial service and write you off."

"No, Paul, it wouldn't be worth it."

"Think it over."

She took a step, but he presented too much weight and mass. He proliferated, listed. He was a solidity she could not get by. "Now I remember you," she said, releasing a smile luminous and enchanting. "You disgusted me. Your brat would disgust me more."

She sidestepped him but did not make it past his chair. The first blow glanced off her face. The second cracked a bone.

Chief Morgan lived beyond Pearson Grammar School on Winter Street in a small gingerbread Victorian in need of painting, caulking, and reshingling, tasks he thought he might one day do himself, though he had no skills. The time spent in it was minimal, the food in the refrigerator was often spoiled, and the dog next door was a nuisance. Anything started it barking. In the kitchen was an old portable television, uncabled. He had seen at least three times every episode of *Kojak* and *The Rockford Files*. Telly Savalas and James Garner were like family.

In the front room he hit a wall switch, and light bulged from a window lamp, a beacon for Kate Bodine, another one outside on the porch. The room, which he and his wife had inexpertly wallpapered, was one he seldom entered, for he learned only too well that the familiar turns sinister in the agony of loss. The summer after Elizabeth's death, her garden had mocked him with its overlush bloom, sweet William flickering like fire, lupine blazing on the stalk, bleeding heart dripping its sorrow. The red maple sapling planted nearby had taunted him with a shadow longer than his until he tore it up by the roots.

In the bathroom he splashed his face with cold water, smoothed his hair back with wet hands, and wondered whether Kate Bodine would show up. He did not like waiting around, which consumed too much energy, all of it nervous. Then he heard the slow slam of a car door and the bark of the neighbor's dog and knew she was out there.

Her snappy little car, a tongue of silver in the moonlight, was parked on the street. Stepping silently out the front door, he saw her pause on the sidewalk as if unsure she had the right house. Then in the small driveway she paused again and scrutinized his old Chevy, public property, eaten at the edges, its official function denoted by the town seal. Looking past him as he descended the porch step, she said, "It's not what I pictured. Do you live in there alone?"

"When I'm here." The dog, a mongrel, was still yapping. Shrubbery separating the narrow properties stood jagged against the night air. "Would you like to come in?"

His neighbor, an elderly widow with whom he did not get along, hollered from an unlit window. "That you out there?"

"Yes," he shouted back.

"Who's that with you?"

"None of your business, Mrs. Winkler."

Kate said, "Why don't we walk?" They moved to the sidewalk and strolled side by side in the direction of the school. The moon seemed bigger and nearer than normal, as if some force had driven it down. Kate dropped her head back. "I want to know who threw all those stars up there."

"I know I didn't," Morgan said. "At least not all of them."

"No mosquitoes," she observed.

"The town sprayed. You people from the Heights demanded it. Your taxes paid for it."

"I won't mention it to my husband. He says the taxes here are exorbitant."

Thin clouds caroused the lit sky. A breeze walked the street. Morgan said, "How are you doing with your husband?"

"He's trying to get me pregnant, but it won't work. I'm on the pill. I'm telling you too much, of course, most of it none of your business."

"Where is he tonight?"

"Out. I don't believe he mentioned where. What do you want to talk to me about?"

"About him. I have certain suspicions."

"He has many about you." Mosquitoes attacked her legs, and she slapped herself below the knees. "Damn it."

"We can't get 'em all," Morgan said fatalistically, his eye on the school. Darkness packaged the brick, and moonlight ribboned it. They gazed at it.

"Did you go there?"

"Yes," he said. "I'm a real townie. Except for Vietnam, Bensington's the only world I know."

"*What* suspicions?"

Slowing his step, he related them in a quiet and reserved voice, no inflections. He mentioned her dead stepson by name and the drowned Gunner girl by age. To his missing prisoner he assigned a kind of perverse truth. At one point, even to his own ear, the drama verged on the preposterous, which temporarily dismayed him. When he finished, she moved away from him with her eyes lifted.

"It's the stars they say that keep the sky pinned in place. Thank God for the stars, James."

"What does the moon do?" he asked.

"It moves oceans. For a dead thing I'd say that's damn good."

He followed her into folds of darkness beneath a tree, where her scent became the heaviest ingredient in the air. He made out only a single line of her face, enough to draw him close. Her white hand came out of nowhere and manacled his bare wrist.

"I don't buy it."

"I didn't think you would," he said.

She let go. "You said it yourself. You live in a vacuum."

In May Hutchins's backyard the shallow pool of the birdbath trapped the moon and toyed with its shape. May, refilling a bird feeder, listening to the soothing murmurs of the night, felt magical. Breezes lifted her colored hair, airing her scalp. Moonlight moved over grass, awakened phlox, gave life to a moribund shrub, gripped a croquet ball, and enameled the face of a man in the fretwork of the gazebo.

"Who's there?" she said, and her voice startled a young raccoon that with racketing claws scrabbled halfway up the pear tree. Through the ghostly dim she could see only the creature's luminous eyes, like fired bullets frozen between two worlds.

She returned to the house.

Her husband spoke to her through the bathroom door. "Who were you talking to out there?"

"Myself," she said, looking at herself in the mirror of the medicine cabinet. Fluorescent lighting could be cruel.

"You shouldn't roam around in the dark."

"Lots of things I shouldn't do," she said, "and, damn it, I don't."

She lingered in the bathroom, ruminating on the state of her hair and the state of herself. Living on memories, she felt undernourished. She thought back to her fortieth birthday, her realization that her youth had vanished, no way to reach it, address unknown. She had had herself a good cry, and later Roland with his flipper arms had tried to please her in bed. Fifty was when she began brooding over mistakes in her life. At sixty, she supposed, she would learn to live with them.

Roland smiled when she came upon him in the kitchen, his face a milky sheen of chubbiness. "What did you mean by that?" he asked, and her mind had to work back.

"I didn't mean anything. Forget it."

He was in old moccasins, which he used for house slippers, and he was only a few years from retirement, which frightened her. Her sister Joan's husband had retired two years ago and turned womanish, usurping Joan's kitchen, soaking bottles in the sink for the redeemable labels, clipping recipes from Mary's magazines before she read them. When one of her friends phoned, he got on the extension to join the conversation, then to monopolize it. He was seldom out of *his* slippers.

Roland said, "You're in a funny mood, May."

"It's my mood. Don't fuck with it."

His eyes jittered, for the language wasn't hers, at least not her public one, but his smile stayed unassuming and uncomplaining. He wasn't one for going deeply into things, but he was, she readily admitted, a good provider, his heyday when the Heights was under development. He had wired most of the grand houses, including the Gunners', the grandest.

Watching him turn away, she softened her feelings. He was shelter, he was groceries on the table, he was the balance in her checkbook, and he was more than that. He had to be. Watching him rub the nape of his neck, she knew he was ready for bedtime television.

In the bedroom, he placed his coin purse on the dresser, and they began readying themselves for bed with their backs turned, though she could see him in the mirror. With his shirt off, he looked like a boiled potato. His pants gone, his body struggled for shape. Yet, she wondered, would Fred Fossey, her would-be lover, look any different in the round? Fred Fossey, she suspected, did not wear pajamas.

Roland switched on the television. *Law & Order.* "Okay?" he asked and padded to the window to raise the shade for air. Moonlight bathed him, breezes blew in.

"I think I'd like to watch Barbara Walters," she said, propping her pillows. Head bent, he stood tranced looking out the window. She waited. "Did you hear me, Roland?"

He didn't move. His eyes were cast into the night. "Somebody's out there."

She reached across the bed for the clicker and changed channels and raised the volume. Her interest was in Barbara Walters's hairdo, which her own at times resembled.

Roland's voice was a rasp. "A man's in the gazebo."

Settling back against the propped pillows and curling her legs under the covers, she said, "I know who it is. Let him be."

"Let me out here," Regina Smith said when they made the turn into the gateway of the drive. The headlights, supernovas, cast fogbows. Harley Bodine's foot was on the brake.

"We're not hiding anything," he said in the tone of a younger man. "We're not children."

"I would hope not, Harley."

"Friends can't have dinner?"

"It was a fine dinner," she said, opening her door. "Thank you."

"No," he said. "Thank *you.*"

She accepted a kiss on the cheek, climbed out, and stepped aside, her mind elsewhere when the car gave a leap back, righted

itself on the road, and fled into the night. She began the long
walk up the drive at a smart pace. The moon seemed too much
stone for the sky, in danger of tearing from its setting. Only a
few lights in the large house beckoned.

Inside the front door, mirrors recording her entrance, she
slipped her pumps off. Her purse she deposited on a table where
a plume of ferns gave off the scent of cinnamon. She clicked on
no extra lights. Her ascent up the grand stairway was silent and
attended with a kind of unalterable dignity usually seen in older
women, dowagers of the first rank.

Her daughter's room was lit but vacant, the television tuned
to a music video of Prince or Michael Jackson (she could not
tell them apart) rolling epicene eyes, rubbing an androgynous
crotch, and gyrating an ebony ass buggered, she supposed, by
the wild fancies of adolescent millions. She moved far down the
dim passage, well beyond the sound of the video, carrying with
her the badge of high purpose and a perverse thrill of anticipation.

The door to her stepson's room was half open, and the air
pumping out was potent, the scent stronger than what she had
drawn from the ferns. The sounds she heard loosed a pulsing
vein at her temple, and after fighting through a moment of pa-
ralysis in her legs, she looked in. There were clothes on the floor
and a rumpus on the bed, the sight at once a grotesque comedy
of abuse and an exquisite conspiracy against her. Defiant muscles
in her stepson's taut legs raced into his buttocks, which were
banged together like cobblestones. The soles of his feet were
dirty, the knees of her daughter rosy. Outrage struck her with
the force of a tidal wave.

She reeled away and retreated, for she did not want to witness the mockery of a crescendo. Passing a guest room, she
nearly gave out an hysterical horse laugh that would have
brought down the roof on her head. As silently as she had
climbed the stairs she descended them.

Harley Bodine returned home and, though he heard his wife at
work at her typewriter, knew she had gone out and come back

not much before he. This he knew because he had laid a hand
on the hood of her car. In a room of her own, her back to him,
she sat at a sturdy table in a small chrome and leather swivel
chair. "How's it going?" he asked in a forceful voice, and her
fingers slid off the keys.

"Not well," she said, turning in the chair.

"I didn't think so." He idly thumbed the wheel of his
lighter, not hard enough to scratch up a flame for the cigarette
that hung from his mouth. "Why bother?"

"I want to make my own money again."

"I give you enough."

"You make it seem painful."

"It's not about the money, is it? It's something else." He
produced a flame and lit a cigarette. "Tell me what it is."

"I don't know what you're talking about."

"Yes, you do. It's in your face."

She said, "How much did you love your son?"

Dudley stood outside the gazebo on bare feet, his toes gnawing
the grass, and gazed up at the calm calamity of stars, some burning beyond their existence, emitting flames no longer there. He
was aware of the figure advancing toward him but chose to ignore it until, bearing a burden, it was upon him.

"My wife says you might need these."

His arms accepted a puffy pillow and a folded blanket,
which assured his comfort on the cushioned bench in the gazebo. His gaze returned to the night sky, which he saw as a battle
in which many shots are fired at an enemy never seen. "This is
too kind."

"She wants to know if you've eaten."

"I could use a bite."

"We'll leave something for you on the back step."

His gaze focused on a protuberance of stars strung up like
the cocked hind leg of a dog. He had never had a dog, never
wanted one. A cat had been his love. "That will be wonderful."

"Then I'll say good night."

"And I won't let the bogeyman get me."

In the glassy light of the moon Roland Hutchins's departure was a shuffle. His footsteps were leavings on the grass, his shadow his skeleton. A stunted tree that had not borne leaves in years gave out posthumous rustlings in the breeze. From the dark of a window came May Hutchins's voice.

"Sleep tight."

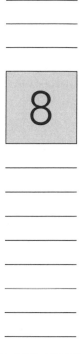

8

BEVERLY GUNNER ENTERED HER HOUSE LIKE A STRANGER AND avoided mirrors. God knows what she looked like. She had put on lipstick but had not done her hair and had ruined her dress. In the sun room, where a pruned ficus mushroomed its pointed leaves, she gazed out at the pool. Her sons were floating belly up on rubber rafts, though she saw only one clearly, her vision blurred, as if an eyeball had sprung loose. With painful and strenuous effort, she forced the shrunken pumps from her swollen feet and let out two hurt cries of relief, the first the fiercest.

She entered the kitchen from one wide entrance, her husband from the other. Wearing only pajama bottoms, he looked more maternal than masculine. Shambling on slow, fat feet, he burst open a cabinet door and plucked out a glass. Without looking at her, he spoke first.

"I'm not going to ask what last night was all about."

"You're wise not to," she said in a tone never used with him before. She stood near the breakfast nook and saw that the boys had fed themselves. The milk had been left out, a spill of it on the table, next to the skins of two bananas. Spoons had been left clunked in their cereal bowls. The box was thrown on its side, as if they had fought over it.

His back to her, her husband gulped orange juice. His rear end was massive and eternal. When he faced her, he said, "You look like hell."

She said, "What did you do to Phoebe Yarbrough?"

They took note of each other, he with his mouth drawn down. Seconds passed. "What did she say?"

"You hit her."

"That's her story."

"You broke her cheekbone."

"She'll be all right." He put aside the empty juice glass and tugged at his pajama pants. Sizable nipples depended from the mush of his chest. "You want to hear what really happened?"

"I don't trust you."

"She came on to me."

She smiled in the abstract behind too much lipstick. Her dress hung heavy on her. "I've never trusted you."

"Things about Phoebe Yarbrough you don't know," he said.

"And don't want to know."

"In New York she was a call girl. That's what Yarbrough married. A fancy whore."

She turned away from him. "That's what I wish I had been," she said, with certain crashes inside her head, tilted thoughts exploding like spilled dishes, through which she heard him snort.

"You don't have the body."

In high school, sought after, she had almost allowed a fellow to have fun with her. He was later killed in Vietnam. She wished she had given joy to him. Looking back, she was sure she had.

"But I like what you've got," he said, his face increasing.

She sheered away when the edge of his hand sought the groove of her rump. "Don't touch me," she said and watched his face burn.

"You've got nothing without me."

She had her grandmother's jewelry, inexpensive pieces embossed with memories, and pictures of her daughter handled always with love. Her smile was back, still in the abstract. "And I have nothing with you," she said.

Sunlight trembled on the grass. Carrying a tray of buttered toast, coffee, and juice, May Hutchins saw that Dudley was not in the gazebo but behind it. When she realized he was urinating, she stopped in her tracks, turned her head, and waited. A small bird, blurred by its speed, flew by like a bullet.

"Good morning," she said when, decent, he made his way toward her with an easy step. "Did you sleep all right?"

Indeed he had, he told her, and with much appreciation took the breakfast tray from her hands. The toast was oatmeal bread, and from inside the gazebo he nodded his satisfaction. He sat on the cushioned bench he had slept on, with the tray balanced nicely on his lap, as if he were accustomed to tea time with women who made of him. She had absolutely no fear of him, though Roland had voiced reservations.

"I looked in on you earlier," she said, "but you were dead to the world."

"I heard you," he replied, "but I didn't want to open my eyes yet."

A wasp flew at her, and, in swiping at it, she discovered a curler dangling from the back of her head. Swiftly she dislodged it and clenched it inside her fist. "My husband says you can use the garden hose to wash up. I left soap and towel on the step." Then, hesitantly, she added, "You can bathe all over. We won't look."

"Nudity doesn't embarrass me," he said. "I've been an artist's model."

She wasn't sure she believed that, though neither did she disbelieve it, for he said it in such a natural and offhand way, as if his experiences were well beyond the scope of hers. Hers were bound and gagged in Bensington, her only adventures abortive ones with Fred Fossey, who was no prize but whose attentions touched a need. Her eye spotted the library book she had delivered to his cell.

Following her gaze, munching toast, he said, "I haven't finished it yet."

"Take your time."

This thing she had with Fred was rudimentary, some touching here and there when she allowed it, though always quickly putting a stop to it. She was unconvinced that sex was the means to what she wanted, which was an edge against slipping too fast into old age. She said, "Are they looking for you?"

He dunked a piece of toast into his coffee, which he had lightened with the real cream she had provided. She wished now that she had served him eggs, not store-bought, but fresh from Tish Hopkins's chickens.

"Don't worry," she said. "I won't tell."

She returned to the house. It was Saturday, but Roland, readying to leave, had a job to do in Andover. Spotlessly clad in his electrician's coveralls, he personified competence except when he clicked his teeth. Her thoughts on leaving him had always been lame, clubfooted, dink-toed, never a full stride.

"I don't like leaving you alone, him still here," he said, a worry line scoring his rosy face.

"Don't talk rubbish. There was anything to worry about, he wouldn't be loose. Besides, I can tell a person by his eyes."

"That may not be the best way."

"Go," she said, and he did.

In the bathroom she heard water charging through the pipes and knew that her guest was using the hose. In the mirror, while inspecting the small parts of her face, she looked for a wrinkle that appeared only when she was melancholy. It wasn't there. She restored her hair with a brush and brought color to her cheeks with pinches. When the pipes went silent, she pictured him rubbing himself down in one of her better bath towels. She felt bad that he would be getting back into the same clothes.

She gave him ample time to get decent and let the screen

door slam behind her to give him warning. The grass sparkled where he had dropped the hose. The soap was on a rock and the wet towel draped over a currant bush, but he was nowhere in sight. Looking into the vacancy of the gazebo, she frowned at the cluttered breakfast tray but brightened when she saw the Thornton Burgess book, a slip of paper marking his place. He would, most certainly, be back.

Cool to her daughter, ice to her stepson, Regina Smith confronted neither but chose to hold her tongue, control her rage, and bide her time, none of which was easy. At the breakfast table she watched Patricia try to play eye games with Anthony, who was wise enough not to reciprocate but not clever enough to hide his unease. She grimaced over her coffee cup when Patricia announced that they planned another day at the beach. Frowning at Anthony, she said, "Watch the way you drive. You have my daughter's life in your hands."

Twenty minutes later they were gone.

She phoned her husband, who was busy but never too busy to talk with her. Washington, he said, was stifling. The war memorials, he joked in a weary tone, were sweating bullets, and Republicans, among whom he was a moderate one, were under a state of siege. And the business that had brought him down there was a royal mess, worse than he had expected. None of this was what she had called about.

"Listen to me," she said and rushed out her story in a bitter voice that expurgated nothing, for the image of the crime was lurid in her mind. Vivid was her stepson's rearing bottom, the cheeks pinched together, creating the tight focus from which the rest of his body sprang. She said, "I want him out of here."

"We'll straighten it out when I get back."

"I'll call the academy," she said, her head at an angle, her hand sweeping back her dark hair. "I'm sure there's room in one of the dorms. If not, maybe that teacher, Pitkin, can take him in until the school year."

"That's something to deliberate, not necessarily to act upon. I don't excuse any of it, but—"

"You're not listening, Ira. I want him *gone*."

"Regina, we're talking about my son."

"Not at all. We're talking about my daughter. She's number one and always will be. I made that plain when we married, did I not?"

"It would seem Patricia was complicit," he said in his lawyer's voice, which infuriated her, as if he expected Patricia to yield to cross-examination. Again she pushed back her hair, a sense of traffic in her head, thoughts coming and going.

"She's fifteen, Ira. Complicity is irrelevant."

"And Tony's sixteen. Surely that's relevant."

She dared pursue it no more, for she was pitched high, in danger of saying things that would make yesterday remote and tomorrow unimaginable. "When will you be back?"

He wasn't sure. He spoke with a heavy sigh. "I'm dealing here with a felony."

"So am I," she said, though not for his ear. Quietly she had disconnected.

Smoking a furtive cigarette, Beverly Gunner spilled an ash and walked it into the carpet without compunction, without constraint. She was in an airy front room, the walls pale blue, the moldings white, her own shadow more company than she wanted. She was still in yesterday's dress, which now seemed to be some sort of uniform, as if she had entered a battle and bore wounds. The seam in the right underarm was ruptured, and the hem in back hung short.

Her posture was slack until a sound from the outside jerked her to attention. Her cigarette stub she buried in the moist soil of a potted plant flourishing on a pedestal. At the window she saw an old car with the town seal on the side and recognized the man stepping out of it. Good, she thought, Phoebe has pressed charges, and the police chief has come to make an arrest.

When the bell rang, she didn't move. She waited, her breath half held, and finally, after two more rings, her husband went to the door. She heard pieces of their voices. The chief wanted to come in.

Of course he could come in. He could read Paul his rights and then take him away, and the boys too, in handcuffs if necessary. She reeled. The possibility of a new life touched her down to her toes.

She heard the door close. What were they saying? Submerging her thoughts, she tried to attend only to the voices, particularly the chief's, but Paul's, fat and intrusive, kept getting in the way.

"What did you say your name was, Chief? Moran?"

"Morgan."

She slipped across the room to hear them better, but they were moving away. The chief was being led to the study, where her husband could flump himself into a club chair, brim over it, and act like the lord of a manor, though she imagined the chief would soon have him back on his feet. After a few moments she crept after them.

The door to the study was ajar. Peering through the crack, she saw the roundness of her husband's head and glimpsed a quarter of the chief's face, which she found reassuring, though she wished he would speak louder. She listened hard.

Her husband said, "What's your interest? It didn't happen here."

Of course it did. Where else would he have dared to do it? The formal rigor of his voice had nothing to do with the truth. She stood straight, with her hands pressed to her thighs.

The chief said, "Are you satisfied it was an accident?"

It was no accident! He had split Phoebe's face, cracked a bone, and her face, tended to at the hospital in Lawrence, was swollen and bandaged. Good God, Chief, don't be taken in!

"She was clumsy, mentally and physically," her husband said. "Look here, this is not something I enjoy discussing."

"I understand."

"No, you don't. But I understand where you're coming from. I know about your business with Bodine, which I consider cruel and suspect on your part."

What was this about? Something was going over her head and curving away from her. Paul, with no allegiance to the facts, was muddling things the way he did when she tried to speak her mind. In the end it was she left muddled.

"What disturbs me the most about you, Chief, is your business with Bodine's wife."

This was getting out of hand. What did Kate Bodine have to do with it? She could see most of the chief's face now, and it was no longer reassuring but blank and harmless. Disappointment came up on her like phlegm in her throat.

"My suspicion," Paul said, "is you're performing for her."

"May I speak with your wife?"

"Absolutely not. You're not going to upset her the way you have Bodine."

She felt she was being drawn to the center of something unsavory, and she remembered a blood uncle whose kisses had left slaver on her young mouth. She ran a hard hand across her lips as if it were there now and found herself remembering silly things, like the grit on her teeth after eating spinach and the stain in her urine after enjoying asparagus.

"Three years my wife's still not herself."

Three years? Then she understood, and her face went hard and tight as if to stem bleeding. It wasn't Phoebe the chief had come about. It was her baby. It was Fay.

Dudley appeared in the garden as if blown in, and the Reverend Mr. Stottle, who relished intangibles, put aside the pad of paper on which he had composed Sunday's sermon and gestured from his canvas chair. "Watch your step."

A fiercely green creeper threw tentacles at Dudley's sneakered feet. The thorns of rosebushes endangered the path. "I'm a bird on the wing," he said.

"Then you've flown the coop," the reverend said, in a marvelous mood from the balance in his life, the worldly ingrained in the ether. Earlier he had intruded upon his wife's privacy and found her deliciously vulgar in bra and bloomers. If Dorothea Farnham had not chosen that moment to ring up on garden club business, he would have exerted himself with a gluttony usually reserved for young lovers. Picking from a plate, he said, "Help yourself. My wife made them."

Pink cupcakes occupied a ring of glazed cookies. A milk scum sheathed the tumbler the reverend had been drinking from. Dudley said, "I'm not a bad fellow."

"We're not angels, none of us," the reverend said. "Nor would we want to be."

"I have a question."

Reverend Stottle smiled from a deeply inner delight, happy to have his thoughts scattered perhaps to another plane, to un-charted landscape. At that moment came a great honking from a wedge of Canada geese, whose summer place was Paget's Pond. The reverend said, "They always shout when they pass over my house. What was your question again?"

"I haven't asked it yet."

"Please do."

Dudley had frosting on his chin and cupcake in his mouth. "In the scheme of things," he asked, "how much of a dent is one person's death? Does it disturb in any way the course of the planet? Is it noted anywhere among the stars?"

The reverend, who preferred to talk around things, the way Jesus Christ had, was slow to respond. His eye was on a lush patch of big-buttoned daisies in which, wired upright, was an immense sun-dazzled spiderweb that looked like a stringed in-strument on which one could pluck a deadly tune. The marvel-ous creator was a living jewel clasped to the air, no sight of a thread. Finally, stealing from his sermon, the reverend said, "We never experience the limits of anything. There are joys far greater and sorrows much deeper than those we know. God has reserved those for himself."

"God lives on, we die."

"Does that trouble you?"

"No, it pleases me."

Reverend Stottle, pondering, placed a finger under his chin. "Have you suffered night sweats?"

"I've woken wet."

"Then I must ask myself what Freudian darkness you've slipped out of. I'm not only a servant of God, I'm a student of psychology, and the truth is we are each alone under the skin, from cradle to grave, which makes perfect sense. God, who is utterly alone, made us in his image."

"He may be playing jokes on us," Dudley said, picking up a second cupcake and eating the frosting. "I mean, what else has he to do, he's done it all."

The sun was a blossom in Dudley's hair, and the reverend wondered, fleetingly, whether he behaved himself in men's rooms. A sadness seemed to pass between them. Stirring, the reverend said, "The most anyone can ask for is his sanity. When a person has that, he has a chance to make it through the later years."

A sound came from the house, and he saw his wife coming out the side door. In no way was she heavy, but her legs were large and frankly revealed in khaki hiking shorts. He looked at her with love. In their younger years they had read poetry to each other, he with the richer voice, she with the better diction.

Dudley bit into a glazed cookie.

"Don't make yourself sick," the reverend cautioned.

His wife, approaching with a measured stride and a wary smile, was a thoroughly Christian woman who, however, did not share all his views or accompany him on all his flights of fancy. But always she was his strength during his deepest doubts and greatest needs.

"This is the fellow I told you about," he said.

"Yes, I guessed that," she said, taking in the sloppy shirt and threadbare jeans and the cookie in his hand.

"He's from another world," the reverend said, smiling.

"And what world is that?"

"My own," Dudley replied.

"The police chief is looking for you," she said.

Reverend Stottle said, "We won't tell."

Orville Farnham, acting in his official capacity of selectman, summoned Chief Morgan to his insurance agency, which was housed next to the fire barn. In the Saturday quiet, ensconced behind his desk, Farnham said, "I know what you've been doing, it's got to stop." He waved a nervous hand. "Sit down, for God's sake."

The chair possessed Morgan, locked him in. "Who called you? Gunner or Bodine?"

"Makes no difference," Farnham said, his tone defensive only for a moment. Business at his agency had increased greatly in the years that the Heights had been developed and populated. "You can't go around prying into people's tragedies, especially ones that didn't even happen here. It's not right. It's certainly not professional."

Morgan's face was immobile. In high school he had dated one of Farnham's younger sisters, the cheeriest of three, the family favorite. A few months ago he had gazed down upon her at Drinkwater's, where death looked innocent in a padded box. Fluids sterilized the remains, flowers scented the air, and the ghost of the deceased, unseen and unfelt, edged through the crowd, a world apart.

Farnham said, "You take too much upon yourself."

He imagined the bouqueted funerals of the Bodine boy and the Gunner girl, each child special in a different way, each put to rest by a renegade fate. "I think I'm on to something, Orville."

"Look me in the eye and tell me you've got nothing going with Bodine's wife. See, you can't. You've got no credibility in this investigation of yours."

"Can't a woman be just a friend?"

"Not in this town."

He heard a chain of falling sound from the outside. Fellows from the fire barn, Zach and Chub, were playing with a ladder, yanking and loosening its ropes. He heard Zach's curse and Chub's laughter. For some reason he remembered when Miss Rushmore, well before Holly Pride's time, regularly reconnoitered the stacks at the library to deter couples from fooling around. That was where he and Gloria Farnham used to kiss.

"You have to learn your place, James. It's not in the Heights."

He remembered when Tuck's was still an old country store warmed by a wood stove and pervaded by the odor of men who worked in manure, pig and cow, and when veterans of very old wars, some in wheelchairs, paraded around the green in meticulously preserved regimentals. And he remembered his childhood wonderment over the way Paget's Pond could reflect the bulk and weight of trees on its fragile surface.

"I hate talking to you like this, James. It pains me."

Breaking the chair's grip, Morgan struggled upright with a memory of breasts warm as muffins and feet cold as ice, his wife's. How in hell had he gone on this long without her?

Farnham's voice trailed him to the door. "That crazy tramp that started all this, have you let him go yet?"

"More or less," he said and stepped out into the heat of the day.

At the station he always seemed to catch Sergeant Avery when Eugene was not quite on his feet, just getting up or sitting down, tilting one way or another, always with the air of a redundant worker trying to look busy. Meg O'Brien was eating soup from a thermos cup at her desk. Their presence, their nearness, encased him in the protection of old habits. Letting out a breath, he hoped Meg had not noticed his staring at the veins in her hands.

"He's at the Stottles'," she said. "I'm not supposed to say who called, but it was the reverend's wife."

"Want me to go get him?" Sergeant Avery asked, hitching up his trousers.

Morgan went into his office. Before closing the door, he said, "Forget him."

Regina Smith answered the telephone on the second ring and heard echoes on the line and then her daughter's voice, breathy and impetuous. In her ear it was disruptive, and she stood in a harsh attitude of impatience, not yet ready to confront and in no mood to forgive. "What do you want, Patricia?"

"We're still at the beach."

"I figured."

"Tony's run into a friend whose parents have a summer place here. They've asked us to stay over. They're the Goodmans, wonderful people. Do you know them?"

A lie, she was sure. Anthony putting her up to it, embroidering the lie for her and attaching fancy lace to make it more believable. "No, Patricia, I don't know them."

"Is it all right, Mom?"

Her thoughts treaded through a silence. When she spoke, her voice thickened. "Do what you want."

She changed her clothes, shed hot colors for cool ones, forsook stockings, deodorized her underarms, and poured sherry into a small glass. She was sipping it and thumbing *Vogue* when the phone rang again. She thought it might be her husband, with whom she was furious for trivializing what she considered egregious. The voice was Harley Bodine's.

"Have I called at a bad time?"

It was as if he had appeared at her elbow without warning, his face hanging close, the scent of his aftershave bearable. "No," she said with only the faintest air of reproach. "The kids are away, Ira's still in Washington."

"I was wondering whether you'd like to go out for dinner again tonight."

"No," she said, "but come over anyway."

Her body hot, her brain cooking, Beverly Gunner wavered with indecision and stood vulnerable, as if stripped of clothing, her bulges and pinch marks exposed. Suspicions never articulated flared at every nerve ending, and for the very first time since little Fay's drowning she did not pray for a blank mind. Then she heard her husband's ponderous footsteps and the heave of his breath. The air shook with his entrance into the room.

"What are you doing?" he asked, his smile crescent, meaning he wanted to make up.

She didn't answer. Were she to place another woman inside her dress, pitch her to the light, walk her through the house, how many hours would pass before he or the boys would notice? His hand reached out.

"Don't touch me," she shot back, bristling, aware of a phantom strength. From outside came raucous sounds. The boys had friends over, no manners, no feelings except for themselves, all of them capering fatly at the pool's edge, their round faces only faintly stamped by life. Her grimace was automatic.

"They're only having fun."

"Of course," she said, aware of her role. She was expected to keep an eye on them, maintain order, serve sandwiches, entertain them if need be. She had the hilarious notion of joining them in the water and letting them play with her tits.

"What's funny?"

An angry cry of pain from outside gave her ignominious satisfaction. Gustav perhaps—not Herman, who would have shrieked—had stubbed a toe or bruised a shin, probably while bullying someone, showing off, throwing his weight around. "Nothing's funny, Paul. When has anything been funny?"

He scowled. "One of us should see to them."

"Yes, one of us should." Tilting sideways, she opened a dresser drawer and fished through underwear.

"What are you doing?"

"Looking for a cigarette."

The frog in her throat and the gravel in her voice drove him away, which didn't surprise her. She was a pull on his strength and a carrier of memories he didn't want and wouldn't accept under any conditions.

His departure altered her appearance. She felt taller, bolder, in some ways striking, which a mirror validated. An ash spilled on her way to the window, where she heard foul language. Gustav and another boy had raised fists to each other but were too cowardly to use them, which made their language fouler.

Downstairs, she gathered up her husband's newspapers and carried them to the kitchen table, where she read headlines and first paragraphs, perused photographs, smiled at a political cartoon, scanned the review of a book she would never buy, read obits of people she didn't know, and foresaw the sum of her evening on the TV page of the Boston *Globe*. She was still at the table an hour later when her sons looked in on her, Paul behind them.

"Let her be," he said.

"Don't worry about it," Regina Smith said when the phone rang and she let it. She enlarged Harley Bodine's sensitivities. She bared her thighs, and he saw tusks. When she batted her eyes, he saw two dark moments on the face of a high clock. The marriage bed, soon to be sullied, was her idea, which filled him with unkillable urges and the same sense of marvelously good fortune as when he had captured Kate. "Go do what you have to do," she said.

In her bathroom he lifted an oval of pristine soap, breathed in the fragrance, and washed his hands. He used her husband's mouthwash and gargled deep. Suited in light wool appropriate for August, he made undressing an occupation. With his chin tucked in, his fingers particularized each step like someone loosening screws, removing pegs, sliding bolts. Anticipation tensed him.

Stepping from the bathroom, he instantly felt he was under scrutiny and revealing himself as unpleasant and unremarkable. He straightened his shoulders and sucked up the fold from his belly. His part stood erect in a condom, as if masquerading.

She said, in a curiously harsh voice, "I would have done that for you."

Curtains had been drawn against the evening sun. On the bed she was a torso of lunar white and more of a mystery. When he stumbled in his approach, embarrassment seared his face. Why was he feeling the fool? Standing still, he said, "Who was calling?"

"I wouldn't know."

Their nakedness more clinical than sensual, they were scanning each other for flaws. He had wilted.

"For God's sake, take it off."

Denuded, he drove a shin onto the bed with a force that surprised him and a spasm of confidence that recharged him.

His manhood quaked like something astonished by its own audacity. She spoke through the rush of his kiss.

"You smell like Ira."

"Is that bad?"

"It's appropriate."

He kissed the scraped flesh beneath her arms. Nothing was
inhibiting. Her navel was a coin a Roman might have hammered
into being, and he kissed it for the sheer delight of knowing he
was spending another man's money. With a wrench she placed
wealth in his face, forcing him to grapple joyously with his
greed, a formidable opponent and an unprincipled fighter. He
groped for breath.

"For Christ's sake, don't stop!"

When it was time to, actually past the time, he looked up
and said, "Does he do that?"

She touched his head where the accurate part in his hair,
the chalk of a property line, now ran crooked. "You may want
to outdo him," she said.

When he rose to his knees, she threw hers back. He fought
for purchase, which came like a vise, and she gripped his shoulders. At one point they rolled from side to side. It was entirely
mindless, a sexual madness, which sprang him into a perpetual
state of increase. He strained an arm and wedged a finger where
it hadn't belonged until now. She shredded skin from a shoulder,
his left one, a small price to pay.

When it was over, he lay with his head high in her husband's pillow, his prick still a post, an emblem of prosperity.
The whole of summer, he knew without a doubt, would be
wrapped in this single evening, fat and succulent, oozing its own
juice.

"Don't look so smug."

"This is more than I expected," he said.

"It may not have been what I intended."

He touched her. She was open. "Like the comb of a
rooster," he said.

"How's your shoulder?"

"Burning."

"There are risks in everything."

"Perhaps I know that better than you," he said.

The room was dark, a breeze billowing the curtains, when the shrill of the phone jolted them. Like before, she let it ring and ring. When it stopped, he said, "What does Ira mean to you?"

"Nearly everything, but he's let me down."

"How?"

"You wouldn't understand."

"Try me." He felt they could say anything to each other now, reveal any secret with no fear of censure or loss of stature.

"It's about my stepson," she said.

"What about him?"

"He's a toad in my house."

"Am I calling at a bad time?"

"He's not here, if that's what you mean."

"Are you writing?"

"It's more like I'm kidding myself."

"Tell your husband I won't be bothering him anymore. Tell him . . . I'm sorry."

"Have you scared me for nothing, James? Are you saying you were wrong?"

"I'm telling you I don't know where the truth lies and probably never will."

"Where does that leave me?"

"I don't know, Kate. I don't even know where it leaves me."

When he put the phone down, his face was drawn, his head heavy. Alone in the small kitchen of his house, he ghost-walked to the refrigerator and held the door open longer than needed because he enjoyed the cool. At the table he ate cheese on crackers, drank dark beer, and read an article in a police magazine detailing crimes in which the perpetrators walked the streets because the evidence never fell into place, too many missing pieces. Thumbnail photos showed detectives, some retired, haunted by their frustrations.

He felt little in common with them, instead picturing himself as someone who, occasionally aflame with empty purpose, sees life only from the tail of his eye. With comfortable creases in his face, with still no gray in his hair, of which he was inordinately proud, he looked as if nothing bothered him when nearly everything did. He was clearing the table when the telephone rang.

A woman said, "Are you investigating something?"

The voice was unfamiliar, perhaps disguised, a flavoring agent added to it. A woman named Bowman used to call the station and ask for Chief Cock. Christine Poole, who still lived in the Heights, would lower her voice so that she sounded like a man.

"Hello?"

"Yes, I'm here," he said. "Who is this, please?"

"Can't you answer my question?"

He was dealing with a crank, he was sure. And not sure. A quality of desperation lurked in the voice. "What investigation are you referring to?"

"This one."

"Which one?"

"Please," she said, "could we meet somewhere? Maybe we know different things. We could put them together."

He looked at his watch, seven exactly, time for the network news. "Where do you want to meet?" he asked, true to form, ready to pluck evidence from the wind instead of from reality.

"Away from town," she said quickly.

"There's a place called Rembrandt's in Andover, right off the square. We could meet in the lounge."

"What time?" Her voice sounded giddy.

"Eight all right?"

"I'll be there."

"How will I know you?"

"I'll come naked."

9

THEIR TABLE WAS A SMALL ONE AGAINST THE WALL. CHIEF Morgan glugged Heineken beer into a frosted glass. "Are you sure you won't have something?" he asked.

"Positive."

"You're not naked."

"I thought better of it."

A wide-brimmed straw hat, aided by dark glasses, gave her the parody of a Garbo look. All he could see of her face was the tip of her nose, the movement of her mouth, and the softness of her chin. "You're Mrs. Gunner," he said.

"Once," she said, "for a very thrilling moment, I considered lacing his soup with weed killer."

"Whose soup?"

"My husband's."

A maroon paper doily stuck to the bottom of his glass. The cold beer iced his throat. "Could you take off your hat, Mrs. Gunner? And you don't really need those glasses."

She did as she was asked, without fuss. Her shell of hair fell

161

loose on one side. Her hand went to her brow. She was off color, a touch of something. "Maybe I will have a drink."

A glass of white wine was delivered. The waitress, a sprightly Frenchwoman who frequently chatted with Morgan when he was there alone, sensed drama and vanished quickly.

"He won't allow me to give meaning to my daughter's life."

"Why not?"

"Perhaps because he feels it had none."

"I understand she was retarded," he said gently.

"No, Chief Morgan, she was special. She went to a special school, here in Andover. I drove her there every day and picked her up at three-thirty. He *never* did."

"Tell me about her death."

"A class trip to Cambridge, a picnic on the bank of the Charles, and my Fay wandered off. Someone should have been watching, but no one was. They found her in the river."

He started to speak and stopped himself. Tables near them stood vacant. A cluster of couples at the far corner of the bar were joking with the bartender.

"I'm sorry," she said. Tears had made her face a torn thing. With a napkin she blotted one eye and then the other. "Paul sued the school. Harley Bodine negotiated a settlement, and Paul gave it all to charity in Fay's name. It was the only good thing he did."

"What do you mean?"

"He wasn't sad at the funeral. He only pretended to be. A wife knows."

Morgan sipped his beer. He waited. When he felt it was safe, he said, "Do you have any reason to think Fay's death might not have been accidental?"

"What else could it have been? I want you to tell me."

He lifted the Polaroid of Dudley from his shirt pocket and handed it over. She looked at the back to see if anything was written on it. Nothing was. She turned the front of it to the light and, peering hard, held it this way and that.

"I've never seen him before, but I feel I have. Who is he?"

"He may be no more than a vagrant, one of those crackpots

who read newspapers and intrude into other people's tragedies."
"Please." Her features tightened. "Be honest with me."

He feared telling her too much, fearing she couldn't handle it, but he told her everything, suspicions only mildly tempered by doubts, thoughts with flimsy claims on logic, purging himself of speculations not entirely consistent or reasonable. All the while he watched her closely and hoped to God he wasn't feeding a fire, placing arson among his crimes.

When he finished, she was quiet, removed. Finally she said, "Are you on my side, Chief Morgan?"

He knew the proper response, the one a real policeman would be obliged to give. He gave, instead, his own. "Yes, I am."

They were, it now seemed, snarled in each other's existence. She said, "For years I've wished it possible to rent someone's kindness for an evening, long enough to get me into a sleep so sound no dream would be remembered. Do you know what I'm talking about, Chief Morgan?"

He knew only of a loneliness that could strike without warning, even with companions at his side. "Don't you want your wine?"

"I want something stronger. A gin and tonic."

He ordered her one, and soon she wanted another. "Sometimes," she said, "I make myself fall into a mood in which my mother and father are still alive and my brother rides his bicycle around the block. My brother's in the leather business and travels around the world, China, South Africa, everywhere. In Poland, he says, the coffee is a pretense, the milk chunky, and the water unfit. Their cigarettes tear at your lungs. Do you mind if I smoke?"

He lit the cigarette for her, concern in his eyes. "Does your husband know you're here?"

"I do things on my own now."

He waited for her to say more, to tell him what was now in her head. Her thoughts were still on her brother, from whom she received postcards, seldom a phone call, so many demands on his time. She understood. She understood much, she said.

A while later she said, "I'm perfectly fine, but you may have to drive me home."

He used the phone at the bar to call Sergeant Avery, who was off duty and at home. In a low voice he said, "I want you to pick me up in twenty minutes, in the Heights. I'll be on the street near the Gunners' house."

"Sure, Chief. What's up?"

"Just do as I say, Eugene."

When he returned to the table, she was on her feet, stiff and deliberate in her stance, her hat held flush against her leg. Leaving the lounge, she accepted his arm trustingly. The night sky was rose-tinged. "All falling stars are named Icarus," she said and surrendered the keys to her car, a blue Volvo that still smelled brand-new when he opened the passenger door for her.

"Beautiful automobile," he said.

"If it were in my name, I'd give it to you."

He stepped around to the driver's side and climbed in. It took him a few moments to sort out the right key and to find the ignition switch. She smiled, offering no help, giving him no clue of what was percolating through her brain. She sat collected, bound up, the smile incongruous, as if she didn't know it was there.

When he ran the car onto the street, she said, "I'd like to talk to the man in the picture."

"I don't have him in custody at the moment."

"You let him go?"

"I can round him up."

The drivers of two Camaros poised at a set of lights were trying to out-rev each other. When the lights flashed green, one Camaro blasted off with a blood-curdling screech that brought to Morgan's mind flares around a highway tragedy. He drove around the other Camaro, which had stalled.

Beverly Gunner said, "I wonder how many killers lurk in my husband's ancestry."

They walked the beach in the darkening air, and people strolling by them knew they were lovers, young and glorious creatures tuned a pitch higher than anyone else. Glossy black hair and vanilla skin, Patricia wore an open white shirt over her bikini. Anthony, bare-chested, unyieldingly slim, pushed fair hair from his eyes. The beach was aluminum under a glassy moon. It was high tide. Waves heaved and surged, thundered when they broke.

"Do you think your mother believed you?"

"She expects to be lied to," Patricia replied.

"Why do you say that?"

"My dad lied to her, all the time. He was unfaithful. That's why she divorced him." The crash of a wave dismembering itself hurled up an arc of spray. In the salt breeze Patricia's white shirt floated behind her. "Would you lie to me, Tony?"

"Why would I want to?"

"Boys like to."

"I have no need."

Up ahead ghostly figures were poised in the mist of the surf. Patricia stopped in her tracks. Kneeling, she scooped up sand and shifted it from hand to hand, some of it sifting through her fingers. "I'd like to stay longer."

"That would be pushing it."

She went quietly, entranced by the way each muscular wave, like a lover, reared up, crested white, and hesitated inside a shiver before collapsing. Anthony was looking up at the night sky, at the flashlight quality of stars.

"Mr. Pitkin says if the big bang theory is correct, the universe is simply far-flung debris with a lot of fires still burning."

"Tell your Mr. Pitkin I only know about the fire below," she said, rising with sand printed on each knee. Her voice deepened. "We'll be going back to school soon. I won't see you."

"We can write, talk on the phone."

"It's not the same. Tony, what do I mean to you?"

"A lot. Why are you asking this stuff?"

She moved close to him. "Don't you know?"

"Know what?"

"How much I love you."

He looked disturbed, embarrassed. "I thought you were just playing with me."

"It's not play. It's me, Tony. Everything I do is a way to get your attention."

Their bellies touched. She had sand on hers, which grated on his. Waves rousting pebbles gave out a language, and water spumed over their feet. She kissed his shoulder and licked the skin for the taste of tanning lotion.

"Please, Tony, let's stay through the weekend." They had a room at the Dunes, a motel on the boulevard with a public dining room that served a variety of pancakes, a choice of several syrups. "We could go back on Monday."

"Your mother would kill us."

"How long will we be young, Tony?" She held him in the depths of her dark eyes. "How long will we be able to do this?"

Regina Smith stiffened and turned her head on the pillow. Harley Bodine had fallen asleep, his face visible in a patch of light from the bathroom. She shook him awake. "You'd better go."

"What time is it?"

"I don't know. Late."

He rubbed an eye.

"Move, Harley. You have a wife waiting."

His big toe touched her heel. "You're my wife."

"Don't talk nonsense."

"You know something, Regina? Kate was never for me, I only thought she was. I've never really been comfortable with her."

"For better or worse, Harley, that's how it's supposed to work. If you can't hack it, that's your problem."

He flung an arm over her. "May I see you again? Soon?"

"It's something to think about," she said.

"You're still on my face and fingers."

"Then you'd better have a wash."

"No, it stays."

"At least comb your hair."

"I'll have to use Ira's comb."

She watched him rise reluctantly in a new temper of circumstance and movement. He swayed on his feet. "Don't leave hairs in it," she said.

Later, when he was finally gone, she slipped from the bed and pattered into the bathroom with a pleasurable lightness. A large mirror gave her a lurid and fantastic look at herself. A feminine solution, antiseptic and odorless, left her smarting and clean. She felt her own eyes commenting on herself, making statements, judgments, all of which she could live with.

Downstairs, a cup of decaf in front of her, she picked up the telephone. Despite the hour she rang up the hotel in Washington, woke her husband, and said, "Did you call earlier?"

"Yes."

"Twice?"

"Yes. Why didn't you answer?"

"I didn't want to be disturbed."

Paul Gunner moved like a bear to the window and glimpsed two sets of headlights at the distant gates, then only one set, which tottered up the long drive. He was waiting at the door when she came in wearing that straw wheel of a hat he found ridiculous. His face massive, he said, "Where the hell have you been?"

She tossed her hat negligently on a table. With no repairing hand to her hair, she said distractedly, "None of your business."

"What have you been drinking?" A part of his mind that always stayed cool warned him to be careful. He saw a glitter of tears. "What's the matter?"

"What could be the matter?" she said, dropping her bag on the table. "You have everything you want. You may even have more than you want."

"What's that supposed to mean?"

She moved away as if his voice had glided in and out of her hearing. He followed her up the grand stairway. Her shoulders were set and her hand firmly on the banister with each step. At the landing, her other hand brushed over ferns in a floor vase.

In her bedroom, he said, "I want to know who you were with."

She moved to a window, and he moved with her. Flood-lights blazed over the grounds. Like acid, they ate into the dark and kept the greater dark at bay. "I was with a friend," she said.

"What friend?"

"A dear one."

"Is that all you're going to tell me?"

"That's all you need to know." Turning, she pushed around him and seated herself at a vanity table, where she ran both hands through her hair and began removing her makeup. He hovered. She said, "Please don't watch me age."

He fell back a single step. Her face in the glass looked drained, wan, diminished, like that of a little girl bleached of her childhood. "Beverly," he said. Authority was back in his voice. "You can't bring Fay back. She's gone. Can't you get that through your head?"

"Yes," she said. "I have."

In the parking lot behind Rembrandt's, Chief Morgan stepped out of Sergeant Avery's automobile and returned to his own. Twenty minutes later he was back in Bensington, semicircling the green and pulling up at the church, behind which he could see lights burning in Reverend Stottle's house.

The reverend, in shirt sleeves and stocking feet, answered his knock and then his question. "He was here, but he's gone. It's Chief Morgan, dear."

"I can see him," Mrs. Stottle said. Her voice had the ring of a church bell. Her blouse, worn over khaki shorts, was the same maroon as the prayer books in the pews. She appeared over her husband's shoulder with a reproving look at Morgan. "Too bad you didn't come earlier."

Morgan agreed with his eyes, her secret kept. He said to the reverend, "Did he behave himself?"

"A perfect gentleman."

"My husband says he's a lost soul. I think he's loony. What's your assessment, Chief?"

"He's different," Morgan said. "I just want to keep an eye on him."

Mrs. Stottle, lately stiffened in her ways, said, "We don't see you in church much. In fact, I can't remember the last time."

The reverend poked her. "Different snores, different dreams. Remember that, Sarah. Hope you're not going to stay up all night looking for him, Chief."

"He can wait till morning. Sorry to have bothered you."

Morgan went home. His unmade bed awaited him, his pillow bared loyally for his head, but he was too loose for sleep. In the kitchen he turned on the black-and-white TV and uncapped a beer. Tuned to a public channel, a nature film on desert life in Arizona, he watched with distaste a snake called a sand-swimmer break surface to embrace a scorpion, then to crush it and swallow it whole. He wondered whether the scorpion was suicidal and seemed to recall reading it was.

A sound from the outside, out of the ordinary, alerted him, and he sprang from his chair with an urgency he welcomed. His foot slipped on the floor where something had been spilled. When he flung open the back door and threw on the light, his neighbor's mutt scampered off like a fugitive from justice.

He drove to the police station. Bertha Skagg, whose large floral dress made her look like an arrangement, was slumped back behind Meg O'Brien's desk, her eyes closed and her lips fluttering. From the cell, where Officer Wetherfield was sacked out, he heard snores. Different snores, different dreams. Bertha Skagg opened her eyes and glared as if he had no right intruding.

"What are you doing here, Chief?"

"I thought he might be here."

"Who?"

He remembered Bertha when she was pounds lighter and had a better disposition. "No one," he said.

"Have you been drinking, Chief?"

"You call a beer drinking?"

"One leads to two."

Mr. Skagg, soft-spoken, diminutive, hardly there unless one had stared directly at him, had died a quiet drunk. "Why don't you go home, Bertha? I'll be here for a while."

"You think I'm not doing my job?"

"I didn't say that."

She rocked forward and planted her elbows. "I'm here for the night."

So was he, and he slipped into the dark of his office.

Slipping out of bed, May Hutchins robbed her husband of covers and exposed his rump to the night breeze, which woke him. "Where are you going?" he asked, his unfocused eyes seeking her in the dim of the room. Sheathed in old nylon, her body was smoke in a bottle. "I know what you're up to, May. Don't go out there."

"I just want to see," she said.

"I'll go."

"No, you stay here."

She stepped out the back door and let the night air soak her face. Grass wetted her ankles. Stars burning through distances too great to imagine gave her a sensation of otherness, and breezes snipping at her gown made her feel she had stepped out of her skin and was one with the flash of lightning bugs. The gazebo was empty, but a sound sneaked through the rippling air and reached her ear.

"I hear you," she said.

The darkness was total behind the gazebo. Moving into it, she felt she heard the trees breathing like elephants. As a schoolgirl she had envied those chums of hers with predilections for folly. She felt a wheel was turning, coming around.

"Where are you?" she called out, expecting his face to burn a hole in the dark.

"I'm peeing," Dudley said.

"I won't bother you." She stood still, no idea what part of the darkness he occupied. "Try not to go on the flowers."

"I think I'm standing in some."

It didn't matter. She was poised on her toes, trying to get a fix on him. "Don't you worry about a thing," she said. "I'll protect you."

"Against what?"

She had to think through a moment of confusion, from

which high school memories emerged, feelings swelled. "Against the world," she said.

Lights blazing in her studio, Mary Williams showed Soldier her latest sketch of him. His balls, she told him, were the bells of his body, which that big tongue of his rang. He liked none of it. "You're doing caricature again," he said, fiercely prideful of his sinewy physique, hard work gone into every muscle. "I don't have a belly. You gave me one."

Her smile was uncanny. She'd had too much white wine. He was in his skivvies, ready for bed an hour ago. She reached out playfully.

"Cut it out," he said. He did not like anyone to touch his navel. His prick, fine; his balls, tenderly; but his navel, no. "I don't like being made fun of."

"You're thin-skinned."

"I deserve respect."

"How about a salute?"

"I was seventeen when I joined the fucking army. Doesn't that mean anything to you?"

"It's military history, Soldier. I've heard it."

His eyes burned. He missed the Oriental women who had bathed his body reverently, and he missed the olive drab of the old Ike jacket, which had stressed the youthfulness of his waist. "I was just a kid fighting in Korea, and I was an old pro when I went to 'Nam, two tours of duty."

"War is meant to put youth in its place, Soldier. That's usually the ground."

She did not understand the patriotism inherent in the roll of a drum or the lathered emotions in the draping of a flag. He did not have the words to tell her, and even if he had, they would not have cohered into a sentence.

Her voice was thick. "Smart fellow like you should've realized that by now."

She had no idea of the pomp, fuss, and effect that went with the wearing of a uniform, nor did he expect her to. After his retirement, she never would have comprehended his dismal feelings at an American Legion dance where the women were gussied up and the men sported big knots in their ties, warriors who had let themselves go.

"Come on," he said. "It's late."

When a leg leaned out of her split skirt, he slung an arm around her, and for a moment they stood static, a balance of extremes. He guided her out of the studio, sniffed her hair, and remembered a woman in Munich who had uttered her frustrations in German, which he understood, and her joys in French, Greek to him. Before entering her room, he peered into Dudley's.

"If he's not coming back, I'd like to wear some of his clothes. He's got some nice things."

"No way, Soldier."

He led her to the four-poster bed and sat her down on the frilly edge. He looked down at the center part of her hair and watched her cross a leg to slip off a shoe. "You look like a little girl playing a woman."

"What I am," she said, "is grace under pressure."

Roland Hutchins heard sounds on the margin of his sleep. He woke up, pricked his ears, and, reaching through the covers, roused his wife, who had been sleeping soundly. "Someone's in the house," he whispered.

"You're crazy."

"No."

"I don't hear anything."

"Listen."

Her head rose from the pillow. "You're right."

Roland, coping with the banjo beat of his heart, rolled cautiously out of bed and sought his trousers in the dark. "I bet it's him. Who else could it be? Good God, May, he could've killed us in our sleep."

She moved like fire from the bed and groped for her bathrobe. "He's our friend."

"Your friend, not mine," he whispered, ransacking a drawer.

"What are you doing?"

"Getting a weapon." It was a flashlight. "Call the police station."

"It's not necessary."

"Please, May, do as I say for once."

But she didn't. Together they crept downstairs, the beam of the flashlight leading the way. Roland nearly tripped. May brushed a wall for a light switch and missed it. There was a glow from the pantry, but the intruder was in the dark of the kitchen.

"We see you," May said.

"I want to use your phone," Dudley said.

They saw him only in chunks, by flashlight. Roland said, "You have no right coming in here."

"Let him make his call," May said. "Is it local?"

"May, this isn't right."

Dudley took a crumpled dollar bill from his pocket and placed it on the table. "It's a toll call," he said.

They talked in the dark, the covers pulled half over their heads. Soldier exulted in the warm-seasoned smell of a woman with her clothes off, her nearness enough to smother chills, stifle hysteria, the threat of which had been with him since birth. Thoughts rolling in his head, he said, "I don't want him to come back."

"You have no say in it, Soldier." Her voice tried to be kind. "This is his home."

"Who needs you more?"

"That's not a question you really want to ask."

His hand slid over the warmth of her. "Who gives you more?"

"You don't know what he gives me. You can never know."

His hand, which had hurled grenades and fed bazookas, glided at will. In his head was roller-skating music. "He's not that much younger than me, Mary. Sixty years old, I still fuck like a rabbit."

"It's not a rabbit a woman wants."

"Is it him or me you want, you know for sure?"

"He's my friend, Soldier. He's like my blood brother."

"What am I?"

"I don't know."

"Maybe you won't let yourself know." He moved closer, aware of dead notes in his voice. "I never told you this, but I was married once. She was a stripper. Her ass was in lights. The marriage didn't last, six weeks, I think."

"Long enough, I would wager."

"I never knew my parents. My sister and I were brought up in foster homes, never the same one."

"That's not my problem, Soldier."

"What is your problem?"

"I don't know. You'll have to speak to my shrink."

"I didn't know you had one."

"I used to."

He dredged up souvenirs from his memory—the taste of this woman's skin, the quality of that one's voice—and knew what he wanted. "Who knows how long I'm going to live, Mary, the pension would be yours. Do you know what I'm telling you?"

She did not answer, but he felt a knot in her loosen, just a little, just enough. After a moment she said, "Did your sister know your parents?"

"Yes."

"What did she say about them?"

"They were no good."

From Beacon Street the occasional rumble of traffic, along with the random toot of a horn, was music to his ears as he applied himself. A breeze capped his shaved head like the liner in a steel helmet, and he felt the strong sensual pleasure he'd gotten from firing weapons or simply marching with one, the blood racing to his loins. Then a whistle shrieked. Not a whistle. It was the ring of the telephone.

"Get off me," she said.

Reaching over him, the breath of her underarm in his face, she grabbed the receiver from its cradle. He heard her voice and the distinct one on the other end, and then he refused to listen.

He muffled one ear in the pillow and hit the other with the heel of his hand, which hurt.

In 'Nam, the medics had ignored shattered men bleeding from the ears, from the rectum, and administered to those with glimmers of hope, of which he was one. *Easy does it, fella.*

The stripper, high on coke, soon to be his wife, liked the naked look of him, thought he was a riot. He grinned at her. His thing saluted her. *I do*, she said.

Mary was reaching over him again, replacing the receiver, then falling back, collapsing in what was almost a swoon. Her face waxed in the dim. They were less than a foot apart, but he might have been looking at her from another shore.

"That was Dudley," she said.

"Where is he?"

"He didn't say, but he's coming home."

"When?"

"He'll let me know."

She was crying, her face joyful.

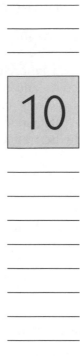

10

IT WAS A BRIGHT PINK SUNDAY MORNING. ROLAND HUTCHINS, who had slept late and was still in his underwear, peered out the bedroom window and said, "Good! He's gone!"

May, behind schedule for church, still in her gown, gave him a critical look. Fully clothed or buck naked, nothing about him was significant. Though she detested tattoos, she thought it too bad he didn't have a few, evidence he'd had a life.

"I don't want him back, May. I mean that."

Her face flared up. "Don't give me orders."

He turned around with a listless move. "When, May, when have I ever been able to do that?"

"Then maybe that's a message," she said and wheeling about, showed contempt with the breadth of her backside.

She bathed and, stepping from the tub, used a rough towel that felt good on her skin. Stepping on a scale, she viewed the result with splendid indifference. At the mirror she spent ten minutes on her face and another ten on her hair, over which she bounced a light hand. Five minutes were consumed choosing a dress.

Roland was in the other bathroom. Rapping on the door, she said, "We don't have time for breakfast if we're going to make church."

"I don't feel all that great," he said. "For one thing, I didn't get enough sleep."

"Then stay home," she said.

Arriving late, she slipped into a back pew and was unmoved by the resounding voice of the organ. A fair-sized crowd for a summer Sunday, she noted with a sweeping eye, though certainly no one from the Heights was in evidence. Noses in the air, they went, if they went at all, to places of worship in Andover.

Picking up a maroon hymn book, she sang with the rest of them, all the while aware of Dorothea Farnham's high soprano, an irritant since school days. Dorothea, in her estimation, was a bitch who always got more than she deserved.

Choirboys accepted brimming collection plates, and Reverend Stottle began his sermon, which too often she found full of nonsense. She knew for a fact she wasn't the only one who suspected that the waxing of the moon influenced his behavior.

"Time," the reverend began resonantly, "contracts as you grow older. To a child, a year is enormous. To us, it's nothing. A whole decade can slip away without our knowing it."

"Tell me about it," she muttered under her breath. "Every tick of the clock means less of me, I know that."

"Human history represents only a few lines in the larger scheme of things. For some forms of life, a nanosecond is all they have."

"I hope to hell they make the most of it," she said without moving her mouth, her eyes down the front of her dress. She had, if she did say so herself, a nice set.

"When you're young, your life is outward, stretching beyond you, but when you're older, it's inward, winding you together for the ultimate space you'll occupy."

"Christ, what a thing to say!" She ceased to listen. The hymn book wedged between her knees, she yawned, closed her eyes, and dozed. Fifteen minutes later, the sound of shuffling feet brought her to attention, just as the hymn book fell on her toe.

Outside in the hot sun, Reverend Stottle stationed himself to shake hands with the departing faithful, some of whom sported faces as gloriously bright and quietly hysterical as his own. She tried to avoid him, but his godly hand reached toward her and she stopped short, like an ax thrown into the ground.

"Where's Roland?" the reverend asked.

Probably reading the papers, the funnies first. "Under the weather," she replied.

The reverend's throat quivered like a songbird's. "We don't see you much at our coffees."

"The truth is, I have better things to do."

He sidled close, spoke in confidence. "For that matter, so do I."

At Minerva's Tea Room, a favorite of women from the Heights, she ordered Belgian coffee and buttered scones, despite the outrageous price. Sitting alone at a corner table was a woman with a golden shell of hair that was breaking apart, tendrils glittering against both cheeks, the careless look that women from the Heights thought they could get away with. Try again, sister! The woman's lips were pursed as if something were dissolving inside her overly painted mouth. A No Smoking sign was prominently posted, but she was smoking anyway. Some nerve! May looked at her watch, relished the last crumbs of the scone, paid her bill, and left.

Sunday hours at the library were from noon to four. Fred Fossey wasn't at the tables, but she heard a shuffle in the stacks and found him in Biography, a book about Eisenhower in his hands. He twisted around. "I was afraid you wouldn't come."

She leaned past him to scan the shelves. "I had nothing better to do."

He sniffed her hair. His questioning eyes were full of excitement; indeed, downright lust. His hand was on her hip.

"Careful, Fred."

"Don't you know, May? Don't you have any idea?"

"Of course I do." She glanced down at him. "I'm not blind."

"One of these days, May? Please? Promise?"

Until Dudley—that childlike, questionable man whom she didn't understand and didn't need to—there had been no strong urge in her toward life. She had weeded her garden more than she had watered it. "I'm in the autumn of my life, Fred."

"We could be dead tomorrow, May."

"The whole world could cave in."

"The sun could explode."

Her mouth was set in a receptive way. "Do you want to kiss me, Fred?"

"God, yes!"

She shot a look over her shoulder. "Then do it quick."

Sunstruck, Paget's Pond was a shimmer of prisms. Dudley, who had just washed his face and hands, stood where floating flowers rimmed the water. Chief Morgan, keeping his distance, said, "Don't run."

"Have you been looking for me?"

"Now and then." Morgan took no solid steps, only tentative ones.

"Please, stop right there," Dudley said, and Morgan did, tilting his head when the sun threw a beam straight into his eyes. "I heard the bells," Dudley said. "Why aren't you in church?"

"It must be over by now."

"I'm an Episcopalian."

"I'm something less," Morgan said, relaxing. Dudley stood straight, soft, and peaceful, and Morgan read gentle madness in the friendly smile.

"I like your town, Chief, I really do."

"Are you thinking of staying?"

"Not forever."

"Right. You have to be born here to do that." Morgan shaded his eyes. "You're beginning to look seedy again."

"You're not so neat yourself."

Morgan passed a hand over his stubble, stepping sideways for the firmer ground. "There's someone who wants to meet you, Dudley. It won't take long."

"Who is it?"

"I don't think you know her, though you may know her husband. That's a guess."

"I see."

"I wonder. Will you come with me?"

"I'll wait here."

Morgan considered the weight of mistakes made during his career, some of which had left him feeling inadequate and besmirched. He remembered a dream in which he raced in full uniform onto a frozen pond and fell through weak ice. "You won't run away?"

Dudley nodded.

"You swear?"

"I swear."

Harley Bodine phoned first, arrived ten minutes later, and stared at her so intently she became singular, a being apart from all others. She looked beautiful in an austere white shirt tucked into a straight skirt, her black hair as glossy as the pelt of a panther. He was not all that certain she was glad to see him and felt his presence was provisional, dependent upon her mood. Her voice was casual, simply tossed at him.

"Do you want coffee?"

She served it in the sunroom, which overlooked small squares, cones, and spheres of evergreens. The house was abnormally quiet. Every little noise he made stood out. They sat in precisely facing chairs of white wicker.

"I've had only one other affair," she said. "He was quite handsome, exciting, an assistant district attorney with political ambitions. For a while he was my pagan god."

Bodine felt a rush of jealousy he would not have thought possible. "Was he married?"

"Yes."

"Did Ira ever find out?"

"Not Ira. My first husband, a liar and a cheat. Yes, inevitably he found out. I wanted him to. It hurt him deeply."

"You took revenge."

"Call it what you like."

He put his coffee cup aside because his hands were trembling, which was unlike him. Usually he had a strong hold on his emotions. "Where's your assistant D.A. now?"

"In Washington. He's a senator. Ira will doubtless run into him. They were at Harvard together."

Yes, Harvard. Of course. He brooded for a moment, then reminded himself what he had had from her, more than he had ever expected. "I think Kate plans to leave me," he said.

"I hope that has nothing to do with me."

"No, nothing."

"Will you try to stop her?"

The coffee cup was back in his hands, the ear almost too narrow for his finger. The saucer had a wavy edge. "I don't know, too many variables. The only certainties are death, taxes, and ragweed in August."

"Do you suffer from it?"

"Ragweed? I take medication." An unwanted emotion pushed at him, took control. "Tell me more about the assistant D.A. The senator. Was he a good lover?"

"I thought so."

A hot flush coloring his face lessened him, the way it did when he failed to catch a waiter's eye. "How about me?"

The telephone rang in the next room. She rose with her coffee cup in hand and glanced down at him. "Let's put it this way, Harley. You surprised me."

Elbows on the table, Beverly Gunner sat silent and still, like a cup of tea gone cold. She watched the clock, she smoked, she waited and waited, and finally he came. He had not shaved. He was wearing, she noticed, the same clothes he'd had on at Rembrandt's. He did not look like a policeman of any sort, but she trusted him.

"You found him?"

"Yes," he said.

Leaving Minerva's, she clung to his sleeve like a child. He opened a door of his car, and she climbed in with her heart racing and her confidence evaporating. She gave a start when the radio crackled, but nothing came on. She clutched her chest.

"What's the matter?"

"Some things the heart can't stand," she said. He was alarmed. "I'm all right," she assured him.

They drove up Summer Street and onto Fieldstone Road, which she knew well, too well, and soon her senses eddied. The poultry farm on the left was where an old woman in rubber boots had let Fay cuddle a newborn chick. On the right was an ice cream stand where Fay's choice had invariably been black raspberry, a single scoop in a sugar cone, the drippings on her dress.

When they stopped, she looked out at a picnic bench and a No Swimming sign and said, "I don't know where we are."

Then she was out of the car, with the sun hot on her face. Walking into woods seemed a wrong thing to do, but she did it without question, along a path that ran rough and hurt her heels. She should have worn flats. Snagged in the pine tops was a blue tissue of sky she needed to know was there. The path wandered into a clearing, where she saw the flash of the pond and the figure of a man joyously naked. She turned her head.

Chief Morgan yelled, "Put your clothes on, Dudley."

"Do we know what we're doing?" she asked.

"Not entirely," Morgan replied.

She shivered. "Can I call you something other than Chief?"

"James."

The man, who had gotten into jeans and a roomy shirt, called back in a happy voice, "I've been swimming."

The voice was in no way familiar, yet it gnawed at her ear. James, dear James, her strength, looked at her.

"Are you afraid?"

"I'm beyond that," she said, though the man's look, even

from a distance, was unnerving. His eyes absorbed whatever they rested on, and they were resting on her.

"This is Mrs. Gunner, Dudley."

"How do you do."

Alone, aware of the endless threat of water, she went to him and felt the world retreating. Flat moments of silence spread between them as they stared at each other, as if they were relatives meeting for the first time, strangers sharing blood. Her voice came gradually.

"Do you know my husband?"

"Some people I've forgotten."

"He's a fat man."

"But not a burden, I hope."

A butterfly floated between them. As a girl she had fancied that delicate Japanese hands patterned the colors, that factories in Tokyo existed for that single purpose. She took a snapshot of Fay from her bag. "Did you know my daughter?"

He would not take the picture from her hand. He merely looked at it. "Was she sweet?"

"Very."

"Some things I can't talk about."

"About this you have to." Trembling, she had spoken loud enough for James, wise James, to hear.

"You mustn't gang up on me."

"I'm doing what a mother has to do," she said.

His eyes were sympathetic, his smile collusive. "You're not right in the head, are you?"

"I haven't been for a long while."

"You get used to it, you must believe me."

She experienced a blast of visual sensations, none of them in sync, each carrying its own coloring noise. She recalled dreams in which sums on a blackboard never totaled correctly and written words failed to correspond.

"We may have been fed from the same spoon," he said.

"No, I don't believe that." Her look communicated urgency. "Help me."

"Yes, I should do something." Words, kindly spoken, welled out of him. "I know a place you could go. You could rest, read, forget."

This wasn't what she wanted to hear. "What are you talking about?"

"A very exclusive place. Privileged. Your mother-in-law is there."

She continued to stare at him, but her essential self floated away like the monarch that had passed between them.

She backed off, turned slowly, and on hurt heels returned to Chief Morgan, who stood with a thumb wedged in his belt and an unsettled expression on his waiting face.

"Did you hear?"

"Not all of it," he said.

"He killed my daughter," she said.

"How do you know?"

"I know."

The chief took a step forward and said to Dudley, "I have to take you in."

Dudley edged toward blueberry bushes denuded of their fruit by jays. "Please don't."

"I have to."

Dudley fled.

"It's all right," the chief said, slipping his hands into his pockets. "I'll get him later."

"It's not necessary," she said.

Myles Yarbrough returned with the Sunday papers, dumped them into a chintz chair, and said, "I met with him. Things are going to be all right for us." Color long absent had returned to his face, along with a bit of life to his receding hair. "Did you hear me, Phoebe?"

She had heard him quite clearly. She sat on a creamy white sofa with her legs drawn under her. The bandage was gone from her face. The bruised and broken skin was violet circled in yellow, but the swelling had subsided.

"He was reasonable," Myles said. "But of course he had to be."

She was slow in looking at him, slower still in replying. Her voice had a smooth, thick texture. "He knows what I was, Myles. He was one of my clients."

"Doesn't matter."

He pulled up an ornate footstool, sat on it, and caressed her ankles while viewing her in a manner she did not want to be viewed, as if she were a portrait other men had painted, her likeness idealized. Whenever he embraced her, it was as if he were lifting her off an easel.

"It might even have worked to our advantage."

His advantage, not hers, though that was expected. Their marriage had been machined on quid pro quo. For her, a fur in her closet, diamonds in her jewelry box, an annuity in her name; for him, a prized courtesan.

Smiling, he gripped her foot and gently squeezed her toes together. "In any event, you're my ace in the hole. We'll never starve."

It was an old joke she had never appreciated. "I'm forty years old, Myles."

"I'm only kidding," he said, his face altering in the instant. "I'm sorry."

She could see that he was. And she knew that he loved her in some boyishly perverse fashion that suited him well. It was a side of his nature hidden from himself but not from her. Her passions, which he considered amusements, were in another room, a wall brightened by books. She had read them all.

"What did you get from him?" she asked, though she really did not want to know.

"A loan, interest-free, a year to pay back. By that time I'll be on my feet."

She casually kicked his hand off her foot. "You extorted him."

"I negotiated a settlement like any lawyer would. He assaulted you, Phoebe. That's a criminal offense, not to mention the civil suit we could've brought."

Abruptly she rose from the sofa and stood on long, shaky legs visible inside an open white robe. "You did wrong, Myles."

"What do you mean?"

"You pushed him. He'll neither forgive nor forget. He'll get back at us."

"How?"

She sorted through the Sundays, brought up the *Times*, and extracted the book review section. "How, Myles?"

"Yes, how?"

She turned pages. "He'll tell everyone in this town about me. It's only a question of when."

Chief Morgan hooked a left onto Wainright Road and drove Beverly Gunner to the cemetery. It was where she wanted to go. Inside the cemetery, where the geometry of erect stones looked like the low ruins of a lost time, she directed the way, this lane, then that one, and then she said, "Pull up." Pausing, she collected strength, which now seemed easier to come by. She managed a smile. "Shall we?"

They stepped out into the swelling sunshine. A cardinal, scarlet on the run, vanished into the blue. A jay that sounded berserk squawked from the distance. Morgan offered his arm, but she didn't need it.

"This one," she said, stopping, and they stood before her daughter's modest stone, an inscription that read SWEETNESS THAT NOW BELONGS TO GOD. "I'm not a believer, but I wanted those words."

He was watching her closely, as if she were on the brink of nervous collapse, which she wasn't. She was simply reliving moments in a field when Fay had been picking a nosegay of violets and other delicate wildflowers in bloom, a gift for her daddy. The chief murmured something that didn't carry.

She said, "Paul never comes here, and he doesn't like it when I do. He says it's morbid."

"We do what we have to do."

"Yes, that's exactly right." She was crying, good tears, not bad ones. His hand was in motion on her back.

"Shall we leave?"

Back in the car, which the sun had heated, she sank deep into the seat. Her collapsing hair shaded her face, and she pushed part of it away with the astonishing sensation that she was breaking threads, severing connections. The chief was staring at her, his face almost an intrusion.

"Mrs. Gunner."

"Yes, James."

"Back at the pond you said you know, but how do you know?"

She smiled, for that was not something easily answered, nor was she sure it had an answer.

"I need something substantial, Mrs. Gunner."

"I don't know what that means anymore," she said with a smile.

"Are you holding anything back, something I didn't hear at the pond?"

"What would be the advantage?"

"I don't know," he said, "but all of a sudden you've changed."

"Yes, I have, haven't I? You've helped me, James." Her smile was nervous. "I feel odd calling you James."

"Then maybe you shouldn't."

"You don't want me to?"

"It's up to you." He wiped the sweat from his brow. "But you must tell me what's in your mind."

She touched his wrist, patted it. "I have to sort it out."

He started up the car. As they drove out of the cemetery she found herself humming a tune that hadn't popped into her head in twenty years or so.

A half hour later, alone, Chief Morgan motored up a straight drive and glided to a stop. Kate Bodine was bent over a flower bed near the last stall of the garage. He did not get out of the car. He waited for her to come to him. When she didn't, he said, "I know, I have no right."

Removing her garden gloves, she straightened. "You're taking a chance."

"Where is he?"

"Playing golf. Or seeing another woman. It's not like him, but it's possible."

"Does it bother you?"

"Not so strangely, it doesn't."

He watched her slow approach, sunlight slipping in and out of her blond hair. Her mouth was set tight, as if she no longer wanted the burden of his confidences, his suspicions. "How's the writing going?" he asked.

"I thought ideas would rush into my head like music. They don't." She placed a hand on the window ledge. "I have an interview coming up with WBZ. It's radio, not TV, but I'll do anything."

"I'll miss you."

"I haven't got it yet, but it looks good. I've told Harley. He didn't seem interested." She leaned forward, both hands on the window ledge. "You planted seeds in my head, James, but I must tell you, I don't think Harley could ever have wanted his son hurt."

Morgan nodded. "Please. Sit in the car with me."

"It looks hot in there."

"It is."

She strode around the front of the car and slipped in, leaving the door open. She was wearing shorts. Her knees were grass-stained. "What's the matter, James?"

"I don't know what I've got myself into. One moment I feel I'm on the right track, the next I feel foolish. Worse than that, I feel responsible for the state of other people's minds."

"Maybe you should worry about your own. You look like hell. Don't you shave anymore?"

"I feel I'm a player in something I don't understand."

"You've made me share the feeling."

"I'm sorry." He dropped a hand on her. "I should talk only to myself, but when I do that I never know when to shut up."

"Your hand is sweaty. Are you making a pass?"

"I've been doing that since the first time I saw you."

"All I want, James, is to get back into the business, or near enough."

"At least you know what your business is. Mine's becoming a mystery."

"You tell me only bits and pieces. The rest I don't know."

"Nor do I."

She crossed her thighs and locked his hand in place. "That's far enough, James."

"Yes," he said sadly, "I knew it would be."

Beverly Gunner yanked at curtains to block the sun, and in the shadowy room she stood before a mirror and saw only parts of herself, which deepened a feeling of estrangement. From herself. From the world, which operated, she had no doubts, at the lowest moral level. Then a light came on, and her parts connected. She viewed herself quickly to make sure she had not been rearranged.

"What's going on?"

The voice came from her husband. Behind him were her sons, who were trying to get a look at her, as if she were a sideshow. She lit a cigarette and stood with her feet planted wide apart to show she didn't give a shit about any of them.

"Look," he said, "are you sick or something?"

"When have I been right?" She spoke through smoke. She glimpsed her eldest. "When have I? Can you tell me, Gustav?"

"Leave the boys out of it."

Her shoes were too small, tight at the toes, cruel at the heels, and she kicked them off with agonized effort, one almost hitting him. "I want to be young again, do you mind?"

"Do what you want."

"Do what I want? Maybe you won't like that."

He turned to the boys. "You go on," he said and shooed them off. Then he stepped in and shut the door behind him. "You dropped an ash."

"My prerogative."

"You got something to say, Beverly, say it."

"I met the man who killed our daughter."

She didn't know what she had expected, but she received nothing other than an oppressive stare that was shrewd and calculating, playing for time. The silence was forceful. It thrust itself upon her and anchored her to her sore feet.

"Do you know what you just said?"

"Oh, yes."

"The police chief's mixed up in this, am I right?"

His sudden smile shouldn't have surprised her, but it did. He was a genius, as his father had been, and his mind moved ten times faster than hers.

"You spilled another ash," he said.

"So I did."

At college, Victorian literature, she had read that in the best of worlds men are muscles of iron and women etherealities, their decisions never their own. Their own restraints see to that.

"So he had you meet this man. A vagrant, right?"

"His name is Dudley," she said.

"Then this man and you, you're both crazy. Certifiable." His smile increased. "Do you know what I mean, Beverly?"

She did and had, for now, nothing more to say. Her look slammed a door on him.

11

MONDAY MIDDAY, THEY CAME BACK. REGINA SMITH HEARD THE slam of car doors and peeped through the drapes. Patricia's black hair was molten in the sun, and her bicycle pants were a bright second skin. Anthony's shirt hung loose, his ballooning trousers tapering to his sandaled feet. Everything wonderful about youth clung to them. They were too absurdly beautiful for their own good, which gave her an unwanted sense of her own accelerating years. She took time to get her face straight and then positioned herself. The front door opened. Her dark eyes swept in the two of them.

"Did you enjoy yourselves?" Her voice was pruned, pointed at Patricia, who stood up to it.

"Weather was great. That's why we stayed longer than expected."

"How nice for you." She aimed her eyes solely at Anthony, who showed less stamina, his energy, she imagined, consumed in copulation. "And how about you? Was it lots of fun?"

Patricia stepped forward. "Be careful, Tony. I think my mother has a hair across."

"That's enough, Patricia!"

She let them go. She watched them ascend the stairs to their rooms, nothing more to be said for the moment. In the corner bathroom she picked up a tube and did her lips. She brushed her hair, which wasn't as glossy as her daughter's but was still vibrant and would grow lush if she let it, which was the way Patricia's father had liked it. The week before they divorced, he had turned forty and had furry dice hanging from the rearview of his Corvette. The last time she had seen him, a theater in New York, he had worn a young new wife on his arm, large smiles on their faces, as if they'd just gotten it off. How sweet!

She mounted the stairs.

She entered Anthony's room without knocking, a presumptive right now that he had betrayed the family. He stood clean as a knife in skin-biting Jockey briefs, the pouch too explicit to ignore.

"Put some pants on," she said.

"I was just getting ready to take a shower." He was flustered, grabbing his voluminous slacks. He got them on quickly. "You should've knocked."

"You forget, this is my house."

"My father's too."

"Yes, but that doesn't include you." Her gaze ground into him. "You, my friend, have taken advantage. You've made fools of your father and me."

"No," he said, "I wouldn't do that. I respect you and Dad. I especially respect you."

She smiled at him with derision, confident that in his imaginings she was ladylike in loving his father, knees only slightly lifted, eyes appropriately closed, decorum in her climaxes. Along with lies waiting to be told, she saw on his face the flush of naivete, a babe in the woods.

"I warned you, didn't I, Anthony? I told you to keep your hands off Patricia, but you did what you wanted."

"No."

"You, my friend, are a liar." Her voice, though low and contained, struck with as much force as if she'd reached in and squeezed his testicles. His recoil was immediate and painful. "My real concern for Patricia is disease. You *have* heard of AIDS, haven't you?"

"I don't have that," he said. "And there's no possible way I could."

"But I don't know that. I have no idea what you do in school. Sexual ambiguity is not uncommon with boys your age. And I'm not comfortable with all your teachers. What's that fellow Pitkin like?"

"I swear to God," he said, beet red, tears in his eyes.

That was what she wanted. She wanted him on his knees, groveling. She was keyed up. Her blood raced, her body sang. "You are rather disgusting, Anthony, but we'll let it rest for now," she said and moved to the door.

"Regina."

She turned sharply and gave a scornful twist to her lips. He had never called her that before. He had never called her anything. "Yes, what?"

"You're a bitch," he said.

In prime pasture land Tish Hopkins buried a dead cow with the help of a hired hand, Vernon, who said, "I betcha gonna miss that animal."

Tish wore a man's flat cap and rubber boots and had tears in her eyes. When her husband was alive, they had had two dozen cows and a henhouse, but after Mr. Hopkins died she sold off the cows except the one and added more henhouses.

Vernon, whose hair was like the gray from a soft pencil, had large drastic eyes, veiny arms, and socks that wrinkled into his shoes. He tossed the last shovelfuls over the grave and said, "Almost like we oughta say a prayer."

"Something dies, there's always sadness. That's because we're mortal. Mortal means we're temporary. Temporary means we ought to be good to each other because some of us won't be here tomorrow."

"You're good to me, Mrs. Hopkins. You pay me more than you oughta."

"You're only part-time, Vernon. You were full-time, I'd only pay you what you're worth, which might not satisfy you."

Vernon deliberately planted his shovel in the ground and said, "Somebody's watchin' us."

Some thirty yards away near a section of unmended fence was the figure of a man that looked like a scarecrow, breathlessly still in the heat. Tish mopped her face with the sleeve of her elbow. She couldn't see close up without glasses, but she could still see for distance without them.

"I know him," she said. "Fellow I fed."

"He the one the chief locked up? I'd be careful I was you."

"He's no more harm than a butterfly," she scoffed.

"They say the chief doesn't know what to do with him and lets him run free."

"Who says that?"

"Guys at the Blue Bonnet. They say his name is Dudley but nothing else. Just that."

"You go on back, Vernon, take the shovels with you. Looks like he's afraid of you."

"I ain't hurt nobody since fourth grade, Malcolm Crandall, and he deserved it."

"You're smart not to mess with him anymore. You go on back like I told you."

She waited, gestured to Dudley, and looked up at the sky. A magnificent fair-weather cloud loitered in the distance. Birds in flight were a pebbled path. Then she splashed through clover toward Dudley because he wouldn't come to her. Something about him pulled at her heart. The sun beating at him, he looked like boyhood burnt out.

"Who did you put under?" he asked.

"Nobody. Just a cow, but I loved her."

"I could tell."

"I suppose you want something to eat."

"Better not, if he's here."

"He's goin', soon as he puts the shovels away."

"Then best we wait awhile." He put a hand to his face. "I don't suppose you have a razor."

"I had a husband, I guess I still got the razor."

"Do you have any clean clothes?"

She sized him up and saw her husband's bones. "Well, I can dress you better than you are. I can even give you a fine pair of shoes worn only on Sundays. What size do you wear?"

"Eight and a half."

"Close enough. My husband was a nine."

They began the trek to the house. Halfway there, he said, "Afterward, can I use your phone?"

One of the brothers, Herman, dozed off with a computer science book in his lap and many minutes later woke with a scare from a bad dream, which meant his brain had been misbehaving. He went to the doorway of his brother's room. Gustav was sitting Indian fashion on a cushion near an oxeye window and gazing at a wall papered with *Playboy* centerfolds. Herman said, "Can I come in?"

"Ask right."

"*May* I come in?"

"Just don't stay too long."

Herman closed the door behind him, and they viewed each other through a grainy filter of sunlight, their porky faces nearly identical, though Herman's had the tendency to overbulge from emotional disturbances. Down deep, they had an honest liking for each other, but Gustav would never show it and Herman didn't know how.

"What's the matter with Mama?" Herman asked. He wanted his world always the same. Thanksgiving was turkey, Christmas was goose, and Mama was Mama ready to serve, ready to do.

"Papa says it's the time of life women go through," Gustav said. "Makes them crazy."

"Something's wrong between her and Papa."

"Mama's a ballbreaker."

"No, she isn't. We break hers."

"Women don't have balls."

Herman turned his gaze to the wall, from one centerfold to another, and said, "That bottom one looks like Mama. I mean, if Mama was young."

Gustav looked at him with extreme impatience. "If that was Mama, I wouldn't look at it. Besides, Mama was never young."

"She's got a picture of Fay in her bag," Herman said abruptly. "I've seen it."

"So what?"

"She loved Fay more than us."

"But Papa loves us more."

"I'd rather she did."

"Papa's a genius. She's not."

Overstrung, Herman felt a tightening in his chest, which he tried to ignore. "Do you miss Fay?" he asked.

"No, I don't miss her. She was a cretin."

"I know, but don't you miss her at all?"

"Maybe a little, but now we don't have to explain her."

He was thinking too many thoughts, fanning emotions he wanted to share. "Do you ever dream of her, Gustav?"

"Sure, that's normal."

"Good dreams or bad?" he asked. In his dream she had reached out, but he had stepped beyond her touch. He wished he hadn't. "Good dreams or bad, Gustav?"

"None of your business."

"She was afraid of you, but she wasn't of me. I used to pet her head, tie her shoes."

"She should've learned to do that herself."

Her face took possession of Herman's mind, and an especially poignant memory pressed tightly against his heart. "She shouldn't have drowned. She could be here now, and Mama would be okay."

Gustav was growing cross, nervous, as if Herman's feelings had become too much of a burden. He looked at the wall, at his favorite centerfold, a nurse wearing only a cap and a single garter. "Get out of here," he said. "I want to jerk off."

Herman nodded. He understood. "That's what I do when I've got things on my mind."

"You don't do it right. You don't know how to make it last."

May Hutchins was rinsing a pan at the sink. Her husband, who had come home at the noon hour, was seated at the table, at the edge of her attention. She didn't want him underfoot, in her way, in her light. Peering through the window over the sink, she said, "I suppose you want something to eat."

Roland shook his head. "I'm not all that hungry."

"Then why'd you come home?"

"I was worried about *him* being here."

"The book's still in the gazebo, but I don't think he's coming back for it. I don't think he's coming back, *period*." Stepping away from the sink, she sighed. "I wonder if I'll ever see him again. I bet not."

"Why would you want to?"

"When I figure that out I'll tell you. Or maybe I won't." She ripped off a paper towel, the last sheet on the cylinder, and dried her hands. Her face was pulled tight, lips pinched in. She was having a bad moment, which had come upon her without warning.

"May."

She turned. She was indifferent to both his presence and his absence. Either one, it made no difference. She was looking through him.

"May."

"Yes, what?"

His face was pink and nearly a perfect roundness. "Remember when we were first married, how I'd sneak home at noon for a little of this and that?"

She remembered his short arms could make it around her, which was not the case now. She remembered the quick sex, his delight, her lethargy afterward, Peggy Lee's song, "Is That All There Is?" She said, "My ankles were pretty then."

"They're still pretty, May. They're the best."

"I was fifteen pounds lighter." Twenty-five was more like it. She was aware more than ever that her present self stumbled along while her younger ones thrived in memory, sometimes adding to themselves, other times subtracting, never holding still.

Suddenly he was blushing. "May, what d'you say?"

"Don't be silly."

His eyes brimmed with hope. "May, why not?"

She owed him. Christ, she owed him. And yes, why not? Maybe he'd surprise her, though she doubted it. They climbed the stairs together, and at the top he playfully banged his hip against hers. She smiled, not with her whole face. She felt she was being generous enough.

Thirty minutes later he was gone. He had, she knew, an afternoon job in Stoneham, work that would take him into the evening. She was relieved. In one way she felt used and in another untouched, simply breathed upon.

She washed, she dressed, and, her bra loosened to give her breasts a measure of independence, she sauntered out for the mail, but there was none, not even a flyer, which offended her, as if the world wanted nothing to do with her—worse, had forgotten her.

Coffee freshly made, a cup poured, she sat at the kitchen table and thumbed through her high school yearbook, in which the best moments of her life were preserved. She had been popular, perhaps not the most popular but popular all the same. She played girls' basketball, worked for the school paper, sang in mixed chorus, had a role in the senior play. Eyes filled, she closed the book as if on herself.

In the bathroom mirror she gave herself a new mouth, and over the sink she clipped her nails. She raised an arm. Nap in the socket resembled a preserved rose. With a razor she plucked the petals and washed them down the drain. Looking again in the mirror, she sucked in her lower lip, then let it protrude. With adolescent intensity she continued work with the razor, the scissors too.

Later, perhaps twenty minutes later, after giving herself a long, thoughtful look, she phoned the town hall, Veterans Affairs office, and disguised her voice. "Is Mr. Fossey there?"

Fred Fossey said, "May, it's me."

The shirt was white, though yellowed from lying so long in a drawer. The trousers were a trifle short but a good fit around the waist. The shoes, dusted, had a shine, and Dudley, shaved, fed, ready for the world, had a smile. "I knew I was saving those things for something," Tish Hopkins said, looking at him with satisfaction. "You're a proper man now."

She sensed something resilient and sly floating through him but was not deterred from investing him with a value perhaps he didn't deserve but suited her fancy. Though he was too old to have been one of hers, she said, "My husband and I never had children, just animals. Chickens and cows."

"Could I use your phone now?" he said in a tone that immediately distanced them, which saddened her only a little. Their relationship had a beat but no melody.

She took him to the telephone, a boxy black thing set on a side table in the parlor, and left him alone. Puttering in the kitchen, she tried not to listen, which wasn't difficult. His singsong voice was in a low key. Then he called to her.

"A taxi will come for me, but I need to give directions."

She went to him. "Let me have it," she said and took the receiver from him. "Who is this?"

"Please," said a woman's voice. "The directions."

Tish recited route numbers and street names, mixing in landmarks comprehensible only to the locals. "You got that? . . . You sure? . . . At the green you get onto Summer Street . . . What? . . . Right, Fieldstone Road." When she replaced the receiver, she looked at the clean line of Dudley's face. "She sounded awfully worried. She your wife?"

"No," he said, "but I'm her lamb."

"For all I know," Tish said, "you could be Jesus Christ with a shave."

Sunlight gashed the kitchen windows. Beverly Gunner opened
a container of eggs, country fresh, and one by one began dropping them on the floor. Herman, walking in on her, cried out,
"Mama, what are you doing?"

She smiled. "Making a mess, dear."

"Mama, don't!" He stared at smashed shells drooling yolk.
"Who's going to clean it up?"

"I'm sure I don't know." She dropped another and another,
then the last one.

"Mama, don't step in it. You might fall."

Her own sensations consumed her. "If I do, you can pick
me up and put me in the garbage."

"Don't talk that way." His face, stripped of protection, was
fat with panic. "You're scaring me."

"A smart boy like you doesn't have to be scared. You have
the world by the balls."

"Mama, don't talk dirty."

Her smile verging on the terrible, she reached out and patted his head. "Mama's no good at shaping her thoughts. She
just says what comes into her head, and it's not always the right
thing."

He spoke through tears. "I love you."

"Of course you do. You love me dearly."

"And I miss Fay. I bet you think I don't, but I do."

"Yes, we all miss her," she said in a stronger voice and with
a belief in the radiant energy of ghosts. She imagined Fay drifting in the form of a grown woman, like Emily Dickinson dressed
in white.

"Gustav misses her too, but he won't say so."

"Souls hibernate, then come back."

He began ripping away at fresh paper toweling with such
force that the whole business fell into his hand. "I'll clean it all
up, Mama, don't you worry. Papa won't see."

"Papa sees everything," she said and moved away from the
mess, tracking some of it.

"Don't worry, Mama."

"I won't," she said, turning a corner and confronting her

reflection in a pane of glass, which baffled her. She reeled back like a stroke victim failing to recognize himself in the mirror, an introduction needed each day. "Herman," she hollered. "Come tell me who I am."

"Remember Will Harris?" May Hutchins asked.

"Sure I remember him." Fred Fossey rocked on worn heels. "We both went to Korea. He didn't come back."

"But you did."

"And here I am, May." He'd been eying her keenly all the while, his first time alone with her in her house. They stood in her parlor, and she had their high school yearbook open, certain pages overly thumbed through the years.

"Here's your picture, Fred."

Slipping to her side, he peered at the thumbnail photo. "I was funny-looking then."

"You still are."

"We guys used to walk around with our pants turned up, our white socks showing. Sweat socks, that's what we wore with our penny loafers. Do you remember, May?"

"Now that you mention it." Memories squeezed her heart, she turned pages, skipped the one on which Dorothea Farnham appeared, and came to her own. "Recognize her?"

His cool hand was on her warm bottom. "You were beautiful, May."

"I was attractive."

"Guys wanted you."

She'd been burdened with too much embarrassing bloom and racked with fugitive desires consigned to a diary, the entries penned in glaring red ink, valentines pierced with arrows drawn around the dates. "Inside I was a hot number, but nobody got to me."

"How about Malcolm Crandall?"

"He came close, my mistake."

His hand, which had heated up, was still on her. He pulled it away. "May, you're not wearing anything underneath."

"That's right, I'm not."

The yearbook was cast aside. His face loomed. Standing pelvis to pelvis with her, swaying as if at a school dance, he kissed her like a novice.

"Not like that," she said and, demonstrating, felt him spring to life.

"May," he murmured, his hand tentative at her breast, as if cupping a flame. His body was a quivering exercise in expectation.

"Upstairs," she said.

They left the room and moved through another, which smelled of floor wax and furniture polish. They climbed stairs to forbidden territory, where the carpeting was springy and the smells more intimate.

"Jeez, May, don't you make your bed?"

"The clock's running out on us, Fred. Don't you hear it?"

"Don't talk sad, May. Talk happy." He was fumbling with his belt, jamming the buckle, getting nowhere.

"At our age," she said, weighing implications and tipping the scale, "so much is to be gained, so little to be lost."

He triumphed over the buckle and stumbled out of his pants. His boxer shorts were tapered, unlike Roland's, which bagged to the knees. "I can't believe I'm in your bedroom."

"Turn around. Don't watch." She yanked off her dress and flung it at a chair as if it didn't belong to her. There was little else to remove. She kept on her watch and the gold chain around her neck. "Okay, you can look." On the bed she appeared as a prize, unwrapped, the swells of her thighs exaggerated, the push of her belly diminished. She was bounty for any man's eyes and more than enough for Fred's. He gawked at her.

"Jeez, May, what did you do?"

For a moment embarrassment garnished her face. "Don't you like it?"

"I do."

With nail scissors and razor she had made her cunt cute by trimming the rusty hair into a heart. "I did it for you," she said and had second thoughts. "No, I didn't. I did it for me."

They made love belly to belly, and then he snoozed. Ten minutes later he woke with a start. "I'd better go, May."

"I was about to suggest it."

"I'd rather stay."

"You don't have a choice."

He looked skinny, uncertain. He leaned over to kiss her. "Having you, May, Roland's got to be the luckiest man alive."

"No, Fred. You are."

Dudley said good-bye to Tish Hopkins and then, as an after-thought, struggled to remove his ring. "Here," he said, "I want you to have this. Harvard College, class of fifty-seven. Or fifty-eight, I forget which."

"Oh, no." She protested in a voice crackling like brittle parcel paper. Her flat cap sat square on her head. "It's too valuable."

"I got it in a pawnshop."

"I still can't take it."

His eyes bled blue, his shaved face hung white. "People have been good to me here," he said and pressed the ring into her callused hand. "Please."

"What will I do with it?"

"You can wear it."

He trekked past chicken coops to the road and waited on the shoulder, where the late afternoon sun blazed against his white shirt, the cuffs turned back at the wrists. The taxi that finally arrived all the way from Boston was a rattletrap with a noisy throb in the motor. Looking in through the open window, he said, "Can I sit in front?"

"It's not allowed," the driver said, clearing the seat beside him of debris. "But I'll make an exception."

The taxi took time to achieve speed. A crow eating some-thing on the road flew away only at the last second. Dudley enjoyed taxis. For the length of the ride his wishes were su-preme. The wheels rolled for him, the driver his bearer.

"You're a black man," he said.

"Some of us are."

"I could have been," he said, "you never know. The dice decide that. My name's Dudley. What's yours?"

"John." John, turning onto Summer Street, gave him a look. "Your missus said you might be a mess, but you look pretty clean and proper."

"Folks were wonderful to me." Maples shaded the street. Dudley pointed at a particularly well-groomed Victorian. "But the lady lives there was mean. I did a poop on her porch."

John tossed him another look. "Why don't you relax now, enjoy the ride."

The taxi breathed in more than it breathed out, and Dudley took the heat in his face. They bypassed the green and on Ruskin Road followed a lawn-chemical truck on its way into the Heights, where the grand houses kept their distance on rising grounds and flower gardens exported their scent in long drifts.

"Rich people," John commented.

"Roll of the dice," Dudley said, closing his eyes. "My stomach's upset."

"You're not going to be sick, are you?"

"No, but I think I'll nap for a while, may I?"

When he opened his eyes again, the taxi was cruising an inner lane on Interstate 93 and withstanding the shock of the faster traffic. The car ahead of theirs exhibited bumper stickers hyping the sport of bowling and glorifying the ownership of guns. When he woke from another nap, they were in the snarl of Boston, in the drumbeat of stop and go.

"Let me off here," he said. "I can walk the rest of the way."

"She said for me to take you to the door."

Dudley's hand was on the latch. "It's not for her to say."

"You're the boss," John said.

"Can you lend me some money? She'll pay you back."

"How much you want?"

"Twenty dollars, that would do it."

"I'll let you have ten."

Stepping out into the stationary traffic, he was startled by the hoot of a horn and hustled to the wide sidewalk, where well-dressed bodies swept by him. The lesser-dressed, nowhere to go, billowed around him. He felt at home, too much at home. Up ahead was a squad of skinheads whose violet scalps and bald faces gave them the look of death and evoked flashes of Sweeney, the cat killer.

He plowed through the crowd to a display window, where a naked dummy, a sexless male, was another evocation of Sweeney. Eyeballs rolled back. No vital signs. Gore at the base of the head.

He had let Sweeney stalk him up four flights of stairs to the flat pebbled roof, where he taunted him by walking the slender wooden edge. He knew where it was safe and where it wasn't, and Sweeney didn't.

"I bet you don't dare look down," he said, and that was when Sweeney, teetering on rot, swung out a sudden arm for balance.

With cramps in his stomach, he moved into the human sea, now with the tide, then against it. A tattooed arm on which a dragon snorted fire jostled him. Through a window he saw a jeweler with a loupe in his eye and a gentleman with a tightly furled umbrella that could be used for defense. Ahead of him two youths were swearing in broken sentences. Slipping by them, he entered a coffee shop, ensconced himself on a stubby seat at a low counter, and ordered milk.

He had soared skyward when Sweeney plunged into the void. Pure spirit, he was jostling clouds in an ocean of air when Sweeney burst into blood and bone on the asphalt. Never before had he flown so high, seen so much, been so big.

His eyes lit, he sipped his milk through a straw and smiled appropriately when the woman on the next seat looked at him from a face void of cosmetics, which reminded him of his mother, who, unlike Sweeney, should not have died.

"Aren't you feeling well?" the woman asked.

"My tummy's upset."

"Milk is good, but warm water is better."

His mother had been ill off and on and then had gotten worse. Mrs. Cronin, who lived on the first floor, huffed up the stairs twice a day. A public nurse came once a week. His mother ate soup. Anything solid she couldn't keep down.

"Bottled water is best," the woman beside him said.

From his breast pocket he removed the folded bill John had given him and placed it on his napkin. His mother's weight had always fluctuated, though she had never been fat. In the final weeks she'd been skinny. "You ought to find a good girl and get married," she had told him.

He smelled something musty laced with spearmint. The woman had opened her purse. "Everything is so expensive," she complained.

"Are you leaving?"

"Don't you want me to?"

With a soft step he had entered the dim of his mother's room. She was a still figure under the covers, her face turned to the wall. After a few minutes, slowly and unerringly, he backed out. Seated at the chrome-legged table was Mrs. Cronin, in whose life priests were the controlling force, though gin did more to soothe her soul. "Did she finish her soup?" The breezy voice altered with the next breath. "What is it, luv?" Her chair scraped. "She's gone," he said, and the cuckoo came out of the kitchen clock to mock the moment.

"I didn't cry," he said. "Some things are too sad for tears."

"I'm sorry," the woman said. "Did I miss something?"

The word *death* did not scare him. The other word did, *oblivion*.

Soldier, drinking beer from a can, stared at an oil Mary Williams had dug out of storage and hung in her studio. It was an abstract festooned with ostentation, convoluted with overstatement, and overcharged with rebellious colors bleeding into one another. Soldier didn't like it. "It's a joke," he said.

"It belonged to my grandmother."

"It's still a joke."

"It's Expressionism," she said. "I identified with this stuff when I came out."

"Came out of where?"

Three months, when she was sixteen, she had been confined in an institution where the mirrors were metal and the doors had handles like those on ships. Three months had seemed like

three years. No razors allowed. An attendant who had read
Auntie Mame said she looked like King Kong under the arms.

"Out of where, Mary?"

"Out of myself."

Soldier went into deep thought, lips pressed in, eyes narrowed, when she looked at her watch. "What's going to happen
to me, he gets here?"

"Maybe we can work something out," she said, with no idea
if anything could be.

"He'll sponge off you."

"The last three years he's paid for everything."

"I don't believe it."

"It's not necessary you do."

"You need me in other ways, admit it."

"Don't make me choose, Soldier. You'd lose."

He finished off his beer. His hand, cold from the can, was
an ice pack on hers. He kissed the stain on her cheek. "Don't
be so sure."

But she was perfectly sure and looked at him with a twinge
of regret. He brought forward the flaps of his ears.

"Who makes you laugh?"

She ran a hand over his shaved head and down the side of
his jaw. His presence had a weight and reality hers did not.
"We'll talk about it later."

When the bell sounded, she dashed through the passageway
to buzz open the downstairs door. Tremors in her legs, she was
waiting at the top of the stairs when John came up them, alone.
Her face fell in the instant.

"Where is he?" she asked.

"He made me let him off, few blocks away. Said he wanted
to walk."

Her voice went bare bones. "I depended on you."

"I'm just a taxi driver, ma'am. I can't make people do what
they don't want to do."

"Don't call me ma'am. My name is Mary. You let me
down."

"No, Mary, he did."

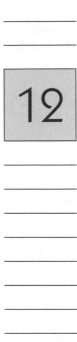

12

THEY MET IN THE MORNING AND WALKED THROUGH THE PINES to the pond. Fronds of ferns arched toward them. The sky was mackerel. "I got the job," Kate Bodine said, and Chief Morgan's smile vanished into his face, to be saved for another time.

"I was sure you would."

"Aren't you glad for me?"

"Give me awhile."

"It's different from what I thought. The station's going all news, and I'm on the team. News I can write, James, and I can read it well. I won't have butterflies. The camera used to terrify me."

They sat on flat rock, which was mossy and would probably stain them. He wore chinos and she white shorts that showed her fine thighs and strong calf muscles. "When do you start?" he asked.

"Next week."

"What did your husband say to that?"

"I told you, James. He's not interested. And he's not touching me anymore, which is a relief." She picked up a twig and tossed it into the rim of the pond, disturbing a dragonfly. "I'm an uncomplicated person. I realize a career is all I want, not a bunch of things."

"Sounds like you're settling for a career."

"You could put it that way, but I prefer my words. I'm going to look for a place to live in Boston."

"Then the marriage is over."

"It scares me a little. I had high hopes." She ran a hand over his forearm, gripped it for a moment, then withdrew. "The funny thing is now I find myself worrying about you. I loaded a lot on your shoulders."

"It was a pleasure."

"This stuff about Harley's son, I can't help asking myself how much is personal with you."

"Twenty-five percent," Morgan said. "Maybe fifty. It fluctuates."

"You heard only my side of the story about the marriage. I'm not peaches and cream, James, and I probably wasn't the easiest woman to live with. I don't need a man in my bed every night. I never have."

"You just wanted to get pregnant."

"I'm glad it didn't happen." She tossed another twig into the water. The clouds began casting doubt on the day. "I'll miss you, James."

"I won't miss you. All I'll have to do is turn on the radio. WBZ, you said?"

"Be happy for me, I'd appreciate it."

"I'm happy."

"It's going to rain," she said, and together they rose to their feet.

Ira Smith, back from Washington, drank his morning coffee at the table in the bow window. His eyes were heavy inside his horn-rims. Fatigue marked his face. He enjoyed being tested, but only if the test was reasonable. The business in Washington, a betrayal of the firm, had not been reasonable. Nor was it reasonable what his wife was demanding he do. Regina, looking extremely beautiful, sat across from him.

"I don't understand you," she said. "A man steals from you, you protect him."

"A scandal would have cost us more. We hope to recoup some of the money from him. Not all, I grant you."

"Small punishment, Ira. In other words, no punishment at all. Is that how you intend to deal with Anthony?"

Adjusting his horn-rims, he looked out the window. His son, wearing only shorts, was stretched out on a chaise with a book. With affection and admiration he gazed at the healthy glow of Anthony's body and hoped the years would not dim it too soon. "I'd rather handle the situation in my own way, Regina."

"What way is that?"

He wished he could remove himself from her stare. She was driving a nail. "I can't cast him out, Regina. He's not Ishmael."

"He raped my daughter."

"It wasn't rape. It couldn't have been."

"Statutory rape."

"They're *both* minors."

"*Something* has to be done," she said and pushed her chair back.

He went outside, where white roses frothed under a sky that looked as if it had gone gray for good, the air warm and unsettled. Canada geese passing over the house sounded like a conference that had got out of hand. Anthony jumped to his feet. They stood face to face, father and son, and talked quietly, man to man.

"It wasn't that way, Dad."

"I know it wasn't."

The cover of the book was mildewed, and pages clung precariously to the buckram. May Hutchins carried it with great care. She had meant to return it to the library but instead settled on a bench on the green and read from it. Jenny Wren was a little busybody, Peter Rabbit an irresponsible love, and Reddy Fox a rascal easily forgiven. So easily she could fancy herself dipping a bare toe into the Smiling Pool and drinking from the Laughing Brook, the water purer than from her tap. She would have read another chapter had a shadow, jagged at the edges, not fallen over her.

"Improving your mind, May?"

She slapped the book shut and planted a hand over the cover. "No," she said, "pleasing it."

Hands on his hips, Reverend Stottle stood tall and tilted while she tried to ignore him. "Is Roland feeling better?"

"Roland has his good days and his bad ones, like all of us. Don't tell me there aren't times you don't feel like going to church."

"Not a morning goes by I don't feel like staying in bed, but Jesus calls, your savior and mine."

"Yours, Reverend. My sins I cherish."

"He died for you, May."

"Damn presumptuous of him. He shouldn't have done it."

"You're putting me on," Reverend Stottle said, all smiles. He sat beside her, which she didn't want. "Besides, what sins do you have?" he said, as if hers would be too inane for discussion.

"I'm two-timing Roland, would that be sin enough?"

"Yes," he said, with more smiles, "if it were true."

He sensed no mystery in her, for which she despised him. She wanted to slap his face. Her voice unpleasant, she said, "How about you? You have any sins worth repeating?"

"I sin in heart and mind, but I'm on my knees at night. Jesus hears. He's always within earshot. And you, May?" His voice seemed inside her where she couldn't spit it out. "Are you on your knees?"

"Not the way you think."

"Are you trying to shock me, May?" He had a way of looking at her with his whole face. "You're troubled, aren't you?"

"What do you think of God?" she said. "You think he's doing a good job?"

"Between you and me, May?" With a different sort of smile, he laid a finger against the side of his nose. "It's a good thing his office isn't elective."

She no longer wanted to slap him and felt instead a touch of sympathy. What kind of life did he have, preaching on Sunday and poking about the rest of the week with a voice full of irrelevancies?

"The fact is, May, God made the world in such a manner that leaves a bit of a lie in every truth. Any reputable scientist will tell you that."

He spoke nonsense bound to get on anybody's nerves. Looking away, she felt a quickness on her skin from a change in the air. The day had dimmed. Reverend Stottle shot to his feet.

"It's going to rain."

"Let it," she said.

"You'd better come on, May. You'll get soaked."

She felt a drop and brought the book to her bosom. The reverend scurried off, and after a few moments she left the bench and took shelter under a billowing red maple. The shower was brief, hardly enough to kiss the leaves.

Chief Morgan secluded himself in his office, sat himself behind an old manual typewriter, and summarized suspicions and doubts about the derelict who called himself Dudley and seemed to claim responsibility for the deaths of an adolescent named Glen Bodine and a child named Fay Gunner—claims that seemed to implicate a parent of each victim. The summary ran six pages, single spaced, and was long on supposition and short on facts. In postscript, he wrote: "Dudley's gone again, and I don't know if he's worth looking for. The truth is, I don't know which way to move."

He stapled the pages together and stashed them in a bottom drawer. Stepping out of his office, he said to Meg O'Brien, "I'm going to lunch, then home. Anything major comes up, call me. Otherwise you handle it, but let Eugene think he's doing it."

"Don't I always?"

"No, you give him the pin."

"That's to get him off his ass." She scrutinized him, like an older sister. "You're acting funny."

"It's how I always act, Meg. You just haven't noticed."

The knotty pine paneling at the Blue Bonnet was permanently stained with grease from the grill. The blackboard menu, the fare virtually unchanged in decades, was screwed to a wall. It was past the lunch hour, no one sitting at the counter. Morgan crunched crackers into a bowl of clam chowder. Malcolm Crandall, consuming a cheeseburger, ignored him, which was just as well. Ben Foxx, sitting closer, looked at him out of an age-spotted face. Years ago Ben had been a reporter for a now-defunct Boston paper when it had morning and evening editions. Ben had worked the bulldog, never a byline. He said, "Anything happening, Chief?"

"You'd be the first to know."

"Good, paper's practically put to bed. I wouldn't want to tear a page apart."

The chowder was salty. "I wouldn't ask you to do that."

Malcolm Crandall said with a full mouth, "Ask him whatever happened to that tramp, Ben."

"What tramp's he talking about, Chief?"

"Beats the hell out of me, Ben," Morgan said and didn't finish his soup. His water glass he emptied with a silent swallow.

At home, plumping a pillow and stretching out on the sofa, he began watching a vintage movie, Deborah Kerr playing a young Irishwoman duped by a Nazi spy. Halfway through, he fell asleep and woke in a sweat to credits creeping onto the screen. He read them all. Then he got up and made a phone call. If the voice was male, he intended to hang up. The voice was Beverly Gunner's.

He said to her, "I've been working it and reworking it, and I can't believe someone would want his child done away with. It goes against the grain."

"You shouldn't worry about it, James. It's my problem."

"No," he said. "It's a police matter. I mean, if it's that at all."

"He's a genius. He thinks he can do anything he wants."

"I'm worried about you."

There was a silence. Then she said, "That's the nicest thing anyone has said to me in years."

Paul Gunner drove his sons to Andover and dropped them off at the academy for preterm activities. Then, back in Bensington, lunching at the country club, he stuffed himself. His stomach, an avalanche, lay in his lap. When Anne Lapierre, dining with Regina Smith, stopped at his table, he was a politician with his impromptu smile.

"God, you're lovely. Tell Armand he's the luckiest man alive."

When he returned home he avoided his wife. His shirt off, he was a sea of moving flesh. He dropped his trousers, donned voluminous Bermuda shorts, and padded out to the pool, where he filled a collapsible chair and thumbed a copy of *Fortune*.

His eyes blinking at the glossy page, he read an article on the hubris and suspicious death of newspaper tycoon Robert Maxwell, never a hero of his, merely a foreign upstart with an Anglicized name. Tossing the magazine, he prided himself in living without backward glances, no memories capable of disturbing his sleep. Closing his eyes, he slept.

He slept an hour and the better part of another one when the collapsible chair bent, twisted, and splintered under his weight. He rose from the shambles rubbing his back and looking for someone to blame: no one in sight.

In the house he listened for his wife and heard nothing. He wasn't even sure she was home. He was nursing his hurts and watching television in his study when she appeared in the doorway, dressed to step out, though her golden shell of hair was tippy. She was letting herself go. Yet never had he seen her looking so attractive.

"The boys won't be home till tomorrow," he said, but she was not interested. The expression on her face was airy, opaque, unexplained, the same expression she had shown when manifestly pregnant. He said, "You going somewhere?"

"Phoebe's."

This mutinous attitude was a phase of hers, unsustainable. He looked at his watch. Five o'clock. "I want you back by seven," he said.

"You want me back by seven?" Her voice was low. Her eyes showed that her mind was working. "Do you know what seven means to me, Paul? The number of fingers you have left after sticking three up your ass."

They met at the Marriott. Harley Bodine had booked the room from Boston, left his office early, and was waiting for her when she arrived. Entering the room, Regina Smith seemed only vaguely in her clothes and soon, he knew, would be out of them. His mind whirled over boundaries that such a short time ago had lain one way and now meandered in different directions.

"I thought you might not want to see me again," he said.

"What gave you that idea?"

He fumbled for something clever to say and then simply smiled. The nearly imperceptible cast in one eye added to her allure and doubled his excitement. The single noise in his head was her name.

"Let's not stand on formality," she said, glancing at her watch.

He loosened his tie. The delicious novelty and stunning achievement of the first time could not be repeated, but now there was this time, which also would never be repeated. Her breasts, abruptly gaining their freedom, frolicked for a moment.

"A story about Phoebe is going around the country club," she said. "Remind me to tell you about it later."

He had an uncle who played the accordion and got people dancing. He wondered whether she'd care to hear about that. A man's rough cough came through the wall. The cough had depth and gravel and grated on their ears.

"I hope the walls don't have eyes," she said.

She was on the bed, the covers peeled back. What had been etched in his brain was now before the eye again. He had a great desire to know what she looked like in the morning, whether

her face was puckered and splotched or pure enamel as it was now.

"Easy," she said, for he was overanxious, ubiquitous, addicted.

Later—he couldn't help himself—he questioned her.

"It was good, Harley. Take my word for it." The man in the next room had quit coughing. Maybe he had left. "Thank God," she said.

They lay apart. He appropriated her hand, confidence in his grip, and told her about his uncle and a certain musical ability that ran in the family. He had played piano as a boy. Gradually, without realizing it at first, he began talking about his first wife, who had gotten the better of him in the divorce. He had been obliged to deal generously with her because his firm insisted on utmost probity when its members' personal lives were exposed to the public.

"I can see how that caused problems," Regina said. She had a cramp in her knee. Would he mind moving a bit?

"Sorry," he said, shifting, still holding her hand. "Glen's medical bills were bleeding me. Insurance doesn't pay for everything. And he wanted to go to medical school. That would have been throwing money into the grave."

"There was no hope for him?"

"None." Bodine sighed heavily. "The accident was a blessing, I guess. It ended his suffering."

"If I were dying," she said, "I'd want to get it over with. None of this hanging around, stringing it out."

"I've learned to view the accident as God's will."

"God's?"

"Yes," he said, looking at her sharply.

"Don't upset yourself," she said and kissed him, their joined hands coming between them. He wanted her again.

Dudley had returned. He started to speak, but Mary Williams put a finger to his lips. "Just let me look at you." She believed they had joined hands in a previous life and had reunited in this one. She stroked his hair. So much to be said, so much that needn't be. Always they had divined the most important of each other's thoughts, which now disquieted her.

"Who's living here?" he asked.

She spoke quickly. "Soldier, you remember Soldier."

They were in the kitchen. He looked about, as if something were missing. "The toaster belongs next to the bread box. He's moved things around."

"He won't again. I promise."

His smile was a thin glint. "Are you sleeping with him?" When she didn't answer, he said, "I don't mind."

"It doesn't mean anything."

"I know that," he said and touched her cheek, warmed his whole hand against it. "I missed you."

"I missed you more," she said and made him sit down. "Where did you get those shoes?" Crouching, she loosened them and pulled them off, along with socks she didn't recognize, and counted his toes like a mother fearful her newborn might not be sound. "You need a bath."

Hot water steamed the bathroom and misted chrome and mirrors. When he eased into the tub, she scrutinized him, again like a mother, to make sure he was intact. She poured water over his head, put suds in his hair, and massaged his scalp. She cleaned an ear, the debris like the black chunk of seeds inside a poppy, and she soaped the back of his neck and shoulders. When he lifted an arm, she soaped him there. "I borrowed ten dollars," he said. "Did you pay him back?"

"John? Yes."

"Do you want to tell me where you've been all the rest of the time?"

He took the soap from her and used it on his chest. He straightened his back. Quite suddenly he was more his grown self. "I had many places to stay. One was a gazebo. Another was a chicken coop."

"You're fooling."

"I'm not." He soaped a sponge and squeezed it over his shoulders. "Mostly I was in a jail cell."

"Now I *hope* you're fooling," she said with a shudder. "We'll talk about it later."

"Yes, later," he said. Alone, he soaked for a while and then dried himself in a luxurious towel. He dressed himself in the clothes she had laid out. A shirt that fitted him. Lightweight trousers that remembered him. Slippers that greeted him. He used a blower on his hair.

She smiled broadly when he returned to the kitchen. "You're your old self, I can tell." Her eyes went to him. "I want you to stay this way. No more of that awful business."

"The money is important."

"You pay a bigger price." She moved closer. "Face it, Dudley, you go off the deep end."

"No, I don't." His face was luminous from the repeating lights of his eyes. "I swim."

Phoebe Yarbrough had been drinking, the best gin and tonic, more than enough to give her a glow. Wearing a silk shirt tucked into denim shorts, she stood tall and erect on legs that looked like bright spears. "Sure you won't have one, Bev?"

"No, I need to be perfectly sober," Beverly Gunner said from the depth of a large upholstered chair. "Are you sure Myles can't hear us?"

"Positive."

"Then please, Phoebe, tell me more about your life back then."

Memories pelted her. She wore a bra under the silk but nothing under the denim. The fly was neglected, and feminine hair escaped like down from a milkweed pod. "You've heard, I'm sure, how the overbred Englishman pants for the blood of a fox. Well, that's not a bad analogy."

"That's the way they were with you?"

"The older ones."

"But they were good to you."

"They had to be. That was a rule." She took a sip of gin and settled in a wing chair, placing her feet on an ottoman. Her white canvas shoes were long and narrow. "I never tolerated vulgarity." She took another sip. "Some wanted to videotape me. I never allowed that."

"Then it wasn't all fun."

"It was work, that's all it was. The challenge was to make the man think you enjoyed every minute of it." Her head dropped back for a moment, with a random thought of her father, his hands weathered by coins, the constant traffic at his toll booth. She remembered the roughness of those hands on her arms, her legs.

"Most," she continued, "came on too strong, wanted too much, as if money bought everything. But they were all manageable and predictable. Men who'd married virgins, more or less, far as they knew, wanted me in white lingerie. Repeat honeymoons. Guys long dissatisfied wanted me in black."

"You must've learned so much."

"I did a short story about it for my writing class. The professor was one of my clients. Needless to say, I got an A." Sitting with splayed knees, she glanced down and made a face. "Why didn't you tell me?" She patted herself in and fixed the fly.

Beverly said, "There must've been some excitement, a certain glamour."

"Sometimes a little fun." Smiling over her gin, she told of strolling Fifth Avenue in high-heel suede boots, stark naked under a full-length mink, her arm linked to a man's.

"The man wanted you to do that?"

"It was Myles. The evening he proposed."

"Oh, Phoebe, that was romantic. Were you in love?"

"No, but I wanted a different life."

"Has he been good to you?"

"He doesn't know who I am. The problem is I know who he is." She threw her feet off the ottoman and uncoiled from the chair to refill her glass. "Are you sure you don't want one, Bev?"

"No, I must be clear-headed. I want you to know, Phoebe, I won't repeat anything you've told me. Ever."

"Don't fret about it." Phoebe returned to her chair with less energy, a smile locked into her bruised face. "I'm sure your husband has already let the story out."

"Yes, that's something he would do," Beverly said after a small hesitation. "Was he a client?"

"It's taken me awhile to place him, but I remember him quite clearly now."

"Was he disgusting?"

"He wasn't a gentleman."

"I'm sorry, Phoebe."

"Not your fault," she said, her smile turning mysterious, as if there existed no situation from which she could not disengage herself, if not physically, then mentally. Her feet were back on the ottoman, her ankles crossed. A restful silence grew until Beverly broke it.

"I've come to a decision, Phoebe."

"Have you? I'm glad."

"I've decided to change my life, and I feel quite good about it."

"Are you leaving Paul?"

"He's leaving me."

"Then make sure you have a good lawyer. I don't recommend Myles. And remember, the only sure thing in a woman's life is disappointment. Or worse."

"I've had the worst," Beverly said.

Regina Smith stepped into her daughter's room. Patricia, watching television, ignored her until a commercial came on. Then she said, "I love him, Mom. You may as well know that."

Regina bristled. "You think you love him. You're enthralled with sex."

"No, I'm enthralled with Tony."

"The boy's a fag."

"No, he isn't! Only *you* would say that."

"But he could be. How do you know anything about anyone in today's world? You're a child, Patricia. You don't have sense, you have whims."

"I don't care to discuss it, Mom. I really don't."

"Yes, you're right. You'll be going back to school soon. You won't be seeing him, thank God."

Patricia's face shot up. "We'll find ways."

Regina reared back at the insolence and felt infinitely fatigued and betrayed by forces impinging on her daughter's life and now on her own. She remembered imagining her uncle's whole hand going up in flames when he lit wooden matches with a thumbnail. Now she imagined flames engulfing her flesh-and-blood child. "I love you, Patricia."

"Then let me live."

She retreated. Downstairs she wandered. Darkness shrouded one room, lamplight opened another. The silence pinged. At an open window a curtain billowed in.

"What are you doing?" she asked.

"Just sitting," Ira said, one leg over the other. He was in shirtsleeves, his tie loosened. "Isn't it time we went to bed?"

"You go ahead," she said coolly. "I'm not tired."

His brow wrinkled, as if all his thoughts were uneasy, which did not displease her. It seemed ages ago that she had loved him. He said, "Should I expect you within a reasonable time?"

"I wouldn't count on it."

Rising, he attempted a smile, a joke, a poor one. "Punishing me for the sins of the son?"

"You may end up punishing yourself," she said.

Soldier drank beer in a bar around the corner from Charles Street, near Massachusetts General Hospital. Part of the time he sat with the nurse he knew. The remote quality of her voice had always placed a distance between them and placed a greater one now that they no longer lived together. She asked how things were going for him with his new friend, and he said he wasn't sure, too much was up in the air. "She's complicated," he said, "like you."

The nurse, who didn't intend to be unkind, said, "Maybe you should lower your sights."

He walked back to Beacon Street, clinking coins in his pocket, passing a homeless man who had kenneled himself in a carton. The sight gave him a chill.

When he entered the apartment with a key he might soon

have to surrender, he knew Dudley was back. The air told him. Then Mary Williams's face did. He said, "Well, what about me?"

"Shh," she said, "he's asleep." She took his arm, ignored the beer on his breath, and edged him into the kitchen. "I'll make you a nice supper. You're hungry, aren't you?"

He laid out dishes in the dining room. She lit candles, instant jewels, then served him and herself an omelette shot with bits of onion, the way he liked it. He said, "You haven't answered my question."

"He says you can stay."

"*He* says. What do you say?"

"I want you to."

"The three of us, huh? That what you want?"

"It'll work," she said, "if you make the effort."

He felt he had cards to play. "I don't like it."

"It's your decision."

He threw his hand in fast. For the first time in his life he feared old age, feared shrinking into a half-life of sicknesses, detested the ugly thought of death. The famous live on in books and movies. The ordinary dead, grunts like himself, just get deader. "We can try it," he said.

The omelette was delicious, the coffee a choice blend, and he began to relax. She had gone out of her way for him. The nurse never had, had never even pretended to care for him, and had kicked him out unceremoniously. Mary had feelings for him.

She said, "I've made a bed up for you on the sofa."

His face fell. "What?"

"It has to be that way, Soldier."

"Where's he sleeping?"

"In his own bed. I'll be in mine."

In the dark he lay under a blanket on the sofa, unable to sleep, unable to control his thoughts, every sound from the street an irritation, sometimes a jolt. The anger grew until he could not cope with it.

He stole through the dark, a soldier on a mission, a certain cadence in his creep, armed only with what God had given him.

Over Mary's bed, he deepened his voice. "This isn't right."
"I know," she said, and made room for him.

Beverly Gunner entered her house without a sound and turned
on only necessary lights, her resolve steeled with the strength of
pure purpose. Ascending stairs, she pictured herself as a series
of arrangements, of which her breasts were the fiercest, her hips
the heaviest, her thighs the meanest. In her bedroom she did
her eyes, poked red on her lips, and dabbed scent behind each
ear. Her hair, returned to its perfect shell, gleamed gold. In the
bathroom she sought something useful, efficient.

Letting light leak in after her, she entered her husband's
bedroom, which smelled both of him and the outdoors. His
snores were flutters; moths buffeted the screens. He had kicked
half out of the covers, and she saw not the flesh and fat of a man
but the near hairless body of a beast ready to be skinned. She
had scissors in hand, the kind for cutting hair. When she stabbed
him, parts of him jumped. He chomped for air.

She struck again, but he seemed to feel no pain, only surprise, then shock. He couldn't breathe. Wonderful. He was a
man drowning.

He gaped at her in disbelief, tangling a frantic arm in the
sheet.

"A woman bleeds," she said, "why shouldn't you?"

She smelled blood but couldn't see any, which was frus-
trating. A knee on the bed, she made another hit, like piercing
butter, no positive strike, which was more frustration.

They fought. His lurid face was heated up the way water
boils, and hers was merely determined. The clenched scissors
again found flesh. She was too large for him. Her hair was a
helmet, her thighs were expansive, her hips explosive. Her knee
dug in.

"You killed my daughter."

His fist shot up. It knocked her back but left him with no
strength to raise his head.

"Now I've killed you," she said.

13

BEVERLY GUNNER WENT OUT INTO THE DARK, WHERE SHE WAS met by phantom breezes and the restlessness of trees. The night was a symphony. Every insect and tree frog for miles around was making music. The dark air, which would have chilled another woman, warmed her.

She dragged a deck chair along with her and some distance from the house erected it on open ground. A beautiful night, many stars, a chunk of the moon remaining. She sat with her head tipped back and under the spread of the sky viewed history, though all that was visible was the punctuation. A little later, she closed her eyes with a smile, no longer obliged to think deeply about anything, her mind uncluttered, her conscience spotless.

In his bedroom Paul Gunner lay without movement. His mind worked, but his body didn't. Every muscle was tightening, his universe regressing, contracting. Somehow he moved an arm, found the phone, and straightened a thick finger. His memory for numbers did not desert him. He called the Stoneham home

of a doctor in whose health clinic he had a substantial invest-
ment. He spoke quickly, his mind moving faster than his words,
which tended to grip his tongue.

The doctor, nevertheless, grasped everything.

Gunner said, "You'll have to restrain her."

Two silent ambulances and the doctor's Infiniti arrived in
thirty minutes, time enough for him to go into cardiac arrest,
but he didn't. He was breathing with difficulty when the doctor,
whose face was sharply cut, the details poignant, scanned his
wounds and administered a shot. Two ambulance attendants,
both burly, gripped him, said, "Heave ho," and landed him on
the stretcher.

On the way down the stairs, Gunner gave further instructions, wheezing each word. His breath was fire, which reached
out and tried to pull the doctor in. "And call Bodine," he said.

"It can wait," the doctor said.

"It can't."

The attendants loaded him into the ambulance and drove
away as silently as they had arrived. The doctor stood with the
men from the other ambulance, both black, one tall like a basketball player. The tall one had a gentle voice. "He gonna make
it, Doc?"

"If he does, he can thank his blubber. You two find the
woman."

"She's not in the house."

They went behind the house and walked the grounds beyond the reach of the floodlights. They called out in one direction, then another, their voices knocking about in the dark.
When they came upon her, she rose from the chair. "I don't
believe there's any blood on me," she said. "Shouldn't there be
some?"

The tall man approached her first. "You just take it easy."

"Something really happened, didn't it?"

"Yes, ma'am, something did."

She smiled. "I was afraid it was only a dream."

Each man took her by an arm, one firmly, the other gently.

At Hanover House, Isabel Williams's sleep was always broken. If her bladder didn't wake her, a dream did. She dreamed of a past lover, a jazz guitarist from the forties, the tips of his long playing fingers worn smooth and producing an eerie melody over her skin. The dream, or perhaps a sound from the depths of the building, woke her. Unable to fall back to sleep, she rose, donned a fitted robe, and stepped into the bathroom, where the mirror mocked her with the skin of her stretched face, as smooth as the guitarist's fingers had been.

She slipped out of her room and in soft slippers traveled the long, well-lit corridor. Here and there a door was ajar, a light on, the occupant unable to sleep without it. Reaching the grand stairway, she paused at the painting of nymphs bathing in a brook. Her eye saw what the guitarist had seen with his some fifty years ago when she was exquisite and he a white woman's dream.

Downstairs, she entered the common room, where coffee was available through the night for those like herself, the small hours a trial, sanity always a chore. Mr. Skully in silk pajamas was slurping coffee from a mug under subdued lamplight, a cane hooked to the arm of his chair. The trace of smoke that once was his hair was wafting into the light. Always he had something out. This time it was his teeth, which he thoughtfully returned to his face.

"They brought somebody in," he said in a crusty voice. "Half hour ago. They got Mrs. Nichols up to see to it."

"Who is it? Anyone famous?"

"A woman. They gave her something. She's out cold."

"Where'd they put her?"

"Heard Mrs. Nichols say the third floor."

She poured coffee from a Silex, half a cup, and carried it with her to the birdcage elevator. Any break in routine was a gift. Any hint of drama was cherished. In the elevator she sipped her coffee and smoothed her hair. On the third floor, some distance down, she approached an open door and heard low voices. A nurse stood at one side of the occupied bed, Mrs. Nichols at the other. Mrs. Nichols's robe was satin, and the glint from her round glasses was sharp.

"What are you doing here, Mrs. Williams?"

She craned her neck for a look at the face in the bed. She saw a crushed helmet of hair and features supremely at rest. "Good Christ, that's Hilda's daughter-in-law."

"Let's keep it to ourselves," Mrs. Nichols said.

"Is she alive?"

"She's quite alive."

"You sure? She doesn't look it."

"Take my word for it."

"Who's going to tell Hilda?"

"I'll attend to it, Mrs. Williams. In the morning."

Clasping her coffee cup in both hands, she took the staircase down to the second floor. A line of light lay under Hilda Gunner's door. With a rap, she entered the room. Mrs. Gunner, a childish sight, was occupied.

"Jesus Christ, Hilda, why use that when you have a perfectly good toilet?"

"This is my place, I'll do what I want."

"I had something to tell you, but it can wait."

"Tell me now," Mrs. Gunner demanded.

"They brought your daughter-in-law in. Feet first."

Harley Bodine, who had got little sleep but was as fresh and alert as ever, arrived in Boston early, law offices of Phelps, Finberry and Monk, where he was valued for his close association with Paul Gunner, through the years an esteemed client worth his weight in gold. Bodine worked twenty minutes at his desk and then called in a young associate. He tossed a sturdy folder across the desk and said, "Think you can handle it on your own, Winger?"

"No problem," the young man said.

Bodine threw out another folder. "This needs tighter language. Don't fudge, you understand?"

"Yes, sir. No problem."

Bodine stared at the part in Winger's hair, as precise as his own. Winger was a Dartmouth grad and had a smooth face pink with confidence. Bodine trusted his brain but nothing else about him. "I'll be with Mr. Gunner all day. Double-bill him." Bodine shut a drawer and rose. "How come everything's no problem for you? Things that easy for you, Winger?"

"There are always ways of doing things, sir. You taught me that."

Some minutes later, in traffic, his well-polished BMW purred for him as no woman ever had, though he had passionate hope for Regina Smith, who could invade his thoughts without warning, her image vivid one instant and wavering the next, as if she were a gift that might be taken from him. He steered onto a ramp. No other woman, not Kate, not his first wife, had had such a hold on him. Merely thinking about her made him large.

On the interstate, he drove with uncustomary speed, slowing only when the number of lanes diminished. Regaining too much speed, he had to swerve to avoid overshooting the Stoneham turnoff.

The medical clinic lay beyond a stand of maples with great sprawls of leaves, some turning before their time. He parked in a reserved space, not for him, near an electrical contractor's van, and entered the building through a sleek double door. The doctor was waiting for him beyond the reception desk. In the doctor's office, he said, "Is he going to make it?"

"He's a lucky man. I'm concerned about infection, but I don't think we have too much to worry about. We set up a special room for him."

"Can I talk to him?"

"I don't know if he's awake. We just gave him more medication."

Alone in Gunner's room, Bodine leaned over him. Gunner's head was deep in a pillow, his face flattened out and yellowish. The eyes burned. He looked like a man unable to die. He gave Bodine instructions in torn whispers. He could not wipe his mouth. Bodine did it for him. "The boys," he said.

"Yes, I'll arrange it." Bodine stepped back. "I'll let you rest."

With what could not have been a smile, too much of a twist, Gunner said, "She's certifiable."

"Yes, that's a plus."

He drove to Andover, to Phillips Academy, parked beyond the Andover Inn, where he had occasionally taken Kate to dinner, and bumped into Ted Pitkin before he had a chance to look for him. Pitkin was with three students, who went on their way. "This is a surprise," Pitkin said, smiling out of his beard. Bodine led him to a bench.

"Mr. Gunner's sons have been here since yesterday. He's due to pick them up this afternoon."

"I know," Pitkin said. "They're at the gym. Volleyball. They're not skilled, but they show spirit."

"Mr. Gunner would like you to look after them for a few days. I'm sure there's dormitory space."

"Of course. Most certainly." Pitkin wore no socks. His ankles ran raw into tennis shoes. "Is anything the matter?"

"Mrs. Gunner is having some personal problems, rather serious. Mr. Gunner doesn't want anything spilling onto the boys." Bodine handed him a check. "This is for your help."

"No need of that!"

"Mr. Gunner prefers it that way." Bodine rose from the bench. "He knows the boys are in good hands."

"Wait a minute." Pitkin glanced at the check. "What'll I tell them?"

"You'll think of something."

Bodine returned to his car, the finish reflecting his approach and the mischievous beauty of blossoming ivy creeping over stone. The rest of the day was his. His and Regina's.

At ten and again near noon, Chief Morgan rang up the Gunners' number, each time reaching only the answering machine, with Paul Gunner's voice telling him to leave his name and number, which he didn't do. He had nothing really to say to Beverly

Gunner, but he felt acutely responsible for whatever might be in her mind. After lunching at the Blue Bonnet, he drove to the Heights.

Newspapers—*Times*, *Journal*, and *Globe*—lay on the wide steps leading to the Gunners' grand front door. He stepped over them and rang the impressive bell, several times. Pushing through shrubbery, he looked in windows and saw only stately furniture in a context of fine walls and floors. Glass strips in the garage doors revealed a handsome automobile in each stall.

He reconnoitered. Nothing foreign floated in the pool. Gardens sprang up only flowers. Walking over the clipped lawn, he saw a deck chair in the distance and went to it, though it told him nothing. He sat in it, feeling both foolish and uneasy.

He drove back not to the station but to the Blue Bonnet. Reverend Stottle was coming out, and he walked with him onto the green. The reverend had a dreamy look. Their pace was slow.

"Ever feel you made the wrong career choice, Reverend?"

"I've had doubts all my life," he said. "Doubts are what make us human. Today distorts yesterday, and tomorrow surely will give today a different twist. It may even bend it all out of shape."

Morgan waved to a woman he'd known since the first grade. She had sons in high school and a daughter in college. He said, "I never seem to come up with clear answers, only more of a muddle."

"Central truths are all that matter," Reverend Stottle said with force and clarity. "The peripheral you don't have time for."

"I'm not sure I'd know the truth if it hit me in the face. That's scary for a policeman."

"Our small darknesses grow deeper as we grow older, Chief. And each of us lives different, rich man, poor man, fat fella, thin one, but we die the same. The lights go out, we eat the ground."

Morgan suspected he and the reverend were a little out of sync, but it didn't bother him. Birdsong filled a void, the sound touching him. "I thought we went to heaven, Reverend."

"We do, and the vehicle that will take us there is a beam of light, nonpolluting, energy-efficient. How does that grab you?"

"How do we get to hell?"

"No transportation needed. Hell is here."

Morgan let the reverend wander on without him. Flower beds on the green were never the same from week to week. Much multiplied, sprang loose, roamed. After several steps Reverend Stottle looked back.

"My wife is worried about you."

"I'm a little worried myself."

"A psychiatrist using hypnotism can bring you back to the baby bottle but not back to God. Come to church this Sunday, Chief."

"That'll do it?"

"No, but you'll hear a super sermon."

Harley Bodine was in her house. "You shouldn't be here," she said, the reproof mildly delivered. She was attending to plants, picking off dead leaves, her back to him. He embraced her from behind and told her how good she felt. Then he told her about the Gunners, the aftermath, Stoneham, Hanover House. "Christ," Regina said, staying in his grip. "She really stabbed him? Scissors?"

"Several times."

She was shocked. Then she wasn't. "He must've had it coming."

"Nobody deserves that."

"You'd be surprised," she said, still in his grip, his face in her hair. Hanover House. She'd heard of it. A discreet place for the rich and famous. Bette Davis was said to have dried out there—or was that at Baldpate? Bodine's hands ran up to her armpits.

"Can we go somewhere?" he whispered.

"Where do you want to go? No, don't tell me."

"I could meet you there."

She inclined her head. "You're getting too much of a good thing."

"You're teasing me," he said.

"You complaining?"

"Never."

Through his voice she heard a sound, which her keen ear interpreted. Her head dropped back. "Kiss me," she said in her most seductive tone, and he did, protracting it. She took his hands and ran them over her. Her stepson stood in the doorway.

"Are you spying, Anthony?"

Bodine leapt back as the boy vanished, like a fish that had been still. With a jolt it was gone. "My God!" Bodine said, his face pale. "I'm sorry, Regina. I'm really sorry."

She smoothed her hair, her dress. "You'd better go."

"Yes." He turned. He stopped. "What can I do?"

"Nothing, Harley. Seems you've already done it."

"Will I see you again?" he asked, his eyes panicking. Hers were quite steady.

"We'll talk about it later."

When he was gone, she picked a sere leaf off the floor. It was brittle as a bug, and she crushed it in her hand. She walked over hardwood. She had a long, gliding step, purpose to it. She mounted the stairs. Anthony stood at a window in his room. His legs ran straight. Such a handsome boy.

"I wouldn't say anything about this if I were you, Anthony. Not a word. It would break your father's heart."

He wouldn't look at her. "I know that, *Mother*."

"Don't call me 'Mother,' I'm not your mother."

"I know that too."

"This will be our secret," she said. "You'll tell no one and live with it. Not a word to Patricia. If you do, I'll tell your father myself."

"You're good," he said. "You're better than anyone."

"I'm glad you see that. From now on, you keep your hands off my daughter, and I'll do what I can to keep Bodine's off me. Deal?"

"Please," he said. "Get out of my room."

———

May Hutchins took time doing her face, muting the liner around her eyes, adding peach to her cheeks. Her lips, brightly painted, were a careful flame. Hearing sounds, she gave a final look at herself and stepped out of the bathroom. Downstairs, she gave a little screech and turned on her husband with anger.

"You scared me half out of my wits!"

"Who'd you think it was?" Roland said. "I made plenty of noise."

"You didn't make enough." The anger disguised anxiety. "What are you doing home?"

"Can't I come home if I want? What are you all fixed up for?"

"I like to look nice. That a crime? I thought you were still on the Stoneham job."

"Job's finished." He washed his hands at the sink. Clean white coveralls gave him the appearance of a milk bottle. May imagined tipping him upside down and pouring him down the drain.

"I suppose you want something to eat."

"No," he said. "I'm going to lie down for a while."

Frustration joined her anxiety. "What's the matter? You sick?"

"I'm fine. Can't I take a nap if I want?"

He stretched out on the sofa in the parlor, his shoes off. She waited a few minutes and then hurried upstairs and used the bedroom phone. Her voice was low and peremptory and blew hot and cold while her eyes counted age spots on her arms, too God-damn many. Replacing the receiver, she assigned blame for her personal predicament on the way the world is run.

Her great-grandfather, fumigated and deloused in Liverpool, was thirteen days in steerage coming to America, where he was turned back at Ellis Island. His voice, so the story went, was shrill and one eye rolled, which put off the doctor, who promptly rejected him as a mental defective. A year later, smart bugger that he must've been, he entered the States through Can-

ada and found work in an apple orchard in Bensington. And here
she was more than a century later, sitting on the edge of a bed
like a cow in heat afraid to moo.

She picked up the phone, punched out the same number as
before, and said, "Meet me at the library."

Regina Smith stood in a wide window and looked out at the
pool. Patricia and Anthony, wearing nearly nothing, were lolling
on chaises, laughing. Anthony's laughter was not altogether natural, nor was the expression on his face when he rose from his
chaise as if someone had cued him, freed him from a chain.

Regina watched him hover over her daughter and press
down with his fingertips. Patricia, responding, opened and
bloomed, the merest material holding her tits together.

Fists clenched, Regina saw him insinuate his hands over
Patricia the way she had manipulated Bodine's over herself.

Slowly Anthony looked up and locked eyes with her. He
was mocking and challenging her all at once.

An ice pick in her heart, she stood frozen. Her vision
blurred.

When she could focus again, Anthony was perched on the
diving board and lobbing a kiss to Patricia. Then he seemed to
lob one at her, which put a second pick in her heart.

She stepped back. The skirmish was his. She conceded it
without a second glance.

Chief Morgan, beside himself, made a third visit to the Gunner
house and came upon a BMW parked in the drive. Harley Bodine was collecting the newspapers from the stone steps. Morgan
slipped out of his car and approached him with a casual step,
the casualness forced. "How are you doing?" he said.

"I'm doing fine, Morgan. What are you doing here?"

"Looking for them. Where are they?"

"If they wanted you to know, I'm sure they'd have told
you."

Stepping closer to him, Morgan said, "I want to know
where Mrs. Gunner is."

"It's not my place to tell you."

"I think you'd better."

Bodine's smile was faint and indulgent, that of a man with the upper hand. "Someone seems to have tipped Mrs. Gunner over the edge. We suspect it was you."

"What are you saying?"

"She had a nervous breakdown, in the course of which she assaulted her husband."

"I don't give a damn about him, I want to know about her."

"Isn't Kate enough for you?"

Morgan let that pass. He had no choice. "Tell me where Mrs. Gunner is."

"It's not a police matter, strictly domestic."

Morgan grabbed the front of Bodine's shirt, crushing up the tie with it. "Tell me!" he said, panic rising in him, as if all facts were imperfect and primed to create only confusion.

"Take your hands off me," Bodine said with utter disdain and cold superiority.

Morgan let go.

Bodine smoothed his shirt, checked buttons, and straightened his tie. His voice unaffected, he said, "Mr. Gunner is recovering from stab wounds at a private clinic. Get the picture, Morgan? Best thing you can do is lie low, though it probably won't help. I'll be surprised if Mr. Gunner doesn't tell me to bring suit against you and the town."

Morgan watched him shift the newspapers and lift a key from a pocket. The key was to the front door. "You're his lackey, aren't you?"

"Gratuitous remarks like that don't help your cause. Don't you know the deep shit you're in?"

"I think you and Gunner have had business with Dudley. You remember Dudley, don't you?"

"Quite well, and yes, your kind of mind would eat up his garbage."

"I think you had your son killed. And Gunner his daughter."

"How criminally stupid you are."

Morgan watched him key open the door and then looked away. The day was tilting toward evening. A single dark cloud looked as if it had been hammered into the sky. His thoughts were of Beverly Gunner. Where was she? Bodine pushed open the door.

"I'm curious, Morgan. Don't you have a life of your own? Yours so empty you have to get into others'?"

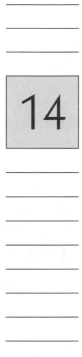

14

THE SAME AMBULANCE THAT HAD TAKEN PAUL GUNNER AWAY brought him back four days later, though the doctor had wanted him to stay longer. His color was off, his strength lacking, and pain remained throughout his upper body. The same attendants who had lugged him out assisted him in. Harley Bodine greeted him. Two Hispanic women who had worked part-time at the house were now full-time. A male nurse was there to monitor him around the clock. The nurse, who had a serene face and arms like a wrestler's, shifted him into the hospital bed that had been set up downstairs, a room near his study.

Gunner said, "I want the boys back."

"This afternoon," Bodine promised.

"They'll have to know what their mother did. I don't want her back in this house. She's homicidal."

"She's comfortable at Hanover House."

Gunner licked his lips, which were dry, and through a bent glass straw sipped orange juice the nurse had provided. "I'm thinking of moving to California, Palm Springs. Get in touch with a real estate agent there."

"What about this house?"

"Put it on the market."

"The market's soft."

"Not for a house like this. Not for money people." Abruptly he lifted an arm, which he shouldn't have done. The pain was sharp. "No VCR on the TV!"

"We'll get you one."

The climate of his body affected his moods. His thumb mashed the button of a buzzer attached to a cord. "Where the hell is he?" The nurse, briefed on his moods, brought him cognac. A taste warmed him. "What the hell was that?" A burst of rain had come while the sun shined. Light foamed the windows. "I'm jittery. Any minute I expect to see her with those fucking scissors."

"No need to worry about that," Bodine said quietly as the nurse left.

"Where's my weapon?" Bodine opened the drawer in the bedside table and showed him. "Give it to me." Bodine placed it in his hand, and he inspected it with respect and pride. It was a semiautomatic pistol with a ventilated barrel, a gift from the National Rifle Association, to which he was a generous donor. "What do you think?"

"Fine means of defense," said Bodine.

"She comes at me again, I'll blow her away."

"The police chief thinks you already have."

"Good. Let him make a fool of himself."

"He's already that," Bodine said and returned the pistol to the drawer.

At Hanover House Beverly Gunner knew long nights, too many wakeful hours, but enjoyed the daytime. On the sun porch she made a path between wheelchairs, walkers, and canes, struck by the seductive way the very old smiled out of their robes for attention. She spent time with each, no more with one than another, for jealousies arose. She read chapters from a storybook to Miss Whittleton, small, sere, and ethereal, who, she was certain, would scatter like pastry crumbs if left unattended too long.

At the indoor pool, in the far wing, she sat with her feet dangling in the heated water beside Mrs. Aldrich, whose body age had given its own idiom of twists and turns. Mrs. Aldrich complained that women far outnumbered men at Hanover House, which made it a hennery.

In the common room, Mr. Skully showed her his pecker.

His voice creaked. "Would you be my girlfriend?"

"I'm spoken for," she said gently.

She and Isabel strolled near a shower of willows to a listing stand of birches. A squirrel clawing the grass stopped, stood up, and stared. Isabel said, "Some day you must meet my Mary, though I'm not sure you'd get along with her. You're much more stable than she is."

The thought of meeting someone from the outside did not engage her. Isabel did. Isabel's face, brimming with blush, apricot makeup, cerise lipstick, and magenta eye shadow was a baroque ornament. Most of the time Isabel looked angry, but it was possible she was not. Beverly said simply, "I like it here."

When they turned back, Isabel said, "We must do something with your hair."

Evenings she spent with her mother-in-law, who was a trial, a voice too much in her ear, a pressure on her sensibilities. Lolling in the consoling heat of a bath, old Mrs. Gunner demanded explanations. "Tell me why you're here."

"It's for the best," she said, waiting with a towel.

Later, bundled in a robe and sunk in a club chair, Mrs. Gunner wanted her hair brushed, her feet massaged. "The others don't do it as well as you," she said, her voice heavy with presumptions. Her potty needed emptying. There was a stool in it. Beverly, drawing the line, told her she would have to do that herself.

They watched Home Box Office until Mrs. Gunner indignantly changed channels. "I don't like all those sex scenes in today's movies," she said with a snort. "You never saw Greer Garson tearing at Clark Gable's fly."

Beverly's eyes were closed. She had not been watching.
"You asleep?"

Her eyes opened. She sat in the fixed glow of a lamp that had the effect of confining her, isolating her. Her voice was clear. "I think Paul was responsible for Fay's death."

Mrs. Gunner reached into a dish of hard candy. "It wouldn't surprise me."

"I think he paid a man to do it."

"I wouldn't put it past him." Candy rattled against Mrs. Gunner's dentures. "Time you went to bed."

Dick English spotted Kate Bodine sitting alone at the country club bar and lavished on her the same look he gave to fine automobiles. Altering his course, he approached her with a pampered abundance of silvery hair, a brilliant smile, and a fine baritone voice. "May I?" Waving away the bartender, he perched beside her. She was a bold figure in tennis whites. "True you're back in television?"

"Radio," she said, unprepared for his company, which she had never encouraged. He was a repeat, a rerun of too many other men she had known in the business.

"That a step down?"

His voice was resonant in her ear. He'd be splendid reading news. She gave him a dig. "When are you getting a job?"

He motioned to the bartender. He decided to have a drink after all, a martini, two olives. "I'm allergic to hard work, makes me break out in a sweat."

He had no money, but his wife did. "How's Germaine?" she asked.

"In New York for a few days. Theater, museums, that sort of thing. Did you hear that stuff about Phoebe Yar—"

"I don't believe any of it," she said swiftly. He was full of gossip, another thing she didn't like about him.

"Have you seen the Gunners?"

"Not lately," she said.

"Something's happening between them," he said mysteriously.

"I wouldn't know."

"I thought Harley might." He had his martini. He lifted up an olive. "One's for you."

"I'll pass." His attention was stifling, his knee touched hers. This was what she despised about him, his drive to reduce a woman to her cunt.

"How is it between you and Harley?" he asked.

"Why do you ask?"

"Things I've heard."

"Something I should tell you, Dick." She finished off her drink, a small Chablis. "I'm not looking for action. Nor am I one of those women who can't bear to be alone. What I want is a companion who'll spring for dinner at a good restaurant, a sensitive and undemanding fellow who can lighten a mood, knows when to hold my hand, and can lie quiet when a presence is all I need."

He was quiet for a dramatic moment. "I could be that."

"You're full of shit," she said. "Besides, I have a true love."

"Don't tell me it's Harley."

She slid off the chair. "Our police chief," she said.

May Hutchins and Fred Fossey were in the sheets, tearing at each other as if Death were at the door. Their bodies ran with sweat and at times slipped away from each other. "It came out," she said. He thrust it back in, but she pulled away. "Did you hear that?" He heard nothing. She pushed him, and he went up on his knees, his head bent back. They each listened hard. "Christ, he's home!" she gasped.

In the instant she was on her feet. She didn't bother with underwear, simply threw her dress on, dug her toes into flat shoes, and gave short shrift to the state of her hair. The state of Fossey enraged her. He had a foot in the wrong leg of his pants.

"Hide!" she said. "Not here, another room!"

For the first time in her life she was frightened of her husband. Frantic but not out of control, she descended the stairs and remembered entering puberty with her eyes averted. Look at her now. Between the dining room and the kitchen, she faced her husband, her smile grotesquely bright.

"You're home." What a silly, stupid thing to say, but she repeated it. "You're home, I said."

Roland stood motionless. Penguin-shaped in his coveralls, a battery of ballpoint pens bulging the breast pocket, he looked tired, understated, played out, like an improbable soldier with too many campaign ribbons. "Yes, May. I'm home."

"Come on," she said shrilly. "I'll make you something to eat."

She forced him into the kitchen and hurled open the refrigerator door. "How about a sandwich? Cream cheese and olive." She already had the bowl out and skinned the Handi-Wrap off it. He was still on his feet. "Sit down, Roland. Aren't you feeling well?"

He sat down. "I need an oil change, that's all."

Busying herself at the butcher's block, her breasts flopping as if unhinged, she said, "After you eat, you can take a nice nap on the sofa." She kept her back to him. "I'm giving you rye bread, that all right?"

"That's fine, May."

She served him the sandwich on a transparent plate, potato chips sprinkled on the side. "How's that for fast work?"

She waited for him to eat.

"May," he said. "Is someone upstairs?"

Myles Yarbrough looked at his watch. Reservations for dinner at the country club were for seven o'clock. He climbed the stairs with a buoyancy lately returned to his step. At present his financial situation was satisfactory, and he was confident that in an emergency he could depend on Paul Gunner for more help.

"You dressed yet?" he called out.

"Getting there," Phoebe called back.

Humming, he approached the bedroom and glimpsed her through the partly open door. She wore nothing. He stood still. He remembered the first night he'd had her company, the absolute precision of her movements multiplied in the wings of a full-length triple mirror. To hell with reservations. He barged in.

Expecting him, she turned on him. "It's not yours."

The quality of her voice affected him physically. He had not heard it before. Viewing her reverently, he stepped closer. "Phoebe, what is it?"

"Don't touch the merchandise."

He didn't understand. What was sailing over his head? When he reached out, she pushed him back.

"You want it, you pay for it."

"I was scared to death I wouldn't see you again," Harley Bodine said, stroking her hair, touching her face, reaffirming she was there, which let her know he didn't want to do without her, ever. She was in his car under pines near Paget's Pond, in the deepening dusk of evening. Her car, needles on the roof, was parked nearby. Bodine was happy, overwhelmed. "I can't believe you're here."

Her head turned. "Anyone could come."

"No one will," he said, a guarantee in his tone. "I don't know how you feel about me, Regina, but I love you. That's the way it plays."

"Play it slow," she said. Handling him, she could not help comparing. Her first husband's dark thing, she remembered, was bent at the top like a farm implement. Ira's, like Bodine's, ran straight to the knob. What did it matter which man she had?

"What brought us together?" he murmured. "I can't remember."

"Cats smell each other out. Maybe we did that."

"You never gave me a look before."

"Now it's different," she said, peering into the shadows of a man who could not believe his good fortune. What irked her was that of the men in her life memory gave her first husband pride of place. It softened his lies and even excused some. Concentrating her gaze, she pleased Bodine with her fist and no doubt would have pleased him more had she not made it seem like labor. Tossing a tissue out the window, she let his head fall

against her. When he looked up, a smugness squatted on his
face.

"Have you noticed? I don't smoke anymore."

"Yes, I've noticed."

"Kate's leaving me."

Idly she touched his sleeve. "Does that distress you?"

"Not in the least," he said from a contentment she was sure
she had never known. "She won't get anything out of me, not
a penny. I'm the aggrieved party."

"Smart, Harley. Very smart."

"Do you know what she asked when the police chief was
bothering me? She asked how much I loved my son. I told her
it was none of her business."

"How much did you love him?"

"More than enough to do what was best for him."

"What was that?"

He sat up, smoothing his hair, then reaching for her hand
to hold. "Let's not talk about Glen. He's gone."

"He's at peace."

"Yes." Loose and relaxed, he was sinking toward her again.
Then he was telling her things she doubted he had told anyone
else, events in his childhood, times he had been left standing
with his face out, incidents when money would have made a
difference. He spoke of his mother. "She wasn't a whore, but
she acted like one."

That was nothing she wanted to hear, and she said sharply,
"It's easy to blame things on our mothers."

"I don't blame her. I think I understand her now."

The separation between the seats made his weight against
her awkward, and she eased him away. Darkness scaled the pines.
A drawn breath increased her chest. When he spoke, she scarcely
heard him, her face vague with inattention. He spoke again, with
concern.

"What's wrong, Regina?"

She expelled her breath. "Everything's right for you, nothing is for me."

"Regina. It can't be that bad."

"You're telling me it can't? I'm telling you it can. My stepson has poisoned the air in my own house. He's turned Patricia against me. You want to hear more? He's holding you over my head."

"Yes, I was afraid of that," Bodine said. "But he'll be back in school soon. So will Patricia—Connecticut, isn't it?"

"That won't stop him." She shuddered. "I can't stand the sight of him."

Bodine wanted to comfort her but was hesitant to touch her. "Then it's that bad."

"Worse," she said. "I wish he was dead."

A car passed on the road, but the headlights failed to reach them. "You don't mean that," he said.

"Then you don't know how much I hate him."

The darkness had patched out the day's heat. The air actually had a chill. Bodine raised his window. "I could help," he said, "but I don't want to shock you."

"Shock me," she demanded.

Kate Bodine, wearing a light jacket over her tennis whites, sat waiting on Chief Morgan's front steps in the evening's diffuse light. A neighbor peered from a window. Coming up the walk, Morgan smiled through a squint of surprise and said, "How did you know I needed a shoulder?"

"A problem, James?"

"Nothing that won't work itself out."

"A positive attitude is what counts." She rose slowly, some of the gallop gone from her sturdy legs. She swept the hair from her eyes. "How about giving a gal a kiss?"

"Mrs. Winkler's looking."

"Mrs. Winkler? Oh yes, Mrs. Winkler." They converged, embraced, and then stepped to the door, a key not needed. "Don't you ever lock up?"

"Never."

He made coffee. He poked about in a cupboard for doughnuts he thought he had. From the table she said, "Don't worry about it. Coffee's enough." For a while her face was free of meaning. It echoed that of a former screen star he could not place a name to. She said, "I've found a place. In Brookline. The irony is that it's a block from the first Mrs. Bodine. Perhaps we'll become friends, though I doubt it."

Morgan said, "Maybe I could come in and see you sometime."

"It's a thought, James."

He had an uncomfortable feeling of being left out, excluded. He sipped coffee. Her voice skimmed to him as if on ice.

"Harley and I have agreed to a no-fault divorce. I want nothing from him, but of course he doesn't believe that. I worry he has something up his sleeve, though I can't imagine what it could be."

"I've tried to quit suspecting things."

She sighed. "My first love was in college, a very charming poli-sci major. First love is forever special, for your eyes are closed. Ever after, they're open. That's what I can't understand. When I met Harley, what didn't I see?"

"You probably weren't looking."

"What makes me so sad? I don't love him."

Morgan got up and poured more coffee. The pot was shiny, and his reflected face reared up like evidence against him. He reseated himself across from her.

"What was your first love like, James?"

"It wasn't special, but my wife was. Later there was someone else, but she did what you're doing. She moved out of town."

"You're not blaming me for something, are you?"

"No, not at all. I've learned to take what comes, and I've learned to wave good-bye. That should earn me some sort of diploma."

"That's a doctorate."

They finished their coffee. She wanted to know the time. Her watch was fast, his was true. He didn't want her to leave, nor did she want to, but she was tired. She had a headache, she said. She was shedding private blood, which in adolescence had been like sopping up some old shame.

"You telling me you have your friend?"

"Sorry, old pal."

He managed a rueful smile. "I knew it would be something."

"You must have a sofa somewhere. Let's stretch out on it like two old farts and watch TV."

They left the table, and he slung an arm around her as they entered the living room. "Actually, except for the other," he said, "I can't think of anything else I'd rather do."

Harley Bodine returned to a dark house and was clicking on lights when the telephone rang. It was Paul Gunner's doctor. Gunner had had a stroke. It didn't surprise him. It almost didn't interest him. His thoughts clustered on a woman the likes of whom he'd never encountered before, a woman with steel and purpose that matched his own, a woman who exceeded his expectations.

"How bad?" he asked.

"Bad enough," the doctor said. "The problem is, he won't let me move him to a hospital."

"Then he can talk."

"He can make himself understood."

"What do you want from me?"

"I have problems here, Bodine. That gun of his. He wants me to shoot him."

"A man has a right to choose. Ask the nurse to do it."

The doctor exploded. "Are you serious?"

"Just joking. I'll be over in a while."

He washed up in the small bathroom off the kitchen. In the glass, his face was keener than he'd ever seen it, as close to the bone as it could get. His eyes overran the sockets. A towel slung around his neck, he returned to the telephone and tapped out a number he felt was his own.

———

Regina Smith made herself a cup of tea. Patricia was up in her room, the door closed. Anthony was dining with his father at the Andover Inn, Ira's invitation, Ira's grope for a compromise that would mollify everyone, no longer a concern to her. She sat over her tea with an elbow on the table and her chin in her hand, her head clearer and calmer than it had been in months. Her assessment of Harley Bodine had risen, and she had to give him his due. Only diamond can cut diamond. Then the phone on the wall rang, jarring her mood. She knew who it was. She grabbed the receiver and spoke curtly.

"What is it, Harley?"

"Are you sure? Absolutely sure?"

"Please don't ask me that again," she said and hung up on him.

She was exercising her mind and her memory with a cross-word puzzle when her husband and stepson arrived home. Anthony went straight up to his room. Ira, looking at once weary and relieved behind his horn-rims, sat near her, crossed his legs, and swayed a well-shod foot.

"We've worked something out," he said.

She shrugged. His words were mere breath as far as she was concerned. His time to act had passed, and now it was hers.

"He's going back to school early. It's all arranged."

"It's too late," she said.

"Regina, what more can I do?" He leaned out of his chair as if snared between two uncertainties, wife and son. Her arm jerked.

"Don't touch me."

It was a stunted hour of the morning when the telephone shrilling from the kitchen woke Morgan. He was still on the sofa, the television murmuring. Kate Bodine was gone. The only evidence she'd been there was the scent on his arm from her hair. The phone rang five or six times before he reached it, his mind groggy, then instantly alert. He recognized the voice, a woman's, right away.

"Thank God you've called."

"I hope I didn't wake you."

"It's all right."

"I'm not sleeping well. The nurse gave me a pill, but she says my body fights it."

"Where are you?"

"I've forgotten, but I'll think of it in a minute. Will you answer something truthfully, James? Quite truthfully?"

"Yes."

"Is he dead?"

"No."

"A pity," she said.

15

IT WAS THAT TIME IN AUGUST WHEN A BREATH OF AUTUMN sneaks into the soul of summer, the summer never a long enough response to the winter, which is never short enough. From the window over the sink, May Hutchins noted that the lilies near the gazebo were past their prime, the once glorious blossoms now hanging like long teardrops. Beyond the bird bath were sprays of goldenrod, among which Queen Anne's lace sought space. For a moment she thought the bird bath had caught fire, but it was only a cardinal splashing about.

Stepping from the sink, she was overly conscious of her own presence and that of Roland's, who was watching morning television in the den. He was spending too much time at home, neglecting his business, leaving too many jobs for his assistant, who was slipshod unless watched. She moved into the doorway of the den. Sitting there in a coat sweater and trousers that had seen better days, he was watching the Disney Channel. Family fare, which irked her. He was rubbing it in.

"Look," she said, "I'm not going to spend the rest of my life feeling guilty."

He glanced up. "No, May, I wouldn't want you to."

Punishing her with too much forgiveness. That was it in a nutshell. "I know what you're doing," she said with acrimony.

"I'm not doing anything, May."

"Fred means nothing to me. It just happened." Her foot stamped the floor. "Why am I explaining?"

"You don't have to."

His eyes didn't reach out, they gathered in. She wanted to scream. She wanted him out of the house. "Why aren't you working?"

"Just not myself," he said, offering a smile. "I think my oil pressure's down. My bearings might be gone."

"You're sick, see a doctor."

"I'm not sick, May. Just not up to snuff."

She turned on her heels. She changed her dress. She put a face on. Returning to the doorway of the den, she waved a book at him. "I never brought it back. I should have, but I didn't, and Holly Pride's dunning me for it."

"Yes," he said, "I've seen the notices."

She could have walked, she usually did, but she drove to the library. When she pushed through the doors, Holly Pride, prim and correct in a lacy blouse, gave her a smile reserved for delinquents. The smile faded and an eyebrow arched at the condition of the book.

"No lecture, please. Just take the book and stamp it in."

"It's mildewed, and the binding's loose. What in the world happened, Mrs. Hutchins?"

A spinster who wouldn't say shit if she had a mouthful belonged in a library. What did she know about the trials and torments of a married woman, of the hammering forces at work in a marriage? At thirty, what did she know about being fifty? "Never should've taken it out in the first place. You want, I'll pay for it."

After a thoughtful pause, Holly reexamined the cover and the binding. "Possibly we can fix it. Did you enjoy it?"

"It wasn't for me, you damn fool. It was for that idiot."

Holly flushed but held on hard to her poise. "This is a book for children, Mrs. Hutchins. Not idiots."

"Don't tell me who it's for. I should've listened to Roland." May's eyes were filled.

"Oh, Mrs. Hutchins, I didn't mean to—"

"Of course you didn't. You don't have the brains you were born with." She pivoted sharply, almost too sharply, and headed toward the doors.

"Mrs. Hutchins."

She grappled with the doors, one of which nearly struck her face. "What do you want?"

"Have a nice day."

Harley Bodine found his daily visits to Paul Gunner's house an increasing chore and an imposition on his thoughts. The doctor, who was leaving, the front door yanked open, said, "I've gone to a lot of trouble for him, all because he won't let me move him out of that goddamn room."

"It's his show," Bodine said.

"I had to turn it into an ICU."

"It's his money."

"That gun of his," the doctor said, his gray hair beaten back in an obedient way, "you'd better get rid of it."

"What's the danger? He can't use it."

The doctor plunged out the door, and Bodine proceeded to Gunner's room, where Gunner lay like a body on water, dead man's float. He was wired to a monitor, his heart spikes on a screen. His feeding was intravenous. Two nurses were now on hand, the second one female, neither needed for the moment. Bodine shooed them away. The Gunner boys were in the room, of negligible concern to him. He disliked one as much as the other.

"You go on now," he said to the elder. "Take your brother with you."

The younger, his face swollen with fright, left at once. Gustav, displaying giant curiosity and obvious concern over the in-capacitated bulk of his father, did so grudgingly, suspiciously.

Bodine approached the bed. The left side of Gunner's face, paralyzed, was aimless. Bodine had never liked him, only his money, all prudently invested, here in bonds and there in the growth industries of health care, pharmaceuticals, genetic en-gineering, medical equipment. The returns would last several lifetimes, but Gunner had only the one. Bodine knew why he was still alive. There was too much of him to die all at once.

Gunner's mouth twitched. It was twisted, crippling the voice. Bodine had to lean close. "I don't want her near the boys," Gunner managed. The effort was not pleasant to look at, or to listen to. "She got me, she'll go for them."

"We'll see that she doesn't."

One eye was nearly closed, the other fully open. "I want security people here."

"I'll arrange it." Bodine had a crick in his neck and straight-ened. Gustav was listening outside the door. Bodine went to the door and closed it. When he returned to the bedside, Gunner was trying to raise his right arm, which had movement but little strength.

"Where's my weapon?"

Bodine opened a drawer and reached in. The weight of the loaded gun frightened his hand, an impossible weight for Gun-ner's. "It's here if you need it," he said and returned it to its place.

Gunner struggled. "I'm not going to make it."

"Perhaps not."

"I want you to be their guardian."

"Of course," Bodine said, pleased.

"Papers."

"I'll draw them up."

"Witnesses."

"We'll have plenty."

The door opened. The female nurse looked in, her hair a hazy bouffant. "How's he doing?"

"I'm afraid he's agitated," Bodine said. "You'd better take over."

Dudley, who seldom received a phone call, received one. Mary Williams, listening only for a moment, got up and went to her studio. Standing at a table, she turned the glossy pages of an oversize art book. Truly good paintings let you see what isn't there. No cry is louder than Munch's. Van Gogh saw the world as one of God's rough sketches. Classical sculptors gave gods heroic penises to set them apart from mortal men. She closed the book and said, "What do you want, Soldier?"

He had come up quietly behind her, his jaws scented with English Leather, which was Dudley's, not his. "Who's he talking to?"

"That's his business."

Soldier stayed close. "He doesn't like me. He doesn't like us sleeping together."

"Has he said anything?"

"No, but—"

"Then forget it." She looked toward the large windows. "If you could travel at the speed of light, Soldier, what you'd see is Picasso."

"What's that?"

"Everything."

Dudley, quiet and immaculate in a white dress shirt and slacks, entered the studio. His tousled hair exhaled a fragrance, her shampoo. A private apology was in his eyes. Mary glanced at Soldier.

"Would you leave us alone, please?"

Soldier left. Opening the book she had browsed, Dudley rubbed one ankle against the other and viewed a graphic of a male figure reduced to scaffolding. Another, heartrending, depicted a mother in death and her children in agony. Mary observed him with an unsparing eye.

"You promised."

"Don't you understand, Mary?"

"No. If it's Soldier, say so. I'll send him packing now."

"It's not Soldier."

Her voice bore in. "Then why are you doing this?"

"It's what I'm good at, Mary. It's the only thing."

Her face embayed in a bonnet, Beverly Gunner said, "I'm quite comfortable here. It's like I'm living in an egg."

"But you can leave anytime."

"Yes, but where would I go? Harley Bodine has had my clothes sent here, and I'm nicely settled in. Besides, he says if I leave I'll be charged with grievous assault with intent to commit murder. Is that true?"

"I wouldn't worry about it," Chief Morgan said.

"I don't. Not in the least."

They were strolling the grounds under a few high-flung clouds and passed a gigantic willow full of murmurs. Birches leaned toward them. Her step was casual, Morgan's self-conscious, as if someone were clocking him. The administrator, Mrs. Nichols, had not believed he was a policeman and demanded identification, then viewed it with suspicion. She was authority, he was not.

Beverly removed her bonnet.

"You've cut your hair," he said.

"Yes, do you like it? Mrs. Williams did it for me."

"Who's Mrs. Williams?"

"I'm not sure you'd like her, but she's good to me and my mother-in-law."

"Your mother-in-law?"

"Oh, yes. We're both here inside the egg."

"I'm not sure you sound happy about it."

"But I am. I'm starting up an exercise class for some women who haven't exerted a muscle in years. Did you know I was a physical education major?"

"I didn't," Morgan said with a smile. "Does that mean you didn't shave your legs?"

She smiled back. "I feel at home with you, James. And I

feel at peace here. Last night I dreamed it was a May morning and all the flowers were awake and smiling at me. My daughter was sitting among them. I woke not sad but happy."

They reached the limits of the grounds. Vines bound a low, crumbling wall as if it were cargo. Ground ivy scrawled dark earth. Morgan gave a start when thunder cannoned out of the distance. She seemed not to hear it.

"I've lost the picture of that man. Dudley. Would you have another?"

"For some reason I carry one around with me."

She took it from him, tucked in into her skirt pocket. "I watch police shows on TV. I know how to be a detective."

The sky threatened. "We'd better turn back," he said, and she swung her bonnet as she pivoted with him.

"You're not afraid of a little rain, are you?"

"I don't like electrical storms. A childhood fear, I guess." He tried to hurry her along, but her step was programmed. She continued to swing the bonnet, which made her seem like a figure from another period.

"I could be wrong about Paul. You see, I hate him so much I blame him for everything. Actually, I hope you'll sort it all out. I trust you to do that."

He wished he held the same trust and was aware of a few past failures likely to haunt him the rest of his life. Their footsteps flattened the grass.

"Sometime, James, could we go out to dinner? Two friends. You see, deep down I don't know if I can go on."

He looked at her sharply. "But you will."

"Yes, James, I will."

They saw a flash of lightning, a white rope across the sky. "Give me your hand," he said, and she did. Together they began to run.

She entered the reception area of Smith, Judkins, Hill & Hall, the decor so much more sedate and elegant than that of the law offices where her husband had a desk but with less and less to do. There, the atmosphere was of malcontents, fault finders, whiners, and a few crooks. Here, an air of propriety hung heavy, which did not prevent, however, a distinguished balding gentleman from letting his attention stray to her lengthy figure. She spoke to the receptionist, a smartly dressed woman with impeccable diction, who said, "I'm sorry, but he doesn't see anyone except by appointment."

"Tell him," she said, "it's Phoebe Yarbrough."

Moments later she entered Ira Smith's office, his surprise evident, his graciousness more so. They sat well away from his desk in dark embroidered chairs, a low table between them. Within minutes coffee arrived. Ira poured.

"I suppose you've heard," she said.

He did not feign ignorance. She'd known he wouldn't, he wasn't the sort. He said, "I don't listen to stories."

"I was Frances then. I changed it to Phoebe."

A small assortment of pastry had come with the coffee. She shook her head when he proffered the dish, only a hint of strain in the gesture. She crossed her legs daringly.

"I had something. Why give it away? Especially when I needed tuition. I entered college late."

He blushed. She'd known he would. No recklessness, only respectability in those horn-rimmed eyes. He was a man of the world only in the narrow sense: Harvard, the Heights, his fiefdom here, which she was sure he ruled benignly, no decapitations.

"You mustn't think badly of me. Whores are wishing wells in which men throw pennies."

"Why do you need to tell me any of this?" he said.

The coffee was rich and fragrant. Cream or sugar would have tainted it. "I want to divorce Myles."

He was startled. "That's a big step, Phoebe."

"Please don't question it." She rattled the cup in the saucer, beautiful bone china. "I'd like you to be my lawyer."

"I don't handle divorces."

"Make an exception. For me. Will you?"

"Myles is a brother lawyer and a neighbor. It's really not fair of you to ask."

"But I am." Cup and saucer were put aside and her legs recrossed, her unshrouded past placed on the table. "Haven't you ever wanted to throw a penny in a well, Ira?"

He was slow to answer, but the answer was firm. "I have a happy home, Phoebe. I've really nothing more to wish for." His eyes went to her, those of a true gentleman. "I'm sorry."

Uncoiling from the chair, she rose with a smile. "It's all right. I understand."

He walked her to the door. She'd known he would. His gaze pressed upon her. "Think twice about a divorce," he said. "I suspect Myles needs you."

She picked a phantom piece of lint from his finely woven lapel. "But you don't."

May Hutchins was glad he was outdoors. In his old coat sweater and shapeless trousers, he was puttering about in the yard. She shuddered when he started weeding a flower bed, for he was sure to pull up something he shouldn't. He stayed at the task until lightning and thunder came out of nowhere and brought him back inside. When rain beat against the windows, she frowned at him as if it were his doing. Nerves stretched, she said, "Please go to work."

"May, I've been thinking it over. I'd like to retire."

"Good God," she said under her breath.

The next day, Friday, the high temperatures of summer returned. Eight in the morning, Fred Fossey's wife, Ethel, left to baby-sit for their daughter, who lived in a newly built bungalow on County Road. Mid-morning, Fossey sneaked home from the town hall and fifteen minutes later let May in through the back door, which shamed her but didn't stop her. In the spare bedroom that had belonged to the daughter, they tumbled about in the heat, striving for more than was there. When they finished, she spun away and fought a forlorn feeling. Fossey, on his knees, said, "What's the matter, May?"

"I like it when it's happening, but not afterward." An arm was flung over her eyes, a bracelet resting on her nose. "Do you have any idea what I'm talking about?"

"No, May."

"I didn't think so."

The next day she went to the library, simply to get away from the house. She flipped through *Cosmopolitan* and *Elle*. When he showed up and sat across from her, she promptly moved to another table, despite Holly Pride's lifted eyebrow and presumptuous smile, as if Holly had keyhole knowledge of her. When she was leaving, Fossey pressed a note on her, easier to take it than not. The penciled words were passionate and conciliatory. At home, she read it again and, setting the paper aflame, watched it writhe in her fingers.

Sunday, without Roland, she listened to Reverend Stottle's sermon but didn't believe a word of it, life being too short for so much avoidance of sin. What's sin now might not be later. The language of Jesus, the reverend said in an aside, was Aramaic, which sounded to her like a shampoo. With other congregants she dropped to her knees to address her maker, whom she suspected had little or no interest in her.

"You want to do something for me, make me eighteen again."

While she was picking up the Sunday papers at Tuck's, Roland was pruning a hedge, though his crocodile arms lacked reach. Wearying of the work and of the sun on his neck, he entered the cellar through the bulkhead and returned the clippers to the proper place. Climbing stairs, he thought about things that had vanished, the soda fountain at Pearl's Pharmacy, Jiggs and Maggie in the funny papers, the spring from his step. He was tired. In the front room he sat on the sofa and removed his shoes while awash in a tide of memories. Stretching out, he closed his eyes, and all in a moment his world was gone.

He lay stone still while his watch told time. Death molded his face into another self, which had little to do with what had been the live one. After eight minutes at room temperature, his brain sensed it was no longer needed and began decomposing.

May glimpsed him on the sofa, thought he was asleep, and didn't disturb him. She lay the Sunday papers on the kitchen table and used the bathroom. Fixing the back of her hair, she was clumsy with the hand mirror and dropped it, breaking the glass, her image with it. Seven years' bad luck. She returned to the table and read parts of the Sunday *Globe*.

A half hour later, she went into the front room. When she couldn't wake him, she didn't scream. She phoned Dr. Skinner and stood immobile near the window all the time it took him to arrive, which could not have been as long as it seemed. He was presentable. His fly was zipped.

"Nothing we can do, May."

She didn't quite believe him. She had thought he would administer a shot to the arm, a pound to the chest. "Are you sure?"

"He's gone, May. He's with God."

Those were the lies in life one had to prepare for. She folded her arms tightly high over her chest. Dr. Skinner's fatalistic stare was an affront to her intelligence.

"I'll call for an ambulance," he said and went to the telephone. When he got off it, she was tottering. "May, I'd better give you something."

"I'm all right." Her voice, though unnaturally high, was steady. "Does death come as a shock to the body or is it a blessing?"

"A bit of both," Dr. Skinner replied. "The body has its own way of dealing with things."

"Fine for him," she said. "What about me?"

Sunday evening, tuned to the Bravo Channel, Chief Morgan watched an old French detective movie, *film noir*, in which a police inspector, habitually wearing a fuming cigarette on his lower lip, traced a killer of women to the depths of a public latrine, a dungeon of no return, the humid walls running with graffiti. The killer, unable to urinate in the presence of others, busied himself at a sink until he thought he had the place to himself. The inspector stood mute in a supposedly vacant stall. When he revealed himself, pistol in hand, a knife came at him like a flash of underground water. His body drank it. His cigarette clung to his lip as he fired off a single reverberating shot and collapsed outside the stall. In dubbed English, he thought of his soul as an erose leaf tearing loose from the twig. Dying on his feet, the killer pissed on him.

The ending flattened Morgan, and he had to force himself from the sofa, his thoughts burdened with the conviction he lacked the stuffing for his job. A sense of fraud followed him to the refrigerator, in which nothing looked appetizing. When the phone rang, he was heavy on his feet, each step a stamp.

It was Beverly Gunner.

"The man in the picture. Dudley. I know who he is."

The receiver wedged between his jaw and shoulder, Morgan shook cornflakes into a chipped bowl. "What does it prove?"

Her voice trembled. "You're the policeman, James."

He did not have the heart to disabuse her.

One side of his face empty, Paul Gunner gazed up asymmetrically at his elder son and spoke in the crippled voice. "She comes here, you know what to do."

"Yes, Papa," Gustav replied, prideful his father had chosen to speak privately to him, without Herman.

"You don't want her to get you."

"She won't get up the stairs, Papa. I'll see to that."

"Your papa's helpless," Gunner said, his voice wavering.

"You'll get better!"

"I know numbers." Gunner's eyes were teary. "I know the odds."

"Don't cry, Papa."

"You boys will get everything."

A few moments later Herman came into the room. His face hung out like an apology for being there. "How's Papa?"

"Leave us alone," Gustav said.

The male nurse appeared, displaced both boys, and looked down at the bed. "How are we doing, Mr. Gunner?"

Gunner didn't respond.

Isabel Williams stood splendidly straight, extended a hand, and said in a charming voice, "A pleasure to meet you, though I must say I've never been interviewed by a policeman. You look much too pleasant to be one." She led him into a small sitting room off the vestibule, where there was privacy, cushioned captain's chairs, and vases of wildflowers.

Seated, Chief Morgan said, "It's very nice here."

She smiled through the seamless glaze of her stretched face. "Never has an inmate lived so comfortably. Almost obscene, wouldn't you say?"

"You're not confined."

"Not in the sense you mean." She leaned forward in her chair, an elbow propped on her knee. The low top of her dress revealed modest breasts the pale yellow of certain apples, the nipples the button caps of mushrooms. The scent of her perfume fanned out. "If you don't mind my asking, how old are you, Chief Morgan? Older, I suspect, than you look."

"I'm vain about my age," he said.

"Ah, like me. I won't ask you to guess *my* age." She sat back, crossing her legs and exhibiting the waxy smoothness on her knees. "What is it you want to know about Dudley?"

"What's his full name?"

"I'm not sure I ever knew."

"Dudley his first or his last name?"

"Could be either."

"Tell me about him."

"A frivolous man—effete, to my mind—and a born liar. He claims he went to Harvard, which is pure bullshit. He lives in a fantasy world, though I'll admit he's clever, clever enough to sponge off my daughter. Pains me to say this, but she's also a fruitcake. Do you have children, Chief Morgan?"

"No."

"You're fortunate. What in the world do you want with Dudley? Beverly Gunner was very mysterious passing around that picture. I'm afraid she's in her own world too."

"Dudley claims he kills children."

"Sounds like something the silly ass would say. What can I tell you? He enjoys shocking people."

"He claims he does it for money."

"Bully for him. It would be the first time he earned a dime of his own."

"Then you don't believe a word of it?"

"No, but it's interesting you do."

"I didn't say I did," Morgan said, shifting in the chair. "Could he have known Harley Bodine?"

"I don't know any Harley Bodine."

"Paul Gunner?"

"Hilda's son? Yes, indeed, some time ago when my daughter visited me more. Dudley used to tag along and wait in the lobby. He was never shy about introducing himself. Paul Gunner during his visits took a shine to him. God knows what they talked about, but I'm sure Dudley amused him. I remember thinking a genius and an idiot. They go together."

Morgan, quiet for an extended moment, said, "Do you have Dudley's address?"

"You'd have to ask my daughter."

"May I have her number?"

He provided a ballpoint and a slip of paper. The paper was a cash register receipt, on the face of which she jotted a Boston number. "You won't upset her?"

A stillness hung over his face. "I promise."

"Does this have anything to do with Hilda's granddaughter?"

"Why do you ask?"

"It's not hard to put two and two together, though don't be surprised if you come up with five."

"I usually do," Morgan said.

Sitting uneasily on a bench in the Public Garden, Regina Smith frequently consulted her watch to give passersby the impression that time mattered to her. Only the useless and forsaken sat alone on public benches and watched bits and pieces of life float by. It bothered her that strangers might think her devoid of destination and purpose. Her worst fear growing up was being thought common.

A poorly dressed man shambled up the walkway with a face

in danger of being a mere skull. Auschwitz and AIDS, each at the same time, popped into her head. Christ, let it not be him. A trash barrel abruptly occupied him. A noisy passel of children paraded by, two women in their midst. Then someone dropped down beside her. She glimpsed a boyish tousle of gray locks and crested buttons on a blue blazer, which looked brand-new.

"Beautiful day," he said.

That was what he was supposed to say whether the day was that way or not. "If it doesn't rain." She said that on her own. Then: "Dudley?"

He dimpled when he smiled. "I would have liked to have been born with a silver spoon in my mouth, but it wasn't there."

A number of overly fed men and women tramped by, one after the other, as if obesity were contagious and epidemic. "I don't need explanations," she said.

"Do you have the money?"

She had booty from her first marriage, wise investments she had converted to cold cash, contained in a weighty accordion folder secured by sturdy laces. She passed it over, and he undid the laces, reached inside, and rubbed a thumb over one of the bands of bills as if to determine authenticity.

"The correct amount, I presume." He placed the folder beside him. "I believe we're in business. I may have questions."

"You won't."

"If he has an automobile, I'd like you to disable it."

She looked at him coldly.

"It's really not that tricky," he said. "I'll tell you how."

In his office, with a feeling he was winding inward, Chief Morgan rang up the Boston number and got a woman's voice, quite pleasant, somewhat professional. He said, "Miss Williams, my name is James Morgan. I'm the police chief in Bensington. Your mother gave me your number."

"She's all right, isn't she?"

"She's fine. She said you could tell me the address of your friend Dudley."

"I could have," Mary Williams said without hesitation, "but

I haven't seen him since last spring. He was living here, you see."

"You don't know where he is now?"

"I wish I did. He left owing me money. I attract the wrong kind of men, my mother probably told you that. What has he done?"

Morgan let a pencil slide from his grasp. "Would you know his full name?"

"He was rather theatrical. Dudley was all he went by."

"Where's he from?"

"I don't know. He told many stories."

"Where did you meet him?"

"In the Public Garden. I do tend to pick up strays. I have one now. You haven't told me what Dudley's done."

"I merely want to talk to him."

"I wish I could help you."

"I may get back to you."

"Please do."

Morgan, loosening his shirt, made another phone call and learned from a man identifying himself as a nurse that Paul Gunner had suffered a stroke. The pencil he had allowed to escape he retrieved and broke in two. He stepped from his office and sank into a chair alongside Meg O'Brien's desk.

"What's happening, James?"

"Too much," he said, "and not enough."

16

THE SUN FLOODED THE FRONT ROOM AND RACED THROUGH
May Hutchins's hair, in which she had let the gray creep back.
Roland's ashes were in a brown paper parcel, as if delivered in
the mail. Everett Drinkwater, the undertaker, had placed the
parcel beside Roland's picture on the table near the window. She
had not wanted the ashes in the house but eventually had come
around. "Not much to show for him, is there?" she said.

Seated on the sofa, Drinkwater said, "The shame of it, May,
is he wasn't that old."

"He was running on failing batteries," she said, her eye
moving to the picture.

"Death does what it wants," Reverend Stottle said from an
armchair. She had served sherry, which he appreciated. His second glass, which he held by the stem, had begotten a mood, one
not all that different from Drinkwater's.

Drinkwater, who usually didn't like to explore the subject,
said, "The greatest mystery in the world is what it's like to be
dead. I still haven't figured it out."

"He didn't have enough fuel in him to continue the fight," May said. She sat herself in a chair near the reverend, diagonal to Drinkwater, and unknowingly flaunted her legs.

"In death," the reverend said, "one joins the speed of light. In near-death experiences the light is glorious. In death it's blinding."

"Then how do we see God?" Drinkwater asked.

"There's no need."

May had left her sherry glass somewhere and didn't feel like fetching it. Drinkwater, divining the bind, lifted himself from the sofa and retrieved it for her. He also freshened the reverend's glass and his own. "When I was a girl," May said, "I saw Jesus in a dream. I've never forgotten it, but I wonder if he'll remember me. I've changed so."

"Age is a disguise," Reverend Stottle said. "When you enter the kingdom of heaven, you can tear the mask off and be that girl again."

"When I die," Drinkwater said, "what are they going to do for me in heaven? If they give me my teeth back, I'll settle for that."

May put her glass aside and brought her hands together under her chin. "My daughter's upset because I had him cremated."

"It was your choice," the reverend said.

"My son is even more upset. He won't speak to me."

"You can't please everybody."

Drinkwater said, "There are some who say you come back."

"Reincarnation is just another word for recycling," Reverend Stottle said. "So it's quite possible."

May's head swayed to one side, as if overtaken by consuming passivity. "I was a giddy piece of ass, that's what I was."

Drinkwater pretended he hadn't heard. Reverend Stottle said, "The idiot exists in all of us."

"A woman does what she has to do, even if it's wrong. You men wouldn't understand. Too many differences between us."

"The only difference, May, is between the legs. Everett and I have stubs, you have an ellipsis."

"What's an ellipsis?"

"This is getting a bit thick," Drinkwater said, and cleared his throat. "I think caskets should be womb-shaped so that the deceased may be placed in the fetal position. This would not only return the person to his beginnings but suggest the anticipation of rebirth."

May put her hands to her head. "You were right the first time, Everett. This is too much." She stretched an arm. "Will one of you help me up?"

Drinkwater was the gentleman, though the effort put a strain on his back. A kind of strangeness came over May, who stood flat-footed, her gaze inward.

"When you lose your mate," she said, "you have nothing to look forward to."

Reverend Stottle, on his feet, said, "Only if you let yourself think that way."

Her face was in sunlight streaming through two windows. Emotions had obliterated one mask and were revealing another. "Please," she said, "the two of you get out of here."

The bed was cranked up, hiking Paul Gunner's head and shoulders. His left arm drooped uselessly while the right struggled for strength. "Let me help," Harley Bodine said and gripped the wrist. With supreme effort, the pen loose in his curved hand, Gunner affixed a signature, little more than a hen track, to a redrawn will, to which the male nurse was a witness. Bodine notarized it. The nurse left.

"I have no patience for this," Gunner murmured. His large, loose face lacked texture, as if the essential oil were gone from the skin. "About the other matter."

"You'd better be sure about that," Bodine said.

"You have it on paper?"

"Yes."

"You fix it up, tighten the language." The voice swerved away from itself, then straggled back. "If I could do it in equations, I wouldn't need you."

"You'll need me even more afterward," Bodine said. "For the boys."

"They'll carry on my name. Gustav has my brain."

Bodine lowered the top of the bed, which was like lowering a shrine. Gunner's pajamas were gold-trimmed, the breast pocket monogrammed. Bodine said, "You understand I can't implicate myself."

"Time comes, just put it in my hand."

Bodine's expression, remote, impersonal, softened. "The least I can do," he said.

The three of them, early risers. From her studio window, with a morning song of emotion, Mary Williams watched the sun creep through the Boston sky. It was like paint on a canvas. Her mood altered when she heard Dudley go out, a whistle on his lips. Moments later, his regimen of push-ups and sit-ups cut short, Soldier came into the studio.

"He goes out, where's he go all day? What's he do?"

"He has friends," she lied, for truth was an enemy. It could wrap you into a bundle of nerves.

"One of these days he won't come back. Somebody will run him over."

That was merely one of several scenarios, by far not the worst, running through her mind. The worst could wake her in the night, only Soldier to cling to. She said, "One of these days it'll be over."

"You got me, Mary. Forever, if you want."

"What's 'forever,' Soldier? Ten years, twelve?"

"I take care of myself. You want, I'll live to be ninety. I could go to a hundred." He stepped toward her, his head rearing out of a gray athletic shirt, his jaws shaved close. "There's another factor. With me, you're a woman. With him, you're not. You want to deny that?"

Much later in the day, she walked the length of Charles Street and around the corner to the Harvard Gardens, where the bar was busy and most of the booths occupied. She caught sight of a nurse's uniform in a rear booth, strode to it, and slipped into the opposing seat. "I'm Mary Williams. Thank you for being here."

The nurse, Lydia, said, "Your call surprised me." The work-worn uniform gave her a vague resemblance to a rumpled bride. Her hair, blends of brown, was whipped back and gripped in the snarl of a rubber band. "That's white wine if you want it. I don't have much time."

"I won't waste it. Was Soldier good to you?"

"You want me to give a reference, is that it?"

The other booths were noisy. She didn't want to raise her voice, so she leaned over a wineglass, nearly tipping it. "I need to know. Was he good to you?"

"He knew where he stood with me. He filled a temporary need, and then he got on my nerves. *I* wasn't good to him."

She trusted the face and, entranced by the hard play of bones, wished she could sketch it. Maybe later, from memory. "Thank you," she said.

Lydia gathered herself to go. "What is it, Mary Williams? You in love with him or something?"

She took out money for wine neither of them had touched. "I don't want to be alone."

"Then you could do worse."

His car on the blink, Anthony Smith was one of many waiting on Main Street near the academy for a Boston bus. It was a soft and sunny, irresponsible day, slightly breezy. A student he knew distorted the corner of his mouth with a hooked finger to amuse his girlfriend. Two faculty wives, slight of figure but robust in voice, were sharing thoughts. Beyond them all, a man he didn't know but had seen on campus, a new teacher perhaps, smiled at him. Then the bus came.

He met his stepsister in South Station, where she arrived from Connecticut by Amtrak. She flew into his arms, her overnight bag tumbling between them. They kissed, they hugged. "Did you miss me, Tony?" He'd missed her much more than he'd thought he would. He'd missed her the way he would have one of his arms. "Do you have a place for us?"

"Marriott Long Wharf," he said. "We can walk there."

The room was high up, and the large window overlooked the murk of the harbor, the white stillness of pleasure boats, the ribbed archways of Christopher Columbus Park, the beaded glitter of traffic on the Central Artery, and the shooting sapphire lights of a police cruiser. Patricia said, "I don't want ever to lose you. Don't let them do anything."

He saw a loveliness he'd taken for granted and sought to make amends. His hand in her clothes stuck to her like a stamp. "You're letting the hair grow back."

"Summer's over."

"I do love you," he said in a tone that left no doubts, no questions.

"Then why did you keep me guessing so long?"

A push landed him slant-wise across the quiet cobbles of a down comforter. Her knees bestrode him. Sloping over him with palms planted on his chest, she ground against him as if the joy of life were overwhelming, every piece of it encased in the urgent. She rode him with her eyes clamped shut, her nostrils flared, and her jaw shoved to one side. When she collapsed upon him, she shed tears—happy ones, she said, but they alarmed him, heightening a sense of responsibility.

Her hair covered a pillow when they made love again, he the aggressor this time, with the same air of necessity she had shown. Afterward, they went straight off to sleep, nothing to disturb them except an unremembered dream or two.

It was evening when they rode the elevator to the lobby. On their way to the dining room they passed a man sitting on one of the leather couches, a magazine in his lap. Patricia glanced back and poked Anthony.

"Did you see how he stared at us?"

Anthony looked over his shoulder, narrowed his eyes, and said, "He was on the bus with me."

———

Ira Smith played golf that afternoon and played it badly. When he teed off, the ball failed to make head against a stiff breeze. Shots usually made he missed. Everything was off, his step, his rhythm, his reaction, as if something had untuned him. He stuffed an iron into the bag and quit early. Much pressed upon him. He suspected his wife of having poured sugar into the gas tank of his son's car, the engine rendered useless. Worse, he suspected her of infidelity, but did not want to confront her. He was reasonably certain that if guilty she would not deny it.

He let an attendant take away the motorized cart and his bag of clubs. A maple full of leaves shook some loose and yielded birds. Curving overhead, dipping a wing like an oar, a small pleasure plane was carried by a current. On his way into the car lot, he glimpsed Myles Yarbrough's sun-scraped face and saw no way to avoid him.

Looking up, sweeping back his thinning hair, Yarbrough said, "When I was a little kid I used to wonder if airplanes did harm to the sky. You know, if the propellers tore holes."

Ira exchanged his prescription sunglasses for his horn-rims. Yarbrough fell in stride with him.

"I'm stupid about so many things. To this day, I don't know how ocean water can support the weight of a ship."

"I used to know," Ira said, "but I've forgotten."

Yarbrough rubbed his forehead, a rusted surface of faint freckles. He looked as if he needed a drink of water. "Phoebe said she saw you. I guess you know everything."

"I'm a lawyer same as you, Myles. Everything's in confidence."

"I guess you think I'm a fool."

"There are all kinds of fools. You could be one kind and I another."

They approached their cars. Yarbrough drove a Jaguar he could not afford but felt he owed to himself. "But you must wonder why I married her. The thing is, Ira, it was different. It was like playing with fire."

Not that far away, oblivious of the world, Anne Lapierre

and Dick English were engrossed in conversation. A headband gave Anne a girlish look, adding to her considerable appeal. English obviously enjoyed looking at her. Her eyes were promises. Her lips were never quite together.

Yarbrough said, "I want to keep her, I really do. Do you think I have a chance?"

"Don't ask me what you know I can't answer."

"I'm just trying to ride it out, it's all I can do."

"Occasionally that's enough."

Anne, the sun blazing in her red hair, noticed them and waved, but only Myles waved back. Ira felt queer in the face and light in the head. Eyes brimming, he saw too much.

Yarbrough said, "What would you do?"

"Exactly what you're doing," he replied.

When Chief Morgan arrived at the police station, Meg O'Brien had a mouthful from a sandwich and struggled to speak. She half rose from her desk and gesticulated. Sputtering, she said, "Get over to the Heights . . . been a shooting."

His heart sank. "Where in the Heights?"

She told him the number, the name. She wiped mayonnaise from her upper lip and added, "Eugene's already there."

"What next?" he said, not to her.

He drove with a wind up Ruskin Road to the Heights and swerved through the Gunners' stone gateway and up an avenue of tapered arborvitae. Sergeant Avery's cruiser was parked between an Infiniti and a BMW. The cruiser was leaking oil. The Infiniti bore an M.D. plate.

As Morgan approached the front entrance, Sergeant Avery came out of it. The man behind him, tailored smartly, looked every inch a doctor. Sergeant Avery said, "Ambulance just left, Chief. Guy named Gunner shot himself."

The doctor stepped forward. "You'll excuse me."

Morgan grabbed his arm. "Tell me about it."

"Mr. Gunner had suffered a serious stroke and was depressed. That's it."

"If he had a stroke, how'd he manage to hold a gun?"

"Not very well," the doctor said and pulled free. "In a manner of speaking, he's still alive."

"If you can call it that," Harley Bodine said from the doorway and stepped out with a cold smile.

The doctor pushed on. Sergeant Avery stood with his hands in his pockets. Morgan let his arms dangle.

Bodine said, "I feel sorry for the both of you, him more than you. Poor bastard doesn't know how to die."

He was back the next morning, sitting in Christopher Columbus Park, the air festive. Stainless steel pushcarts under umbrellas of flaming colors dispensed ice cream, popcorn, croissants, German sausages. Peddlers hawked leather goods, handcrafted jewelry, silk scarves, pocket tabulators. From the street a bannered car with a roof sign and speaker promulgated a political candidacy. A breeze from the harbor smelled human. Dudley reckoned they would sleep late and was right. At noon they emerged from the Marriott. He bought a croissant and followed them.

With silly abandon they cut through traffic surging through the streets under the steel fretwork of the Central Artery. Dudley had to dodge cars to keep them in sight. He figured they'd head for Quincy Market and was wrong. They went all the way to Summer Street and walked it to Washington. The boy had the build of a runner, the girl a healthy robustness that made him think of things to eat. He ate the croissant while they window-shopped Filene's.

On busy Bromfield Street they stepped into the doorway of the Massachusetts Bible Society and talked quietly, deep into each other. They looked melancholy, in need of a laugh. Poised across the street, shielded by a streaming sidewalk crowd, Dudley saw love in their faces, beauty in their youth. In their melancholy he read a relationship not unlike his and Mary's. When they stepped from the doorway, the girl drew her arm through the boy's.

On Tremont Street, traffic held still for a moment and then

plunged ahead. The boy and girl muscled through a crowd in which Dudley, prone to head colds, was aware of sniffling noses and hectic sneezes. He drew too close when the girl stopped at a display window and produced a tube to do her lips. "I want always to be pretty for you," he heard her say.

When the lights allowed, he followed them across the street to the wide sidewalk along the Common and fell to a reasonable distance behind them. But when a man behind him made a spitting sound, he quickened his step. A woman, blown sideways by a new rush of traffic, held onto her dress.

He trailed them to Boylston Street, where the girl looked over her shoulder as if she sensed eyes aimed at them from the distance. Two men cut in front of him, one ranting, his heavy hand butchering the air. A caravan of silver and green buses, monster-size, jolted by. The fumes offended him, but a woman casting crumbs for pigeons pleased him.

Near the corner of Charles, where traffic ran breakneck, he caught up to them. The girl's name he didn't know and didn't need to. Anthony was enough. He liked the way the three syllables bonded themselves together. He liked the way Anthony's fair hair flopped over his head and spilled to the nape of his neck. The girl's hair was a rush of blackness embracing her shoulders.

Lights, which had held the traffic, released it. When he drew up behind them at the curb's edge, he saw the girl's face in bold profile and heard her say, "It's that creep." The tone was Sweeney's, and the words seemed to lie against the air like the faint ink on an old letter, the writer long vanished. A crowd compacted against them. The girl, barely turning her head, said, "Fuck off."

Cars shooting around the corner were perilous in pursuit of each other, one after another, tires squealing. A taxi charged. It was not Anthony he pushed in the small of the back, it was the girl, but Anthony lunged after her. Cars immediately began slamming against one another, the noise thunderous. The reek

of antifreeze and gasoline was fierce as hoods flew up and ra-
diators gushed. Anthony had been thrown, the girl dragged.
Dudley, an anonym in the hysterical crowd, slipped away.

Chief Morgan heard the report on the radio, Kate Bodine's
voice: a teenage couple had been struck at the corner of Boylston
and Charles. The girl was pronounced dead at the scene, and
the boy was in critical condition at Massachusetts General Hospital. Police were withholding their names until the families
could be notified. Morgan was at his desk. He'd been sorting
through the contents of a bottom drawer, but now he sat back
in his chair with no skill in keeping his mind from racing. Ten
minutes later he phoned WBZ, got hold of Kate, but she knew
nothing other than what she had reported.

"Why are you interested, James? This is Boston, not
Bensington."

"I'm a news junkie."

"Don't play games with me."

"It's an excuse to hear your voice," he said. "How are
things? Are you happy or sad?"

"Too busy to be either."

"I miss you."

"When I get five minutes to myself, I'll miss you too."

His next call was to the Boston Police, Division A, but the
sergeant who talked to him said that the investigating officers
were not available and their report not yet prepared. "Would
you call me when it is?" he said, doubting the likelihood that
anyone would.

He went home.

His mind was hot, overpacked. TV was an anodyne. Lying
on the sofa, his shoes off, a blanket thrown over him, he watched
a sitcom, which he tried to find funny. During a commercial he
fell into a deep sleep that carried him well into the night and
would have lasted until morning had the telephone not shattered
the quiet.

"Is this the residence of James Morgan?"

He didn't recognize the voice, which lacked a human quality and could've been piped into a court of law where justice was truly blind and all judgments final. "Yes," he said.

"The police chief?"

He tried to get a focus on his watch. He thought it read eleven-fifteen. It was five to three. "Yes."

"My name is Ira Smith. I live on Bellevue Drive in the Heights. I want you to come here."

Mary Williams couldn't sleep and woke Soldier, who said, "What are you worried about? He's back, that's what you wanted."

"I know," she said, the covers pulled to her chin. Her voice was tinny. She had only a faint hold on her emotions and would have had none at all without Soldier, whose hand rested on her stomach. "This time he's gone too far," she said.

"Too far for what?"

Her eyes fought the dark. She wanted to see the ceiling. "This time they'll get him."

"Get him for what? What's he done?"

"What I told him not to do."

"You say things, Mary, but they don't tell me anything."

She thought of things that saddened her: a butterfly deprived of its wings, rain on the window in November. In November her father had submitted to the terror of depression. "The girl," she said, "was a beautiful child."

"What girl? You'd better start clueing me in."

"How much do you love me, Soldier?"

"You already know. How much do you trust me?"

She told him about the child Fay, the afternoon on the bank of the Charles, a picnic for many children, with games and music. The little girl, wandering off, accepted Dudley's hand along a stretch of paved bank, where he took his hand away and told her to look down. Keep looking. Keep looking.

"Jesus Christ, Mary."

She told him about the boy Glen, who looked fourteen but was sixteen to the day and wore braces. Who'd had a newspaper opened to his horoscope. "Both were flawed."

"That's why he did it?"

"There was money involved, but that was not the reason."
Her eyes pierced the dark. The ceiling glimmered. "The thing
is, Soldier, he's done it again."

"Jesus Christ."

They rose from the bed and went into the bathroom. She
used the toilet. Then Soldier did. He showered, and she washed
up at the sink. Drying himself, he said, "I don't get it. Why does
he do it if not for the money?"

"It releases him. It lets him soar. It makes him special."

"And you let him do it?"

A sigh came from her depths. "You don't understand. I
wouldn't have been able to stop him, and I didn't want to lose
him."

"What about the money?"

"He always gives it to me."

She put on a robe, and Soldier donned fatigues. In the dark
of the passage she put an ear to Dudley's door and heard the
sound of his sleep, which she knew was deep, as if drugged. In
the kitchen she made herbal tea for herself, instant coffee for
Soldier.

"He'd never survive a state prison," she said, and for moments her features lacked prominence, like a headstone too often
rubbed. "They'd tear him apart."

"Loony bin is where they'd send him."

"He wouldn't survive that either. He'd drown."

Soldier tested his coffee, enjoyed the swallow, and took another. "You're asking me something."

"Yes," she said.

"What do I get out of it?"

"What you've never had. A home."

In the predawn dark Chief Morgan drove to the Heights, to
Bellevue Drive. Lights blazed in the Smiths' house, a near mansion less intimidating than the Gunners' presumptuous one.
Climbing out of the car, Morgan was put on edge by the restless
number of birds already awake, the chirping emanating from

trees he couldn't see. His footsteps resounded on a brick walk flanked by ground ivy. A door hung open for him. Stepping inside, he saw the heat of hell in Ira Smith's face.

"My wife has something to tell you."

"What's it about?"

"This way."

He was led deep into the house to a room where ceiling plants festooned the windows and other plants stood tall in massive pots. Regina Smith sat in a wicker chair with her arms folded tightly, her knees glued together. Nothing in her face moved. Like an air-brushed photo, it bore no imperfections except an almost imperceptible cast in one eye.

"Tell him what you told me," Ira Smith said.

Her eyes came alive in a glare. "Call the police."

"This man is the police. You don't tell him, I will."

"Go to hell."

"I am in hell." His voice was bone-dry.

She looked at Morgan. "His son killed my daughter."

"No," Ira Smith said. His arms slackened, then his legs, and he touched a table for support. "Tell him the truth."

The first light on the dew-drenched lawn was tentative, mirage-like. The two men walked through it. Ira Smith needed air. He took great gulps of it, his throat parched from repeating everything into a tape recorder. He said to Chief Morgan, "I have to get back to Boston. I have to be with my son."

"I'll have someone drive you," Morgan said.

"No. I need time alone."

Meg O'Brien, though she lacked official status, sat with Regina Smith in the plant room. Neither spoke. Sergeant Avery, unshaved, was in the kitchen and drinking coffee he had brought in a thermos. Morgan poured a cup and told him to join Meg in the plant room. Sergeant Avery nodded. "I think she scares Meg."

"That's why you're here, Eugene."

A little later Morgan telephoned Kate Bodine at her apartment in Brookline and woke her from an apparent sound sleep.

"Sorry, Kate, but I have to warn you that Bodine's likely to be arrested before the day's over."

She went dead silent, and Morgan counted the seconds ticking away. Then she said, "Are you telling me you were right?" Her voice rose. "Are you saying I was sleeping with the devil?"

At eight o'clock he phoned his friend, Lieutenant Bakinowski, at the state police barracks in Andover and said, "I have something for you."

"This is absurd," Harley Bodine said when, mid-afternoon, state troopers escorted him from his office in Boston. During the drive to Andover he spoke not at all, his gaze on the racing landscape and glyphic road signs of Interstate 93. In the interrogation room at the barracks, where Lieutenant Bakinowski laced the air with pipe smoke and Chief Morgan sat silently to one side, he was composed, formal, and indeflectable. At times he showed concern but not alarm, which prompted Bakinowski to whisper to Morgan, "The son of a bitch is good."

With a passing nod at Morgan, Bodine said from the side of his mouth, "That man broke up my marriage. And he's responsible for the attempted suicide of Paul Gunner and the mental breakdown of Mr. Gunner's wife. Suits are pending against him."

Bakinowski said, "Let's stick to my questions."

"In light of her tragedy," Bodine asked, "is Mrs. Smith in her right mind?"

The interrogation went on, with nothing altering Bodine's composure, except Bakinowski's pipe smoke, which from time to time he batted away. He asked for a soft drink and was given a can of Pepsi, from which he took only a single swallow. A sandwich was brought in, but he didn't touch it. Morgan could feel a terrible headache coming on.

A few minutes after eight o'clock, Bodine said, "Unless you intend to charge me, I'll answer no more questions without counsel."

Bakinowski and Morgan stepped out of the room. "I don't know, Chief. I just don't know what I've got yet." In his hands was the report Morgan had prepared a month ago. "I'm on your side, you know that, but the Smith woman is a basket case."

"You have Mr. Smith's statement."

"This Dudley character, you sure we can find him?"

"We have a shot." Morgan tore a slip of paper from his breast pocket. "Here's a phone number."

A few minutes later Harley Bodine was placed in a holding cell.

They ate in Chinatown, Soldier's treat. A chance to get to know each other better, Soldier said, and to clear the air between them. To let Dudley know that if there were any major problems, jealousies, things like that, he, Soldier, would pack his duffel bag and push off, no hard feelings. He wanted only what was best for Mary.

The Chinese food did not sit well in Dudley's stomach, which had troubled him since morning. The message in his fortune cookie promised sweetness in life.

They left the restaurant for the melody of the nighttime streets. Soldier wanted the air. He wanted to walk off the meal. Prostitutes in frippery gave him the eye. When a platoon of youths crossed their path, Dudley felt safe in his company. A drunk of mixed race stumbled out of an alley, and Soldier shoved the fellow to one side.

"I know what you mean to Mary," he said. "It's something I never had. My sister and I were separated young."

Dudley stuffed his hands into the pockets of his blazer. No one would know what Mary meant to him except Mary herself. It went beyond words, beyond touch, and narrowed to a point where one would always do what was best for the other.

On Summer Street some of the stores had vanished for the night under metal shutters. A dog clawed at a loaded trash bag. Approaching South Station, Soldier said, "Mary's got a heart big enough for the both of us, but I know my place. You've got center stage."

"My stomach's bothering me," Dudley said as they skipped from one traffic isle to another. Soldier told him to take deep breaths. They walked beyond South Station, along South Street where the moon was visible, unusually bright, and seemed to be everywhere. Each glass front had a copy. "I can't keep up," he said when Soldier led him down a side street.

"I need my exercise, Dudley. My body won't let me do without it."

He felt decisions slipping from his grasp. The street was dead-end, folding up fast against the blank wall of an industrial building. He drank the night air against his will. Soldier tugged at his arm.

"This way. I've got to take a leak."

He stumbled past a dumpster into an alley half lit by a bulb burning high over a door. On the ground were pieces of bright plastic from a broken plate, a tennis ball robbed of its felt, a styrofoam cup weighted by rainwater, and the remains of a small bird. He saw Soldier lift his fatigue jacket. Soldier shoved a clip into a large pistol, the sound clean and businesslike.

"Mary says you shouldn't know, but I feel you should. A man has the right."

He stained his underpants with a silent spindrift from his bowels and smiled as if everything happening were forewritten, surprising only to himself. "What are you going to do?"

"A public service," Soldier said.

The shot knocked him to the ground and gave him the immediate sensation of an everlasting present, the past no longer a burden, the future a fantasy. When he realized he was dying, he felt it in every joint, in the ends of his fingers, in the back of his throat. Tucking in his chin, he peered at the wound, saw beauty in the blood, and felt elevated in status, exalted. When he heard Soldier moving away, his eyes reached out. He wanted someone to watch him go. "Please," he said.

Soldier took three or four steps and turned. He fired off another shot, which took the lid off Dudley's head.

17

FOR THE MAN IT WAS LOVE AT FIRST SIGHT. HE WAS A WIDOWER from Vermont, Yankee to his toes, and well aware that there's no fool like an old fool, but it didn't matter. When Phoebe Yarbrough walked into the bar at the Ritz, he saw a tulip high on the wand. "Please, join me for a drink," he said and shed the weight of his years. He kept himself in shape, he told her. He jogged. He awaited the ski season. His face bound in tough leathery skin, he told her he loved the outdoors.

"Yes, I can see that," she said.

He told her she was beautiful. He said he could not take his eyes off her. He loved, he said, the sound of her name.

"It used to be Frances," she said.

He was in Boston on bank business and due to return to Burlington in the morning. He might, however, stay an extra day. He quivered with enthusiasm when she agreed to dinner, over which she told him that her stab at marriage hadn't worked. She was in the process of divorce. Over after-dinner drinks, she said, "Why does childhood outweigh the whole rest of your life? Do you have an answer for that?"

"That's when everything counts double," he said.

The next day they strolled through the Public Garden, where each tree was lit with an October color. An American ash stood golden. A sassafras ran from banana yellow to red orange. He took deep breaths, she seemed to take none at all. Her gait was weightless. "I love this time of year," she said. "The world in glorious ruin."

He guided her to a bench, where she sat with her legs crossed, her trousers skin-tight satin. He told her he wanted to be married again, a woman to share the years he had left, and he made a proposal that she countered with a suggestion of hard coin. Could he afford her? What, she asked in so many words, was his bottom line? His loneliness and his appetites owned him. "I have a lawyer," he said, "who can lay it all out for you."

"Aren't lawyers wonderful," she said.

May Hutchins was in the library. Her hair was streaky, her coat didn't hang right, and her stomach gurgled, none of which mattered to her. Nor did any of the books. The titles blurred. The faces of magazines glared. A gaggle of girls were acting up in the stacks, and she absorbed their voices without hearing a word, though she suspected one was mocking her. A hand touched her.

"May, are you taking care of yourself?"

The voice was Fred Fossey's. His hand dropped away because of the look on her face, which welcomed nothing. She backed off, and he regarded her helplessly.

"I thought you'd need me more than ever."

The words offended her. Her heart racing, she felt she was killing time when she had none to spare. She put on her wool cap and said, "I have to go."

The air nipped at her. The smash of autumn colors around the green assaulted her eye and made the familiar alien, herself an intruder. Children were splashing through leaves. Who among them would care that she had won the spelling bee in sixth grade? Who would care that in high school she had had a part in the class play?

Women were coming out of the side of the church. When one of them waved, she tugged at her wool cap. She was a lamb outside the fold, a stranger in her own town. Who in the whole of Bensington could fathom the bittersweet loss of her long-ago girlhood and the emptiness of her soul?

In Tuck's, she went to the deli counter and bought bologna and American cheese, which George Tuck weighed and wrapped and handed to her. Lying in her refrigerator, the bologna would spoil and the cheese would wilt unless she forced herself to eat it.

"I'm s-s-sorry about Roland, May."

Roland was home. He was in an urn. Could she shake the ashes and tell him she missed him? "I'm sorry too, George."

"Is there anything I can do?"

"Can you bring him back?"

"I g-guess not, May."

"Then mind your own business."

She walked up Pleasant Street to her house. The vinyl siding, installed seven or eight years ago, still looked new. When she was gone her children would sell the house, which was just as well. After a few years in the ground, who in town would remember her? Fred Fossey perhaps, but he no longer counted.

She started up the front path where the Boston fern, glorious throughout the summer, had fallen to rust. Out back, dying sunlight fell on the gazebo, and for a stunning second she thought she glimpsed Dudley through the latticework. With a sudden chill she rummaged through her bag for the door key and couldn't find it, which didn't matter. She hadn't locked the door. She opened it and stepped in.

"Roland, I'm home."

Beverly Gunner, home from Hanover House, had her hair recut and reshaped. She had a facial. She had lost ten pounds and bought a dress of the sort she'd never worn before. It was autumn. She was summer seeking a second bloom.

The first time Chief Morgan took her to dinner at Rem-

brandt's, she stumbled on the way to the table and would have
fallen had Morgan not caught her. Seated, she said, "This is like
a first date." Gradually, under his attention, along with a glass
of wine, she relaxed. The conversation led gently to her state of
mind. Gone were the dreams in which the pull of gravity was
threatening, consuming her with the fear she would not awake.
"I'm really in good shape," she said, "mentally, physically, and
financially. As long as Paul stays alive the money's mine, all
mine. I've been feeling quite greedy and enjoying it."

The second time they dined together, same restaurant,
same table, she spoke of feelings left unexpressed for years.
When she mentioned her daughter, her eyes filled, but then she
went on to other things. She felt comfortable with Morgan.
Voices ringing loud at the next table drew them closer together.
He listened to each word she said. Waiting for her coat, she
stood in a way that gave drama to her new figure. An air of
seduction hovered close when he helped her into her coat, but
neither made a gesture. They valued the friendship too much to
disturb it.

Her sons were boarding students at the academy, but one
weekend they came home. Gustav avoided her, but Herman was
affectionate, and had he a tail he'd have swept it from side to
side. He was too big to sit on her lap, but he seemed to want
to. He settled for a place on the arm of her chair, where she
told him how his great-grandfather had driven salesmen from
the door by removing his glass eye and querying the length of
them with his good one.

"You never told me that story before."

"You had other things to amuse you," she said.

They both went quiet when Gustav entered the room with
something behind his back, which he revealed presently. It was
a knife from the kitchen. He didn't raise it, but he held it ready.
His eyes were his father's, and in time his weight would be. She
smiled at him.

"Are you going to kill me with that, Gustav?"

His lips puckering, he began to cry.

———

Harley Bodine, charged with conspiracy in a homicide and free on bail, was on leave from his law firm and working daily with the nationally known trial attorney who was preparing his defense. A possible witness for the defense was Mary Williams, who was prepared to testify that her companion, whereabouts unknown, was a gentle soul incapable of violence. The attorney, focusing his gaze upon her, pondered the possibility of Dudley's reappearing. Mary's eyes closed for a moment. In her bag was a month-old newspaper clip about frustrated attempts to identify a man found slain in an alley off South Street. Her silence seemed to satisfy him.

The Essex County district attorney was banking on the recovery of Anthony Smith, who had twice undergone major surgery for head injuries. The district attorney needed Anthony to identify Dudley's photograph and to place him at the scene. The trial was scheduled for next month but was expected to be delayed. No trial date had been set for Regina Smith, whose mental condition at Bridgewater State Hospital was deteriorating.

The district attorney had read Chief Morgan's report and for the present was not pursuing its deeper implications. Paul Gunner, brain dead, was on a life-support system at a clinic in Stoneham.

Sitting with Soldier in a narrow glassed-in café on Newbury Street, Mary Williams gripped a glass of Perrier and grieved over the fact that Dudley lay anonymously in a pauper's grave, Fairview Cemetery, Boston's Hyde Park section. Her voice shallow, she said, "I'll wait a couple of years and have him reburied in a proper place."

"That's not smart," Soldier said.

"I'll wait five years, then."

"Better wait till I'm dead."

Drinking German beer from a frozen metal mug, he cramped his stomach and then imagined his own funeral blazoned with flags and resounding from a volley of rifle shots. Mary clenched the Perrier glass and stamped her prints on it, as if leaving evidence.

"Did I do right, Soldier?"

"You didn't do wrong, let's put it that way."

She looked out at the street, headlights beginning to flash, and said, "It gets dark so early now. Long nights scare me."

"What do you think eating alone used to do to me?" His hand reached across the table and touched her. "But we got each other now, right?"

She thought of the winter that lay ahead and the long wait for spring to reinvent itself. Looking at Soldier with a sense of gratitude, she forced affection into her smile. "Right," she said.

On a day off Kate Bodine visited an art gallery on Newbury Street and viewed representative works of several local artists, all of the human figure, none of which pleased her eye. One was an acrylic of Christ with ghostly genitalia. Another, Manet-like, was of a woman sitting on a park bench with her legs open, as if for public consumption.

"No one has painted a female nude as Matisse did," said an authoritative voice behind her. "He captured the rhythms of a woman's body. He came the closest to bringing out her being." Turning, she looked into the face of a man with a silver mane of hair pampered to perfection. "Someone should do you," he said.

She stepped away gracefully and found her way to the bathroom, which was walled with mirrors, startling her. It was the second time in her life she was viewing herself on a toilet. She looked distracted, unguarded, vaguely sacrificial. Someone jiggled the doorknob. "It's occupied," she said forcefully.

The authoritative voice said, "Take your time."

She left the bathroom quickly, the gallery even faster, and took a cab to her apartment building in Brookline. A security guard manned a desk in the lobby. A painting of a meadow imbued with the calm of a Corot hung on the wall. The elevator whisked her to an upper floor. Inside her apartment, she telephoned Chief Morgan.

"When are you going to visit me?" she asked.

He arrived an hour later. He looked tired, older, as if a year or two had passed since she had seen him, and she wondered whether he was coming to a similar conclusion about her.

She had put food on the table, but they ignored it. In the bedroom she felt all of him, for he made love with his whole body, the momentum carried up from his toes. When they finished, she lay sprawled with an arm hanging over the side.

"James."

"What?"

"That was swell."

"You wouldn't kid me?"

"I wouldn't know how."

Much later, the darkness total, she tried to wake him, which took some doing. His sleep was deep, as if he had gone without it for some time. His arm found her and drew her close.

"Do you think we could make a go of it, James?"

His hand drooped over her head, seemed to clasp it. "Let's talk about it in the morning."

"We could see each other off and on. Why don't we try that?"

Late in the evening at Hanover House, too restless to sleep, Isabel Williams slipped on a robe and went to Hilda Gunner's room, where a single lamp burned weakly, the shadows profound. Mrs. Gunner, wearing a flannel nightshirt, occupied a club chair, her cockled legs firmly crossed. In a low voice she said, "I told him not to get any ideas. I've been buggered enough."

"Then what's he doing here?" Isabel said sharply.

Mr. Skully was ensconced in the other club chair, a sallow hand on the curve of his cane, which rested between his pajama'd legs. His leather slippers were slit to accommodate the bulges in his feet. A clock radio, tuned low, was playing old standards. After the first bar or two, Mr. Skully knew what was coming and who would sing it.

" 'Mona Lisa,' " he said. "Nat King Cole."

"He's lonely," Mrs. Gunner murmured. "He can't sleep."
Cords pulled at Isabel's throat as she raised her chin.
"We're all lonely here, Mr. Skully. What else is new?"

Gripping his cane, he sank deeper into the chair. In his
prime, he could leap abysses. Now he couldn't take a straight
step. From the trenches in his face, he said, "They never come
to see me. Not one of them."

"He's talking about his sons," Mrs. Gunner said.

"Tell me about it," Isabel said, lighting a cigarette. "The
only one of my daughters comes to see me is the weird one, and
she's taken up with another lunatic. The guy shaves his head and
wears jungle clothes." Ruby lipstick splotched her cigarette.
Picking up the ashtray kept out for her, she drifted into shadows
and sat on the edge of Mrs. Gunner's tightly made bed. "The
one before him was the Grim Reaper posing as Little Boy Blue."

Mrs. Gunner ran a nervous hand through her tainted white
hair, her scalp shining through. "You have a child, you're never
sure what you're gonna get. Could be a monster."

Isabel drew on the cigarette, illuminating her stretched-
tight face while deepening the bullet-hole eyes. "My Mary was
late in my life. I didn't want her, you know. I should've dropped
her on her head."

"My Paul is a duplicate of his father."

"Mary was every bit her father, no real stuff to him. He
kept a rope in his closet for when he could get up the nerve. It
was Mary who found him."

Mrs. Gunner put a hand to her nose. Mr. Skully blessed
her when she sneezed. A crumpled tissue came out of her fist.
She had a lingering chest cold and a ragged cough like the rattle
of broken glass inside a thermos. Several moments passed, and
Mr. Skully mumbled out another song and singer.

Isabel, no longer smoking, dropped back on the bed and
extended her legs, intact and shapely. "One of these days," she
said, "genetic engineering will ensure perfect lovers, ideal fa-
thers, and wonderful children."

Mrs. Gunner closed her eyes. Mr. Skully half lifted his cane and smiled. His teeth had the gleam of nickel. "I was one of each," he said.

Isabel spoke in a drifting voice of the poet Lowell, the only man, she said, with whom she had been musical when struck, sonorous when brought about. Her head sought more of the pillow. "The affair ran its course too fast. We both knew it would. He went back to his other life and I to mine."

Mrs. Gunner nodded off into a dream and woke a few minutes later with her conviction strengthened that other worlds meandered beyond the grave. Without opening her eyes, she said, "I'm not afraid of pushing off, don't think for a minute I am. My granddaughter awaits me. I just spoke to her."

"He was too morose, he got on my nerves," Isabel said from the pillow, her legs stretched to their limits. "I told him to straighten up and fly right."

"Lowell?" Mr. Skully asked.

"My husband."

" 'Honeysuckle Rose,' Lena Horne," he said quietly, awash in memories. Haltingly, with strain, he rose from the chair, abandoned his cane, and tottered into the shadows, where he lost his bearings. "Where are you?"

Mrs. Gunner had a coughing spell and thumped her chest, after which she needed many moments to regain her breath. The air in the room was close, heavy, active, touched with sounds of drama. Her ears told her what her eyes could not manage. "I know what you're doing," she said through congestion.

Mr. Skully pulled out and ejected three small drops of semen on the sunken surface of Isabel's abdomen. Then, still triggered, he fell away and lay with his face in collapse. Rising slowly, Isabel fixed her robe, raked her hair back, and lit a cigarette.

"He's not dead, is he?" Mrs. Gunner asked roughly.

The cigarette threw a spark. Isabel advanced from the shadows and sat on the fat armrest of Mrs. Gunner's chair. Holding the cigarette in one hand, she blew on the other. She had broken a nail, the finger defanged. Both women were conscious of the hour, of the darkness outside, of the man sleeping like a baby on the bed. Isabel stroked her friend's shoulder.

"We did our best, didn't we, Hilda?"

"Our best? I never had the opportunity to know what my best is."

For more than a minute they existed in separate silences like two actors deprived of applause, the curtain dropping, the audience frozen. An ash fell.

"What did you say to her, Hilda?"

"Say to who?"

"Your granddaughter."

"I told her not to be afraid. Nana's coming."